# IF IT BLEEDS

If It Bleeds

# IF IT BLEEDS

## STEPHEN KING

**THORNDIKE PRESS**
A part of Gale, a Cengage Company

LIBRARY OF CONGRESS CIP DATA ON FILE.
CATALOGUING IN PUBLICATION FOR THIS BOOK
IS AVAILABLE FROM THE LIBRARY OF CONGRESS

ISBN-13: 978-1-4328-7755-2 (hardcover alk. paper)

Published in 2020 by arrangement with Scribner, an imprint of Simon & Schuster, Inc.

Printed in Mexico
Print Number: 01          Print Year: 2020

*Thinking of Russ Dorr*
*I miss you, Chief.*

# CONTENTS

# CONTENTS

# MR. HARRIGAN'S
# PHONE

My home town was just a village of six hundred or so (and still is, although I have moved away), but we had the Internet just like the big cities, so my father and I got less and less personal mail. Usually all Mr. Nedeau brought was the weekly copy of *Time,* fliers addressed to Occupant or Our Friendly Neighbors, and the monthly bills. But starting in 2004, the year I turned nine and began working for Mr. Harrigan up the hill, I could count on at least four envelopes hand-addressed to me each year. There was a Valentine's Day card in February, a birthday card in September, a Thanksgiving Day card in November, and a Christmas card either just before or just after the holiday. Inside each card was a one-dollar scratch ticket from the Maine State Lottery, and the signature was always the same: *Good Wishes from Mr. Harrigan.* Simple and formal.

My father's reaction was always the same,

too: a laugh and a good-natured roll of the eyes.

"He's a cheapster," Dad said one day. This might have been when I was eleven, a couple of years after the cards began arriving. "Pays you cheap wages and gives you a cheap bonus — Lucky Devil tickets from Howie's."

I pointed out that one of those four scratchers usually paid off a couple of bucks. When that happened, Dad collected for me at Howie's, because minors weren't supposed to play the lottery, even if the tickets were freebies. Once, when I hit it big and won five dollars, I asked Dad to buy me five more dollar scratch-offs. He refused, saying if he fed my gambling addiction, my mother would roll over in her grave.

"Harrigan doing it is bad enough," Dad said. "Besides, he should be paying you *seven* dollars an hour. Maybe even eight. God knows he could afford it. Five an hour may be legal, since you're just a kid, but some would consider it child abuse."

"I like working for him," I said. "And I like *him,* Dad."

"I understand that," he said, "and it's not like reading to him and weeding his flower garden makes you a twenty-first-century Oliver Twist, but he's still a cheapster. I'm surprised he's willing to spring for postage to mail those cards, when it can't be more than a quarter of a mile from his mailbox to ours."

We were on our front porch when we had this conversation, drinking glasses of Sprite, and Dad cocked a thumb up our road (dirt, like most of them in Harlow) to Mr. Harrigan's house. Which was really a mansion, complete with an indoor pool, a conservatory, a glass elevator that I absolutely *loved* to ride in, and a greenhouse out back where there used to be a dairy barn (before my time, but Dad remembered it well).

"You know how bad his arthritis is," I said. "Now he uses two canes instead of one sometimes. Walking down here would about kill him."

"Then he could just hand the damn greeting cards to you," Dad said. There was no bite to his words; he was mostly just teasing. He and Mr. Harrigan got along all right. My dad got on all right with everyone in Harlow. I suppose that's what made him a good salesman. "God knows you're up there enough."

"It wouldn't be the same," I said.

"No? Why not?"

I couldn't explain. I had plenty of vocabulary, thanks to all the reading I did, but not much life experience. I just knew I liked getting those cards, looked forward to them, and to the lottery ticket I always scratched off with my lucky dime, and to the signature in his old-fashioned cursive: *Good Wishes from Mr. Harrigan.* Looking back, the word *ceremo-*

*nial* comes to mind. It was like how Mr. Harrigan always wore one of his scrawny black ties when he and I drove to town, even though he'd mostly just sit behind the wheel of his sensible Ford sedan reading the *Financial Times* while I went into the IGA and got the things on his shopping list. There was always corned beef hash on that list, and a dozen eggs. Mr. Harrigan sometimes opined that a man could live perfectly well on eggs and corned beef hash once he had reached a certain age. When I asked him what that age would be, he said sixty-eight.

"When a man turns sixty-eight," he said, "he no longer needs vitamins."

"Really?"

"No," he said. "I only say that to justify my bad eating habits. Did you or did you not order satellite radio for this car, Craig?"

"I did." On Dad's home computer, because Mr. Harrigan didn't have one.

"Then where is it? All I can get is that damn windbag Limbaugh."

I showed him how to get to the XM radio. He turned the knob past a hundred or so stations until he found one specializing in country. It was playing "Stand By Your Man."

That song still gives me the chills, and I suppose it always will.

On that day in my eleventh year, as my dad and I sat drinking our Sprites and looking up

14

at the big house (which was exactly what Harlowites called it: the Big House, as if it were Shawshank Prison), I said, "Getting snail-mail is cool."

Dad did his eye-roll thing. "*Email* is cool. And cellular phones. Those things seem like miracles to me. You're too young to understand. If you'd grown up with nothing but a party line and four other houses on it — including Mrs. Edelson, who never shut up — you might feel differently."

"When can I have a cell phone?" This was a question I'd asked a lot that year, more frequently after the first iPhones went on sale.

"When I decide you're old enough."

"Whatever, Dad." It was my turn to roll my eyes, which made him laugh. Then he grew serious.

"Do you understand how rich John Harrigan is?"

I shrugged. "I know he used to own mills."

"He owned a lot more than mills. Until he retired, he was the grand high poobah of a company called Oak Enterprises. It owned a shipping line, shopping centers, a chain of movie theaters, a telecom company, I don't know whatall else. When it came to the Big Board, Oak was one of the biggest."

"What's the Big Board?"

"Stock market. Gambling for rich people. When Harrigan sold out, the deal wasn't just in the business section of the *New York Times,* it was on the front page. That guy who drives a six-year-old Ford, lives at the end of a dirt road, pays you five bucks an hour, and sends you a dollar scratch ticket four times a year is sitting on better than a billion dollars." Dad grinned. "And my worst suit, the one your mother would make me give to the Goodwill if she was still alive, is better than the one he wears to church."

I found all of this interesting, especially the idea that Mr. Harrigan, who didn't own a laptop or even a TV, had once owned a telecom company and movie theaters. I bet he never even went to the movies. He was what my dad called a Luddite, meaning (among other things) a guy who doesn't like gadgets. The satellite radio was an exception, because he liked country music and hated all the ads on WOXO, which was the only c&w station his car radio could pull in.

"Do you know how much a billion is, Craig?"

"A hundred million, right?"

"Try a *thousand* million."

"Wow," I said, but only because a wow seemed called for. I understood five bucks, and I understood five hundred, the price of a used motor scooter for sale on the Deep Cut Road that I dreamed of owning (good luck there), and I had a theoretical understanding of five thousand, which was about what my dad made each month as a salesman at Parmeleau Tractors and Heavy Machinery in Gates Falls. Dad was always getting his picture on the wall as Salesman of the Month. He claimed that was no big deal, but I knew better. When he got Salesman of the Month, we went to dinner at Marcel's, the fancy French restaurant in Castle Rock.

"Wow is right," Dad said, and toasted the big house on the hill, with all those rooms that went mostly unused and the elevator Mr. Harrigan loathed but had to use because of his arthritis and sciatica. "Wow is just about goddam right."

Before I tell you about the big-money lottery ticket, and Mr. Harrigan dying, and the trouble I had with Kenny Yanko when I was a freshman at Gates Falls High, I should tell you about how I happened to go to work for Mr. Harrigan. It was because of church. Dad and I went to First Methodist of Harlow, which was the *only* Methodist of Harlow. There used to be another church in town, the one the Baptists used, but it burned down in 1996.

"Some people shoot off fireworks to celebrate the arrival of a new baby," Dad said. I couldn't have been more than four then, but I remember it — probably because fireworks interested me. "Your mom and I said to hell with that and burned down a *church* to welcome you, Craigster, and what a lovely

17

blaze it made."

"Never say that," my mother said. "He might believe you and burn one down when he has a kid of his own."

They joked a lot together, and I laughed even when I didn't get it.

The three of us used to walk to church together, our boots crunching through packed snow in winter, our good shoes puffing up dust in summer (which my mom would wipe off with a Kleenex before we went inside), me always holding Dad's hand on my left and Mom's on my right.

She was a good mom. I still missed her bad in 2004, when I started working for Mr. Harrigan, although she had been dead three years then. Now, sixteen years later, I still miss her, although her face has faded in my memory and photos only refresh it a little. What that song says about motherless children is true: they have a hard time. I loved my dad and we always got along fine, but that song's right on another point, too: there's so many things your daddy can't understand. Like making a daisy chain and putting it on your head in the big field behind our house and saying today you're not just any little boy, you're King Craig. Like being pleased but not making it out to be a big deal — bragging and all — when you start reading Superman and Spider-Man comic books at the age of three. Like getting in bed with you if you wake up in the middle of the night from a bad dream where Dr. Octopus is chasing you. Like hugging you and telling you it's okay when some bigger boy — Kenny Yanko, for instance — beats the living shit out of you.

I could have used one of those hugs on that day. A mother-hug on that day might have changed a lot.

Never boasting about being a precocious reader was a gift my parents gave me, the gift of learning early that having some talent doesn't make you better than the next fellow. But word got around, as it always does in small towns, and when I was eight, Reverend Mooney asked me if I would like to read the Bible lesson on Family Sunday. It might have been the novelty of the thing that fetched him; usually he got a high school boy or girl to do the honors. The reading was from the Book of Mark that Sunday, and after the service, the Rev said I'd done such a good job I could do it every week, if I wanted.

"He says a little child shall lead them," I told Dad. "It's in the Book of Isaiah."

My father grunted, as if that didn't move him much. Then he nodded. "Fine, as long as you remember you're the medium, not the message."

"Huh?"

"The Bible is the Word of God, not the

Word of Craig, so don't get a big head about it."

I said I wouldn't, and for the next ten years — until I went off to college where I learned to smoke dope, drink beer, and chase girls — I read the weekly lesson. Even when things were at their very worst, I did that. The Rev would give me the scriptural reference a week in advance — chapter and verse, as the saying is. Then, at Methodist Youth Fellowship on Thursday night, I'd bring him a list of the words I couldn't pronounce. As a result, I may be the only person in the state of Maine who can not only pronounce Nebuchadnezzar, but spell it.

One of America's richest men moved to Harlow about three years before I started my Sunday job of delivering scripture to my elders. The turn of the century, in other words, right after he sold his companies and retired, and before his big house was even completely finished (the pool, the elevator, and the paved driveway came later). Mr. Harrigan attended church every week, dressed in his rusty black suit with the sagging seat, wearing one of his unfashionably narrow black ties, and with his thinning gray hair neatly combed. The rest of the week that hair went every whichway, like Einstein's after a busy day of deciphering the cosmos.

Back then he only used one cane, which he

leaned on when we rose to sing hymns I suppose I'll remember until the day I die . . . and that verse of "The Old Rugged Cross" about water and blood flowing from Jesus's wounded side will always give me chills, just like the last verse of "Stand By Your Man," when Tammy Wynette goes all out. Anyway, Mr. Harrigan didn't actually sing, which was good because he had kind of a rusty, shrieky voice, but he mouthed along. He and my dad had that in common.

One Sunday in the fall of 2004 (all the trees in our part of the world burning with color), I read part of 2 Samuel, doing my usual job of imparting to the congregation a message I hardly understood but knew Reverend Mooney would explain in his sermon: "The beauty of Israel is slain upon thy high places: how are the mighty fallen! Tell it not in Gath, publish it not in the streets of Askelon; lest the daughters of the Philistines rejoice, lest the daughters of the uncircumcised triumph."

When I sat down in our pew, Dad patted me on the shoulder and whispered *You said a mouthful* in my ear. I had to cover my mouth to hide a smile.

The next evening, as we were finishing up the supper dishes (Dad washing, me drying and putting away), Mr. Harrigan's Ford pulled into the driveway. His cane thumped up our dooryard steps, and Dad opened the

21

door just before he could knock. Mr. Harrigan declined the living room and sat at the kitchen table just like home folks. He accepted a Sprite when Dad offered, but declined a glass. "I take it from the bottle, the way my pa did," he said.

He got right to the point, being a man of business. If my father approved, Mr. Harrigan said he'd like to hire me to read to him two or perhaps three hours a week. For this he would pay five dollars an hour. He could offer another three hours' worth of work, he said, if I would tend his garden a bit and do some other chores, such as snow-shoveling the steps in winter and dusting what needed dusting year-round.

Twenty-five, maybe even thirty dollars a week, half of it just for reading, which was something I would have done for free! I couldn't believe it. Thoughts of saving up for a motor scooter immediately rose to mind, even though I would not be able to ride one legally for another seven years.

It was too good to be true, and I was afraid my father would say no, but he didn't. "Just don't give him anything controversial," Dad said. "No crazy political stuff, and no overboard violence. He reads like a grownup, but he's just nine, and barely that."

Mr. Harrigan gave him this promise, drank some of his Sprite, and smacked his leathery lips. "He reads well, yes, but that's not the main reason I want to hire him. He doesn't *drone,* even when he doesn't understand. I find that remarkable. Not amazing, but remarkable."

He put his bottle down and leaned forward, fixing me with his sharp gaze. I often saw amusement in those eyes, but only seldom did I see warmth, and that night in 2004 wasn't one of them.

"About your reading yesterday, Craig. Do you know what is meant by 'the daughters of the uncircumcised'?"

"Not really," I said.

"I didn't think so, but you still got the right tone of anger and lamentation in your voice. Do you know what *lamentation* is, by the way?"

"Crying and stuff."

He nodded. "But you didn't overdo it. You didn't ham it up. That was good. A reader is a carrier, not a creator. Does Reverend Mooney help you with your pronunciation?"

"Yes, sir, sometimes."

Mr. Harrigan drank some more Sprite and rose, leaning on his cane. "Tell him it's *Ashkelon,* not *Ass*-kelon. I found that unintentionally funny, but I have a very low sense of humor. Shall we have a trial run Wednesday, at three? Are you out of school by then?"

I got out of Harlow Elementary at two-thirty. "Yes, sir. Three would be fine."

"Shall we say until four? Or is that too late?"

23

"That works," Dad said. He sounded bemused by the whole thing. "We don't eat until six. I like to watch the local news."

"Doesn't that play hell with your digestion?"

Dad laughed, although I don't really think Mr. Harrigan was joking. "Sometimes it does. I'm not a fan of Mr. Bush."

"He is a bit of a fool," Mr. Harrigan agreed, "but at least he's surrounded himself with men who understand business. Three on Wednesday, Craig, and don't be late. I have no patience with tardiness."

"Nothing risqué, either," Dad said. "Time enough for that when he's older."

Mr. Harrigan also promised this, but I suppose men who understand business also understand that promises are easy to discard, being as how giving them is free. There was certainly nothing risqué in *Heart of Darkness,* which was the first book I read for him. When we finished, Mr. Harrigan asked me if I understood it. I don't think he was trying to tutor me; he was just curious.

"Not a whole lot," I said, "but that guy Kurtz was pretty crazy. I got that much."

There was nothing risqué in the next book, either — *Silas Marner* was just a bore-a-thon, in my humble opinion. The third one, however, was *Lady Chatterley's Lover,* and that was certainly an eye-opener. It was 2006 when I was introduced to Constance Chatterley and her randy gamekeeper. I was ten. All these years later I can still remember the verses of "The Old Rugged Cross," and just as vividly recall Mellors stroking the lady and murmuring "Tha'rt nice." How he treated her is a good thing for boys to learn, and a good thing to remember.

"Do you understand what you just read?" Mr. Harrigan asked me after one particularly steamy passage. Again, just curious.

"No," I said, but that wasn't strictly true. I understood a lot more of what was going on between Ollie Mellors and Connie Chatterley in the woods than I did about what was going on between Marlow and Kurtz down there in the Belgian Congo. Sex is hard to figure out — something I learned even before I got to college — but crazy is even harder.

"Fine," Mr. Harrigan said, "but if your father asks what we're reading, I suggest you tell him *Dombey and Son.* Which we're going to read next, anyway."

My father never did ask — about that one, anyway — and I was relieved when we moved on to *Dombey,* which was the first adult novel I remember really liking. I didn't want to lie to my dad, it would have made me feel horrible, although I'm sure Mr. Harrigan would have had no problem with it.

Mr. Harrigan liked me to read to him because his eyes tired easily. He probably didn't need me to weed his flowers; Pete Bostwick, who mowed his acre or so of lawn, would have been happy to do that, I think. And Edna Grogan, his housekeeper, would have been happy to dust his large collection of antique snow-globes and glass paperweights, but that was my job. He mostly just liked having me around. He never told me that until shortly before he died, but I knew it. I just didn't know why, and am not sure I do now.

Once, when we were coming back from dinner at Marcel's in the Rock, my dad said, very abruptly: "Does Harrigan ever touch you in a way you don't like?"

I was years from even being able to grow a shadow mustache, but I knew what he was asking; we had learned about "stranger danger" and "inappropriate touching" in the third grade, for God's sake.

"Do you mean does he grope me? No! Jeez, Dad, he's not *gay.*"

"All right. Don't get all mad about it, Craigster. I had to ask. Because you're up there a lot."

"If he was groping me, he could at least send me *two*-dollar scratch tickets," I said, and that made Dad laugh.

Thirty dollars a week was about what I made, and Dad insisted I put at least twenty of it in my college savings account. Which I did, although I considered it mega-stupid; when even being a teenager seems an age

26

away, college might as well be in another lifetime. Ten bucks a week was still a fortune. I spent some of it on burgers and shakes at the Howie's Market lunch counter, most of it on old paperbacks at Dahlie's Used Books in Gates Falls. The ones I bought weren't heavy going, like the ones I read to Mr. Harrigan (even *Lady Chatterley* was heavy when Constance and Mellors weren't steaming the place up). I liked crime novels and westerns like *Shoot-Out at Gila Bend* and *Hot Lead Trail*. Reading to Mr. Harrigan was work. Not sweat-labor, but work. A book like *One Monday We Killed Them All,* by John D. MacDonald, was pure pleasure. I told myself I ought to save up the money that didn't go into the college fund for one of the new Apple phones that went on sale in the summer of 2007, but they were expensive, like six hundred bucks, and at ten dollars a week, that would take me over a year. And when you're just eleven going on twelve, a year is a very long time.

Besides, those old paperbacks with their colorful covers called to me.

On Christmas morning of 2007, three years after I started working for Mr. Harrigan and two years before he died, there was only one package for me under the tree, and my dad told me to save it for last, after he had duly admired the paisley vest, the slippers, and the briar pipe I'd gotten him. With that out of the way, I tore off the wrappings on my one present, and shrieked with delight when I saw he'd gotten me exactly what I'd been lusting for: an iPhone that did so many different things it made my father's car-phone look like an antique.

Things have changed a lot since then. Now it's the iPhone my father gave me for Christmas in 2007 that's the antique, like the five-family party line he told me about from back when he was a kid. There's been so many changes, so many advances, and they happened so fast. My Christmas iPhone had just sixteen apps, and they came pre-loaded. One of them was YouTube, because back then Apple and YouTube were friends (that changed). One was called SMS, which was primitive text messaging (no emojis — a word not yet invented — unless you made them yourself). There was a weather app that was usually wrong. But you could make phone calls from something small enough to carry in your hip pocket, and even better, there was Safari, which linked you to the outside world. When you grew up in a no-stoplight, dirt-road town like Harlow, the outside world was a strange and tempting place, and you longed to touch it in a way network TV couldn't match. At least I did. All these things were at your fingertips, courtesy of AT&T and Steve Jobs.

28

There was another app, as well, one that made me think of Mr. Harrigan even on that first joyful morning. Something much cooler than the satellite radio in his car. At least for guys like him.

"Thanks, Dad," I said, and hugged him. "Thank you so much!"

"Just don't overuse it. The phone charges are sky-high, and I'll be keeping track."

"They'll come down," I said.

I was right about that, and Dad never gave me a hard time about the charges. I didn't have many people to call anyway, but I did like those YouTube videos (Dad did, too), and I loved being able to go on what we then called the three w's: the worldwide web. Sometimes I would look at articles in *Pravda,* not because I understood Russian but just because I could.

Not quite two months later, I came home from school, opened the mailbox, and found an envelope addressed to me in Mr. Harrigan's old-fashioned script. It was my Valentine's Day card. I went into the house, dropped my schoolbooks on the table, and opened it. The card wasn't flowery or sappy, that wasn't Mr. Harrigan's style. It showed a man in a tuxedo holding out a tophat and bowing in a field of flowers. The Hallmark message inside said, *May you have a year filled with love and friendship.* Below that: *Good*

*Wishes from Mr. Harrigan.* A bowing man with his hat held out, a good wish, no sticky stuff. That was Mr. Harrigan all over. Looking back, I'm surprised he considered Valentine's Day worth a card.

In 2008, the Lucky Devil one-dollar scratchers had been replaced by ones called Pine Tree Cash. There were six pine trees on the little card. If the same amount was beneath three of them when you scratched them off, you won that amount. I scratched away the trees and stared at what I had uncovered. At first I thought it was either a mistake or some kind of joke, although Mr. Harrigan was not the joke-playing type. I looked again, running my fingers along the uncovered numbers, brushing away crumbles of what my dad called (always with the eye-roll) "scratch-dirt." The numbers stayed the same. I might have laughed, that I can't recall, but I remember screaming, all right. Screaming for joy.

I grabbed my new phone out of my pocket (that phone went everywhere with me) and called Parmeleau Tractors. I got Denise, the receptionist, and when she heard how out of breath I was, she asked me what was wrong.

"Nothing, nothing," I said, "but I have to talk to my dad right now."

"All right, just hold on." And then: "You sound like you're calling from the other side of the moon, Craig."

30

"I'm on my cell phone." God, I loved saying that.

Denise made a *humph* sound. "Those things are full of radiation. I'd never own one. Hold on."

My dad also asked me what was wrong, because I'd never called him at work before, even on the day the schoolbus left without me.

"Dad, I got my Valentine's Day scratch ticket from Mr. Harrigan —"

"If you called to tell me you won ten dollars, it could have waited until I —"

"No, Daddy, it's the big prize!" Which it was, for dollar scratch-offs back then. *I won three thousand dollars!*

Silence from the other end of the line. I thought maybe I'd lost him. In those days cell phones, even the new ones, dropped calls all the time. Ma Bell wasn't always the best mother.

"Dad? Are you still there?"

"Uh-huh. Are you sure?"

"Yes! I'm looking right at it! Three three thousands! One in the top row and two in the bottom!"

Another long pause, then I heard my father telling someone *I think my kid won some money.* A moment later he was back to me. "Put it somewhere safe until I get home."

"Where?"

31

"How about the sugar cannister in the pan-try?"

"Yeah," I said. "Yeah, okay."

"Craig, are you positive? I don't want you to be disappointed, so check again."

I did, somehow convinced that my dad's doubt would change what I had seen; at least one of those $3000s would now be something else. But they were the same.

I told him that, and he laughed. "Well, then, congratulations. Marcel's tonight, and you're buying."

That made *me* laugh. I can't remember ever feeling such pure joy. I needed to call someone else, so I called Mr. Harrigan, who answered on his Luddite landline.

"Mr. Harrigan, thank you for the card! And thank you for the ticket! I —"

"Are you calling on that gadget of yours?" he asked. "You must be, because I can barely hear you. You sound like you're on the other side of the moon."

"Mr. Harrigan, I won the big prize! I won three thousand dollars! Thank you so much!"

There was a pause, but not as long as my father's, and when he spoke again, he didn't ask me if I was sure. He did me that courtesy. "You struck lucky," he said. "Good for you."

"Thank you!"

"You're welcome, but thanks really aren't necessary. I buy those things by the roll. Send em off to friends and business acquaintances

32

as a kind of . . . mmm . . . calling-card, you could say. Been doing it for years. One was bound to pay off big sooner or later."

"Dad will make me put most of it in the bank. I guess that's okay. It will certainly perk up my college fund."

"Give it to me, if you like," Mr. Harrigan said. "Let me invest it for you. I think I can guarantee a better return than bank interest." Then, speaking more to himself than to me: "Something very safe. This isn't going to be a good year for the market. I see clouds on the horizon."

"Sure!" I reconsidered. "At least probably. I have to talk to my dad."

"Of course. Only proper. Tell him I'm willing to also guarantee the base sum. Are you still coming to read for me this afternoon? Or will you put that aside, now that you're a man of means?"

"Sure, only I have to be back when Dad gets home. We're going out to dinner." I paused. "Would you like to come?"

"Not tonight," he said, with no hesitation. "You know, you could have told me all of this in person, since you're coming up, anyway. But you enjoy that gadget of yours, don't you?" He didn't wait for me to answer that; he didn't need to. "What would you think of investing your little windfall in Apple stock? I believe that company is going to be quite successful in the future. I'm hearing the iPhone

33

is going to bury the BlackBerry. Pardon the pun. In any case, don't answer now; discuss it with your father first."

"I will," I said. "And I'll be right up. I'll run."

"Youth is a wonderful thing," said Mr. Harrigan. "What a shame it's wasted on children."

"Huh?"

"Many have said it, but Shaw said it best. Never mind. Run, by all means. Run like the dickens, because Dickens awaits us."

I ran the quarter of a mile to Mr. Harrigan's house, but walked back, and on the way I had an idea. A way to thank him, even though he said no thanks were necessary. Over our fancy dinner at Marcel's that night, I told Dad about Mr. Harrigan's offer to invest my windfall, and I also told him my idea for a thank-you gift. I thought Dad would have his doubts, and I was right.

"By all means let him invest the money. As for your idea . . . you know how he feels about stuff like that. He's not only the richest man in Harlow — in the whole state of Maine, for that matter — he's also the only one who doesn't have a television."

"He's got an elevator," I said. "And he uses it."

"Because he has to." Then Dad gave me a grin. "But it's your money, and if this is what

34

you want to do with twenty per cent of it, I'm not going to tell you no. When he turns it down, you can give it to me."

"You really think he will?"

"I do."

"Dad, why did he come here in the first place? I mean, we're just a little town. We're *nowhere.*"

"Good question. Ask him sometime. Now what about some dessert, big spender?"

Just about a month later, I gave Mr. Harrigan a brand-new iPhone. I didn't wrap it up or anything, partly because it wasn't a holiday and partly because I knew how he liked things done: with no foofaraw.

He turned the box over a time or two in his arthritis-gnarled hands, looking bemused. Then he held it out to me. "Thank you, Craig, I appreciate the sentiment, but no. I suggest you give it to your father."

I took the box. "He told me you'd say that." I was disappointed but not surprised. And not ready to give up.

"Your father is a wise man." He leaned forward in his chair and clasped his hands between his spread knees. "Craig, I rarely give advice, it's almost always a waste of breath, but today I'll give some to you. Henry Thoreau said that we don't own things; things own us. Every new object — whether it's a home, a car, a television, or a fancy phone like that one — is something more we must carry on our backs. It makes me think of Jacob Marley telling Scrooge, 'These are the chains I forged in life.' I don't have a television, because if I did, I would watch it, even though almost all of what it broadcasts is utter nonsense. I don't have a radio in the house because I would listen to it, and a little country music to break the monotony of a long drive is really all I require. If I had *that* —"

He pointed to the box with the phone inside.

"— I would undoubtedly use it. I get twelve different periodicals in the mail, and they contain all the information I need to keep up with the business world and the wider world's sad doings." He sat back and sighed. "There. I've not only given advice, I've made a speech. Old age is insidious."

"Can I show you just one thing? No, two."

He gave me one of the looks I'd seen him give his gardener and his housekeeper, but had never turned my way until that afternoon: piercing, skeptical, and rather ugly. These years later, I realize it's the look a perceptive and cynical man gives when he believes he can see inside most people and expects to find nothing good.

"This only proves the old saying that no good deed goes unpunished. I'm starting to wish that scratch ticket hadn't been a winner." He sighed again. "Well, go ahead, give me your demonstration. But you won't change my mind."

Having received that look, so distant and so cold, I thought he was right. I'd end up giving the phone to my father after all. But since I'd come this far, I went ahead. The phone was charged to the max, I'd made sure of that, and was in — ha-ha — apple-pie working order. I turned it on and showed him an icon in the second row. It had jagged lines, sort of like an EKG print-out. "See that one?"

"Yes, and I see what it says. But I really don't need a stock market report, Craig. I subscribe to the *Wall Street Journal,* as you know."

"Sure," I agreed, "but the *Wall Street Journal* can't do this."

I tapped the icon and opened the app. The Dow Jones average appeared. I had no idea what the numbers meant, but I could see they were fluctuating. 14,720 rose to 14,728, then dropped to 14,704, then bumped up to 14,716. Mr. Harrigan's eyes widened. His mouth dropped open. It was as if someone had hit him with a juju stick. He took the phone and held it close to his face. Then he looked at me.

"Are these numbers in *real time?*"

"Yes," I said. "Well, I guess they might be a minute or two behind, I don't know for sure. The phone's pulling them in from the new phone tower in Motton. We're lucky to have one so close."

He leaned forward. A reluctant smile touched the corners of his mouth. "I'll be damned. It's like the stock tickers magnates used to have in their own homes."

"Oh, way better than that," I said. "Tickers sometimes ran *hours* behind. My dad said that just last night. He's fascinated with this stock market thingy, he's always taking my phone to look. He said one of the reasons the stock market tanked so bad back in 1929 was because the more people traded, the farther behind the tickers got."

"He's right," Mr. Harrigan said. "Things had gone too far before anyone could put on the brakes. Of course, something like this might actually accelerate a sell-off. It's hard to tell because the technology is still so new."

I waited. I wanted to tell him some more, sell him on it — I was just a kid, after all — but something told me waiting was the right way to go. He continued to watch the minuscule gyrations of the Dow Jones. He was getting an education right in front of my eyes.

"But," he said, still staring.

"But what, Mr. Harrigan?"

"In the hands of someone who actually knows the market, something like this could . . . probably already *does* . . ." He trailed off, thinking. Then he said, "I should have known about this. Being retired is no

38

excuse."

"Here's the other thing," I said, too impatient to wait any longer. "You know all the magazines you get? *Newsweek* and *Financial Times* and *Fords*?"

"*Forbes,*" he said, still watching the screen. He reminded me of me at four, studying the Magic 8 Ball I'd gotten for my birthday.

"Yeah, that one. Can I have the phone for a minute?"

He handed it over rather reluctantly, and I was pretty sure I had him after all. I was glad, but I also felt a little ashamed of myself. Like a guy who's just clonked a tame squirrel on the head when it came up to take a nut out of his hand.

I opened Safari. It was a lot more primitive than it is today, but it worked just fine. I poked *Wall Street Journal* into the Google search field, and after a few seconds, the front page opened up. One of the headlines read COFFEE COW ANNOUNCES CLOSINGS. I showed it to him.

He stared, then took the newspaper from the table beside the easy chair where I'd put his mail when I came in. He looked at the front page. "That isn't here," he said.

"Because it's yesterday's," I said. I always got the mail out of his box when I came up, and the *Journal* was always wrapped around the other stuff and held with a rubber band. "You get it a day late. Everybody does." And

39

during the holiday season it came two days late, sometimes three. I didn't need to tell him this; he grumbled about it constantly during November and December.

"This is today's?" he asked, looking at the screen. Then, checking the date at the top: "It is!"

"Sure," I said. "Fresh news instead of stale, right?"

"According to this, there's a map of the closing sites. Can you show me how to get it?" He sounded positively greedy. I was a little scared. He had mentioned Scrooge and Marley; I felt like Mickey Mouse in *Fantasia,* using a spell he didn't really understand to wake up the brooms.

"You can do it yourself. Just brush the screen with your finger, like this."

I showed him. At first he brushed too hard and went too far, but he got the knack of it after that. Faster than my dad, actually. He found the right page. "Look at that," he marveled. "Six hundred stores! You see what I was telling you about the fragility of the . . ." He trailed off, staring at the tiny map. "The south. Most of the closures are in the south. The south is a bellwether, Craig, it almost always . . . I think I need to make a call to New York. The market will be closing soon." He started to get up. His regular phone was on the other side of the room.

"You can call from this," I said. "It's mostly

what it's for." It was then, anyway. I pushed the phone icon, and the keypad appeared. "Just dial the number you want. Touch the keys with your finger."

He looked at me, blue eyes bright beneath his shaggy white brows. "I can do that out here in the williwags?"

"Yeah," I said. "The reception is terrific, thanks to the new tower. You've got four bars."

"Bars?"

"Never mind, just make your call. I'll leave you alone while you do it, just wave out the window when you're —"

"No need. This won't take long, and I don't need privacy."

He touched the numbers tentatively, as if he expected to set off an explosion. Then, just as tentatively, he raised the iPhone to his ear, looking at me for confirmation. I nodded encouragingly. He listened, spoke to someone (too loud at first), and then, after a short wait, to someone else. So I was right there when Mr. Harrigan sold all of his Coffee Cow stock, a transaction amounting to who knows how many thousands of dollars.

When he was finished, he figured out how to go back to the home screen. From there he opened Safari again. "Is *Forbes* on here?"

I checked. It wasn't. "But if you're looking for an article from *Forbes* you already know about, you can probably find it, because

41

someone will have posted it."

"Posted — ?"

"Yeah, and if you want info about something, Safari will search for it. You just have to google it. Look." I went over to his chair and entered *Coffee Cow* in the search field. The phone considered, then spewed a number of hits, including the *Wall Street Journal* article he'd called his broker about.

"Will you look at this," he marveled. "It's the Internet."

"Well, yeah," I said, thinking *Well, duh.*

"The worldwide web."

"Yeah."

"Which has been around how long?"

*You should know this stuff,* I thought. *You're a big businessman, you should know this stuff even if you're retired, because you're still interested.*

"I don't know exactly how long it's been around, but people are on it all the time. My dad, my teachers, the cops . . . everyone, really." More pointedly: "Including your companies, Mr. Harrigan."

"Ah, but they're not mine anymore. I do know a little, Craig, as I know a little about various television shows even though I don't watch television. I have a tendency to skip the technology articles in my newspapers and magazines, because I have no interest. If you wanted to talk bowling alleys or film distribu-

42

tion networks, that would be a different matter. I keep my hand in, so to speak."

"Yeah, but don't you see . . . those businesses are *using* the technology. And if you don't understand it . . ."

I didn't know how to finish, at least without straying beyond the bounds of politeness, but it seemed he did. "I will be left behind. That's what you're saying."

"I guess it doesn't matter," I said. "Hey, you're retired, after all."

"But I don't want to be considered a *fool*," he said, and rather vehemently. "Do you think Chick Rafferty was surprised when I called and told him to sell Coffee Cow? Not at all, because he's undoubtedly had half a dozen other major clients pick up the phone and tell him to do the same. Some are no doubt people with inside information. Others, though, just happen to live in New York or New Jersey and get the *Journal* on the day it's published and find out that way. Unlike me, stashed away up here in God's country."

I again wondered why he'd come to begin with — he certainly had no relatives in town — but this didn't seem like the time to ask.

"I may have been arrogant." He brooded on this, then actually smiled. Which was like watching the sun break through heavy cloud cover on a cold day. "I *have* been arrogant." He raised the iPhone. "I'm going to keep this after all."

The first thing that rose to my lips was *thank you,* which would have been weird. I just said, "Good. I'm glad."

He glanced at the Seth Thomas on the wall (and then, I was amused to see, checked it against the time on the iPhone). "Why don't we just read a single chapter today, since we've spent so much time talking?"

"Fine with me," I said, although I would gladly have stayed longer and read two or even three chapters. We were getting near the end of *The Octopus* by a guy named Frank Norris, and I was anxious to see how things turned out. It was an old-fashioned novel, but full of exciting stuff just the same.

When we finished the shortened session, I watered Mr. Harrigan's few indoor plants. This was always my last chore of the day, and only took a few minutes. While I did it, I saw him playing with the phone, turning it on and off.

"I suppose if I'm going to use this thing, you better show me *how* to use it," he said. "How to keep it from going dead, to start with. The charge is already dropping, I see."

"You'll be able to figure most of it out on your own," I said. "It's pretty easy. As for charging it, there's a cord in the box. You just plug it into the wall. I can show you a few other things, if you —"

"Not today," he said. "Tomorrow, perhaps."

"Okay."

"One more question, though. Why could I read that article about Coffee Cow, and look at that map of proposed closing sites?"

The first thing that came to mind was Hillary's answer about climbing Mount Everest, which we had just read about in school: *Because it's there.* But he might have seen that as smartass, which it sort of was. So I said, "I don't get you."

"Really? A bright boy like you? Think, Craig, think. I just read something for free that people pay good money for. Even with the *Journal* subscription rate, which is a good deal cheaper than buying off a newsstand, I pay ninety cents or so an issue. And yet with this . . ." He held up the phone just as thousands of kids would hold theirs up at rock concerts not many years later. "Now do you understand?"

When he put it that way I sure did, but I had no answer. It sounded —

"Sounds stupid, doesn't it?" he asked, reading either my face or my mind. "Giving away useful information runs counter to everything I understand about successful business practices."

"Maybe . . ."

"Maybe what? Give me your insights. I'm not being sarcastic. You clearly know more about this than I do, so tell me what you're thinking."

I was thinking about the Fryeburg Fair,

where Dad and I went once or twice every
October. We usually took my friend Margie,
from down the road. Margie and I rode the
rides, then all three of us ate doughboys and
sweet sausages before Dad dragged us to look
at the new tractors. To get to the equipment
sheds, you had to go past the Beano tent,
which was enormous. I told Mr. Harrigan
about the guy out front with the microphone,
telling the passing folks how you always got
the first game for free.

He considered this. "A come-on? I suppose
that makes a degree of sense. You're saying
you can only look at one article, maybe two
or three, and then the machine . . . what?
Shuts you out? Tells you if you want to play,
you have to pay?"

"No," I admitted. "I guess it's not like the
Beano tent after all, because you can look at
as many as you want. At least, as far as I
know."

"But that's crazy. Giving away a free sample
is one thing, but giving away the *store* . . ."
He snorted. "There wasn't even an *advertise-
ment*, did you notice that? And advertising is
a huge income stream for newspapers and
periodicals. Huge."

He picked the phone up, stared at his
reflection in the now blank screen, then put
it down and peered at me with a queer, sour
smile on his face.

"We may be looking at a huge mistake here,

Craig, one being made by people who understand the practical aspects of a thing like this — the *ramifications* — no more than I do. An economic earthquake may be coming. For all I know, it's already here. An earthquake that's going to change how we get our information, when we get it, where we get it, and hence how we look at the world." He paused. "And deal with it, of course."

"You lost me," I said.

"Look at it this way. If you get a puppy, you have to teach him to do his business outside, right?"

"Right."

"If you had a puppy that wasn't housebroken, would you give him a treat for shitting in the living room?"

"Course not," I said.

He nodded. "It would be teaching him the exact opposite of what you want him to learn. And when it comes to commerce, Craig, most people are like puppies that need to be housebroken."

I didn't much like that concept, and don't today — I think the punishment/reward thing says a lot about how Mr. Harrigan made his fortune — but I kept my mouth shut. I was seeing him in a new way. He was like an old explorer on a new voyage of discovery, and listening to him was fascinating. I don't think he was really trying to teach me, either. He was learning himself, and for a guy in his mid-eighties, he was learning fast.

"Free samples are fine, but if you give people too much for-free, whether it's clothes or food or information, they come to expect it. Like puppies that crap on the floor, then look you in the eye, and what they're thinking is, 'You taught me this was all right.' If I were the *Wall Street Journal . . .* or the *Times . . .* even the damn *Reader's Digest . . .* I'd be very frightened by this gizmo." He picked up the iPhone again; couldn't seem to leave it alone. "It's like a broken watermain, one spewing information instead of water. I thought it was just a phone we were talking about, but now I see . . . or begin to see . . ."

He shook his head, as if to clear it.

"Craig, what if someone with proprietary information about new drugs in development decided to put the test results out on this thing for the whole world to read? It could cost Upjohn or Unichem millions of dollars. Or suppose some disaffected person decided to spill government secrets?"

"Wouldn't they be arrested?"

"Maybe. Probably. But once the toothpaste is out of the tube, as they say . . . i-yi-yi. Well, never mind. You better go home or you'll be late for supper."

"On my way."

"Thank you again for the gift. I probably won't use it very much, but I intend to think about it. As hard as I'm able, at least. My

48

brains aren't as nimble as they once were."

"I think they're still plenty nimble," I said, and I wasn't just buttering him up. Why *weren't* there ads along with the news stories and YouTube videos? People would have to look at them, right? "Besides, my dad says it's the thought that counts."

"An aphorism more often spoken than adhered to," he said, and when he saw my puzzled expression: "Never mind. I'll see you tomorrow, Craig."

On my walk back down the hill, kicking up clods of that year's last snow, I thought about what he'd said: that the Internet was like a broken watermain spewing information instead of water. It was true of my dad's laptop as well, and the computers at the school, and ones all over the country. The world, really. Although the iPhone was still so new to him he could barely figure out how to turn it on, Mr. Harrigan already understood the need to fix the broken pipe if business — as he knew it, anyway — was going to continue as it always had. I'm not sure, but I think he foresaw paywalls a year or two before the term was even coined. Certainly I didn't know it then, no more than I knew how to get around restricted operations — what came to be known as jailbreaking. Paywalls came, but by then people *had* gotten used to getting stuff for free, and they resented being asked to cough up. People faced with a *New York Times* paywall went to a site like CNN or *Huffington Post* instead (usually in a huff), even though the reporting wasn't as good. (Unless, of course, you wanted to learn about a fashion development known as "sideboob.") Mr. Harrigan was totally right about that.

After dinner that night, once the dishes were washed and put away, my dad opened his laptop on the table. "I found something new," he said. "It's a site called previews.com, where you can watch coming attractions."

"Really? Let's see some!"

So for the next half hour, we watched movie trailers we would otherwise have had to go to a movie theater to see.

Mr. Harrigan would have torn his hair out. What little he had left.

Walking back from Mr. Harrigan's house on that March day in 2008, I was pretty sure he was wrong about one thing. *I probably won't use it very much,* he'd said, but I had noted the look on his face as he stared at the map showing the Coffee Cow closings. And how quickly he'd used his new phone to call someone in New York. (His combination lawyer and business manager, I found out later, not his broker.)

And I was correct. Mr. Harrigan used that phone plenty. He was like the old maiden aunt who takes an experimental mouthful of brandy after sixty years of abstinence and becomes a genteel alcoholic almost overnight. Before long, the iPhone was always on the table beside his favorite chair when I came up in the afternoon. God knows how many people he called, but I know he called me almost every night to ask me some question or other about his new acquisition's capabilities. Once he said it was like an old-fashioned rolltop desk, full of small drawers and caches and cubbyholes it was easy to overlook.

He found most of the caches and cubbyholes himself (with aid from various Internet sources), but I helped him out — enabled him, you might say — at the start. When he told me he hated the prissy little xylophone that sounded off when he had an incoming call, I changed it to a snatch of Tammy Wynette, singing "Stand By Your Man." Mr. Harrigan thought that was a hoot. I showed him how to set the phone on silent so it wouldn't disturb him when he took his afternoon nap, how to set the alarm, and how to record a message for when he didn't feel like answering. (His was a model of brevity: "I'm not answering my phone now. I will call you back if it seems appropriate.") He began unplugging his landline when he went for his daily snooze, and I noticed he was leaving it unplugged more and more. He sent me text messages, which ten years ago we called IMs.

51

He took phone-photos of mushrooms in the field behind his house and sent them off via email to be identified. He kept notes in the note function, and discovered videos of his favorite country artists.

"I wasted an hour of beautiful summer daylight this morning watching George Jones videos," he told me later on that year, with a mixture of shame and a weird kind of pride.

I asked him once why he didn't go out and buy his own laptop. He'd be able to do all the things he'd learned to do on his phone, and on the bigger screen, he could see Porter Wagoner in all his bejeweled glory. Mr. Harrigan just shook his head and laughed. "Get thee behind me, Satan. It's like you taught me to smoke marijuana and enjoy it, and now you're saying, 'If you like pot, you'll *really* like heroin.' I think not, Craig. This is enough for me." And he patted the phone affectionately, the way you might pat a small sleeping animal. A puppy, say, that's finally been housebroken.

We read *They Shoot Horses, Don't They?* in the fall of 2008, and when Mr. Harrigan called a halt early one afternoon (he said all those dance marathons were exhausting), we went into the kitchen, where Mrs. Grogan had left a plate of oatmeal cookies. Mr. Harrigan walked slowly, stumping along on his canes. I walked behind him, hoping I'd be able to catch him if he fell.

He sat with a grunt and a grimace and took one of the cookies. "Good old Edna," he said. "I love these things, and they always get my bowels in gear. Get us each a glass of milk, will you, Craig?"

As I was getting it, the question I kept forgetting to ask him recurred. "Why did you move here, Mr. Harrigan? You could live anywhere."

He took his glass of milk and made a toasting gesture, as he always did, and I made one right back, as *I* always did. "Where would you live, Craig? If you could, as you say, live anywhere?"

"Maybe Los Angeles, where they make the movies. I could catch on hauling equipment, then work my way up." Then I told him a great secret. "Maybe I could write for the movies."

I thought he might laugh, but he didn't. "Well, I suppose someone has to, why not you? And would you never long for home? To see your father's face, or put flowers on your mother's grave?"

"Oh, I'd come back," I said, but the question — and the mention of my mother — gave me pause.

"I wanted a clean break," Mr. Harrigan said. "As someone who lived his whole life in the city — I grew up in Brooklyn before it became a . . . I don't know, a kind of potted plant — I wanted to get away from New York in my final years. I wanted to live somewhere in the country, but not the tourist country, places like Camden and Castine and Bar Harbor. I wanted a place where the roads were still unpaved."

"Well," I said, "you sure came to the right place."

‘He laughed and took another cookie. "I considered the Dakotas, you know . . . and Nebraska . . . but ultimately decided that was taking things too far. I had my assistant bring me pictures of a good many towns in Maine, New Hampshire, and Vermont, and this was the place I settled on. Because of the hill. There are views in every direction, but not *spectacular* views. Spectacular views might bring tourists, which was exactly what I didn't want. I like it here. I like the peace, I like the neighbors, and I like you, Craig."

That made me happy.

"There's something else. I don't know how much you've read about my working life, but if you have — or do in the future — you'll find many of the opinion that I was ruthless as I climbed what envious and intellectually clueless people call 'the ladder of success.' That opinion isn't entirely wrong. I made enemies, I freely admit it. Business is like football, Craig. If you have to knock someone down to reach the goal line, you better damn well do it, or you shouldn't put on a uniform and go out on the field in the first place. But when the game is over — and mine is, although I keep my hand in — you take off the uniform and go home. This is now home for me. This unremarkable corner of America, with its single store and its school which will, I believe, soon be closing. People no longer 'just drop by for a drink.' I don't have to attend business lunches with people who always, *always* want something. I am not invited to take a seat at board meetings. I don't have to go to charity functions that bore me to tears, and I don't have to wake up at five in the morning to the sound of garbage trucks loading on Eighty-first Street. I'll be buried here, in Elm Cemetery among the Civil War veterans, and I won't have to pull rank or bribe some Superintendent of Graves for a nice plot. Does any of that explain?"

It did and didn't. He was a mystery to me, to the very end and even beyond. But maybe that's always true. I think we mostly live alone. By choice, like him, or just because that's the way the world was made. "Sort of," I said. "At least you didn't move to North Dakota. I'm glad of that."

He smiled. "So am I. Take another cookie to eat on your way home, and say hello to your father."

With a diminishing tax base that could no longer support it, our little six-room Harlow school did close in June of 2009, and I found myself facing the prospect of attending eighth grade across the Androscoggin River at Gates Falls Middle, with over seventy classmates instead of just twelve. That was the summer I kissed a girl for the first time, not Margie but her best friend Regina. It was also the summer that Mr. Harrigan died. I was the one who found him.

I knew he was having a harder and harder job getting around, and I knew he was losing his breath more often, sometimes sucking from the oxygen bottle he now kept beside his favorite chair, but other than those things, which I just accepted, there was no warning. The day before was like any other. I read a couple of chapters from *McTeague* (I had asked if we could read another Frank Norris book, and Mr. Harrigan was agreeable), and watered his houseplants while Mr. Harrigan scrolled through his emails.

He looked up at me and said, "People are catching on."

"To what?"

He held up his phone. "To this. What it really means. To what it can do. Archimedes said, 'Give me a lever long enough and I will move the world.' This is that lever."

"Cool," I said.

"I have just deleted three ads for products and almost a dozen political solicitations. I have no doubt my email address is being bandied about, just as magazines sell the addresses of their subscribers."

"Good thing they don't know who you are," I said. Mr. Harrigan's email handle (he loved having a handle) was **pirateking1**.

"If someone is keeping track of my searches, they don't have to. They'll be able to suss out my interests and solicit me accordingly. My name means nothing to them. My interests do."

"Yeah, spam is annoying," I said, and went into the kitchen to dump the watering can and put it in the mudroom.

When I came back, Mr. Harrigan had the oxygen mask over his mouth and nose and was taking deep breaths.

"Did you get that from your doctor?" I asked. "Did he, like, prescribe it?"

He lowered it and said, "I don't have a doctor. Men in their mid-eighties can eat all the corned beef hash they want, and they no longer need doctors, unless they have cancer. Then a doctor is handy to prescribe pain medication." His mind was somewhere else. "Have you considered Amazon, Craig? The company, not the river."

Dad bought stuff from Amazon sometimes, but no, I'd never really considered it. I told Mr. Harrigan that, and asked what he meant.

He pointed to the Modern Library copy of *McTeague*. "This came from Amazon. I ordered it with my phone and my credit card.

That company used to be just books. Little more than a mom-and-pop operation, really, but soon it may be one of the biggest and most powerful corporations in America. Their smile logo will be as ubiquitous as the Chevrolet emblem on cars or this on our phones." He lifted his, showing me the apple with the bite out of it. "Is spam annoying? Yes. Is it becoming the cockroach of American commerce, breeding and scurrying everywhere? Yes. Because spam works, Craig. It pulls the plow. In the not-too-distant future, spam may decide elections. If I were a younger man, I'd take this new income stream by the balls . . ." He closed one of his hands. He could only make a loose fist because of his arthritis, but I got the idea. ". . . and I would squeeze." The look came into his eyes that I sometimes saw, the one that made me glad I wasn't in his bad books.

"You'll be around for years yet," I said, blissfully unaware that we were having our last conversation.

"Maybe or maybe not, but I want to tell you again how glad I am you convinced me to keep this. It's given me something to think about. And when I can't sleep at night, it's been a good companion."

"I'm glad," I said, and I was. "Gotta go. I'll see you tomorrow, Mr. Harrigan."

So I did, but he didn't see me.

■ ■ ■

I let myself in through the mudroom door like always, calling out, "Hi, Mr. Harrigan, I'm here."

There was no reply. I decided he was probably in the bathroom. I sure hoped he hadn't fallen in there, because it was Mrs. Grogan's day off. When I went into the living room and saw him sitting in his chair — oxygen bottle on the floor, iPhone and *McTeague* on the table beside him — I relaxed. Only his chin was on his chest, and he had slumped a little to one side. He looked like he was asleep. If so, that was a first this late in the afternoon. He napped for an hour after lunch, and by the time I arrived, he was always bright-eyed and bushy-tailed.

I took a step closer and saw his eyes weren't entirely closed. I could see the lower arc of his irises, but the blue no longer looked sharp. It looked foggy, faded. I began to feel scared.

"Mr. Harrigan?"

Nothing. Gnarled hands folded loosely in his lap. One of his canes was still leaning against the wall, but the other was on the floor, as if he had reached for it and knocked it over. I realized I could hear the steady hiss from the oxygen mask, but not the faint rasp of his breathing, a sound I'd grown so used to that I rarely heard it at all.

"Mr. Harrigan, you okay?"

I took another couple of steps and reached out to shake him awake, then withdrew my hand. I had never seen a dead person, but thought I might be looking at one now. I reached for him again, and this time I didn't chicken out. I grasped his shoulder (it was horribly bony beneath his shirt) and gave him a shake.

"Mr. Harrigan, wake up!"

One of his hands fell out of his lap and dangled between his legs. He slumped a little farther to one side. I could see the yellowed pegs of his teeth between his lips. Still, I felt I had to be absolutely sure he wasn't just unconscious or in a faint before I called anyone. I had a memory, very brief but very bright, of my mother reading me the story of the little boy who cried wolf.

I went into the hall bathroom, the one Mrs. Grogan called the powder room, on legs that felt numb, and came back with the hand mirror Mr. Harrigan kept on the shelf. I held it in front of his mouth and nose. No warm breath misted it. Then I knew (although, looking back on it, I'm pretty sure I actually knew when that hand fell out of his lap and hung between his legs). I was in the living room with a dead man, and what if he reached out and grabbed me? Of course he wouldn't do that, he liked me, but I remem-

bered the look he got in his eyes when he
said — only yesterday! when he'd been alive!
— that if he was a younger man, he'd take
this new income stream by the balls, and
squeeze. And how he'd closed his hand into
a fist to demonstrate.

*You'll find many of the opinion that I was ruth-
less,* he'd said.

Dead people didn't reach out and grab you
except in horror movies, I knew that, dead
people weren't ruthless, dead people weren't
*anything,* but I still stepped away from him as
I took my cell phone out of my hip pocket,
and I didn't take my eyes off him when I
called my father.

Dad said I was probably right, but he'd
send an ambulance, just in case. Who was
Mr. Harrigan's doctor, did I know? I said he
didn't have one (and you only had to look at
his teeth to know he didn't have a dentist). I
said I would wait, and I did. But I did it
outside. Before I went, I thought about picking up his dangling hand and putting it back
in his lap. I almost did, but in the end I
couldn't bring myself to touch it. It would be
cold.

I took his iPhone instead. It wasn't stealing. I think it was grief, because the loss of
him was starting to sink in. I wanted something that was his. Something that mattered.

I guess that was the biggest funeral our

church ever had. Also the longest cortege to the graveyard, mostly made up of rental cars. There were local people there, of course, including Pete Bostwick, the gardener, and Ronnie Smits, who had done most of the work on his house (and gotten wealthy out of it, I'm sure), and Mrs. Grogan, the house-keeper. Other townies as well, because he was well liked in Harlow, but most of the mourn-ers (if they *were* mourning, and not there just to make sure Mr. Harrigan was really dead) were business people from New York. There was no family. I mean zero, zilch, nada. Not even a niece or a second cousin. He'd never married, never had kids — probably one of the reasons Dad was leery about me going up there at first — and he'd outlived all the rest. That's why it was the kid from down the road, the one he paid to come and read to him, who found him.

Mr. Harrigan must have known he was on borrowed time, because he left a handwritten sheet of paper on his study desk specifying exactly how he wanted his final rites carried out. It was pretty simple. Hay & Peabody's Funeral Home had had a cash deposit on their books since 2004, enough to take care of everything with some left over. There was to be no wake or viewing hours, but he wanted to be "fixed up decently, if possible" so the coffin could be open at the funeral.

Reverend Mooney was to conduct the service, and I was to read from the fourth chapter of Ephesians: "Be kind to one another, tender-hearted, forgiving each other, just as God in Christ also has forgiven you." I saw some of the business types exchange looks at that, as though Mr. Harrigan hadn't shown *them* a great deal of kindness, or much in the way of forgiveness, either.

He wanted three hymns: "Abide With Me," "The Old Rugged Cross," and "In the Garden." He wanted Reverend Mooney's homily to last no more than ten minutes, and the Rev finished in just eight, ahead of schedule and, I believe, a personal best. Mostly the Rev just listed all the stuff Mr. Harrigan had done for Harlow, like paying to refurbish the Eureka Grange and fix up the Royal River covered bridge. He also put the fund drive for the community swimming pool over the top, the Rev said, but refused the naming privilege that went with it.

The Rev didn't say why, but I knew. Mr. Harrigan said that allowing people to name things after you was not only absurd but undignified and ephemeral. In fifty years, he said, or even twenty, you were just a name on a plaque that everyone ignored.

Once I had done my scriptural duty, I sat in the front row with Dad, looking at the coffin with the vases of lilies at its head and foot. Mr. Harrigan's nose stuck up like the prow of a ship. I told myself not to look at it, not to think it was funny or horrible (or both), but to remember him as he'd been. Good advice, but my eyes kept wandering back.

When the Rev finished his short talk, he raised his palm-down hand to the assembled mourners and gave the benediction. Once that was done, he said, "Those of you who would like to say a final word of goodbye may now approach the coffin."

There was a rustle of clothes and a murmur of voices as people stood. Virginia Hatlen began to play the organ very softly, and I realized — with a strange feeling I couldn't name then but would years later come to identify as surrealism — that it was a medley of country songs, including Ferlin Husky's "Wings of a Dove," Dwight Yoakam's "I Sang Dixie," and of course "Stand By Your Man." So Mr. Harrigan had even left instructions for the exit music, and I thought, *good for him*. A line was forming, the locals in their sport coats and khakis interspersed with the New York types in suits and fancy shoes.

"What about you, Craig?" Dad murmured. "Want a last look, or are you good?"

I wanted more than that, but I couldn't tell him. The same way I couldn't tell him how bad I felt. It had come home to me now. It didn't happen while I was reading the scripture, as I'd read so many other things for him, but while I was sitting and looking at his nose sticking up. Realizing that his coffin was a ship, and it was going to take him on his final voyage. One that went down into the dark. I wanted to cry, and I *did* cry, but later, in private. I sure didn't want to do it here, among strangers.

"Yes, but I want to be at the end of the line. I want to be last."

My dad, God bless him, didn't ask me why. He just squeezed my shoulder and got into line. I went back to the vestibule, a bit uncomfortable in a sport jacket that was getting tight around the shoulders because I'd finally started to grow. When the end of the line was halfway down the main aisle and I was sure no one else was going to join it, I got behind a couple of suited guys who were talking in low tones about — wouldn't you know it — Amazon stock.

By the time I got to the coffin, the music had stopped. The pulpit was empty. Virginia Hatlen had probably sneaked out back to have a cigarette, and the Rev would be in the vestry, taking off his robe and combing what remained of his hair. There were a few people in the vestibule, murmuring in low voices, but here in the church it was just me and Mr. Harrigan, as it had been on so many afternoons at his big house on the hill, with its views that were good but not *touristy.*

He was wearing a charcoal gray suit I'd never seen before. The funeral guy had rouged him a little so he'd look healthy, except healthy people don't lie in coffins with their eyes shut and the last few minutes of daylight shining on their dead faces before they go into the earth forever. His hands were folded, making me think of the way they'd been folded when I came into his living room only days before. He looked like a life-sized doll, and I hated seeing him that way. I didn't want to stay. I wanted fresh air. I wanted to be with my father. I wanted to go home. But I had something to do first, and I had to do it right away, because Reverend Mooney could come back from the vestry at any time.

I reached into the inside pocket of my sport coat and brought out Mr. Harrigan's phone. The last time I'd been with him — alive, I mean, not slumped in his chair or looking like a doll in an expensive box — he'd said he was glad I'd convinced him to keep the phone. He'd said it was a good companion when he couldn't sleep at night. The phone was password-protected — as I've said, he was a fast learner once something really grabbed his interest — but I knew what the password was: **pirate1**. I had opened it in my bedroom the night before the funeral, and had gone to the notes function. I wanted to leave him a message.

I thought about saying *I love you,* but that would have been wrong. I had liked him, certainly, but I'd also been a bit leery of him.

66

I didn't think he loved me, either. I don't think Mr. Harrigan ever loved anyone, unless it was the mother who had raised him after his dad left (I had done my research). In the end, the note I typed was this: *Working for you was a privilege. Thank you for the cards, and for the scratch-off tickets. I will miss you.*

I lifted the lapel of his suit coat, trying not to touch the unbreathing surface of his chest beneath his crisp white shirt . . . but my knuckles brushed it for just a moment, and I can feel that to this day. It was hard, like wood. I tucked the phone into his inside pocket, then stepped away. Just in time, too. Reverend Mooney came out of the side door, adjusting his tie.

"Saying goodbye, Craig?"

"Yes."

"Good. The right thing to do." He slipped an arm around my shoulders and guided me away from the coffin. "You had a relationship with him that I'm sure a great many people would envy. Why don't you go outside now and join your father? And if you want to do me a favor, tell Mr. Rafferty and the other pallbearers that we'll be ready for them in just a few minutes."

Another man had appeared in the door to the vestry, hands clasped before him. You only had to look at his black suit and white carnation to know he was a funeral parlor guy. I supposed it was his job to close the lid of the coffin and make sure it was latched down tight. A terror of death came over me at the sight of him, and I was glad to leave that place and go out into the sunshine. I didn't tell Dad I needed a hug, but he must have seen it, because he wrapped his arms around me.

*Don't die,* I thought. *Please, Dad, don't die.*

The service at Elm Cemetery was better, because it was shorter and because it was outside. Mr. Harrigan's business manager, Charles "Chick" Rafferty, spoke briefly about his client's various philanthropies, then got a little laugh when he talked about how he, Rafferty, had had to put up with Mr. Harrigan's "questionable taste in music." That was really the only human touch Mr. Rafferty managed. He said he'd worked "for and with" Mr. Harrigan for thirty years, and I had no reason to doubt him, but he didn't seem to know much about Mr. Harrigan's human side, other than his "questionable taste" for singers like Jim Reeves, Patty Loveless, and Henson Cargill.

I thought about stepping forward and telling the people gathered around the open grave that Mr. Harrigan thought the Internet was like a broken watermain, spewing information instead of water. I thought of telling them that he had over a hundred photos of mushrooms on his phone. I thought of telling

them he liked Mrs. Grogan's oatmeal cookies, because they always got his bowels in
gear, and that when you were in your eighties
you no longer needed to take vitamins or see
the doctor. When you were in your eighties,
you could eat all the corned beef hash you
wanted.

But I kept my mouth shut.

This time Reverend Mooney read the
scripture, the one about how we were all going to rise from the dead like Lazarus on that
great gettin-up morning. He gave another
benediction and then it was over. After we
were gone, back to our ordinary lives, Mr.
Harrigan would be lowered into the ground
(with his iPhone in his pocket, thanks to me)
and the dirt would cover him, and the world
would see him no more.

As Dad and I were leaving, Mr. Rafferty
approached us. He said he wasn't flying back
to New York until the following morning, and
asked if he could drop by our house that
evening. He said there was something he
wanted to talk about with us.

My first thought was that it must be about
the pilfered iPhone, but I had no idea how
Mr. Rafferty could know I'd taken it, and
besides, it had been returned to its rightful
owner. *If he asks me,* I thought, *I'll tell him I
was the one who gave it to him in the first place.*
And how could a phone that had cost six
hundred bucks possibly be a big deal when

Mr. Harrigan's estate must be worth so much?

"Sure," Dad said. "Come to supper. I make a pretty mean spaghetti Bolognese. We usually eat around six."

"I'll take you up on that," Mr. Rafferty said. He produced a white envelope with my name on it in handwriting I recognized. "This may explain what I want to talk to you about. I received it two months ago and was instructed to hold it until . . . mmm . . . such an occasion as this."

Once we were in our car, Dad burst out laughing, full-throated roars that brought tears to his eyes. He laughed and pounded the steering wheel and laughed and pounded his thigh and wiped his cheeks and then laughed some more.

"What?" I asked, when he'd begun to taper off. "What's so darn funny?"

"I can't think of anything else it would be," he said. He was no longer laughing, but still chuckling.

"What the heck are you talking about?"

"I think you must be in his will, Craig. Open that thing. See what it says."

There was a single sheet of paper in the envelope, and it was a classic Harrigan communique: no hearts and flowers, not even a *Dear* in the salutation, just straight to business. I read it out loud to my father.

Craig: If you're reading this, I've died. I have left you $800,000 in trust. The trustees are your father and Charles Rafferty, who is my business manager and who will now serve as my executor. I calculate this sum should be sufficient to see you through four years of college and any postgraduate work you may choose to do. Enough should remain to give you a start in your chosen career.

You spoke of screenwriting. If it's what you want, then of course you must pursue it, but I do not approve. There is a vulgar joke about screenwriters I will not repeat here, but by all means find it on your phone, keywords screenwriter and starlet. There is an underlying truth in it which I believe you will grasp even at your current age. Films are ephemeral, while books — the good ones — are eternal, or close to it. You have read me many good ones, but others are waiting to be written. That is all I will say.

Although your father has power of veto in all matters concerning your trust, he would be smart not to exercise it concerning any investments Mr. Rafferty suggests. Chick is wise in the ways of the market.

Even with school expenses, your $800,000 may grow to a million or more by the time you reach the age of 26, when the trust will expire and you can spend

71

(or invest — always the wisest course) as you choose. I have enjoyed our afternoons together.

> Very truly yours,
> Mr. Harrigan

PS: You are most welcome for the cards and the enclosures.

That postscript gave me a little shiver. It was almost as if he'd answered the note I'd left on his iPhone when I'd decided to slip it into the pocket of his burial coat.

Dad wasn't laughing or chuckling anymore, but he was smiling. "How does it feel to be rich, Craig?"

"It feels okay," I said, and of course it did. It was a great gift, but it was just as good — maybe even better — to realize Mr. Harrigan had thought so well of me. A cynic would probably believe that's me trying to sound saintly or something, but it's not. Because, see, the money was like a Frisbee I got stuck halfway up the big pine in our backyard when I was eight or nine: I knew where it was, but I couldn't get it. And that was okay. For the time being I had everything I needed. Except for him, that was. What was I going to do with my weekday afternoons now?

"I take back everything I ever said about him being a tightwad," Dad said as he pulled out behind a shiny black SUV some business guy had rented at the Portland Jetport. "Although . . ."

"Although what?" I asked.

"Considering the lack of relatives and how rich he was, he could have left you at least four mil. Maybe six." He saw my look and started laughing again. "Joking, kiddo, joking. Okay?"

I punched him on the shoulder and turned on the radio, going past WBLM ("Maine's Rock and Roll Blimp") to WTHT ("Maine's #1 Country Station"). I had gotten a taste for c&w. I have never lost it.

Mr. Rafferty came to dinner, and chowed down big on Dad's spaghetti, especially for a skinny guy. I told him I knew about the trust fund, and thanked him. He said "Don't thank *me*" and told us how he'd like to invest the money. Dad said whatever seemed right, just keep him informed. He *did* suggest John Deere might be a good place for some of my dough, since they were innovating like crazy. Mr. Rafferty said he'd take it under consideration, and I found out later that he did invest in Deere & Company, although only a token amount. Most of it went into Apple and Amazon.

After dinner, Mr. Rafferty shook my hand and congratulated me. "Harrigan had very few friends, Craig. You were fortunate to have been one."

73

"And he was fortunate to have Craig," my dad said quietly, and slung an arm around my shoulders. That put a lump in my throat, and when Mr. Rafferty was gone and I was in my room, I did some crying. I tried to keep it quiet so my dad wouldn't hear. Maybe I did; maybe he heard and knew I wanted to be left alone.

When the tears stopped, I turned on my phone, opened Safari, and typed in the keywords *screenwriter* and *starlet*. The joke, which supposedly originated with a novelist named Peter Feibleman, is about a starlet so clueless she fucked the writer. Probably you've heard it. I never had, but I got the point Mr. Harrigan was trying to make.

That night I awoke around two o'clock to the sound of distant thunder and realized all over again that Mr. Harrigan was dead. I was in my bed and he was in the ground. He was wearing a suit and he would be wearing it forever. His hands were folded and would stay that way until they were just bones. If rain followed the thunder, it might seep down and dampen his coffin. There was no cement lid or liner; he had specified that in what Mrs. Grogan referred to as his "dead letter." Eventually the lid of the coffin would rot. So would the suit. The iPhone, made of plastic, would last much longer than the suit or the coffin, but eventually that would go, too.

Nothing was eternal, except maybe for the mind of God, and even at thirteen I had my doubts about that.

All at once I needed to hear his voice.

And, I realized, I could.

It was a creepy thing to do (especially at two in the morning), and it was morbid, I knew that, but I also knew that if I did it, I could get back to sleep. So I called, and broke out in gooseflesh when I realized the simple truth of cell phone technology: somewhere under the ground in Elm Cemetery, in a dead man's pocket, Tammy Wynette was singing two lines of "Stand By Your Man."

Then his voice was in my ear, calm and clear, just a bit scratchy with old age: "I'm not answering my phone now. I will call you back if it seems appropriate."

And what if he *did* call back? What if he did?

I ended the call even before the beep came and climbed back into bed. As I was pulling the covers up, I changed my mind, got up, and called again. I don't know why. This time I waited for the beep, then said, "I miss you, Mr. Harrigan. I appreciate the money you left me, but I'd give it up to have you still alive." I paused. "Maybe that sounds like a lie, but it isn't. It really isn't."

Then I went back to bed and was asleep almost as soon as my head hit the pillow. There were no dreams.

It was my habit to turn on my phone even before I got dressed and check the Newsy news app to make sure no one had started World War III and there hadn't been any terrorist attacks. Before I could go there on the morning after Mr. Harrigan's funeral, I saw a little red circle on the SMS icon, which meant I had a text message. I assumed it was either from Billy Bogan, a friend and classmate who had a Motorola Ming, or Margie Washburn, who had a Samsung . . . although I'd gotten fewer texts from Margie lately. I suppose Regina had blabbed about me kissing her.

You know that old saying, "so-and-so's blood ran cold"? That can actually happen. I know, because mine did. I sat on my bed, staring at the screen of my phone. The text was from **pirateking1**.

Down in the kitchen, I could hear rattling as Dad pulled the skillet out of the cabinet beside the stove. He was apparently planning to make us a hot breakfast, something he tried to do once or twice a week.

"Dad?" I said, but the rattling continued, and I heard him say something that might have been *Come out of there, you damn thing.*

He didn't hear me, and not just because my bedroom door was closed. I could hardly hear myself. The text had made my blood run cold, and it had stolen my voice.

The message above the most recent one had been sent four days before Mr. Harrigan died. It read **No need to water the houseplants today, Mrs. G did it**. Below it was this: **C C C aa**.

It had been sent at 2:40 A.M.

"Dad!" This time it was a little louder, but still not loud enough. I don't know if I was crying then, or if the tears started when I was going downstairs, still wearing nothing but my underpants and a Gates Falls Tigers tee-shirt.

Dad's back was to me. He had managed to get the skillet out and was melting butter in it. He heard me and said, "I hope you're hungry. I know I am."

"Daddy," I said. "Daddy."

He turned when he heard what I'd stopped calling him when I was eight or nine. Saw I wasn't dressed. Saw I was crying. Saw I was holding out my phone. Forgot all about the skillet.

"Craig, what is it? What's wrong? Did you have a nightmare about the funeral?"

It was a nightmare, all right, and probably it was too late — he was old, after all — but maybe it wasn't.

"Oh, Daddy," I said. Blubbering now. "He's not dead. At least he wasn't at two-thirty this morning. We've got to dig him up. We have to, because we buried him alive."

I told him everything. About how I'd taken Mr. Harrigan's phone and put it in the pocket of his suit coat. Because it came to mean a lot to him, I said. And because it was something *I* gave *him.* I told him about calling that phone in the middle of the night, hanging up the first time, then calling back and leaving a message on his voicemail. I didn't need to show Dad the text I got in return, because he'd already looked at it. Studied it, actually.

The butter in the skillet had begun to scorch. Dad got up and moved the skillet off the burner. "Don't suppose you'll be wanting any eggs," he said. Then he came back to the table, but instead of sitting on the other side, in his usual place, he sat next to me and put one of his hands over one of mine. "Listen up now."

"I know it was a creepy thing to do," I said, "but if I hadn't, we never would have known. We have to —"

"Son —"

"No, Dad, listen! We have to get somebody out there right away! A bulldozer, a pay-loader, even guys with shovels! He could still be —"

"Craig, stop. You were spoofed."

I stared at him, my mouth hanging open. I knew what spoofing was, but the possibility that it had happened to me — and in the middle of the night — had never crossed my mind.

"There's more and more of it going around," he said. "We even had a staff meeting about it at work. Someone got access to Harrigan's cell phone. Cloned it. You know what I mean?"

"Yes, sure, but Daddy —"

He squeezed my hand. "Someone hoping to steal business secrets, maybe."

"He was retired!"

"But he kept his hand in, he told you that. Or it could have been access to his credit card info they were after. Whoever it was got your voicemail on the cloned phone, and decided to play a practical joke."

"You don't know that," I said. "Daddy, we have to check!"

"We don't, and I'm going to tell you why. Mr. Harrigan was a rich man who died unattended. In addition to that, he hadn't visited a physician in years, although I bet Rafferty gave him hell on that score, if only because he couldn't update the old guy's insurance to cover more of the death duties. For those reasons, there was an autopsy. That's how they found out he died of advanced heart disease."

"They cut him open?" I thought of how my knuckles had brushed his chest when I put his phone in his pocket. Had there been stitched-up incisions under his crisp white shirt and knotted tie? If my dad was right, then yes. Stitched-up incisions in the shape of a **Y**. I had seen that on TV. On *CSI.*

"Yes," Dad said. "I don't like telling you that, don't want it preying on your mind, but it's better that than letting you think he was buried alive. He wasn't. Couldn't have been. He's dead. Do you understand me?"

"Yes."

"Would you like me to stay home today? I will if you want."

"No, that's okay. You're right. I got spoofed." And spooked. That too.

"What are you going to do with yourself? Because if you're going to brood and be all morbid, I should take the day off. We could go fishing."

"I'm not going to brood and be all morbid. But I should go up to his house and water the plants."

"Is going there a good idea?" He was watching me closely.

"I owe it to him. And I want to talk to Mrs. Grogan. Find out if he made a whatchacallit for her, too."

"A provision. That's very thoughtful. Of course she may tell you to mind your beeswax. She's an old-time Yankee, that one."

"If he didn't, I wish I could give her some of mine," I said.

He smiled, and kissed my cheek. "You're a

80

good kid. Your mom would be so proud of you. Are you sure you're okay now?"

"Yes." I ate some eggs and toast to prove it, although I didn't want them. My dad had to be right — a stolen password, a cloned phone, a cruel practical joke. It sure hadn't been Mr. Harrigan, whose guts had been tossed like salad and whose blood had been replaced with embalming fluid.

Dad went to work and I went up to Mr. Harrigan's. Mrs. Grogan was vacuuming the living room. She wasn't singing like she usually did, but she was composed enough, and after I finished watering the plants, she asked if I'd like to go into the kitchen and have a cup of tea (which she called "a cuppa cheer") with her.

"There's cookies, too," she said.

We went into the kitchen and while she boiled the kettle, I told her about Mr. Harrigan's note, and how he'd left money in trust for my college education.

Mrs. Grogan nodded in businesslike fashion, as if she'd expected no less, and said she had also gotten an envelope from Mr. Rafferty. "The boss fixed me up. More than I expected. Prob'ly more than I deserve."

I said I felt pretty much the same way.

Mrs. G. brought the tea to the table, a big mug for each of us. Between them she set down a plate of oatmeal cookies. "He loved these," Mrs. Grogan said.

"Yeah. He said they got his bowels in gear."

That made her laugh. I picked up one of the cookies and bit into it. As I chewed, I thought of the scripture from 1 Corinthians I'd read at Methodist Youth Fellowship on Maundy Thursday and at Easter service just a few months back: "And when he had given thanks, he brake it, and said, Take, eat: this is my body, which is broken for you: this do in remembrance of me." The cookies weren't communion, the Rev would surely have called the idea blasphemous, but I was glad to have one just the same.

"He took care of Pete, too," she said. Meaning Pete Bostwick, the gardener.

"Nice," I said, and reached for another cookie. "He was a good guy, wasn't he?"

"Not so sure about that," she said. "He was square-dealing, all right, but you didn't want to be on his bad side. You don't remember Dusty Bilodeau, do you? No, you wouldn't. He was before your time."

"From the Bilodeaus over in the trailer park?"

"Ayuh, that's right, next to the store, but I 'spect Dusty isn't among em. He'll have gone on his merry way long since. He was the gardener before Pete, but wasn't eight months on the job before Mr. Harrigan caught him stealing and fired his butt. I don't know how much he got, or how Mr. Harrigan found out, but firing didn't end it. I know you know some of the stuff Mr. H. gave this little town and all the ways he helped out, but Mooney didn't tell even half of it, maybe because he didn't know or maybe because he was on a timer. Charity is good for the soul, but it also gives a man power, and Mr. Harrigan used his on Dusty Bilodeau."

She shook her head. Partly, I think, in admiration. She had that Yankee hard streak in her.

"I hope he filched at least a few hundred out of Mr. Harrigan's desk or sock drawer or wherever, because that was the last money he ever got in the town of Harlow, county of Castle, state of Maine. He couldn't have landed a job shoveling henshit out of old Dorrance Marstellar's barn after that. Mr. Harrigan saw to it. He was a square-dealing man, but if you weren't the same, God help you. Have another cookie."

I took another cookie.

"And drink your tea, boy."

I drank my tea.

"I guess I'll do the upstairs next. Prob'ly change the sheets on the beds instead of just strippin em, at least for now. What do you think's going to happen with this house?"

"Gee, I don't know."

"Neither do I. Not a clue. Can't imagine anyone buying it. Mr. Harrigan was one of a kind, and that goes the same for . . ." She spread her arms wide. ". . . all this."

I thought about the glass elevator and decided she had a point.

Mrs. G. grabbed another cookie. "What about the houseplants? Any idears about them?"

"I'll take a couple, if it's all right," I said. "The rest, I don't know."

"Me, either. And his freezer's full. I guess we could split that three ways — you, me, and Pete."

*Take, eat,* I thought. *This do in remembrance of me.*

She sighed. "I'm mostly just dithering. Stretching out a few chores like they were many. I don't know what I'm going to do with myself, and that's the God's honest. What about you, Craig? What are you going to do?"

"Right now I'm going downstairs to spritz his hen of the woods," I said. "And if you're sure it's okay, I'll at least take the African violet when I go home."

"Course I'm sure." She said it the Yankee way: *Coss.* "As many as you want."

She went upstairs and I down to the base-ment, where Mr. Harrigan kept his mush-rooms in a bunch of terrariums. While I spritzed, I thought about the text message I'd gotten from **pirateking1** in the middle of the night. Dad was right, it had to be a joke, but wouldn't a practical joker have sent some-thing at least half-witty, like **Save me I'm**

**trapped in a box** or the old one that went **Don't bother me while I'm decomposing?** Why would a practical joker just send a double **a**, which when you spoke it sounded kind of like a gurgle, or a death-rattle? And why would a practical joker send my initial? Not once or twice but three times?

I ended up taking four of Mr. Harrigan's houseplants — the African violet, the anthurium, the peperomia, and the dieffenbachia. I spotted them around our house, saving the dieffenbachia for my room, because it was my favorite. But I was just marking time, and I knew it. Once the plants were placed, I got a bottle of Snapple out of the fridge, put it in the saddlebag of my bike, and rode out to Elm Cemetery.

It was deserted on that hot summer forenoon, and I went right to Mr. Harrigan's grave. The stone was in place, nothing fancy, just a granite marker with his name and dates on it. There were plenty of flowers, all still fresh (that wouldn't last long), most with cards tucked in them. The biggest bunch, perhaps picked from Mr. Harrigan's own flowerbeds — and out of respect, not parsimony — was from Pete Bostwick's family.

I got down on my knees, but not to pray. I took my phone out of my pocket and held it in my hand. My heart was beating so hard it made little black dots flash in front of my eyes. I went to my contacts and called him. Then I lowered my phone and put the side of my face down on the newly replaced sod, listening for Tammy Wynette.

I thought I heard her, too, but it must have been my imagination. It would have had to've come through his coat, through the lid of his coffin, and up through six feet of ground. But I thought I did. No, check that — I was sure I did. Mr. Harrigan's phone, singing "Stand By Your Man" down there in his grave.

In my other ear, the one not pressed to the ground, I could hear his voice, very faint but audible in the dozing stillness of that place: "I'm not answering my phone now. I will call you back if it seems appropriate."

But he wouldn't, appropriate or not. He was dead.

I went home.

In September of 2009, I started school at Gates Falls Middle along with my friends Margie, Regina, and Billy. We rode in a little used bus which quickly earned us the jeering nickname of Short Bus Kids from the Gates kids. I eventually got taller (although I stopped two inches short of six feet, which sort of broke my heart), but on that first day of school, I was the shortest kid in the eighth grade. Which made me a perfect target for Kenny Yanko, a hulking troublemaker who had been kept back that year and whose picture should have been in the dictionary next to the word *bully.*

Our first class wasn't a class at all, but a school assembly for the new kids from the so-called "tuition towns" of Harlow, Motton, and Shiloh Church. The principal that year (and for many years to come) was a tall, shambling fellow with a bald head so shiny it looked Simonized. This was Mr. Albert Douglas, known to the kids as either Alkie Al or Dipso Doug. None of the kids had ever actually seen him loaded, but it was an article of faith back then that he drank like a fish.

He took the podium, welcomed "this group of fine new students" to Gates Falls Middle, and told us about all the wonderful things that awaited us in the coming academic year. These included band, glee club, debate club, photography club, Future Farmers of America, and all the sports we could handle (as long as they were baseball, track, soccer, or lacrosse — there would be no football option until high school). He explained about Dress-Up Fridays once a month, when boys would be expected to wear ties and sport jackets and girls would be expected to wear dresses (no hems more than two inches above the knee, please). Last of all, he told us there was to be absolutely no initiations of the new out-of-town students. Us, in other words. Apparently the year before, a transfer student

87

from Vermont had wound up in Central Maine General after being forced to chug-a-lug three bottles of Gatorade, and now the tradition had been banned. Then he wished us well and sent us off on what he called "our academic adventure."

My fears about getting lost in this huge new school turned out to be groundless, because it really wasn't huge at all. All my classes except for period-seven English were on the second floor, and I liked all my teachers. I had been scared of math class, but it turned out we were picking up pretty much where I'd left off, so that was okay. I was feeling pretty good about the whole thing until the four-minute change of classes between period six and period seven.

I headed down the hall to the stairs, past slamming lockers, gabbing kids, and the smell of Beefaroni from the cafeteria. I had just reached the top of the stairs when a hand grabbed me. "Hey, new boy. Not so fast."

I turned and saw a six-foot troll with an acne-blasted face. His black hair hung down to his shoulders in greasy clumps. Small dark eyes peered out at me from beneath a protruding shelf of forehead. They were filled with bogus merriment. He was wearing stovepipe jeans and scuffed biker boots. In one hand he held a paper bag.

"Take it."

Clueless, I took it. Kids were hurrying past

me and down the stairs, some with quick sideways glances at the kid with the long black hair.

"Look inside."

I did. There was a rag, a brush, and a can of Kiwi boot polish. I tried to hand the bag back. "I have to get to class."

"Uh-uh, new boy. Not until you shine my boots."

Clueless no more. It was an initiation stunt, and although expressly forbidden by the principal just that morning, I thought about doing it. Then I thought about all the kids hurrying downstairs past us. They would see the little country boy from Harlow on his knees with that rag and brush and can of polish. The story would spread fast. Yet I still might have done it, because this kid was much bigger than I was, and I didn't like the look in his eyes. *I would love to beat the shit out of you,* that look said. *Just give me an excuse, new boy.*

Then I thought of what Mr. Harrigan would think if he ever saw me down on my knees, humbly shining this oaf's shoes.

"No," I said.

"No's a mistake you don't want to make," the kid said. "You better fucking believe it."

"Boys? Say, boys? Is there a problem here?"

It was Ms. Hargensen, my earth science teacher. She was young and pretty, couldn't have been long out of college, but she had an air of confidence about her that said she took no shit.

The big boy shook his head: no problem here.

"All good," I said, handing the bag back to its owner.

"What's your name?" Ms. Hargensen asked. She wasn't looking at me.

"Kenny Yanko."

"And what's in your bag, Kenny?"

"Nothing."

"It wouldn't be an initiation kit, would it?"

"No," he said. "I gotta go to class."

I did, too. The crowd of kids going downstairs was thinning out, and pretty soon the bell was going to ring.

"I'm sure you do, Kenny, but one more second." She switched her attention to me. "Craig, right?"

"Yes, ma'am."

"What's in that bag, Craig? I'm curious."

I thought of telling her. Not out of any Boy Scout honesty-is-the-best-policy bullshit, but because he had scared me and now I was pissed off. And (might as well admit it) because I had an adult here to run interference. Then I thought, *How would Mr. Harrigan handle this? Would he snitch?*

"The rest of his lunch," I said. "Half a sandwich. He asked me if I wanted it."

If she had taken the bag and looked inside,

90

we both would have been in trouble, but she didn't . . . although I bet she knew. She just told us to get to class and went clicking away on her medium just-right-for-school heels.

I started down the stairs, and Kenny Yanko grabbed me again. "You should have shined em, new boy."

That pissed me off more. "I just saved your ass. You should be saying thank you."

He flushed, which did not complement all those erupting volcanos on his face. "You should have shined em." He started away, then turned back, still holding his stupid paper bag. "Fuck your thanks, new boy. And fuck you."

A week later, Kenny Yanko got into it with Mr. Arsenault, the woodshop teacher, and hucked a hand sander at him. Kenny had had no less than three suspensions during his two years at Gates Falls Middle — after my confrontation with him at the top of the stairs, I found out he was sort of a legend — and that was the last straw. He was expelled, and I thought my problems with him were over.

Like most smalltown schools, Gates Falls Middle was very big on traditions. Dress-Up Fridays was just one of many. There was Carrying the Boot (which meant standing in front of the IGA and asking for contributions to the fire department), and Doing the Mile (running around the gym twenty times in phys ed), and singing the school song at the monthly assemblies.

Another of these traditions was the Autumn Dance, a Sadie Hawkins kind of deal where the girls were supposed to ask the boys. Margie Washburn asked me, and of course I said yes, because I wanted to go on being friends with her even though I didn't like her, you know, *that* way. I asked my dad to drive us, which he was more than happy to do. Regina Michaels asked Billy Bogan, so it was a double date. It was especially good because Regina whispered to me in study hall that she'd only asked Billy because he was my friend.

I had a hell of a good time until the first intermission, when I left the gym to offload some of the punch I'd put away. I got as far as the boys' room door, then someone seized me by the belt with one hand and the back of my neck with the other and propelled me straight down the hall to the side exit that gave on the faculty parking lot. If I hadn't put out a hand to shove the crash bar, Kenny would have run me into the door face-first.

I have total recall of what followed. I have no idea why the bad memories of childhood and early adolescence are so clear, I only know they are. And this is a very bad memory.

The night air was shockingly cold after the heat of the gym (not to mention the humidity exuded by all those adolescent fruiting bodies). I could see moonlight gleaming on the chrome of the two parked cars belonging to that night's chaperones, Mr. Taylor and Ms. Hargensen (new teachers got stuck chaperoning because it was, you guessed it, a GFMS tradition). I could hear exhaust banging away through some car's shot muffler up on Highway 96. And I could feel the hot raw scrape of my palms when Kenny Yanko pushed me down on the parking lot pavement.

"Now get up," he said. "You got a job to do."

I got up. I looked at my palms and saw they were bleeding.

There was a bag sitting on one of the parked cars. He took it and held it out. "Shine my boots. Do that and we'll call it square."

"Fuck you," I said, and punched him in the eye.

Total recall, okay? I can remember every time he hit me: five blows in all. I can remember how the last one drove me back against the cinderblock wall of the building and how I told my legs to hold me up and they declined. I just slid slowly down until my butt was on the macadam. I can remember the Black Eyed Peas, faint but audible, doing "Boom Boom Pow." I can remember Kenny standing over me, breathing hard and saying, "Tell anyone and you're dead." But of all the things I can remember, the one I recall best — and treasure — is the sublime and savage satisfaction I felt when my fist connected with his face. It was the only one I got in, but it was a hell of a shot.

Boom boom pow.

When he was gone, I took my phone out of my pocket. After making sure it wasn't broken, I called Billy. It was all I could think of to do. He answered on the third ring, shouting to be heard over the chanting of Flo Rida. I told him to come outside and bring Ms. Hargensen. I didn't want to involve a teacher, but even with my chimes rung pretty good, I knew that was bound to happen eventually, so it seemed best to do it from the jump. I thought it was the way Mr. Harrigan would have handled it.

"Why? What's up, dude?"

"Some kid beat me up," I said. "I don't think I better go back inside. I don't look so great."

He came out three minutes later, not only with Ms. Hargensen but Regina and Margie. My friends stared with dismay at my split lip and bloody nose. My clothes were also speckled with blood and my shirt (brand new) was torn.

"Come with me," Ms. Hargensen said. She didn't seem upset by the blood, the bruise on

94

my cheek, or the way my mouth was fattening up. "All of you."

"I don't want to go in there," I said, meaning back into the gym annex. "I don't want to get stared at."

"Don't blame you," she said. "This way."

She led us to an entrance that said STAFF ONLY, used a key to let us in, and took us to the teachers' room. It wasn't exactly luxurious, I'd seen better furniture out on Harlow lawns when people had yard sales, but there were chairs, and I sat in one. She found a first aid kit and sent Regina into the bathroom to get a cold washcloth to put on my nose, which she said didn't look broken.

Regina came back looking impressed. "There's Aveda hand cream in there!"

"It's mine," Ms. Hargensen said. "Have some if you want. Put this on your nose, Craig. Hold it. Who brought you kids?"

"Craig's dad," Margie said. She was looking around at this undiscovered country with wide eyes. Since it was clear I wasn't going to die, she was cataloguing everything for later discussion with her gal pals.

"Call him," Ms. Hargensen said. "Give Margie your phone, Craig."

Margie called Dad and told him to come pick us up. He said something. Margie listened, then said, "Well, there was a little trouble." Listened some more. "Um . . . well . . ."

Billy took the phone. "He got beat up, but he's okay." Listened and held out the phone. "He wants to talk to you."

Of course he did, and after asking if I was all right, he wanted to know who had done it. I said I didn't know, but thought it was a high school kid who might've been trying to crash the dance. "I'm all right, Dad. Let's not make a big deal of this, okay?"

He said it *was* a big deal. I said it wasn't. He said it was. We went around like that, then he sighed and said he'd be there as fast as he could. I ended the call.

Ms. Hargensen said, "I'm not supposed to dispense anything for pain, only the school nurse can do that, and only then with parental permission, but she's not here, so . . ." She grabbed her purse, which was hanging on a hook with her coat, and peered inside. "Are any of you kids going to tell on me, and maybe cause me to lose my job?"

My three friends shook their heads. So did I, but gingerly. Kenny had caught me with a pretty good roundhouse to the left temple. I hoped the bullying bastard had hurt his hand.

Ms. Hargensen brought out a little bottle of Aleve. "My private stock. Billy, get him some water."

Billy brought me a Dixie cup. I swallowed the pill and felt better immediately. Such is the power of suggestion, especially when the one doing the suggesting is a gorgeous young woman.

"You three, make like bees and buzz," Ms. Hargensen said. "Billy, go in the gym and tell Mr. Taylor I'll be back in ten minutes. Girls, go outside and wait for Craig's father. Wave him over to the staff door."

They went. Ms. Hargensen leaned over me, close enough so I could smell her perfume, which was wonderful. I fell in love with her. I knew it was sappy but couldn't help it. She held up two fingers. "Please tell me you don't see three or four."

"No, just two."

"Okay." She straightened up. "Was it Yanko? It was, wasn't it?"

"No."

"Do I look stupid? Tell me the truth."

How she looked was beautiful, but I could hardly say that. "No, you don't look stupid, but it wasn't Kenny. Which is good. Because, see, if it *was* him, I bet he'd get arrested, because he's already expelled. Then there'd be a trial and I'd have to go in court and tell how he beat me up. Everyone would know. Think how embarrassing that would be."

"And if he beats somebody else up?"

I thought of Mr. Harrigan then — channeled him, you could even say. "That's their problem. All I care is that he's done with me."

She tried to scowl. Her lips curved in a big smile instead, and I fell more in love with her than ever. "That's cold."

"I just want to get along," I said. Which was the God's honest truth.

"You know what, Craig? I think you will."

When my dad got there, he looked me over and complimented Ms. Hargensen on her work.

"I was a prizefight cut-man in my last life," she said. That made him laugh. Neither of them suggested a trip to the emergency room, which was a relief.

Dad took the four of us home, so we missed the second half of the dance, but none of us minded. Billy, Margie, and Regina had had an experience more interesting than waving their hands in the air to Beyoncé and Jay-Z. As for me, I kept reliving the satisfying shock that had gone up my arm when my fist connected with Kenny Yanko's eye. It was going to leave a splendid shiner, and I wondered how he'd explain it. *Duh, I ran into a door. Duh, I ran into a wall. Duh, I was jerking off and my hand slipped.*

When we were back at the house, Dad asked me again if I knew who had done it. I said I didn't.

"Not sure I believe that, son."

I said nothing.

"You just want to let this go? Is that what I'm hearing?"

I nodded.

"All right." He sighed. "I guess I get it. I was young once myself. That's a thing parents always tell their kids sooner or later, but I doubt if any of them believe it."

"I believe it," I said, and I did, although it was amusing to visualize my father as a five-foot-five shrimpsqueak back in the age of landlines.

"Tell me one thing, at least. Your mother would be mad at me for even asking, but since she's not here . . . did you hit him back?"

"Yes. Only once, but it was a good one."

That made him grin. "Okay. But you need to understand that if he comes after you again, it's going to be a police matter. Are we clear?"

I said we were.

"Your teacher — I like her — said I should keep you up at least an hour and make sure you don't go all woozy. Want a piece of pie?"

"Sure."

"Cup of tea to go with it?"

"Absolutely."

So we had pie and big mugs of tea and Dad told me stories that weren't about party telephone lines, or going to a one-room school where there was just a woodstove for heat, or TVs that only got the three stations (and none at all if the wind blew down the roof antenna). He told me about how he and Roy DeWitt found some fireworks in Roy's cellar and when they shot them off one went into Frank Driscoll's kindling box and set it on fire and Frank Driscoll said if they didn't cut him a cord of wood, he'd tell their parents. He told me about how his mother overheard him call old Philly Loubird from Shiloh Church Big Chief Wampum and washed his mouth out with soap, ignoring his promises to never say anything like that again. He told me about fights at the Auburn Rollodrome — rumbles, he called them — where the kids from Lisbon High and those from Edward Little, Dad's school, got into it just about every Friday night. He told me about getting his bathing suit pulled off by a couple of big kids at White's Beach ("I walked home with my towel wrapped around me"), and the time some kid chased him down Carbine Street in Castle Rock with a baseball bat ("He said I put a hickey on his sister, which I never did").

He really *had* been young once.

I went upstairs to my room feeling good, but the Aleve Ms. Hargensen had given me was wearing off, and by the time I got undressed, the good feeling was wearing off with it. I was pretty sure Kenny Yanko wouldn't come back on me, but not positive. What if his friends started getting on his case about the shiner? Teasing him about it? Laughing about it, even? What if he got pissed and decided

Round 2 was in order? If that happened, I would most likely not even get in one good blow; the shot to his eye had been kind of a sucker punch, after all. He could put me in the hospital, or worse.

I washed my face (very gently), brushed my teeth, got into bed, turned off the light, and then just lay there, reliving what had happened. The shock of being grabbed from behind and shoved down the hallway. Being punched in the chest. Being punched in the mouth. Telling my legs to hold me up and my legs saying *maybe later.*

Once I was in the dark, it seemed more and more likely that Kenny wasn't done with me. Logical, even, the way things lots crazier than that can seem logical when it's dark and you're alone.

So I turned on the light again and called Mr. Harrigan.

I never expected to hear his voice, I only wanted to pretend I was talking to him. What I expected was silence, or a recorded message telling me the number I'd called was no longer in service. I'd slipped his phone into the pocket of his burial suit three months previous, and those first iPhones had a battery life of only 250 hours, even in standby mode. Which meant that phone had to be as dead as he was.

But it rang. It had no business ringing, reality was totally against the idea, but beneath the ground of Elm Cemetery, three miles away, Tammy Wynette was singing "Stand By Your Man."

Halfway through the fifth ring, his slightly scratchy old man's voice was in my ear. The same as always, straight to business, not even inviting his caller to leave a number or a message. "I'm not answering my phone now. I will call you back if it seems appropriate."

The beep came, and I heard myself talking. I don't remember thinking about the words; my mouth seemed to be operating completely on its own.

"I got beat up tonight, Mr. Harrigan. By a big stupid kid named Kenny Yanko. He wanted me to shine his shoes and I wouldn't. I didn't snitch on him because I thought that would end it, I was trying to think like you, but I'm still worried. I wish I could talk to you."

I paused.

"I'm glad your phone is still working, even though I don't know how it can be."

I paused.

"I miss you. Goodbye."

I ended the call. I looked in Recents to make sure I *had* called. His number was there, along with the time — 11:02 P.M. I turned off my phone and put it on the night table. I turned off my lamp and was asleep almost at once. That was on a Friday night. The next night — or maybe early on Sunday morning — Kenny Yanko died. He hung himself, although I didn't know that, or any of the details, for another year.

The obituary for Kenneth James Yanko wasn't in the Lewiston *Sun* until Tuesday, and all it said was "passed away suddenly, as the result of a tragic accident," but the news was all over the school on Monday and of course the rumor mill was in full operation.

He was huffing glue and died of a stroke.

He was cleaning one of his daddy's shotguns (Mr. Yanko was said to have a regular arsenal in his house) and it went off.

He was playing Russian roulette with one of his daddy's pistols and blew his head off.

He got drunk, fell down the stairs, and broke his neck.

None of these stories was true.

Billy Bogan was the one who told me, as soon as he got on the Short Bus. He was all but bursting with the news. He said one of his ma's friends from Gates Falls had called and told her. The friend lived across the street and had seen the body coming out on a stretcher with a passel of Yankos surrounding it, crying and screaming. Even expelled bullies had people who loved them, it seemed. As a Bible reader I could even imagine them rending their clothes.

I thought immediately — and guiltily — of the call I'd made to Mr. Harrigan's phone. I told myself he was dead and couldn't have had anything to do with it. I told myself that even if stuff like that were possible outside of comic book horror stories, I hadn't specifically wished Kenny dead, I just wanted to be left alone, but that seemed somehow lawyerly. And I kept remembering something Mrs. Grogan had said the day after the funeral, when I called Mr. Harrigan a good guy for putting us in his will.

*Not so sure about that. He was square-dealing, all right, but you didn't want to be on his bad side.*

Dusty Bilodeau had gotten on Mr. Harrigan's bad side, and surely Kenny Yanko would have been, too, for beating me up when I wouldn't shine his fucking boots. Only Mr. Harrigan no longer *had* a bad side. I kept telling myself that. Dead people don't *have* bad sides. Of course phones that haven't been charged for three months can't ring and then play messages (or take them), either . . . but Mr. Harrigan's *had* rung, and I *had* heard his rusty old man's voice. So I felt guilty, but I also felt relieved. Kenny Yanko would never come back on me. He was out of my road.

Later that day, during my free period, Ms. Hargensen came down to the gym where I was shooting baskets and took me into the hall.

"You were moping in class today," she said.

"No, I wasn't."

"You were and I know why, but I'm going to tell you something. Kids your age have a Ptolemaic view of the universe. I'm young enough to remember."

"I don't know what —"

"Ptolemy was a Roman mathematician and astrologer who believed the earth was the center of the universe, a stillpoint everything else revolved around. Children believe their entire worlds revolve around *them*. That sense of being at the center of everything usually starts to fade by the time you're twenty or so, but you're a long way from that."

She was leaning close to me, very serious, and she had the most beautiful green eyes. Also, the smell of her perfume was making me a little dizzy.

"I can see you're not following me, so let me dispense with the metaphor. If you're thinking you had something to do with the Yanko boy's death, forget it. You didn't. I've seen his records, and he was a kid with serious problems. Home problems, school problems, psychological problems. I don't know what happened, and I don't want to know, but I see a blessing here."

"What?" I asked. "That he can't beat me up anymore?"

She laughed, exposing teeth as pretty as the rest of her. "There's that Ptolemaic view of the world again. No, Craig, the blessing is that he was too young to get a license. If he'd been old enough to drive, he might have taken some other kids with him. Now go back to gym and shoot some baskets."

I started away, but she grabbed my wrist. Eleven years later I can still remember the electricity I felt. "Craig, I could never be glad when a child dies, not even a bad actor like Kenneth Yanko. But I can be glad it wasn't you."

Suddenly I wanted to tell her everything, and I might have done it. But just then the bell rang, classroom doors opened, and the hall was full of chattering kids. Ms. Hargensen went her way and I went mine.

That night I turned on my phone and at first just stared at it, gathering my courage. What Ms. Hargensen had said that morning made sense, but Ms. Hargensen didn't know that Mr. Harrigan's phone still worked, which was impossible. I hadn't had a chance to tell her and believed — erroneously, as it turned out — that I never would.

*It won't work this time,* I told myself. *It had one last spurt of energy, that's all. Like a lightbulb that flashes bright just before burning out.*

I hit his contact, expecting — hoping, actually — for silence or a message telling me the phone was no longer in service. But it rang, and after a few more rings, Mr. Harrigan was once more in my ear. "I'm not answering my

106

phone now. I will call you back if it seems appropriate."

"It's Craig, Mr. Harrigan."

Feeling foolish, talking to a dead man — one who would be growing mold on his cheeks by now (I had done my research, you see). At the same time not feeling foolish at all. Feeling scared, like someone treading on unhallowed ground.

"Listen . . ." I licked my lips. "You didn't have anything to do with Kenny Yanko dying, did you? If you did . . . um . . . knock on the wall."

I ended the call.

I waited for a knock.

None came.

The next morning, I had a message from **pirateking1**. Just six letters: **a a a. C C x.**

Meaningless.

It scared the hell out of me.

That autumn I thought a lot about Kenny Yanko (the current story making the rounds was that he had fallen from the second floor of his house while trying to sneak out in the middle of the night). I thought even more about Mr. Harrigan, and about his phone, which I now wished I'd thrown into Castle Lake. There was a fascination, okay? The fascination with strange things we all feel. Forbidden things. On several occasions I almost called Mr. Harrigan's phone, but I never did, at least not then. Once I'd found his voice reassuring, the voice of experience and success, the voice, you could say, of the grandfather I'd never had. Now I couldn't remember that voice as it had been on our sunny afternoons, talking about Charles Dickens or Frank Norris or D. H. Lawrence or how the Internet was like a broken water-main. Now all I could think of was the old-man rasp, like sandpaper that's almost worn out, telling me he would call me back if it seemed appropriate. And I thought of him in his coffin. The mortician from Hay & Peabody had no doubt gummed down his eyelids, but how long did that gum last? Were his eyes open down there? Were they staring up into the dark as they rotted in their sockets?

These things preyed on my mind.

A week before Christmas, Reverend Mooney asked me to come into the vestry so we could "have a chat." He did most of the chatting. My father was worried about me, he said. I was losing weight, and my grades had slipped. Was there anything I wanted to tell him? I thought it over and decided there might be. Not everything, but some of it.

"If I tell you something, can it stay between us?"

"As long as it doesn't have to do with self-harm or a crime — a *serious* crime — the answer is yes. I'm not a priest and this isn't the Catholic confessional, but most men of faith are good at keeping secrets."

So I told him that I'd had a fight with a boy from school, a bigger boy named Kenny Yanko, and he'd beat me up pretty good. I said I never wished Kenny dead, and I'd certainly not *prayed* for it, but he *had* died, almost right after our fight, and I couldn't stop thinking about it. I told him what Ms. Hargensen had said about how kids believed everything had to do with them, and how it wasn't true. I said that helped a little, but I still thought I might have played a part in Kenny's death.

The Rev smiled. "Your teacher was right, Craig. Until I was eight, I avoided stepping on sidewalk cracks so I wouldn't inadvertently break my mother's back."

"Seriously?"

"Seriously." He leaned forward. His smile went away. "I will keep your confidence if you will keep mine. Do you agree?"

"Sure."

"I'm good friends with Father Ingersoll, of Saint Anne's in Gates Falls. That is the church the Yankos attend. He told me that the Yanko boy committed suicide."

I think I gasped. Suicide had been one of the rumors going around in the week after Kenny died, but I had never believed it. I would have said the thought of killing himself had never crossed the bullying son of a bitch's mind.

Reverend Mooney was still leaning forward. He took one of my hands in both of his. "Craig, do you really believe that boy went home, thought to himself, 'Oh my goodness, I beat up a kid younger and smaller than me, I guess I'll kill myself'?"

"I guess not," I said, and I let out a breath it felt like I'd been holding for two months. "When you put it like that. How did he do it?"

"I didn't ask, and I wouldn't tell you even if Pat Ingersoll had told me. You need to let this go, Craig. The boy had problems. His need to beat you up was only one symptom of those problems. You had nothing to do with it."

"And if I'm relieved? That, you know, I don't have to worry about him anymore?"

"I'd say that was you being human."

"Thanks."

"Do you feel better?"

"Yes."

And I did.

Not long before the end of school, Ms. Hargensen stood before our earth science class with a big smile on her face. "You guys probably thought you were going to be rid of me in two weeks, but I have some bad news. Mr. de Lesseps, the high school biology teacher, is retiring, and I've been hired to take his place. You could say I'm graduating from

110

middle school to high school."

A few kids groaned theatrically, but most of us applauded, and no one clapped harder than I did. I would not be leaving my love behind. To my adolescent mind, it seemed like fate. And in a way, it was.

I also left Gates Falls Middle behind and started the ninth grade at Gates Falls High. That was where I met Mike Ueberroth, known then — as he is in his current career as a backup catcher for the Baltimore Orioles — as U-Boat.

Jocks and more scholarly types didn't mix much at Gates (I imagine it's true at most high schools, because jocks tend to be clannish), and if it hadn't been for *Arsenic and Old Lace,* I doubt if we ever would have become friends. U-Boat was a junior and I was just a lowly freshman, which made becoming friends even more unlikely. But we did, and we remain friends to this day, although I see him far less often.

Many high schools have a Senior Play, but that wasn't the case at Gates. We had two plays each year, and although they were put on by the Drama Club, all students could audition. I knew the story because I'd seen the movie version on TV one rainy Saturday afternoon. I enjoyed it, so I tried out. Mike's girlfriend, a Drama Club member, talked him into trying out, and he ended up playing the homicidal Jonathan Brewster. I was cast as his scurrying sidekick, Dr. Einstein. That part was played by Peter Lorre in the film, and I tried my best to sound like him, sneering "Yas! Yas!" before every line. It wasn't a very good imitation, but I have to tell you that the audience ate it up. Small towns, you know.

So that's how U-Boat and I became friends, and it's also how I found out what had really happened to Kenny Yanko. The Rev turned out to be wrong and the newspaper obituary turned out to be right. It really had been an accident.

During the break between Act 1 and Act 2 of our dress rehearsal, I was at the Coke machine, which had eaten up my seventy-five cents without giving me anything in return. U-Boat left his girlfriend, came over, and gave the machine's upper right corner a hard whack with the palm of one hand. A can of Coke promptly fell into the retrieval tray.

"Thanks," I said.

"No prob. You just have to remember to hit it right there, in that corner."

I said I would do that, although I doubted I could hit it with the same force.

"Hey, listen, I heard you had some trouble with that Yanko kid. True?"

There was no sense denying it — Billy and both girls had blabbed — and really no reason to at this late date. So I said yeah, it was true.

112

"You want to know how he died?"

"I've heard about a hundred different stories. Have you got another one?"

"I've got the truth, little buddy. You know who my dad is, don't you?"

"Sure." The Gates Falls police force consisted of fewer than two dozen uniformed officers, the Chief of Police, and one detective. That was Mike's father, George Ueberroth.

"I'll tell you about Yanko if you let me hit your soda."

"Okay, but don't backwash."

"Do I look like an animal? Give it to me, you fuckin cheesecake."

"Yas, yas," I said, doing Peter Lorre. He snickered, took the can, downed half of it, then belched. Down the hall, his girlfriend stuck a finger in her mouth and mimed puking. Love in high school is very sophisticated.

"My dad was the one who investigated," U-Boat said, handing the can back to me, "and a couple of days after it happened I heard him talking to Sergeant Polk from the house. That's what they call the cop-shop. They were out on the porch drinking beers, and the Sarge said something about Yanko doing the chokey-strokey. Dad laughed and said he'd heard it called a Beverly Hills necktie. The Sarge said it was probably the only way the poor kid could get off, with a pizza-face like that. My dad goes yeah, sad

113

but true. Then he said what bothered him was the hair. Said it bothered the coroner, too."

"What about his hair?" I asked. "And what's a Beverly Hills necktie?"

"I looked it up on my phone. It's slang for autoerotic asphyxiation." He said the words carefully. With pride, almost. "You hang yourself and beat off while you're passing out." He saw my expression and shrugged. "I don't make the news, Dr. Einstein, I just report it. I guess it's supposed to be an extremely big thrill, but I think I'll pass."

I thought I would, too. "What about the hair?"

"I asked my dad about that. He didn't want to tell me, but since I'd heard the rest, he eventually did. He said half of Yanko's hair had turned white."

I thought about that a lot. On the one hand, if I had ever considered the idea of Mr. Harrigan rising from his grave to extract vengeance on my behalf (and sometimes at night when I couldn't sleep, the idea, however ridiculous, would creep into my mind), U-Boat's story seemed to put paid to those thoughts. Thinking about Kenny Yanko in his closet, pants around his ankles and a rope around his neck, face turning purple as he did the old chokey-strokey, I could actually feel sorry for him. What a stupid, undignified way to die.

"As the result of a tragic accident," the *Sun* obituary had said, and that was more accurate than any of us kids could have known.

But on the other hand, there was that thing U-Boat's dad had said about Kenny's hair. I couldn't help wondering what might cause such a thing to happen. What Kenny might have seen in that closet with him as he swam toward unconsciousness while pulling his poor old pudding for everything he was worth.

Finally I went to my best counselor, the Internet. There I found a difference of opinion. Some scientists proclaimed that there was absolutely no evidence that shock can turn someone's hair white. Other scientists said yas, yas, it really could happen. That a sudden shock could kill the melanocyte stem cells that determine hair color. One article I read said that actually happened to Thomas More and Marie Antoinette before they were executed. Another article threw shade on that, saying it was just a legend. In the end, it was like something Mr. Harrigan sometimes said about buying stocks: you pays your money and you takes your choice.

Little by little, these questions and concerns faded, but I'd be lying if I told you that Kenny Yanko ever completely left my mind, then or now. Kenny Yanko in his closet with a rope around his neck. Maybe not losing consciousness before he could loosen the

115

rope, after all. Kenny Yanko perhaps seeing something — only perhaps — that had frightened him so badly that he had fainted. That he had actually been scared to death. In daylight, that seemed pretty stupid. At night, especially if the wind was high and making little screaming sounds around the eaves, not so much.

A FOR SALE sign from a Portland realty company went up in front of Mr. Harrigan's house, and a few people came up to look at it. They were mostly the kind who fly in from Boston or New York (some of them on charter jets, probably). The kind who, like the business folks who had attended Mr. Harrigan's funeral, pay extra to rent expensive cars. One pair was my first married gay couple, young but clearly well-to-do and just as clearly in love. They came in a snazzy BMW i8, held hands everywhere they went, and did a lot of *wow* and *amazing* over the grounds. Then they went away and didn't come back.

I saw a lot of these potential buyers because the estate (managed by Mr. Rafferty, of course) had kept Mrs. Grogan and Pete Bostwick on, and Pete hired me to help out with the grounds. He knew I was good with plants and was willing to work hard. I got twelve bucks an hour for ten hours a week, and with the big trust fund out of reach until I was in college, that money came in very handy.

Pete called the potential buyers Richie Riches. Like the married couple in their rented BMW, they went *wow* but didn't buy. Considering the house was on a dirt road and the views were only good, not great (no lakes, no mountains, no rockbound seacoast with a lighthouse), I wasn't surprised. Neither were Pete or Mrs. Grogan. They nicknamed the house White Elephant Manor.

In the early winter of 2011, I used some of my gardening money to upgrade my first-generation phone to an iPhone 4. I swapped in my contacts that same night, and when I scrolled through them, I came across Mr. Harrigan's number. Without thinking too much about it, I tapped it. **Calling Mr. Harrigan**, the screen said. I put the phone to my ear with a combination of dread and curiosity.

There was no outgoing message from Mr. Harrigan. There was no robot voice telling me the number I'd called was no longer in service, and there was no ring. There was nothing but smooth silence. You could say my new phone was, heh-heh, as quiet as the grave.

It was a relief.

I took biology my sophomore year, and there was Ms. Hargensen, as pretty as ever, but no longer my love. I had switched my affections to a more available (and age-appropriate) young lady. Wendy Gerard was a petite blond from Motton who had just gotten rid of her braces. Soon we were studying together, and going to movies together (when either my dad or her mom or dad would take us, that was), and making out in the back row. All that sticky kid stuff that's so absolutely fine.

My crush on Ms. Hargensen died a natural death, and that was a good thing, because it opened the way for friendship. I brought plants into class sometimes, and I helped out cleaning the lab, which we shared with the chem kids, after school on Friday afternoons.

On one of those afternoons, I asked her if she believed in ghosts. "I suppose you don't, being a scientist and all," I said.

She laughed. "I'm a teacher, not a scientist."

"You know what I mean."

"I suppose, but I'm still a good Catholic. That means I believe in God, and the angels, and the world of the spirit. Not so sure about exorcism and demonic possession, that seems pretty far out there, but ghosts? Let's just say the jury's out on that one. I'd certainly never attend a séance, or mess around with a Ouija board."

"Why not?"

We were cleaning the sinks, something the chem kids were supposed to take care of before they left for the weekend but hardly ever did. Ms. Hargensen paused, smiling.

118

Maybe a little embarrassed. "Science folks aren't immune from superstition, Craig. I don't believe in messing with what I don't understand. My grandmother used to say a person shouldn't call out unless they want an answer. I've always thought that was good advice. Why do you ask?"

I wasn't going to tell her Kenny was still on my mind. "I'm a Methodist myself, and we talk about the Holy Spirit. Only in the King James Bible, it's the Holy Ghost. I guess I was thinking about that."

"Well, if ghosts exist," she said, "I'll bet not all of them are holy."

I still wanted to be some kind of writer, although my ambition to write movies had cooled. Mr. Harrigan's joke about the screenwriter and the starlet recurred to me every now and then, and had cast a bit of a pall over my show biz fantasies.

For Christmas that year Dad got me a laptop, and I started to write short stories. They were okay line by line, but the lines of a story have to add up to a whole, and mine didn't. The following year, the head of the English Department tapped me to edit the school paper, and I got the journalism bug, which has so far never left me. I don't think it ever will. I believe you hear a click, not in your head but in your soul, when you find the place where you belong. You can ignore it, but really, why would you?

I started getting my growth, and when I was a junior, after I had shown Wendy that yes, I had protcction (it was U-Boat who actually bought the condoms), we left our virginity behind. I graduated third in my class (only 142, but still), and Dad bought me a Toyota Corolla (used, but still). I got accepted at Emerson, one of the best schools in the country for aspiring journalists, and I bet they would have given me at least a partial scholarship, but thanks to Mr. Harrigan I didn't need it — lucky me.

There were a few typical adolescent storms between fourteen and eighteen, but actually not that many — it was as if the nightmare with Kenny Yanko had in some way front-loaded a lot of my adolescent angst. Also, you know, I loved my dad, and it was just the two of us. I think that makes a difference.

By the time I started college, I hardly ever thought of Kenny Yanko at all. But I still thought of Mr. Harrigan. Not surprising, considering that he had rolled out the academic red carpet for me. But there were certain days when I thought of him more often. If I was home on one of those days, I put flowers on his grave. If I wasn't, Pete Bostwick or Mrs. Grogan did it for me.

Valentine's. Thanksgiving. Christmas. And my birthday.

I always bought a dollar scratch ticket on

those days, too. Sometimes I won a couple of bucks, sometimes five, and once I won fifty, but I never hit anything close to a jackpot. That was okay with me. If I had, I would have given the money to some charity. I bought the tickets to remember. Thanks to him, I was already rich.

Because Mr. Rafferty was generous with the trust fund, I had my own apartment by the time I was a junior at Emerson. Just a couple of rooms and a bathroom, but it was in Back Bay, where even small apartments aren't cheap. By then I was working on the literary magazine. *Ploughshares* is one of the best in the country, and it always has a hotshot editor, but someone has to read the slush pile, and that was me. I liked the job, even though many of the submissions were on a par with a memorably, even classically bad poem called "10 Reasons Why I Hate My Mother." It cheered me up to see how many strivers out there were worse at writing than I was. Probably that sounds mean. Probably it is.

I was doing this chore one evening with a plate of Oreos by my left hand and a cup of tea by my right when my phone buzzed. It was Dad. He said he had some bad news and told me Ms. Hargensen had died.

For a moment or two I couldn't speak. The stack of slush pile poems and stories suddenly seemed very unimportant.

"Craig?" Dad asked. "Are you still there?"

"Yes. What happened?"

He told me what he knew, and I found out more a couple of days later, when the Gates Falls *Weekly Enterprise* was published online. BELOVED TEACHERS KILLED IN VERMONT, the headline read. Victoria Hargensen Corliss had still been teaching biology at Gates; her husband was a math teacher at neighboring Castle Rock. They had decided to spend their spring vacation on a motorcycle trip across New England, staying at a different bed and breakfast every night. They were on their way back, in Vermont and almost to the New Hampshire border, when Dean Whitmore, thirty-one, of Waltham, Massachusetts, crossed the Route 2 centerline and struck them head-on. Ted Corliss was killed instantly. Victoria Corliss — the woman who had taken me into the teachers' room after Kenny Yanko beat me up and gave me an illicit Aleve from her purse — had died on the way to the hospital.

I'd interned at the *Enterprise* the previous summer, mostly emptying the trash but also writing some sports and movie reviews. When I called Dave Gardener, the editor, he gave me some background the *Enterprise* hadn't printed. Dean Whitmore had been arrested a total of four times for OUI, but his father was a big hedge fund guy (how Mr. Harrigan had hated those upstarts), and high-priced lawyers had taken care of Whitmore the first three times. On the fourth occasion, after running into the side of a Zoney's Go-Mart in Hingham, he had avoided jail but lost his license. He'd been driving without one and operating under the influence when he struck the Corliss motorcycle. "Stone drunk" was the way Dave put it.

"He'll get off with just a slap on the wrist," Dave said. "Daddy will see to it. You watch and see."

"No way." Just the idea of that happening made me feel sick to my stomach. "If your info's correct, it's a clear case of vehicular homicide."

"Watch and see," he repeated.

The funerals were at Saint Anne's, the church both Ms. Hargensen — it was impossible for me to think of her as Victoria — and her husband had attended for most of their lives, and the one they had been married out of. Mr. Harrigan had been rich, for years a mover and shaker in the American business world, but there were a lot more people at the funeral of Ted and Victoria Corliss. Saint Anne's is a big church, but that day it was standing room only, and if Father Ingersoll hadn't had a microphone, he would have been inaudible beneath all the weeping. They had both been popular teachers, they were a love-match, and of course they had been young.

So were most of the mourners. I was there; Regina and Margie were there; Billy Bogan was there; so was U-Boat, who'd made a special trip from Florida, where he was playing single-A ball. U-Boat and I sat together. He didn't cry, exactly, but his eyes were red, and the big galoot was sniffling.

"Did you ever have her for class?" I whispered.

"Bio II," he whispered back. "When I was a senior. Needed it to graduate. She gave me a gift C. And I was in her birdwatching club. She wrote me a recommendation on my college app."

She had written me one, too.

"It's just so wrong," U-Boat said. "They weren't doing nothing but taking a ride." He paused. "And they were wearing helmets, too."

Billy looked about the same, but Margie and Regina looked older, almost adult in their makeup and big-girl dresses. They hugged me outside the church when it was over, and Regina said, "Remember how she took care of you the night you got beat up?"

"Yes," I said.

"She let me use her hand cream," Regina said, and began to cry all over again.

"I hope they put that guy away forever," Margie said fiercely.

124

"Roger that," U-Boat said. "Lock him up and throw away the key."

"They will," I said, but of course I was wrong and Dave was right.

Dean Whitmore's day in court came that July. He was given four years, sentence suspended if he agreed to go into a rehab and could pass random urine tests for those same four years. I was working for the *Enterprise* again, and as a paid employee (only part-time, but still). I'd been bumped up to community affairs and the occasional feature story. The day after Whitmore's sentencing — if you could even call it that — I voiced my outrage to Dave Gardener.

"I know, it sucks," he said, "but you gotta grow up, Craigy. We live in the real world where money talks and people listen. Money changed hands in the Whitmore case somewhere along the line. You can count on it. Now aren't you supposed to be giving me four-hundred words on the Craft Fair?"

A rehab — possibly one with tennis courts and a putting green — wasn't enough. Four years of piss-testing wasn't enough, especially when you could pay someone to provide clean samples if you knew ahead of time when the tests were going to come. Whitmore probably would.

As that August burned away, I sometimes

thought of an African proverb I'd read in one of my classes: *When an old man dies, a library burns.* Victoria and Ted hadn't been old, but somehow that was worse, because any potential they might have had was never going to be realized. All those kids at the funeral, both current students and recent graduates like me and my friends, suggested that *something* had burned, and could never be rebuilt.

I remembered her drawings of leaves and tree branches on the blackboard, beautiful things done freehand. I remembered us cleaning the bio lab on Friday afternoons, then doing the chem half of the lab for good measure, both of us laughing about the stink, her wondering if some Dr. Jekyll chemistry student was going to turn into Mr. Hyde and go rampaging through the halls. I thought of her saying *Don't blame you* when I told her I didn't want to go back into the gym after Kenny beat me up. I thought of those things, and the smell of her perfume, and then I thought of the asshole who'd killed her graduating from rehab and going about his business, happy as a Sunday in Paris.

No, it wasn't enough.

I went home that afternoon and dug through the drawers of the bureau in my room, not quite admitting to myself what I was looking for . . . or why. What I was looking for wasn't there, which was both a disappointment and a relief. I started to leave, then

126

went back and stood on tiptoe to explore the top shelf in my closet, where junk had a way of accumulating. I found an old alarm clock, an iPod that had busted when I dropped it in the driveway while skateboarding, a tangle of earphones and earbuds. There was a box of baseball cards and a stack of Spider-Man comic books. At the very back, there was a Red Sox sweatshirt much too small for the body I now inhabited. I lifted it and there, underneath, was the iPhone my father had given me for Christmas. Back in my shrimp-squeak days. The charger was there, too. I plugged the old phone in, still not quite admitting what I was up to, but when I think of that day now — not so many years ago — I believe that the motivating force was something Ms. Hargensen had said to me while we were cleaning the chem lab sinks: *A person shouldn't call out unless they want an answer.* That day I wanted one.

*It probably won't even take a charge,* I told myself. *Been up there gathering dust for years.* But it did. When I picked it up that night, after Dad had turned in, I saw a full battery icon in the upper righthand corner.

Man, talk about your trips down Memory Lane. I saw emails from long ago, photos of my dad from before his hair started to go gray, and IMs back and forth between me and Billy Bogan. No news in them really, just jokes, and illuminating information like **I just**

**farted**, and incisive questions like **Did you do your algebra**. We'd been like a couple of kids with Del Monte cans connected by a length of waxed string. Which is what most of our modern communications amount to, when you stop to think of it; chatter for the sake of chatter.

I took the phone to bed with me just as I had back before I needed to shave and when kissing Regina was a huge deal. Only now the bed which had once seemed big seemed almost too small. I looked across the room at the poster of Katy Perry I had put up when she had seemed, to junior high school me, the epitome of sexy fun. I was older than that shrimpsqueak kid now, and I was just the same. Funny how that works.

*If ghosts exist,* Ms. Hargensen had said, *I'll bet not all of them are holy.*

Thinking of that almost made me stop. Then, once more thinking of that irresponsible asshole playing tennis in his rehab, I went ahead and called Mr. Harrigan's number. *It's okay,* I told myself. *Nothing will happen. Nothing* can *happen. This is just a way of clearing your mental decks so you can leave the anger and sorrow behind and move on to the next thing.*

Except part of me knew something *would* happen, so I wasn't surprised when I got a ring instead of silence. Nor was I when his rusty voice spoke in my ear, originating from the telephone I'd put in his dead man's pocket almost seven years before: "I'm not answering my phone now. I will call you back if it seems appropriate."

"Hello, Mr. Harrigan, it's Craig." My voice was remarkably steady, considering that I was talking to a corpse and the corpse might actually be listening. "There's a man named Dean Whitmore who killed my favorite teacher from high school and her husband. The guy was drunk and hit them with his car. They were good people, she helped me when I needed help, and he didn't get what he deserved. I guess that's all."

Except it wasn't. I had at least thirty seconds or so to leave a message, and I hadn't used them all. So I said the rest of it, the truth of it, my voice dropping lower still, so it was almost a growl: "I wish he was dead."

These days I work for the *Times Union,* a newspaper that serves Albany and the surrounding area. The salary is peanuts, I could probably make more writing for BuzzFeed or TMZ, but I have that trust fund as a cushion, and I like working for an actual paper, even though most of the action these days is online. Call me old-fashioned.

I made friends with Frank Jefferson, the paper's go-to IT guy, and one night over beer at the Madison Pour House, I told him I'd once been able to connect with the voicemail of a guy who was dead . . . but only if I called from the old phone I'd had when the guy was still alive. I asked Frank if he'd ever heard of anything like that.

"No," he said, "but it could happen."

"How?"

"No idea, but there were all sorts of weird glitches with the early computers and cell phones. Some of them are legendary."

"iPhones, too?"

"Especially them," he said, swigging his beer. "Because they were rushed into production. Steve Jobs never would have admitted it, but the Apple guys were scared to death that in another couple of years, maybe only one, BlackBerry would achieve total market dominance. Those first iPhones, some of them locked up every time you typed the letter *l*. You could send an email and then surf the web, but if you tried to surf the web and *then* send an email, your phone sometimes crashed."

"That actually happened to me once or twice," I said. "I had to reboot."

"Yeah. There was all kinds of stuff like that. Your thing? I'd guess the guy's message somehow got stuck in the software, same way you can get a piece of gristle stuck between your teeth. Call it the ghost in the machine."

"Yes," I said, "but not a holy one."

"Huh?"

"Nothing," I said.

Dean Whitmore died on his second day in the Raven Mountain Treatment Center, a luxury spin-dry facility in upstate New Hampshire (there were indeed tennis courts; also shuffleboard and a swimming pool). I knew almost as soon as it happened, because I had a Google Alert on his name, both on my laptop and my *Weekly Enterprise* computer. No cause of death was given — money talks, you know — so I took a little trip to the neighboring New Hampshire town of Maidstone. There I put on my reporter's hat, asked a few questions, and parted with some of Mr. Harrigan's money.

It didn't take long, because, as suicides went, Whitmore's was more than a bit out of the ordinary. Kind of like strangling to death while beating off is out of the ordinary, you could say. At Raven Mountain the inpatients were called guests instead of dopers and alkies, and each guest room had its own shower. Dean Whitmore went into his before breakfast and chugged down some shampoo. Not to commit suicide, it seemed, but to grease the runway. He then broke a bar of soap in two, dropped half on the floor, and crammed the other half down his throat.

I got most of this from one of the counselors, whose job at Raven Mountain was to

131

work at breaking drunks and druggies of their bad habits. This fellow, Randy Squires by name, sat in my Toyota drinking from the neck of a Wild Turkey bottle purchased with some of the fifty dollars I'd given him (and yes, the irony was not lost on me). I asked if Whitmore had perhaps left a suicide note.

"He did," Squires said. "Kind of sweet, actually. Almost a prayer. 'Keep giving all the love you can,' it said."

My arms broke out in gooseflesh, but my sleeves covered that, and I was able to manage a smile. I could have told him that wasn't a prayer, but a line from "Stand By Your Man," by Tammy Wynette. Squires wouldn't have gotten it, anyway, and there was no reason why I'd want him to. It was between Mr. Harrigan and me.

I spent three days on that little investigation. When I got back, Dad asked me if I'd enjoyed my mini-vacation. I said I had. He asked me if I was ready to go back to school in a couple of weeks. I said I was. He looked me over carefully and asked if anything was wrong. I said there wasn't, not knowing if that was a lie or not.

Part of me still believed that Kenny Yanko had died accidentally, and that Dean Whitmore had committed suicide, possibly out of guilt. I tried to imagine how Mr. Harrigan could have somehow appeared to them and

132

caused their deaths, and couldn't do it. If that *had* happened, then I was an accessory to murder, morally if not legally. I had wished Whitmore dead, after all. Probably in my deepest heart, Kenny too.

"You sure?" Dad asked. His eyes were still on me, and in the old searching way I remembered from early childhood, when I had done some small thing wrong.

"Positive," I said.

"Okay, but if you want to talk, I'm here."

Yes, and thank God he was, but this wasn't a thing I could talk about. Not without sounding like a lunatic.

I went into my room and took the old iPhone off the closet shelf. It was holding its charge admirably. Why, exactly, did I do that? Did I mean to call him in his grave to say thank you? To ask him if he was really there? I can't remember, and I guess it doesn't matter, because I didn't call. When I powered up the phone, I saw I had a text message from **pirateking1**. I tapped with a trembling finger to open it and read this: **C C C sT**

As I looked at it, a possibility that had never so much as touched my mind before that late summer day dawned on me. What if I were somehow holding Mr. Harrigan hostage? Tying him to my earthly concerns by way of the phone I had tucked into his coat pocket before the lid of his coffin went down? What if the things I had asked him to do were hurting him? Maybe even torturing him?

*Not likely,* I thought. *Remember what Mrs. Grogan told you about Dusty Bilodeau. She said he couldn't have gotten a job shoveling henshit out of old Dorrance Marstellar's barn after stealing from Mr. Harrigan. He saw to it.*

Yes, and something else. She said he was a square-dealing man, but if you weren't the same, God help you. And had Dean Whitmore been square-dealing? No. Had Kenny Yanko been square-dealing? The same. So maybe Mr. Harrigan had been glad to pitch in. Maybe he even enjoyed it.

"If he was ever there at all," I whispered.

He had been. In my deepest heart I knew that, too. And I knew something else. I knew what that message meant: *Craig stop.*

Because I was hurting him, or because I was hurting myself?

I decided that in the end it didn't matter.

It rained hard the next day, the kind of chilly no-thunder downpour that means the first autumn color will begin to show in a week or two. The rain was good, because it meant that the summer people — those who remained — were all tucked up inside their seasonal hideaways and Castle Lake was deserted. I parked in the picnic area at the lake's north end and walked to what we kids had called the Ledges, standing there in our bathing suits and daring each other to jump off. Some of us even did.

I went to the lip of the drop, where the pine needles gave out and the bare rock, which is New England's ultimate truth, began. I reached into the right pocket of my khakis and brought out my iPhone 1. I held it in my hand for a moment, feeling its weight and remembering how delighted I'd been on that Christmas morning when I unwrapped the box and saw the Apple logo. Had I screamed for joy? I couldn't remember, but almost certainly.

It was still holding its charge, although it was down to fifty per cent. I called Mr. Harrigan, and in the dark earth of Elm Cemetery, in the pocket of an expensive suit coat now speckled with mold, I know Tammy Wynette was singing. I listened to his scratchy old man's voice one more time, telling me he would call back if it seemed appropriate.

I waited for the beep. I said, "Thank you for everything, Mr. Harrigan. Goodbye."

I ended the call, cocked my arm back, and threw the phone as hard as I could. I watched it arc through the gray sky. I watched the small splash as it hit the water.

I reached into my lefthand pocket and brought out my current iPhone, the 5C with its colorful case. I meant to throw it into the lake as well. Surely I could make do with a landline, and surely it would make my life easier. So much less chitter-chatter, no more texts reading **What are you doing,** no more dumb emojis. If I got a job on a newspaper after I graduated and needed to keep in touch, I could use a loaner, then give it back when whatever assignment had necessitated it was finished.

I cocked my arm back, held it that way for what felt like a long time — maybe a minute, maybe two. In the end I put the phone back in my pocket. I don't know for sure if everyone is addicted to those high-tech Del Monte cans, but I know that I am, and I know Mr. Harrigan was. It's why I slipped it into his pocket that day. In the twenty-first century, I think our phones are how we are wedded to the world. If so, it's probably a bad marriage.

Or maybe not. After what happened to Yanko and Whitmore, and after that last text message from **pirateking1,** there are a great many things I'm not sure of. Reality itself, for a start. I do know two things, however, and they are as solid as New England rock. I don't want to be cremated when I go, and I want to be buried with empty pockets.

# THE LIFE OF
# CHUCK

## Act III: Thanks, Chuck!

### 1

The day Marty Anderson saw the billboard was just before the Internet finally went down for good. It had been wobbling for eight months since the first short interruptions. Everyone agreed it was only a matter of time, and everyone agreed they would muddle through somehow once the wired-in world finally went dark — after all, they had managed without it, hadn't they? Besides, there were other problems, like whole species of birds and fish dying off, and now there was California to think about: going, going, possibly soon to be gone.

Marty was late leaving school, because it was that least favorite day for high school educators, the one set aside for parent-teacher conferences. As this one had played out, Marty had found few parents interested in discussing little Johnny and little Janey's progress (or lack of it). Mostly they wanted to discuss the probable final failure of the Internet, which would sink their Facebook and Instagram accounts for good. None of them mentioned Pornhub, but Marty suspected many of the parents who showed up — female as well as male — were mourning that site's impending extinction as well.

Ordinarily, Marty would have driven home by way of the turnpike bypass, zippity-zip, home in a jiff, but that wasn't possible due to the collapse of the bridge over Otter Creek. That had happened four months ago, and there was no sign of repairs; just orange-striped wooden barriers that already looked dingy and were covered with taggers' logos.

With the bypass closed, Marty was forced to drive directly through downtown to reach his house on Cedar Court along with everybody else who lived on the east side. Thanks to the conferences, he'd left at five instead of three, at the height of rush hour, and a drive that would have taken twenty minutes in the old days would take at least an hour, probably longer because some of the traffic lights were out, as well. It was stop-and-go all the way, with plenty of horns, screeching brakes, bumper-kisses, and waved middle fingers. He was stopped for ten minutes at the intersection of Main and Market, so had plenty of time to notice the billboard on top of the Midwest Trust building.

Until today, it had advertised one of the airlines, Delta or Southwest, Marty couldn't remember which. This afternoon the happy crew of arm-in-arm flight attendants had been replaced by a photograph of a moon-faced man with black-framed glasses that matched his black, neatly combed hair. He was sitting at a desk with a pen in his hand, jacketless but with his tie carefully knotted at the collar of his white shirt. On the hand holding the pen there was a crescent-shaped scar that had for some reason not been airbrushed out. To Marty he looked like an accountant. He was smiling cheerfully down at the snarled twilight traffic from his perch high atop the bank building. Above his head, in blue, was CHARLES KRANTZ. Below his desk, in red, was 39 GREAT YEARS! THANKS, CHUCK!

Marty had never heard of Charles "Chuck" Krantz, but supposed he must have been a pretty big bug at Midwest Trust to rate a retirement photo on a spotlit billboard that had to be at least fifteen feet high and fifty feet across. And the photo must be an old one, if he'd put in almost forty years, or his hair would have been white.

"Or gone," Marty said, and brushed at his own thinning thatch. He took a chance at downtown's main intersection five minutes later, when a momentary hole opened up. He squirted his Prius through it, tensing for a

141

collision and ignoring the shaken fist of a man who squelched to a stop only inches from t-boning him.

There was another tie-up at the top of Main Street, and another close call. By the time he got home he had forgotten all about the billboard. He drove into the garage, pushed the button that lowered the door, and then just sat for a full minute, breathing deeply and trying not to think about having to run the same gauntlet tomorrow morning. With the bypass closed, there was just no other choice. If he wanted to go to work at all, that was, and right then taking a sick day (he had plenty of them stacked up) seemed like a more attractive option.

"I wouldn't be the only one," he told the empty garage. He knew this to be true. According to the *New York Times* (which he read on his tablet every morning if the Internet was working), absenteeism was at a worldwide high.

He grabbed his stack of books with one hand and his battered old briefcase with the other. It was heavy with papers that would need correcting. Thus burdened, he struggled out of the car and closed the door with his butt. The sight of his shadow on the wall doing something that looked like a funky dance move made him laugh. The sound startled him; laughter in these difficult days was hard to come by. Then he dropped half of his books on the garage floor, which put an end to any nascent good humor.

He gathered up *Introduction to American Literature* and *Four Short Novels* (he was currently teaching *The Red Badge of Courage* to his sophomores) and went inside. He had barely managed to get everything on the kitchen counter before the phone rang. The landline, of course; there was hardly any cell coverage these days. He sometimes congratulated himself on keeping his landline when so many of his colleagues had given theirs up. Those folks were truly hung, because getting one put in this last year or so . . . forget about it. You'd be more likely to be using the turnpike bypass again before you got to the top of the waiting list, and even the landlines now had frequent outages.

Caller ID no longer worked, but he was sure enough about who was on the other end to simply pick up the phone and say, "Yo, Felicia."

"Where have you been?" his ex-wife asked him. "I've been trying to reach you for an hour!"

Marty explained about the parent-teacher conferences, and the long trip home.

"Are you okay?"

"I will be, as soon as I get something to eat. How are you, Fel?"

"I'm getting along, but we had six more today."

Marty didn't have to ask her six more of what. Felicia was a nurse at City General, where the nursing staff now called itself the Suicide Squad.

"Sorry to hear that."

"Sign of the times." He could hear the shrug in her voice, and thought that two years ago — when they'd still been married — six suicides in one day would have left her shaken, heartbroken, and sleepless. But you could get used to anything, it seemed.

"Are you still taking your ulcer medication, Marty?" Before he could reply, she hurried on. "It's not nagging, just concern. Divorce doesn't mean I still don't care about you, y'know?"

"I know, and I am." This was half a lie, because the doctor-prescribed Carafate was now impossible to get, and he was relying on Prilosec. He told the half-lie because he still cared about her, too. They actually got along better now that they weren't married anymore. There was even sex, and although it was infrequent, it was pretty damn good. "I appreciate you asking."

"Really?"

"Yes, ma'am." He opened the fridge. Pickings were slim, but there were hotdogs, a few eggs, and a can of blueberry yogurt he would save for a pre-bedtime snack. Also three cans of Hamm's.

"Good. How many parents actually showed up?"

"More than I expected, far less than a full house. Mostly they wanted to talk about the Internet. They seemed to think I should know why it keeps shitting the bed. I had to keep telling them I'm an English teacher, not an IT guy."

"You know about California, right?" Lowering her voice, as if imparting a great secret.

"Yes." That morning a gigantic earthquake, the third in the last month and by far the worst, had sent another large chunk of the Golden State into the Pacific Ocean. The good news was that most of that part of the state had been evacuated. The bad news was that now hundreds of thousands of refugees were trekking east, turning Nevada into one of the most populous states in the union. Gasoline in Nevada currently cost twenty bucks a gallon. Cash only, and if the station wasn't tapped out.

Marty grabbed a half-empty quart of milk, sniffed, and drank from the bottle in spite of the faintly suspicious aroma. He needed a real drink, but knew from bitter experience (and sleepless nights) that he had to insulate his stomach first.

He said, "It's interesting to me that the parents who did show up seemed more concerned about the Internet than the California quakes. I suppose because the state's breadbasket regions are still there."

"But for how long? I heard a scientist on NPR say that California is peeling away like old wallpaper. And another Japanese reactor got inundated this afternoon. They're saying it was shut down, all's well, but I don't think I believe that."

"Cynic."

"We're living in cynical times, Marty." She hesitated. "Some people think we're living in the Last Times. Not just the religious crazies, either. Not anymore. You heard that from a member in good standing of the City General Suicide Squad. We lost six today, true, but there were eighteen more we dragged back. Most with the help of Naloxone. But . . ." She lowered her voice again. ". . . supplies of that are getting very thin. I heard the head pharmacist saying we might be completely out by the end of the month."

"That sucks," Marty said, eyeing his briefcase. All those papers waiting to be processed. All those spelling errors waiting to be corrected. All those dangling subordinate clauses and vague conclusions waiting to be red-inked. Computer crutches like Spellcheck and apps like Grammar Alert didn't seem to help. Just thinking of it made him tired. "Listen, Fel, I ought to go. I have tests to grade and essays on 'Mending Wall' to correct." The thought of the stacked vapidities in those waiting essays made him feel old.

"All right," Felicia said. "Just . . . you know, touching base."

"Roger that." Marty opened the cupboard and took down the bourbon. He would wait until she was off the phone to pour it, lest she hear the glugging and know what he was doing. Wives had intuition; ex-wives seemed to develop high-def radar.

"Could I say I love you?" she asked.

"Only if I can say it right back," Marty replied, running his finger over the label on the bottle: Early Times. A very good brand, he thought, for these later times.

"I love you, Marty."

"And I love you."

A good place to end, but she was still there. "Marty?"

"What, hon?"

"The world is going down the drain, and all we can say is 'that sucks.' So maybe we're going down the drain, too."

"Maybe we are," he said, "but Chuck Krantz is retiring, so I guess there's a gleam of light in the darkness."

"Thirty-nine great years," she responded, and it was her turn to laugh.

He put the milk down. "You saw the billboard?"

"No, it was an ad on the radio. That NPR show I was telling you about."

"If they're running ads on NPR, it really is the end of the world," Marty said. She laughed again, and the sound made him glad. "Tell me, how does Chuck Krantz rate this kind of coverage? He looks like an accountant, and I never heard of him."

"No idea. The world is full of mysteries. No hard stuff, Marty. I know you're thinking of it. Have a beer, instead."

He didn't laugh as he ended the call, but he smiled. Ex-wife radar. High-def. He put the Early Times back in the cupboard and grabbed a beer instead. He plopped a couple of hotdogs into water and went into his little study to see if the Internet was up while he waited for the water to boil.

It was, and seemed to be running at slightly better than its usual slow crawl. He went to Netflix, thinking he might re-watch an episode of *Breaking Bad* or *The Wire* while he ate his dogs. The welcome screen came up, showing selections that hadn't changed since last evening (and the stuff on Netflix used to change just about every day, not so long ago), but before he could decide on which bad guy he wanted to watch, Walter White or Stringer Bell, the welcome screen disappeared. SEARCHING appeared, and the little worry circle.

"Fuck," Marty said. "Gone for the ni—"

Then the worry circle disappeared and the screen came back. Only it wasn't the Netflix welcome screen; it was Charles Krantz, sitting at his paper-strewn desk, smiling with

148

his pen in his scarred hand. CHARLES KRANTZ above him; 39 GREAT YEARS! THANKS, CHUCK! below.

"Who the fuck are you, Chuckie?" Marty asked. "How do you rate?" And then, as if his breath had blown out the Internet like a birthday candle, the picture disappeared and the words on the screen were CONNEC-TION LOST.

It did not come back that night. Like half of California (soon to be three quarters), the Internet had vanished.

The first thing Marty noticed the next day as he backed his car out of the garage was the sky. How long had it been since he had seen that clear unblemished blue? A month? Six weeks? The clouds and the rain (sometimes a drizzle, sometimes a torrent) were almost constant now, and on days when the clouds cleared, the sky usually remained bleary from the smoke of fires in the Midwest. They had blackened most of Iowa and Nebraska, and were moving on to Kansas, driven by gale-force winds.

The second thing he noticed was Gus Wil-fong trudging up the street with his oversized lunchbox banging against his thigh. Gus was wearing khakis, but with a tie. He was a supervisor at the city's public works depart-ment. Although it was only quarter past seven, he looked tired and out of sorts, as if at the end of a long day instead of just starting one. And if he was just starting one, why was he walking toward his house next door to Marty's? Also . . .

Marty powered down his window. "Where's your car?"

Gus's short laugh was humorless. "Parked on the sidewalk halfway down Main Street Hill, along with about a hundred others." He blew out his breath. "Whoo, I can't remember the last time I walked three miles. Which probably says more about me than you want to know. If you're going to school, buddy, you're going to have to go all the way out Route 11 and then hook back on Route 19. Twenty miles, at least, and there'll be plenty of traffic there, too. You might arrive in time for lunch, but I wouldn't count on it."

"What happened?"

"Sinkhole opened up at the intersection of Main and Market. Man, it's huge. All the rain we've been having might have something to do with it, lack of maintenance probably even more. Not my department, thank God. Got to be twenty cars at the bottom of it, maybe thirty, and some of the people in those cars . . ." He shook his head. "They ain't coming back."

"Jesus," Marty said. "I was just there last evening. Backed up in traffic."

"Be glad you weren't there this morning. Mind if I get in with you? Sit down for a

150

minute? I'm pooped, and Jenny will have gone back to bed. I don't want to wake her up, especially with bad news."

"Sure."

Gus got in the car. "This is bad, my friend."

"It sucks," Marty agreed. It was what he'd said to Felicia last night. "Just got to grin and bear it, I guess."

"I'm not grinning," Gus said.

"Planning to take the day off?"

Gus raised his hands and brought them down on the lunchbox in his lap. "I don't know. Maybe I'll make some calls, see if someone can pick me up, but I'm not hopeful."

"If you do take the day, don't plan to spend it watching Netflix or YouTube videos. Internet's down again, and I've got a feeling it might be for good this time."

"I'm assuming you know about California," Gus said.

"I didn't turn on the TV this morning. Slept in a bit." He paused. "Didn't want to watch it anyway, to tell you the truth. Is there something new?"

"Yeah. The rest of it went." He reconsidered. "Well . . . they're saying twenty per cent of northern California is still hanging in there, which means probably ten, but the food-producing regions are gone."

"That's terrible." It was, of course, but instead of horror and terror and grief, all

Marty felt was a kind of benumbed dismay.

"You could say that," Gus agreed. "Especially with the Midwest turning to charcoal and the southern half of Florida now basically swampland fit only for alligators. I hope you've got a lot of food in your pantry and freezer, because now *all* the major food-producing regions of this country are gone. The same with Europe. It's already famine-time in Asia. Millions dead there. Bubonic plague, I'm hearing."

They sat in Marty's driveway, watching more people walking back from downtown, many dressed in suits and ties. A woman in a pretty pink suit was trudging along in sneakers, carrying her heels in one hand. Marty thought her name was Andrea something, lived a street or two over. Hadn't Felicia told him she worked at Midwest Trust?

"And the bees," Gus continued. "They were in trouble even ten years ago, but now they're completely gone, except for a few hives down in South America. No more honey, honey. And without them to pollinate whatever crops might be left . . ."

"Excuse me," Marty said. He got out of the car and trotted to catch up with the woman in the pink suit. "Andrea? Are you Andrea?"

She turned warily, lifting her shoes as if she might have to use one of the heels to ward him off. Marty understood; there were plenty of loosely wrapped people around these days.

He stopped five feet away. "I'm Felicia Anderson's husband." Ex, actually, but husband sounded less potentially dangerous. "I think you and Fel know each other."

"We do. I was on the Neighborhood Watch Committee with her. What can I do for you, Mr. Anderson? I've had a long walk and my car's stuck in what appears to be a terminal traffic jam downtown. As for the bank, it's . . . leaning."

"Leaning," Marty repeated. In his mind he saw an image of the Leaning Tower of Pisa. With Chuck Krantz's retirement photo on top.

"It's on the edge of the sinkhole and although it hasn't fallen in, it looks very unsafe to me. Sure to be condemned. I suppose that's the end of my job, at least in the downtown branch, but I don't really care. I just want to go home and put my feet up."

"I was curious about the billboard on the bank building. Have you seen it?"

"How could I miss it?" she asked. "I work there, after all. I've also seen the graffiti, which is everywhere — we love you Chuck, Chuck lives, Chuck forever — and the ads on TV."

"Really?" Marty thought of what he'd seen on Netflix last night, just before it went away. At the time he'd dismissed it as a particularly annoying pop-up ad.

"Well, the local stations, anyway. Maybe it's

different on cable, but we don't get that anymore. Not since July."

"Us, either." Now that he had begun the fiction that he was still part of an us, it seemed best to carry on with it. "Just channel 8 and channel 10."

Andrea nodded. "No more ads for cars or Eliquis or Bob's Discount Furniture. Just Charles Krantz, thirty-nine great years, thanks, Chuck. A full minute of that, then back to our regularly scheduled reruns. Very peculiar, but these days, what isn't? Now I really want to get home."

"This Charles Krantz isn't associated with your bank? *Retiring* from the bank?"

She paused for just a moment before continuing her homeward trudge, carrying high heels she would not need that day. Perhaps ever again. "I don't know Charles Krantz from Adam. He must have worked in the Omaha headquarters. Although from what I understand, Omaha is just a great big ashtray these days."

Marty watched her go. So did Gus Wilfong, who had joined him. Gus nodded at the glum parade of returning workers who could no longer get to their jobs — selling, trading, banking, waiting on tables, making deliveries.

"They look like refugees," Gus said.

"Yeah," Marty said. "They kind of do. Hey, you remember asking me about my food supplies?"

154

Gus nodded.

"I have quite a few cans of soup. Also some basmati and Rice-A-Roni. Cheerios, I believe. As for the freezer, I think I might have six TV dinners and half a pint of Ben & Jerry's."

"You don't sound concerned."

Marty shrugged. "What good would that do?"

"But see, it's interesting," Gus said. "We were all concerned at first. We wanted answers. People went to Washington and protested. Remember when they knocked over the White House fence and those college kids got shot?"

"Yeah."

"There was the government overthrow in Russia and the Four Day War between India and Pakistan. There's a volcano in Germany, for Christ's sake — *Germany!* We told each other all this would blow over, but that doesn't seem to be happening, does it?"

"No," Marty agreed. Although he'd just gotten up, he felt tired. Very. "Not blowing over, blowing harder."

"Then there's the suicides."

Marty nodded. "Felicia sees them every day."

"I think the suicides will slow down," Gus said, "and people will just wait."

"For what?"

"For the end, pal. The end of everything. We've been going through the five stages of

155

grief, don't you get it? Now we've arrived at the last one. Acceptance."

Marty said nothing. He could think of nothing to say.

"There's so little curiosity now. And all this . . ." Gus waved an arm. "It came out of nowhere. I mean, we knew the environment was going to the dogs — I think even the right-wing nutjobs secretly believed in it — but this is sixty different varieties of shit, all at once." He gave Marty a look that was almost pleading. "In how long? A year? Fourteen months?"

"Yes," Marty said. "Sucks." It seemed to be the only word that fit.

Overhead they heard a droning sound and looked up. The big jets flying in and out of the municipal airport were few and far between these days, but this was a small plane, bumbling along in the unusually clear sky and belching a stream of white from its tail. The plane twisted and banked, rose and fell, the smoke (or whatever chemical it was) forming letters.

"Huh," Gus said, craning. "Skywriting plane. Haven't seen one since I was a kid."

CHARLES, the plane wrote. Then KRANTZ. And then — of course — 39 GREAT YEARS. The name was already starting to fuzz out as the plane wrote THANKS, CHUCK!

"What the fuck," Gus said.

"My sentiments exactly," Marty said.

He had skipped breakfast, so when he went back inside, Marty microwaved one of his frozen dinners — a Marie Callender's Chicken Pot Pie, quite tasty — and took it into the living room to watch TV. But the only two stations he could pull in were showing the photograph of Charles "Chuck" Krantz sitting at his desk with his pen at the eternal ready. Marty stared at it while he ate his pot pie, then killed the idiot box and went back to bed. It seemed the most sensible thing to do.

He slept for most of the day, and although he didn't dream of her (at least that he could remember), he woke up thinking of Felicia. He wanted to see her, and when he did he would ask if he could sleep over. Maybe even stay. Sixty different varieties of shit, Gus had said, and all at once. If this really was the end, he didn't want to face it alone.

Harvest Acres, the tidy little development where Felicia now lived, was three miles away, and Marty had no intention of risking the drive in his car, so he put on his sweatpants and sneakers. It was a beautiful late afternoon for walking, the sky still an unblemished blue, and plenty of people were out and about. A few looked as if they were enjoying the sunshine, but most just looked down at their feet. There was little talk, even among those who were walking in pairs or trios.

On Park Drive, one of the east side's main thoroughfares, all four lanes were jammed with cars, most of them empty. Marty wove his way between them, and on the other side encountered an elderly man in a tweed suit and matching trilby hat. He was sitting on the curb and knocking his pipe out into the gutter. He saw Marty watching him and smiled.

"Just taking a rest," he said. "I walked downtown to look at the sinkhole and take a few pictures with my phone. Thought one of the local television stations might be interested, but they all seem to be off the air. Except for pictures of that fellow Krantz, that is."

"Yes," Marty said. "It's all Chuck, all the time now. Any idea who —"

"None. I've asked two dozen people, at least. Nobody knows. Our man Krantz appears to be the Oz of the Apocalypse."

Marty laughed. "Where are you heading, sir?"

"Harvest Acres. Nice little enclave. Off the beaten track." He reached into his jacket, produced a pouch of tobacco, and began reloading his pipe.

"I'm going there myself. My ex lives there. Maybe we could walk together."

The elderly gent got up with a wince. "As

long as you don't rush along." He lit his pipe, puffing away. "Arthritis. I have pills for it, but the more the arthritis sets in, the less they do."

"Sucks," Marty said. "You set the pace."

The old guy did. It was a slow one. His name was Samuel Yarbrough. He was owner and chief undertaker of the Yarbrough Funeral Home. "But my real interest is meteorology," he said. "Dreamed of being a television weatherman in my salad days, perhaps even on one of the networks, but they all seem to have a pash for young women with . . ." He put his cupped hands in front of his chest. "I keep up, though, read the journals, and I can tell you an amazing thing. If you want to hear."

"Sure."

They came to a bus bench. Stenciled on the back was CHARLES "CHUCK" KRANTZ 39 GREAT YEARS! THANKS, CHUCK! Sam Yarbrough took a seat and patted the space next to him. Marty sat. It was downwind of Yarbrough's pipe, but that was okay. Marty liked the smell.

"Do you know how people say there's twenty-four hours in a day?" Yarbrough asked.

"And seven days in a week. Everybody knows that, even little kids."

"Well, everybody is wrong. There were twenty-three hours and fifty-six minutes in a stellar day. Plus a few odd seconds."

159

"Were?"

"Correct. Based on my calculations, which I assure you I can back up, there are now twenty-four hours and *two* minutes in a day. Do you know what that means, Mr. Anderson?"

Marty thought it over. "Are you telling me the earth's rotation is slowing down?"

"Exactly." Yarbrough took his pipe out of his mouth and gestured at the people passing them on the sidewalk. Their numbers were thinning now that afternoon had begun to edge into twilight. "I'll bet many of those folks think the multiple disasters we're facing have a single cause rooted in what we have done to the earth's environment. It's not so. I would be the first to admit that we have treated our mother — yes, she's the mother of us all — very badly, certainly molested her if not outright raped her, but we're puny compared to the great clock of the universe. *Puny.* No, whatever is happening is much larger than environmental degradation."

"Maybe it's Chuck Krantz's fault," Marty said.

Yarbrough looked at him in surprise, then laughed. "Back to him, eh? Chuck Krantz is retiring and the entire population of earth, not to mention the earth itself, is retiring with him? Is that your thesis?"

"Got to blame something," Marty said, smiling. "Or someone."

Sam Yarbrough stood up, put a hand to the small of his back, stretched and winced. "With apologies to Mr. Spock, that's illogical. I suppose thirty-nine years is quite a span in terms of human life — almost half — but the last ice age happened quite a bit longer ago. Not to mention the age of the dinosaurs. Shall we mosey?"

They moseyed, their shadows stretching ahead of them. Marty was mentally scolding himself for having slept away the best part of a beautiful day. Yarbrough was moving ever more slowly. When they finally reached the brick arch marking the entrance to Harvest Acres, the old mortician sat down again.

"I think I'll watch the sunset while I wait for the arthritis to settle a bit. Would you care to join me?"

Marty shook his head. "Think I'll go on."

"Check the ex," Yarbrough said. "I understand. It was nice speaking with you, Mr. Anderson."

Marty started beneath the arch, then turned back. "Charles Krantz means *something*," he said. "I'm sure of it."

"You could be right," Sam said, puffing on his pipe, "but the slowing of the earth's rotation . . . nothing's bigger than that, my friend."

The central thoroughfare of the Harvest Acres development was a graceful tree-lined parabola from which shorter streets diverged.

161

The streetlights, which looked to Marty like those in illustrated Dickens novels, had come on, casting a moonlight glow. As Marty approached Fern Lane, where Felicia lived, a little girl on roller skates appeared, banking gracefully around the corner. She was wearing baggy red shorts and a sleeveless tee with somebody's face on it, maybe a rock star or a rapper. Marty guessed her age at ten or eleven, and seeing her cheered him enormously. A little girl on roller skates: what could be more normal in this abnormal day? This abnormal *year*?

"Yo," he said.

"Yo," she agreed, but turned neatly on her skates, perhaps ready to flee if he turned out to be one of the Chester the Molester types her mother had no doubt warned her about.

"I'm going to see my ex-wife," Marty said, standing where he was. "Felicia Anderson. Or maybe she's back to Gordon now. That was her maiden name. She lives on Fern Lane. Number 19."

The little girl pivoted on her skates, an effortless move that would have left Marty flat on his ass. "Oh yeah, maybe I've seen you before. Blue Prius?"

"That's me."

"If you come to see her, why's she your ex?"

"Still like her."

"You don't fight?"

"We used to. We get along better now that

we're exes."

"Miz Gordon gives us ginger snap cookies sometimes. Me and my little brother, Ronnie. I like Oreos better, but . . ."

"But that's the way the cookie crumbles, right?" Marty said.

"Nah, ginger snaps don't crumble. At least not until you crunch em up in your mou—"

At that moment the streetlights went out, turning the main drag into a lagoon of shadows. All the houses went dark at the same time. There had been outages in the city before, some as long as eighteen hours, but the power had always come back. Marty wasn't sure it would this time. Maybe, but he had a feeling that electricity, which he (and everyone else) had taken for granted all his life, might have gone the way of the Internet.

"Booger," said the little girl.

"You better go home," Marty said. "With no streetlights, it's too dark for skating."

"Mister? Is everything going to be all right?"

Although he had no kids of his own, he'd taught them for twenty years and felt that, although you should tell them the truth once they reached the age of sixteen, a kind-hearted lie was often the right way to go when they were as young as this girl. "Sure."

"But look," she said, and pointed.

He followed her trembling finger to the house on the corner of Fern Lane. A face was appearing on the darkened bay window overlooking a small patch of lawn. It appeared in glowing white lines and shadows, like ectoplasm at a séance. Smiling moon face. Black-framed glasses. Pen poised. Over it: CHARLES KRANTZ. Below it: 39 GREAT YEARS! THANKS, CHUCK!

"It's happening to all of them," she whispered.

She was right. Chuck Krantz was rising on the front windows of every house on Fern Lane. Marty turned and saw an arc of Krantz faces stretching out behind him on the main avenue. Dozens of Chucks, maybe hundreds. Thousands, if this phenomenon was happening all over the city.

"Go home," Marty said, not smiling anymore. "Go home to your mom and dad, poppet. Do it right now."

She skated away, her skates rumbling on the sidewalk and her hair flying out behind her. He could see the red shorts, then she was lost in the thickening shadows.

Marty walked quickly in the direction she had gone, observed by the smiling face of Charles "Chuck" Krantz in every window. Chuck in his white shirt and dark tie. It was like being watched by a horde of ghost-clones. Marty was glad there was no moon; what if Chuck's face had appeared there? How would he deal with *that*?

He gave up walking at number 13. He ran the rest of the way to Felicia's little two-room bungalow, pounded up the front walk, and knocked on the door. He waited, suddenly sure she was still at the hospital, maybe working a double, but then he heard her footsteps. The door opened. She was holding a candle. It underlit her frightened face.

"Marty, thank God. Do you see them?"

"Yes." The guy was in her front window, too. Chuck. Smiling. Looking like every accountant who ever lived. A man who wouldn't say boo to a goose.

"They just started . . . showing up!"

"I know. I saw."

"Is it just here?"

"I think it's everywhere. I think it's almost —"

Then she was hugging him, pulling him inside, and he was glad she hadn't given him a chance to say the other two words: *the end.*

## 2

Douglas Beaton, associate professor of philosophy in Ithaca College's Department of Philosophy and Religion, sits in a hospital room, waiting for his brother-in-law to die. The only sounds are the steady *bip . . . bip . . . bip* of the heart monitor and Chuck's slow and increasingly labored breathing. Most of the machinery has been turned off.

"Unc?"

Doug turns to see Brian in the doorway, still wearing his letter jacket and backpack.

"You left school early?" Doug asks.

"With permission. Mom texted me that she was going to let them turn off the machines. Did they?"

"Yes."

"When?"

"An hour ago."

"Where's Mom now?"

"In the chapel on the first floor. She's praying for his soul."

And probably praying that she did the right thing, Doug thinks. Because even when the priest tells you yes, it's fine, let God take care of the rest, it feels wrong somehow.

"I'm supposed to text her if it looks like he's . . ." Brian's uncle shrugs.

Brian approaches the bed and looks down at his father's still white face. With his black-framed glasses put aside, the boy thinks his dad doesn't look old enough to have a son who's a freshman in high school. He looks like a high school kid himself. He picks up his father's hand and plants a brief kiss on the crescent-shaped scar there.

"Guys as young as him aren't supposed to die," Brian says. He speaks softly, as if his father can hear. "Jesus, Uncle Doug, he just turned thirty-nine last winter!"

"Come sit down," Doug says, and pats the empty chair next to him.

"That's Mom's seat."

166

"When she comes back, you can give it to her."

Brian shucks his backpack and sits down. "How long do you think it will be?"

"The doctors said he could go anytime. Before tomorrow, almost certainly. You know the machines were helping him breathe, right? And there were IVs to feed him. He's not . . . Brian, he's not in any pain. That part is over."

"Glioblastoma," Brian says bitterly. When he turns to his uncle, he's crying. "Why would God take my dad, Uncle Doug? Explain it to me."

"I can't. God's ways are a mystery."

"Well fuck the mystery," the boy says. "Mysteries should stay in storybooks, where they belong."

Uncle Doug nods and puts an arm around Brian's shoulders. "I know it's hard, kiddo, it's hard for me, too, but it's all I got. Life's a mystery. So is death."

They fall silent, listening to the steady *bip . . . bip . . . bip* and the rasp as Charles Krantz — Chuck, to his wife and his wife's brother and his friends — takes one slow breath after another, his body's last interactions with the world, each inhale and exhale managed (like the beat of his heart) by a failing brain where a few operations still continue. The man who spent his working life in the accounting department of the Midwest

167

Trust is now doing his final tallies: small income, large disbursements.

"Banks are supposed to be heartless, but they really loved him there," Brian says. "They sent a ton of flowers. The nurses put them in that solarium thing because he's not supposed to have flowers. What did they think? That it was going to kick off an allergy attack or something?"

"He loved working there," Doug says. "It wasn't a big deal in the grand scheme of things, I suppose — he was never going to win a Nobel Prize or get a Medal of Freedom from the president — but he did love it."

"Dancing, too," Brian says. "He loved dancing. He was good. So was Mom — they could really cut a rug, she used to say. But she also said he was better."

Doug laughs. "Used to call himself the poor man's Fred Astaire. And model trains when he was a boy. His zaydee had a set. You know, his granddad?"

"Yeah," Brian says. "I know about his zaydee."

"He had a good life, Bri."

"Not enough of it," Brian says. "He'll never get to take the train across Canada like he wanted to. Or visit Australia — he wanted that, too. He's never going to see me graduate high school. He's never going to have a retirement party where people make funny speeches and give him a gold . . ." He wiped his eyes on the sleeve of his jacket. "A gold watch."

Doug squeezes his nephew's shoulders.

Brian speaks looking down at his clasped hands. "I want to believe in God, Unc, and I sort of do, but I don't understand why it has to be this way. Why God would *let* it be this way. It's a mystery? You're the hotshot philosophy guy and that's the best you can do?"

Yes, because death brings philosophy to ruin, Doug thinks.

"You know what they say, Brian — death takes the best of us and death takes the rest of us."

Brian tries to smile. "If that's supposed to be comforting, you need to try harder."

Doug seems not to have heard. He's looking at his brother-in-law, who is — in Doug's mind — an actual brother. Who has given his sister a good life. Who helped him get his start in business, and that's really the least of it. They had some fine times together. Not enough, but it looks like they'll have to do.

"The human brain is finite — no more than a sponge of tissue inside a cage of bone — but the mind within the brain is infinite. Its storage capacity is colossal, its imaginative reach beyond our ability to comprehend. I think when a man or woman dies, a whole world falls to ruin — the world that person knew and believed in. Think of that, kiddo — billions of people on earth, and each one of those billions with a world inside. The earth their minds have conceived."

"And now my dad's world is dying."

"But not ours," Doug says, and gives his nephew another squeeze. "Ours will go on a little while longer. And your mother's. We need to be strong for her, Brian. As strong as we can."

They fall silent, looking at the dying man in the hospital bed, listening to the *bip . . . bip . . . bip* of the monitor and the slow breaths Chuck Krantz inhales and exhales. Once it stops. His chest remains flat. Brian tenses. Then it rises again with another of those agonal rasps.

"Text Mom," Brian says. "Right now."

Doug already has his phone out. "Way ahead of you." And types: **Better come, sis. Brian is here. I think Chuck is near the end**.

### 3

Marty and Felicia went out on the back lawn. They sat in chairs they carried down from the patio. The power was out all over the city now, and the stars were very bright. Brighter than Marty had ever seen them since he was a boy growing up in Nebraska. Back then he'd had a small telescope and conned the universe from his attic window.

"There's Aquila," he said. "The Eagle. There's Cygnus, the Swan. See it?"

170

"Yes. And there's the North Sta—" She stopped. "Marty? Did you see . . ."

"Yes," he said. "It just went out. And there goes Mars. Goodbye, Red Planet."

"Marty, I'm scared."

Was Gus Wilfong looking up at the sky tonight? Andrea, the woman who'd been on the Neighborhood Watch Committee with Felicia? Samuel Yarbrough, the undertaker? What about the little girl in the red shorts? Star light, star bright, last stars I see tonight.

Marty took her hand. "I am, too."

### 4

Ginny, Brian, and Doug stand beside Chuck Krantz's bed, their hands joined. They wait as Chuck — husband, father, accountant, dancer, fan of TV crime shows — takes his last two or three breaths.

"Thirty-nine years," Doug says. "Thirty-nine *great* years. Thanks, Chuck."

### 5

Marty and Felicia sat with their faces turned up to the sky, watching the stars go out. First in ones and twos, then by the dozens, then by the hundreds. As the Milky Way rolled away into darkness, Marty turned to his ex-wife.

"I love —"

Black.

171

*Act II: Buskers*
With the help of his friend Mac, who has an old van, Jared Franck sets up his drumkit in his favored spot on Boylston Street between Walgreens and the Apple Store. He has a good feeling about today. It's Thursday afternoon, the weather is fucking gorgeous, and the streets are thronged with people looking forward to the weekend, which is always better than the weekend itself. For Thursday afternoon people, that anticipation is pure. Friday afternoon people have to put anticipation aside and get to work having fun.

"All good?" Mac asks him.

"Yes. Thanks."

"My ten per cent is all the thanks I want, bro."

Mac heads out, probably to the comics store, maybe to Barnes & Noble, then to the Common to read whatever he's bought. A big reader is Mac. Jared will call him when it's time to pack up. Mac will bring his van.

Jared puts down a battered tophat (scuffed velvet, tattered silk grosgrain band) he bought for seventy-five cents in a secondhand shop in Cambridge, then places the sign in front of it that reads THIS IS A MAGIC HAT! GIVE FREELY AND YOUR CONTRIBUTION WILL DOUBLE! He drops in a couple of dollar bills to give people the right idea. The weather is warm for early October, which allows him to dress as he likes for his Boylston gigs — sleeveless tee with FRANCKLY DRUMS on the front, khaki shorts, ratty Converse hightops without socks — but even on chilly days, he usually shucks his coat if he's wearing one, because when you find the beat, you feel the heat.

Jared unfolds his stool and gives a preparatory paradiddle across the drumheads. A few people glance at him, but most simply sweep on by, lost in their talk of friends, dinner plans, where to get a drink, and the day gone by to the mystery-dump where spent days go.

Meanwhile it's a long time until eight o'clock, which is when a BPD car usually slides over to the curb with a cop leaning out the passenger window to tell him it's time to pack it up. Then he'll call Mac. For now there's money to be made. He sets up his hi-hat and crash cymbal, then adds the cowbell, because it feels like a cowbell kind of day.

Jared and Mac work part-time at Doctor Records on Newbury Street, but on a good day Jared can make almost as much busking. And busk-drumming on sunny Boylston Street is certainly better than the patchouli atmosphere of the Doc's, and long conversations with the record nerds looking for Dave Van Ronk on Folkways or Dead rarities on paisley vinyl. Jared always wants to ask them where they were when Tower Records was going under.

He's a dropout from Juilliard, which he calls — with apologies to Kay Kyser — the Kollege of Musical Knowledge. He lasted three semesters, but in the end it wasn't for him. They wanted you to think about what you were doing, and as far as Jared is concerned, the beat is your friend and thinking is the enemy. He sits in on the occasional gig, but bands don't interest him much. Although he never says it (okay, maybe once or twice, while drunk), he thinks maybe music itself is the enemy. He rarely thinks about these issues once he's in the groove. Once he's in the groove, music is a ghost. Only the drums matter then. The beat.

He starts warming up, going easy at first, slow tempo, no cowbell, no tom and no rimshots, not minding that Magic Hat stays empty except for his two crumpled dollars and a quarter flipped in (contemptuously) by a kid on a skateboard. There is time. There is a way in. Like anticipating the joys of an

174

autumn weekend in Boston, finding the in is half the fun. Maybe even most of it.

Janice Halliday is on her way home from seven hours at Paper and Page, trudging down Boylston with her head lowered and her purse clasped close. She may walk all the way to Fenway before she starts looking for the nearest T station, because right now walking is what she wants. Her boyfriend of sixteen months just broke up with her. Dumped her, not to put too fine a point on it. Kicked her to the curb. He did it the modern way, by text.

**We r just not right for each other.** ☹

Then: **U will always be in my heart!** ❤

Then: **Friends 4ever OK?** ☺ ✌

Not right for each other probably means he met someone and will spend the weekend with her picking apples in New Hampshire and later on fucking in some B&B. He won't see Janice tonight, or ever, in the smart pink blouse and red wrap skirt she's wearing unless she texts him a photo with a message reading **This is what U R missing, you pile of** 💩.

It was totally unexpected, that's what set her back on her heels, like having a door slammed in your face just as you were getting ready to walk through it. The weekend, which seemed full of possibility this morning, now looks to her like the entrance to a hol-

175

low, slowly turning barrel into which she must crawl. She's not down to work at P&P on Saturday, but maybe she'll call Maybelline and see if she can pick up Saturday morning, at least. Sunday the store is closed. Sunday best not considered, at least for now.

"Friends forever my ass." She says this to her purse, because she's looking down. She isn't in love with him, never even kidded herself that she was, but it's a dismaying shock, just the same. He was a nice guy (at least she thought so), a pretty good lover, and fun to be with, as they say. Now she's twenty-two and dumped and it sucks. She supposes she'll have some wine when she gets home, and cry. Crying might be good. Therapeutic. Maybe she'll cue up one of her big-band playlists and dance around the room. Dancing with myself, as the Billy Idol song says. She loved to dance in high school, and those Friday night dances were happy times. Maybe she can recapture a little of that happiness.

No, she thinks, those tunes — and those memories — will just make you cry more. High school was a long time ago. This is the real world, where guys break up with you without warning.

Up ahead a couple of blocks, she hears drumming.

Charles Krantz — Chuck, to his friends —

makes his way along Boylston Street dressed in the armor of accountancy: gray suit, white shirt, blue tie. His black Samuel Windsor shoes are inexpensive but sturdy. His briefcase swings by his side. He takes no notice of the chattering after-work throngs eddying around him. He's in Boston attending a week-long conference titled Banking in the Twenty-First Century. He has been sent by *his* bank, Midwest Trust, all expenses paid. Very nice, not least because he's never visited Beantown before.

The conference is being held at a hotel that is perfect for accountants, clean and fairly cheap. Chuck has enjoyed the speakers and the panels (he was on one panel and is scheduled to be on another before the conference ends at noon tomorrow), but had no wish to spend his off-duty hours in the company of seventy other accountants. He speaks their language, but likes to think he speaks others, as well. At least he did, although some of the vocabulary is now lost.

Now his sensible Samuel Windsor Oxfords are taking him for an afternoon walk. Not very exciting, but quite pleasant. *Quite pleasant* is enough these days. His life is narrower than the one he once hoped for, but he's made his peace with that. He understands that narrowing is the natural order of things. There comes a time when you realize you're never going to be the President of the United

States and settle for being president of the Jaycees instead. And there's a bright side. He has a wife to whom he is scrupulously faithful, and an intelligent, good-humored son in middle school. He also has only nine months to live, although he doesn't know it yet. The seeds of his end — the place where life narrows to a final point — are planted deep, where no surgeon's knife will ever go, and they have lately begun to awaken. Soon they will bear black fruit.

To those passing him — the college girls in their colorful skirts, the college boys with their Red Sox caps turned around, the impeccably dressed Asian Americans from Chinatown, the matrons with their shopping bags, the Vietnam vet holding out a huge ceramic cup with an American flag and the motto THESE COLORS DON'T RUN on its side — Chuck Krantz must surely look like white America personified, buttoned up and tucked in and all about chasing the dollar. He is those things, yes, the industrious ant trundling its pre-ordained path through flocks of pleasure-seeking grasshoppers, but he's other things as well. Or was.

He's thinking about the little sister. Was her name Rachel or Regina? Reba? Renee? He can't remember for sure, only that she was the lead guitarist's little sister.

During his junior year in high school, long before he became an industrious ant working in that hill known as Midwest Trust, Chuck was the lead singer in a band called the Retros. They called themselves that because they played a lot of stuff from the sixties and seventies, heavy on British groups like the Stones and the Searchers and the Clash, because most of those tunes were simple. They steered clear of the Beatles, where the songs were full of weird chords like modified sevenths.

Chuck got to be the lead singer for two reasons: although he couldn't play an instrument he could carry a tune, and his grandpa had an old SUV which he allowed Chuck to drive to gigs, as long as they weren't too far. The Retros were bad to start with, and only mediocre when they broke up at the end of junior year, but they had, as the rhythm guitarist's father once put it, "made that quantum leap to palatability." And really, it was hard to do too much damage when you were playing stuff like "Bits and Pieces" (Dave Clark Five) and "Rockaway Beach" (Ramones).

Chuck's tenor voice was pleasing enough in an unremarkable way, and he wasn't afraid to scream or go falsetto when the occasion called for it, but what he really liked were the instrumental breaks, because then he could dance and strut his way across the stage like Jagger, sometimes wagging the mike stand between his legs in a way he considered suggestive. He could also moonwalk, which always drew applause.

The Retros were a garage band that sometimes practiced in an actual garage and sometimes in the lead guitarist's downstairs rec room. On those latter occasions, the lead's little sister (Ruth? Reagan?) usually came ditty-bopping down the stairs in her Bermuda shorts. She'd station herself between their two Fender amps, waggle her hips and butt in exaggerated fashion, put her fingers in her ears, and stick out her tongue. Once, when they were taking a break, she sidled up to Chuck and whispered, "Just between you and me, you sing like old people fuck."

Charles Krantz, the future accountant, had whispered back, "Like you'd know, monkey-butt."

Little sister ignored this. "I like to watch you dance, though. You do it like a white guy, but still."

Little sister, also white, also liked to dance. Sometimes after practice she would put on one of her homemade cassettes and he'd dance with her while the other guys in the band hooted and made semi-smart remarks, the two of them doing their Michael Jackson moves and laughing like loons.

Chuck's thinking about teaching little sister (Ramona?) how to moonwalk when he first hears the drums. Some guy is banging a basic

180

rock beat that the Retros might have played back in the days of "Hang On Sloopy" and "Brand New Cadillac." At first he thinks it's all in his head, maybe even the start of one of the migraines that have plagued him lately, but then the crowd of pedestrians on the next block clears long enough for him to see a kid in a sleeveless tee, sitting on his little stool and beating out that tasty old-time rhythm.

Chuck thinks, Where's a little sister to dance with when you need one?

Jared has been on the job for ten minutes now and has nothing to show for it but that one sarcastic quarter flipped into Magic Hat by the skateboard kid. It makes no sense to him, on a pleasant Thursday afternoon like this with the weekend just around the bend, he should have at least five dollars in the hat by now. He doesn't need the money to keep from starving, but man doesn't live by food and rent alone. A man has to keep his self-image in order, and drumming here on Boylston is a big part of his. He is onstage. He is performing. Soloing, in fact. What's in the hat is how he judges who is digging the performance and who is not.

He twirls his sticks between his fingertips, sets himself, and plays the intro to "My Sharona," but it's not right. Sounds canned. He sees a Mr. Businessman type coming toward him, briefcase swinging like a short pendulum, and something about him — God knows what — makes Jared want to announce his approach. He slips first into a reggae beat, then something slinkier, like a cross between "I Heard It Through the Grapevine" and "Susie Q."

For the first time since running that quick paradiddle to gauge the sound of his kit, Jared feels a spark and understands why he wanted the cowbell today. He begins to whack it on the offbeat, and what he's drumming morphs into something like that old joint by the Champs, "Tequila." It's pretty cool. The groove has arrived, and the groove is like a road you want to follow. He could speed the beat up, get some tom in there, but he's watching Mr. Businessman, and that seems wrong for this dude. Jared has no idea why Mr. Businessman has become the groove's focal point, and doesn't care. Sometimes it just happens that way. The groove turns into a story. He imagines Mr. Businessman on vacation in one of those places where you get a little pink umbrella in your drink. Maybe he's with his wife, or maybe it's his personal assistant, an ash blond in a turquoise bikini. And this is what they're hearing. This is the drummer warming up for the night's gig, before the tiki torches are lit.

He believes Mr. Businessman will just go past on his way to his Mr. Businessman hotel, the chances that he'll feed Magic Hat hovering somewhere between slim and none. When he's gone, Jared will switch to something else, give the cowbell a rest, but for now this beat is the right one.

But instead of floating on by, Mr. Businessman stops. He's smiling. Jared gives him a grin and nods to the tophat on the pavement, never missing a beat. Mr. Businessman doesn't seem to notice him, and he doesn't feed the hat. He drops his briefcase between his black Mr. Businessman shoes instead and begins moving his hips side to side with the beat. Just hips: everything else stays still. His face is poker. He seems to be looking at a spot directly over Jared's head.

"Go, man," a young man remarks, and chinks some coins into the hat. For the gently jiving Mr. Businessman, not the beat, but that's okay.

Jared begins working the hi-hat in quick tender strokes, teasing it, almost caressing it. With his other hand he begins knocking the cowbell on the offbeat, using the kick-pedal to add a little bottom. It's nice. The guy in the gray suit looks like a banker, but that hip-sway is something else. He raises a hand and begins ticking his forefinger to the beat. On the back of the hand is a small crescent-shaped scar.

Chuck hears the beat change, becoming a little more exotic, and for a moment he almost comes back to himself and walks away. Then he thinks, Fuck it, no law against dancing a little on the sidewalk. He steps back from his briefcase so he won't trip, then puts his hands on his moving hips and does a jivey clockwise turn like an about-face. It's how he used to do it back in the day, when the band was playing "Satisfaction" or "Walking the Dog." Someone laughs, someone else applauds, and he goes back the other way with the tail of his coat flying. He's thinking about dancing with little sister. Little sister was a booger with a dirty mouth, but she could sure get down on it.

Chuck himself hasn't got down on it — that mystical, satisfying *it* — in years, but every move feels perfect. He lifts one leg and spins on the other heel. Then he clasps his hands behind his back like a schoolboy called on to recite and moonwalks in place on the pavement in front of his briefcase.

The drummer goes "Yow, daddy!" in surprise and delight. He picks up the pace, now going from the cowbell to the floor tom with his left hand, working the kick-pedal, never losing the metallic sighing from the hi-hat. People are gathering. Money is pouring into Magic Hat: paper as well as metal. Something is happening here.

Two young men in matching berets and Rainbow Coalition tees are at the front of the little crowd. One of them tosses what looks like a five into the hat and yells "Go, man, go!"

Chuck doesn't need the encouragement. He's into it now. Banking in the twenty-first century has slipped his mind. He frees the button on his suit coat, brushes the coat behind him with the backs of his hands, hooks his thumbs into his belt like a gunslinger, and does a modified split, out and back. He follows with a quick-step and turn. The drummer is laughing and nodding. "You the cheese," he says. "You the cheese, daddy!"

The crowd is growing, the hat is filling, Chuck's heart isn't just beating in his chest but thrumming. Good way to have a heart attack, but he doesn't care. If his wife saw him doing this she'd shit a brick, and he doesn't care. His son would be embarrassed, but his son isn't here. He puts his right shoe on his left calf, spins again, and when he comes back front and center, he sees a pretty young woman standing next to the beret guys. She's wearing a filmy pink blouse and a red wrap skirt. She's staring at him with wide, fascinated eyes.

Chuck holds his hands out to her, smiling, snapping his fingers. "Come on," he says. "Come on, little sister, dance."

Jared doesn't think she will — she looks like the shy type — but she walks slowly toward the man in the gray suit. Maybe Magic Hat really is magic.

"Dance!" one of the beret guys says, and others pick it up, clapping along with the beat Jared is laying down: "Dance, dance, dance!"

Janice breaks into a what-the-hell smile, tosses her purse down beside Chuck's brief-case, and takes his hands. Jared drops what he's been doing and turns into Charlie Watts, hammering like a soldier. Mr. Businessman twirls the girl, puts a hand on her trim waist, draws her to him, and quick-steps her past the drumkit, almost to the corner of the Wal-greens building. Janice pulls away, waving her finger in a "naughty-naughty" gesture, then comes back and grasps both of Chuck's hands. As if they had practiced this a hundred times, he does another modified split and she shoots between his legs, a daring move that opens the wrap skirt to the top of one pretty thigh. There are a few gasps as she props herself on one tented hand and then springs back up. She's laughing.

"No more," Chuck says, patting his chest. "I can't —"

She springs to him and puts her hands on his shoulders and he can after all. He catches her by the waist, turning her on his hip and then setting her neatly on the pavement. He lifts her left hand and she spins beneath it like a hopped-up ballerina. There must be over a hundred people watching now, they crowd the sidewalk and spill into the street.

They burst into fresh applause.

Jared runs the drums one time, hits the cymbals, then holds up his sticks triumphantly. There's another round of applause. Chuck and Janice are looking at each other, both out of breath. Chuck's hair, just starting to gray, is stuck to his sweaty forehead.

"What are we doing?" Janice asks. Now that the drums have stopped, she looks dazed.

"I don't know," Chuck says, "but that's the best thing that's happened to me in I don't know how long."

Magic Hat is full to overflowing.

"More!" someone shouts, and the crowd picks it up. There are many phones being held up, ready to catch the next dance, and the girl looks like she would, but she's young. Chuck is danced out. He looks at the drummer and shakes his head. The drummer gives him a nod to show he understands. Chuck is wondering how many people were quick enough to video that first dance, and what his wife will think if she sees it. Or his son. And suppose it goes viral? Unlikely, but if it does, if it gets back to the bank, what will they think when they see the man they sent to a conference in Boston shaking his booty on Boylston Street with a woman young enough to be his daughter? Or somebody's little sister. Just what did he think he was doing?

"No more, folks," the drummer calls. "We

gotta quit while we're ahead."

"And I need to get home," the girl says.

"Not yet," says the drummer. "Please."

Twenty minutes later they're sitting on a bench facing the duck pond in Boston Common. Jared called Mac. Chuck and Janice helped Jared pack up his kit and load it in the back of the van. A few people hung out, congratulating them, offering high fives, adding a few more bucks to the overflowing hat. When they're rolling — Chuck and Janice sitting side by side in the back seat, their feet planted among stacks of comic books — Mac says they'll never find parking next to the Common.

"We will today," Jared says. "Today is magic." And they do, right across from the Four Seasons.

Jared counts out the cash. Somebody has actually tossed in a fifty, maybe the beret guy mistaking it for a five. There's over four hundred dollars in all. Jared has never had such a day. Never expected to. He sets aside Mac's ten per cent (Mac is currently standing at the edge of the pond, feeding the ducks from a package of peanut butter crackers he happened to have in his pocket), then begins to divvy up the rest.

"Oh, no," Janice says when she understands what he's doing. "That's yours."

Jared shakes his head. "Nope, we split even.

188

By myself I wouldn't have made half this much even if I drummed until midnight." Not that the cops would ever allow such a thing. "Sometimes I clear thirty bucks, and that's on a good day."

Chuck has the beginnings of one of his headaches and knows it's apt to be bad by nine o'clock, but the young man's earnestness makes him laugh just the same. "All right. I don't need it, but I guess I earned it." He reaches out and pats Janice's cheek, just as he sometimes used to pat the cheek of the lead singer's potty-mouthed little sister. "So did you, young lady."

"Where did you learn to dance like that?" Jared asks Chuck.

"Well, there was an extracurricular called Twirlers and Spinners back in middle school, but it was my grandma who showed me the best moves."

"You?" he asks Janice.

"Pretty much the same," she says, and blushes. "High school dances. Where did you learn to drum?"

"Self-taught. Like you," he says to Chuck. "You were great by yourself, man, but the chick added a whole extra dimension. We could do this for a living, you know it? I really think we could busk our way to fame and fortune."

For a mad moment Chuck actually considers it, and sees the girl is, too. Not in a seri-

189

ous way, but in the way you daydream of an alternate life. One where you play pro baseball or climb Mount Everest or duet with Bruce Springsteen at a stadium concert. Then Chuck laughs some more and shakes his head. As the girl tucks her third of the take into her purse, she is also laughing.

"It was really all you," Jared says to Chuck. "What made you stop in front of me? And what made you start moving?"

Chuck thinks that over, then shrugs. He could say it was because he was thinking about that old half-assed band, the Retros, and how he liked to dance across the stage during the instrumental breaks, showing off, swinging that mike stand between his legs, but that's not it. And really, had he ever danced with such elan and freedom even back then, when he had been a teenager, young and limber, with no headaches and nothing to lose?

"It was magic," Janice says. She giggles. She didn't expect to hear that sound coming from her today. Crying, yes. Giggling, no. "Like your hat."

Mac comes back. "Jere, we gotta roll or you're gonna end up spending your take paying for my parking ticket."

Jared stands up. "Sure you don't want to change career streams, you two? We could busk this town from Beacon Hill to Roxbury. Make a name for ourselves."

"I've got a conference to attend tomorrow," Chuck says. "On Saturday I'm flying home. I've got a wife and son waiting for me."

"And I can't do it by myself," Janice says, smiling. "It would be like Ginger without Fred."

"I hear that," Jared says, and holds out his arms. "But you have to get in here before you go. Group hug."

They join him. Chuck knows they can smell his sweat — this suit will have to be dry-cleaned before he wears it again, and strenuously — and he can smell theirs. It's all right. He thinks the girl nailed it when she used the word magic. Sometimes there is such a thing. Not much, but a little. Like finding a forgotten twenty in the pocket of an old coat.

"Buskers forever," Jared says.

Chuck Krantz and Janice Halliday repeat it.

"Buskers forever," Mac says, "great. Now let's get out of here before a meter maid shows up, Jere."

Chuck tells Janice he's headed to the Boston Hotel, past the Prudential Center, if she's going that way. Janice was, the plan had been to walk all the way to Fenway, brooding about her ex-boyfriend and muttering doleful shit to her purse, but she's changed her mind. She says she'll take the T from Arlington Street.

He walks her there, the two of them cutting across the park. At the head of the stairs, she turns to him and says, "Thank you for the dance."

He gives her a bow. "It was my pleasure."

He watches her until she's out of sight, then heads back down Boylston. He walks slowly because his back hurts, his legs hurt, and his head is throbbing. He can't remember having bad headaches like this in his whole life. Not until a couple of months ago, that is. He supposes if they keep up, he'll have to see a doctor. He supposes he knows what this might be.

All that's for later, though. If at all. Tonight he thinks he'll treat himself to a good dinner — why not, he's earned it — and a glass of wine. On second thought, make it Evian. Wine might intensify his headache. When he's finished his meal — dessert definitely included — he'll call Ginny and tell her that her husband might be the next one-day Internet sensation. That probably won't happen, somewhere right now someone is undoubtedly filming a dog juggling empty soda bottles and someone else is memorializing a goat smoking a cigar, but it's better to get out front with it, just in case.

As he passes the place where Jared set up his drums, those two questions recur: why did you stop to listen, and why did you start to dance? He doesn't know, and would answers make a good thing better?

Later he will lose the ability to walk, never mind dancing with little sister on Boylston Street. Later he will lose the ability to chew food, and his meals will come from a blender. Later he will lose his grip on the difference between waking and sleeping and enter a land of pain so great that he will wonder why God made the world. Later he will forget his wife's name. What he will remember — occasionally — is how he stopped, and dropped his briefcase, and began to move his hips to the beat of the drums, and he will think that is why God made the world. Just that.

## Act I: I Contain Multitudes

### 1

Chuck was looking forward to having a baby sister. His mother promised he could hold her if he was very careful. Of course he was also looking forward to having parents, but none of that worked out thanks to an icy patch on an I-95 overpass. Much later, in college, he would tell a girlfriend that there were all sorts of novels, movies, and TV shows where a main character's parents died in a car crash, but he was the only person he knew who'd had that happen in real life.

The girlfriend thought this over, then rendered her verdict. "I'm sure it happens all the time, although partners can also be taken in housefires, tornadoes, hurricanes, earthquakes, and avalanches while on ski vacations. To name only a few of the possibilities. And what makes you think you're a main character in anything but your own mind?"

She was a poet and sort of a nihilist. The relationship only lasted a semester.

Chuck wasn't in the car when it went flying upside-down from the turnpike overpass because his parents were having a dinner date and he was being babysat by his grandparents, who at that time he was still calling Zaydee and Bubbie (this mostly ended in the third grade, when kids made fun of him and he reverted to the more all-American Grandma and Grandpa). Albie and Sarah Krantz lived just a mile down the road, and it was natural enough for them to raise him after the accident when he became what he first believed to be an orphant. He was seven.

For a year — maybe a year and a half — that was a house of unadulterated sadness. The Krantzes had not only lost their son and daughter-in-law, they had lost the granddaughter who would have been born just three months later. The name had already been picked out: Alyssa. When Chuck said that sounded to him like rain, his mother had laughed and cried at the same time.

He never forgot that.

He knew his other grandparents of course, there were visits every summer, but they were basically strangers to him. They called a lot after he became an orphant, your basic how-are-you-doing-how's-school calls, and the summer visits continued; Sarah (aka Bubbie, aka Grandma) took him on the plane. But his mother's parents remained strangers, living in the foreign land of Omaha. They sent him presents on his birthday and at Christmas — the latter especially nice since Grandma and Grandpa didn't "do" Christmas — but otherwise he continued to think of them as outliers, like the teachers who were left behind as he moved up through the grades.

Chuck began to slip his metaphorical mourning garments first, necessarily pulling his grandparents (old, yeah, but not *ancient*) out of their own grief. There came a time, when Chuck was ten, that they took the boy to Disney World. They had adjoining rooms at the Swan Resort, the door between the rooms kept open at night, and Chuck only heard his grandma crying once. Mostly, they had fun.

Some of that good feeling came back home with them. Chuck sometimes heard Grandma humming in the kitchen, or singing along with the radio. There had been lots of take-out meals after the accident (and whole recyclable bins full of Grandpa's Budweiser bottles), but in the year after Disney World, Grandma began cooking again. Good meals that put weight on a formerly skinny boy.

She liked rock and roll while she was cooking, music Chuck would have thought much too young for her, but which she clearly enjoyed. If Chuck wandered into the kitchen looking for a cookie or maybe hoping to make a brown-sugar roll-up with a slice of Wonder Bread, Grandma was apt to hold out her hands to him and start snapping her fingers. "Dance with me, Henry," she'd say.

His name was Chuck, not Henry, but he usually took her up on it. She taught him jitterbug steps and a couple of crossover moves. She told him there were more, but her back was too creaky to attempt them. "I can show you, though," she said, and one Saturday brought back a stack of videotapes from the Blockbuster store. There was *Swing Time,* with Fred Astaire and Ginger Rogers, *West Side Story,* and Chuck's favorite, *Singin' in the Rain,* where Gene Kelly danced with a lamppost.

"You could learn those moves," she said. "You're a natural, kiddo."

He asked her once, when they were drinking iced tea after an especially strenuous go to Jackie Wilson's "Higher and Higher," what she had been like in high school.

"I was a *kusit,*" she said. "But don't tell your zaydee I said that. He's old-school, that one."

Chuck never told.

And he never went in the cupola.

Not then.

He asked about it, of course, and more than once. What was up there, what you could see

197

from the high window, why the room was locked. Grandma said it was because the floor wasn't safe and he might go right through it. Grandpa said the same thing, that there was nothing up there because of the rotten floor, and the only thing you could see from those windows was a shopping center, big deal. He said that until one night, just before Chuck's eleventh birthday, when he told at least part of the truth.

## 2

Drinking is not good for secrets, everybody knows that, and after the death of his son, daughter-in-law, and granddaughter-to-be (Alyssa, sounds like rain), Albie Krantz drank a great deal. He should have bought stock in Anheuser-Busch, that was how much he drank. He could do it because he was retired, and comfortably off, and very depressed.

After the trip to Disney World the drinking tapered off to a glass of wine with dinner or a beer in front of a baseball game. Mostly. Once in awhile — every month at first, every couple of months later on — Chuck's grandpa tied one on. Always at home, and never making any fuss about it. The next day he would move slowly and eat little until afternoon, then he was back to normal.

One night while watching the Red Sox get thumped by the Yankees, when Albie was well into his second sixpack of Bud, Chuck once more raised the subject of the cupola. Mostly just to have something to talk about. With the Sox down by nine, the game wasn't exactly holding his attention.

"I bet you can see way past the Westford Mall," Chuck said.

Grandpa considered this, then pushed the mute button on the TV controller, silencing an ad for Ford Truck Month. (Grandpa said Ford stood for Fix Or Repair Daily.) "If you went up there you might see a lot more than you wanted," he said. "That's why it's locked, boychick."

Chuck felt a small and not entirely unpleasurable chill go through him, and his mind immediately flashed to Scooby-Doo and his friends, chasing down spooks in the Mystery Machine. He wanted to ask what Grandpa meant, but the adult part of him — not there in person, no, not at ten, but something that had begun to speak on rare occasions — told him to be quiet. Be quiet and wait.

"Do you know what style this house is, Chucky?"

"Victorian," Chuck said.

"That's right, and not pretend Victorian, either. It was built in 1885, been remodeled half a dozen times since, but the cupola was there from the start. Your bubbie and I bought it when the shoe business really took off, and we got it for a song. Been here since 1971, and in all those years I haven't been up to that damn cupola half a dozen times."

"Because the floor's rotted?" Chuck asked, with what he hoped was appealing innocence.

"Because it's full of ghosts," Grandpa said, and Chuck felt that chill again. Not so pleasurable this time. Although Grandpa might be joking. He *did* joke from time to time these days. Jokes were to Grandpa what dancing was to Grandma. He tipped his beer. Belched. His eyes were red. "Christmas Yet to Come. Do you remember that one, Chucky?"

Chuck did, they watched *A Christmas Carol* every year on Christmas Eve even though they didn't "do" Christmas otherwise, but that didn't mean he knew what his grandpa was talking about.

"The Jefferies boy was only a short time later," Grandpa said. He was looking at the TV, but Chuck didn't think he was actually seeing it. "What happened to Henry Peterson . . . that took longer. It was four, maybe five years on. By then I'd almost forgotten what I saw up there." He jerked a thumb at the ceiling. "I said I'd never go up there again after that, and I wish I hadn't. Because of Sarah — your bubbie — and the bread. It's the waiting, Chucky, that's the hard part. You'll find that out when you're —"

The kitchen door opened. It was Grandma, back from Mrs. Stanley's across the street. Grandma had taken her chicken soup because

Mrs. Stanley was feeling poorly. So Grandma said anyway, but even at not quite eleven, Chuck had a good idea there was another reason. Mrs. Stanley knew all the neighborhood gossip ("She's a *yente,* that one," Grandpa said), and was always willing to share. Grandma poured all the news out to Grandpa, usually after inviting Chuck out of the room. But out of the room didn't mean out of earshot.

"Who was Henry Peterson, Grandpa?" Chuck asked.

But Grandpa had heard his wife come in. He straightened up in his chair and put his can of Bud aside. "Look at that!" he cried in a passable imitation of sobriety (not that Grandma would be fooled). "The Sox have got the bases loaded!"

## 3

In the top of the eighth, Grandma sent Grandpa down to the Zoney's Go-Mart at the bottom of the block to get milk for Chuck's Apple Jacks in the morning. "And don't even think of driving. The walk will sober you up."

Grandpa didn't argue. With Grandma he rarely did, and when he gave it a try, the results weren't good. When he was gone, Grandma — Bubbie — sat down next to Chuck on the couch and put an arm around him. Chuck put his head on her comfortably

201

padded shoulder. "Was he blabbing to you about his ghosts? The ones that live in the cupola?"

"Um, yeah." There was no point in telling a lie; Grandma saw right through those. "Are there? Have you seen them?"

Grandma snorted. "What do you think, *hantel*?" Later it would occur to Chuck that this wasn't an answer. "I wouldn't pay too much attention to Zaydee. He's a good man, but sometimes he drinks a little too much. Then he rides his hobby horses. I'm sure you know what I'm talking about."

Chuck did. Nixon should have gone to jail; the *faygelehs* were taking over American culture and turning it pink; the Miss America pageant (which Grandma loved) was your basic meat-show. But he had never said anything about ghosts in the cupola before that night. At least to Chuck.

"Bubbie, who was the Jefferies boy?"

She sighed. "That was a very sad thing, boychuck." (This was her little joke.) "He lived on the next block over and got hit by a drunk driver when he chased a ball into the street. It happened a long time ago. If your grandpa told you he saw it before it happened, he was mistaken. Or making it up for one of his jokes."

Grandma knew when Chuck was lying; on that night Chuck discovered that was a talent that could go both ways. It was all in the way she stopped looking at him and shifted her eyes to the television, as if what was going on there was interesting, when Chuck knew Grandma didn't give a hang for baseball, not even the World Series.

"He just drinks too much," Grandma said, and that was the end of it.

Maybe true. *Probably* true. But after that, Chuck was frightened of the cupola, with its locked door at the top of a short (six steps) flight of narrow stairs lit by a single bare bulb hanging on a black cord. But fascination is fear's twin brother, and sometimes after that night, if both of his grandparents were out, he dared himself to climb them. He would touch the Yale padlock, wincing if it rattled (a sound that might disturb the ghosts pent up inside), then hurry back down the stairs, looking over his shoulder as he went. It was easy to imagine the lock popping open and dropping to the floor. The door creaking open on its unused hinges. If that happened, he guessed he might die of fright.

**4**

The cellar, on the other hand, wasn't a bit scary. It was brightly lighted by fluorescents. After selling his shoe stores and retiring, Grandpa spent a lot of time down there doing woodwork. It always smelled sweetly of sawdust. In one corner, far from the planers and sanders and the bandsaw he was forbidden to touch, Chuck found a box of Grandpa's old Hardy Boys books. They were old-timey but pretty good. He was reading *The Sinister Signpost* one day in the kitchen, waiting for Grandma to remove a batch of cookies from the oven, when she grabbed the book out of his hands.

"You can do better than that," she said. "Time to step up your game, boychuck. Wait right there."

"I was just getting to the good part," Chuck said.

She snorted, a sound to which only Jewish bubbies do true justice. "There are no good parts in these," she said, and took the book away.

What she came back with was *The Murder of Roger Ackroyd.* "Now *this* is a good mystery story," she said. "No dummocks teenagers running around in jalopies. Consider this your introduction to actual writing." She considered. "Okay, so not Saul Bellow, but not bad."

Chuck started the book just to please Grandma, and was soon lost. In his eleventh year he read almost two dozen Agatha Christies. He tried a couple about Miss Marple, but he was much fonder of Hercule Poirot with his fussy mustache and little gray cells. Poirot was one thinking cat. One day, during his summer vacation, Chuck was reading *Mur-*

*der on the Orient Express* in the backyard
hammock and happened to glance up at the
window of the cupola far above. He wondered
how Monsieur Poirot would go about investigating it.

Aha, he thought. And then *Voilà,* which was
better.

The next time Grandma made blueberry
muffins, Chuck asked if he could take some
to Mrs. Stanley.

"That's very thoughtful of you," Grandma
said. "Why don't you do that? Just remember
to look both ways when you cross the street."
She always told him that when he was going
somewhere. Now, with his little gray cells
engaged, he wondered if she was thinking of
the Jefferies boy.

Grandma was plump (and getting
plumper), but Mrs. Stanley was twice her
size, a widow who wheezed like a leaky tire
when she walked and always seemed to be
dressed in the same pink silk wrapper. Chuck
felt vaguely guilty about bringing her treats
that would add to her girth, but he needed
information.

She thanked him for the muffins and asked
— as he'd been pretty sure she would — if
he would like to have one with her in the
kitchen. "I could make tea!"

"Thank you," Chuck said. "I don't drink
tea, but I wouldn't mind a glass of milk."

When they were seated at the little kitchen

205

table in a flood of June sunshine, Mrs. Stanley asked how things were going with Albie and Sarah. Chuck, mindful that anything he said in this kitchen would be on the street before the day was out, said they were doing fine. But because Poirot said you had to give a little if you wanted to get a little, he added that Grandma was collecting clothes for the Lutheran homeless shelter.

"Your gramma's a saint," Mrs. Stanley said, obviously disappointed there wasn't more. "What about your granddad? Did he get that thing on his back looked at?"

"Yeah," Chuck said. He took a sip of milk. "The doctor took it off and had it tested. It wasn't one of the bad ones."

"Thank God for that!"

"Yes," Chuck agreed. Having given, he now felt entitled to get. "He was talking with Grandma about someone named Henry Peterson. I guess he's dead."

He was prepared for disappointment; she might have never heard of Henry Peterson. But Mrs. Stanley widened her eyes until Chuck was actually afraid they might fall out, and grasped her neck like she had a piece of blueberry muffin stuck in there. "Oh, that was so sad! So *awful*! He was the bookkeeper who did your father's accounts, you know. Other companies, too." She leaned forward, her wrapper giving Chuck a view of a bosom so large it seemed hallucinatory. She was still clutching her neck. *"He killed himself,"* she whispered. *"Hung* himself!"

"Was he embezzling?" Chuck asked. There was a lot of embezzling in Agatha Christie books. Also blackmail.

"What? God, no!" She pressed her lips together, as if to keep in something not fit for the ears of such a beardless youth as the one sitting across from her. If that was the case, her natural proclivity to tell everything (and to anyone) prevailed. "His wife ran away with a younger man! Hardly old enough to vote, *and she was in her forties!* What do you think of that?"

The only reply Chuck could think of right off the bat was "Wow!" and that seemed to suffice.

Back at home he pulled his notebook off the shelf and jotted, *G. saw ghost of Jefferies boy* *not long before he died. Saw ghost of H. Peterson 4 or 5 YEARS before he died.* Chuck stopped, chewing the end of his Bic, troubled. He didn't want to write what was in his mind, but felt that as a good detective he had to.

*Sarah and the bread. DID HE SEE GRAND-MA'S GHOST IN THE CUPOLA???*

The answer seemed obvious to him. Why else would Grandpa have talked about how hard the waiting was?

Now I'm waiting, too, Chuck thought. And hoping that it's all just a bunch of bullshit.

On the last day of sixth grade, Miss Richards — a sweet, hippy-dippyish young woman who had no command of discipline and would probably not last long in the public education system — tried to read Chuck's class some verses of Walt Whitman's "Song of Myself." It didn't go well. The kids were rowdy and didn't want poetry, only to escape into the months of summer stretching ahead. Chuck was the same, happy to throw spitballs or give Mike Enderby the finger when Miss Richards was looking down at her book, but one line clanged in his head and made him sit up straight.

When the class was finally over and the kids set free, he lingered. Miss Richards sat at her desk and blew a strand of hair back from her forehead. When she saw Chuck still standing there, she gave him a weary smile. "*That* went well, don't you think?"

Chuck knew sarcasm when he heard it, even when the sarcasm was gentle and self-directed. He was Jewish, after all. Well, half.

"What does that mean when he says 'I am large, I contain multitudes'?"

That made her smile perk up. She propped one small fist on her chin and looked at him with her pretty gray eyes. "What do you think it means?"

"All the people he knows?" Chuck ventured.

"Yes," she agreed, "but maybe he means even more. Lean forward."

He leaned over her desk, where *American Verse* lay on top of her grade book. Very gently, she put her palms to his temples. They were cool. They felt so wonderful he had to suppress a shiver. "What's in there between my hands? Just the people you know?"

"More," Chuck said. He was thinking of his mother and father and the baby he never got a chance to hold. Alyssa, sounds like rain. "Memories."

"Yes," she said. "Everything you see. Everything you know. The *world,* Chucky. Planes in the sky, manhole covers in the street. Every year you live, that world inside your head will get bigger and brighter, more detailed and complex. Do you understand?"

"I think so," Chuck said. He was overwhelmed with the thought of a whole world inside the fragile bowl of his skull. He thought of the Jefferies boy, hit in the street. He thought of Henry Peterson, his father's bookkeeper, dead at the end of a rope (he'd had nightmares about that). Their worlds going dark. Like a room when you turned out the light.

Miss Richards took her hands away. She looked concerned. "Are you all right, Chucky?"

"Yes," he said.

"Then go on. You're a good boy. I've

209

enjoyed having you in class."

He went to the door, then turned back. "Miss Richards, do you believe in ghosts?"

She considered this. "I believe memories *are* ghosts. But spooks flapping along the halls of musty castles? I think those only exist in books and movies."

And maybe in the cupola of Grandpa's house, Chuck thought.

"Enjoy your summer, Chucky."

## 6

Chuck did enjoy his summer until August, when Grandma died. It happened down the street, in public, which was a little undignified, but at least it was the kind of death where people can safely say "Thank God she didn't suffer" at the funeral. That other standby, "She had a long, full life" was in more of a gray area; Sarah Krantz had yet to reach her mid-sixties, although she was getting close.

Once more the house on Pilchard Street was one of unadulterated sadness, only this time there was no trip to Disney World to mark the beginning of recovery. Chuck reverted to calling Grandma his bubbie, at least in his own head, and cried himself to sleep on many nights. He did it with his face in his pillow so he wouldn't make Grandpa feel even worse. Sometimes he whispered, "Bubbie I miss you, Bubbie I love you," until sleep finally took him.

Grandpa wore his mourning band, and lost weight, and stopped telling his jokes, and began to look older than his seventy years, but Chuck also sensed (or thought he did) some relief in his grandpa. If so, Chuck could understand. When you lived with dread day in and day out, there had to be relief when the dreaded thing finally happened and was over. Didn't there?

He didn't go up the steps to the cupola after she died, daring himself to touch the padlock, but he did go down to Zoney's one day just before starting seventh grade at Acker Park Middle School. He bought a soda and a Kit Kat bar, then asked the clerk where the woman was when she had her stroke and died. The clerk, an over-tatted twentysome-thing with a lot of greased-back blond hair, gave an unpleasant laugh. "Kid, that's a little creepy. Are you, I don't know, brushing up on your serial-killer skills early?"

"She was my grandma," Chuck said. "My bubbie. I was at the community pool when it happened. I came back in the house calling for her and Grandpa told me she was dead."

That wiped the smile off the clerk's face. "Oh, man. I'm sorry. It was over there. Third aisle."

Chuck went to the third aisle and looked, already knowing what he would see.

"She was getting a loaf of bread," the clerk

211

said. "Pulled down almost everything on the shelf when she collapsed. Sorry if that's too much information."

"No," Chuck said, and thought, That's information I already knew.

<h1 style="text-align:center">7</h1>

On his second day at Acker Park Middle, Chuck walked past the bulletin board by the main office, then doubled back. Among the posters for Pep Club, Band, and tryouts for the fall sports teams, there was one showing a boy and girl caught in mid-dance step, he holding his hand up so she could spin beneath. LEARN TO DANCE! it said above the smiling children, in rainbow letters. Below it: JOIN TWIRLERS AND SPINNERS! FALL FLING IS COMING! GET OUT ON THE FLOOR!

An image of painful clarity came to Chuck as he looked at this: Grandma in the kitchen, holding her hands out. Snapping her fingers and saying, "Dance with me, Henry."

That afternoon he went down to the gymnasium, where he and nine hesitant others were greeted enthusiastically by Miss Rohrbacher, the girls' phys ed teacher. Chuck was one of three boys. There were seven girls. All the girls were taller.

One of the boys, Paul Mulford, tried to creep out as soon as he realized he was the smallest kid there, coming in at five-feet-nothing. Miss Rohrbacher chased him down and hauled him back, laughing cheerfully. "No-no-no," said she, "you're *mine* now."

So he was. So they all were. Miss Rohrbacher was the dance-monster, and none could stand in her way. She fired up her boombox and showed them the waltz (Chuck knew it), the cha-cha (Chuck knew it), the ball change (Chuck knew it), then the samba. Chuck didn't know that one, but when Miss Rohrbacher put on "Tequila," by the Champs, and showed them the basic moves, he got it at once and fell in love with it.

He was by far the best dancer in the little club, so Miss Rohrbacher mostly put him with the girls who were clumsy. He understood she did it to make them better, and he was a good sport about it, but it was sort of boring.

Near the end of their forty-five minutes, however, the dance-monster would show mercy and pair him with Cat McCoy, who was an eighth-grader and the best dancer of the girls. Chuck didn't expect romance — Cat was not only gorgeous, she was four inches taller than he was — but he loved to dance with her, and the feeling was mutual. When they got together, they caught the rhythm and let it fill them. They looked into each other's eyes (she had to look down, which was a bummer, but hey — it was what it was) and laughed for the joy of it.

Before letting the kids go, Miss Rohrbacher paired them up (four of the girls had to dance with each other) and told them to freestyle. As they lost their inhibitions and awkwardness, they all got pretty good at it, although most of them were never going to dance at the Copacabana.

One day — this was in October, only a week or so before the Fall Fling — Miss Rohrbacher put on "Billie Jean."

"Watch this," Chuck said, and did a very passable moonwalk. The kids oohed. Miss Rohrbacher's mouth dropped open.

"Oh my God," Cat said. "Show me how you did that!"

He did it again. Cat tried, but the illusion of walking backward just wasn't there.

"Kick off your shoes," Chuck said. "Do it in your socks. Slide into it."

Cat did. It was much better, and they all applauded. Miss Rohrbacher had a go, then all of the others were moonwalking like crazy. Even Dylan Masterson, the clumsiest of them, got into it. Twirlers and Spinners let out half an hour later than usual that day.

Chuck and Cat walked out together. "We should do it at the Fling," she said.

Chuck, who hadn't been planning on going, stopped and looked at her with his eyebrows raised.

"Not as a date or anything," Cat hastened on, "I'm going out with Dougie Wentworth

—" This Chuck knew. "— but that doesn't mean we couldn't show them some cool moves. I want to, don't you?"

"I don't know," Chuck said. "I'm a lot shorter. I think people would laugh."

"Got you covered," Cat said. "My brother's got a pair of Cuban heels, and I think they'd fit you. You've got big feet for a little kid."

"Thanks a bunch," Chuck said.

She laughed and gave him a sisterly hug.

At the next meeting of Twirlers and Spinners, Cat McCoy brought her brother's Cubans. Chuck, who had already endured slights to his manhood for being in the dance club, was prepared to hate them, but it was love at first sight. The heels were high, the toes were pointed, and they were as black as midnight in Moscow. They looked a lot like the ones Bo Diddley wore back in the day. So okay, they *were* a little big, but toilet paper stuffed into those pointy toes took care of that. Best of all . . . man, they were *slick*. During freestyle, when Miss Rohrbacher put on "Caribbean Queen," the gym floor felt like ice.

"You put scratches on that floor, the janitors will beat your butt," Tammy Underwood said. She was probably right, but there were no scratches. He was too light on his feet to leave any.

**8**

Chuck went stag to the Fall Fling, which turned out just fine, because all the girls from Twirlers and Spinners wanted to dance with him. Especially Cat, because her boyfriend, Dougie Wentworth, had two left feet and spent most of the evening slouched against the wall with his buddies, all of them sucking up punch and watching the dancers with lordly sneers.

Cat kept asking him when they were going to do their stuff, and Chuck kept putting her off. He said he'd know the right tune when he heard it. It was his bubbie he was thinking of.

Around nine o'clock, half an hour or so before the dance was scheduled to end, the right tune came up. It was Jackie Wilson, singing "Higher and Higher." Chuck strutted to Cat with his hands out. She kicked off her shoes, and with Chuck in her brother's Cubans, they were at least close to the same height. They went out on the floor, and when they did a double moonwalk, they cleared it. The kids made a circle around them and began clapping. Miss Rohrbacher, one of the chaperones, was among them, clapping along with the rest and shouting "Go, go, go!"

They did. As Jackie Wilson shouted that happy, gospel-tinged tune, they danced like Fred Astaire, Ginger Rogers, Gene Kelly, and Jennifer Beals all rolled up into one. They finished with Cat spinning first one way, then the other, then collapsing backward into Chuck's arms with her own held out in a dying swan. He went down in a split that miraculously didn't rip the crotch out of his pants. Two hundred kids cheered when Cat turned her head and put a kiss on the corner of Chuck's mouth.

*"One more time!"* some kid shouted, but Chuck and Cat shook their heads. They were young, but smart enough to know when to quit. The best cannot be topped.

## 9

Six months before he died of a brain tumor (at the unfair age of thirty-nine), and while his mind was still working (mostly), Chuck told his wife the truth about the scar on the back of his hand. It wasn't a big deal and hadn't been a big lie, but he'd reached a time in his rapidly diminishing life when it seemed important to clear the books. The only time she'd asked about it (it really was a very small scar), he told her that he had gotten it from a boy named Doug Wentworth, who was pissed about him cavorting with his girlfriend at a middle school dance and pushed him into a chainlink fence outside the gymnasium.

"What actually happened?" Ginny asked, not because it was important to her but because it seemed to be important to him. She didn't care much about whatever had happened to him in middle school. The doctors said he would probably be dead before Christmas. That was what mattered to her.

When their fabulous dance was over and the DJ put on another, more recent tune, Cat McCoy had run to her girlfriends, who giggled and shrieked and hugged her with a fervency of which only thirteen-year-old girls may be capable. Chuck was sweaty and so hot his cheeks felt on the verge of catching fire. He was also euphoric. All he wanted in that moment was darkness, cool air, and to be by himself.

He walked past Dougie and his friends (who paid absolutely no attention to him) like a boy in a dream, pushed through the door at the back of the gym, and walked out into the paved half-court. The cool fall air doused the fire in his cheeks, but not the euphoria. He looked up, saw a million stars, and understood that for each one of those million, there was another million behind it.

The universe is large, he thought. It contains multitudes. It also contains *me,* and in this moment I am wonderful. I have a right to be wonderful.

He moonwalked under the basketball hoop, moving to the music inside (when he made his little confession to Ginny he could no longer remember what that music had been, but for the record it was the Steve Miller Band, "Jet Airliner"), and then twirled, his

arms outstretched. As if to embrace everything.

There was pain in his right hand. Not big
pain, just your basic ouch, but it was enough
to bring him out of his joyous elevation of
spirit and back to earth. He saw that the back
of his hand was bleeding. While he was doing
his whirling dervish bit under the stars, his
outflung hand had struck the chainlink fence
and a protruding jut of wire had cut him. It
was a superficial wound, hardly enough to
merit a Band-Aid. It left a scar, though. A
tiny white crescent scar.

"Why would you lie about that?" Ginny
asked. She was smiling as she picked up his
hand and kissed the scar. "I could understand
it if you'd gone on to tell me how you beat
the big bully to a pulp, but you never said
that."

No, he'd never said that, and he'd never
had a bit of trouble with Dougie Wentworth.
For one thing, he was a cheerful enough
galoot. For another, Chuck Krantz was a
seventh-grade midget unworthy of notice.

Why *had* he told the lie, then, if not to cast
himself as the hero of a fictional story?
Because the scar was important for another
reason. Because it was part of a story he
couldn't tell, even though there was now an
apartment building standing on the site of
the Victorian house where he had done most

of his growing up. The *haunted* Victorian house.

The scar meant more, so he had *made* it more. He just couldn't make it as much more as it really was. That made little sense, but as the glioblastoma continued its blitzkrieg, it was the best his disintegrating mind could manage. He had finally told her the truth of how the scar actually happened, and that would have to do.

**10**

Chuck's grandpa, his zaydee, died of a heart attack four years after the Fall Fling dance. It happened while Albie was climbing the steps of the public library to return a copy of *The Grapes of Wrath* — which, he said, was every bit as good as he remembered. Chuck was a junior in high school, singing in a band and dancing like Jagger during the instrumental breaks.

Grandpa left him everything. The estate, once quite large, had shrunk considerably over the years since Grandpa's early retirement, but there was still enough to pay for Chuck's college education. Later on, the sale of the Victorian paid for the house (small but in a good neighborhood, with a lovely back room for a nursery) he and Virginia moved into after their honeymoon in the Catskills. As a new hire at Midwest Trust — a humble teller — he never could have bought the place without Grandpa's inheritance.

Chuck flatly refused to move to Omaha to live with his mother's parents. "I love you guys," he said, "but this is where I grew up and where I want to stay until I go to college. I'm seventeen, not a baby."

So they, both long retired, came to him and stayed in the Victorian with him for the twenty months or so before Chuck went off to the University of Illinois.

They weren't able to be there for the funeral and burial, however. It happened fast, as Grandpa had wanted, and his mom's folks had loose ends to tie up in Omaha. Chuck didn't really miss them. He was surrounded by friends and neighbors he knew much better than his mother's goy parents. A day before they were scheduled to arrive, Chuck finally opened a manila envelope that had been sitting on the table in the front hall. It was from the Ebert-Holloway Funeral Parlor. Inside were Albie Krantz's personal effects — at least those that had been in his pockets when he collapsed on the library steps.

Chuck dumped the envelope out on the table. There was a rattle of coins, a few Halls cough drops, a pocket knife, the new cell phone Grandpa had barely had a chance to use, and his wallet. Chuck picked up the wallet, smelled its old limp leather, kissed it, and cried a little. He was an orphant now for sure.

There was also Grandpa's keyring. Chuck

slipped this over the index finger of his right hand (the one with the crescent-shaped scar) and climbed the short and shadowy flight of stairs to the cupola. This last time he did more than rattle the Yale padlock. After some searching, he found the right key and unlocked it. He left the lock hanging from the hasp and pushed the door open, wincing at the squeal of the old unoiled hinges, ready for anything.

## 11

But there was nothing. The room was empty.

It was small, circular, no more than fourteen feet in diameter, maybe less. On the far side was a single wide window, caked with the dirt of years. Although the day was sunny, the light it let in was bleary and diffuse. Standing on the threshold, Chuck put out a foot and toed the boards like a boy testing the water of a pond to see if it was cold. There was no creak, no give. He stepped in, ready to leap back the moment he felt the floor start to sag, but it was solid. He walked across to the window, leaving footprints in the thick fall of dust.

Grandpa had been lying about the rotted floor, but about the view he had been dead-on. It really wasn't much. Chuck could see the shopping center beyond the greenbelt, and beyond that, an Amtrak train moving toward the city, pulling a stumptail of five passenger cars. At this time of day, with the morning commuter rush over, there would be few riders.

Chuck stood at the window until the train was gone, then followed his footprints back to the door. As he turned to close it, he saw a bed in the middle of the circular room. It was a hospital bed.

There was a man in it. He appeared to be unconscious. There were no machines, but Chuck could hear one just the same, going *bip . . . bip . . . bip.* A heart monitor, maybe. There was a table beside the bed. On it were various lotions and a pair of black-framed glasses. The man's eyes were closed. One hand lay outside the coverlet, and Chuck observed the crescent-shaped scar on the back of it with no surprise.

In this room, Chuck's grandpa — his zaydee — had seen his wife lying dead, the loaves of bread she would pull off the shelves when she went down scattered all around her. It's the waiting, Chucky, he'd said. That's the hard part.

Now his own waiting would begin. How long would that wait be? How old was the man in the hospital bed?

Chuck started back into the cupola for a closer look, but the vision was gone. No man, no hospital bed, no table. There was one final faint *bip* from the unseen monitor, then that was gone, too. The man did not fade, as

223

ghostly apparitions did in movies; he was just gone, insisting he had never been there in the first place.

He wasn't, Chuck thought. I will insist that he wasn't, and I will live my life until my life runs out. I am wonderful, I deserve to be wonderful, and I contain multitudes.

He closed the door and snapped the lock shut.

■ ■ ■ ■

# IF IT BLEEDS

■ ■ ■ ■

■ ■ ■ ■

# If It Bleeds

■ ■ ■

*In January of 2021, a small padded envelope addressed to Detective Ralph Anderson is delivered to the Conrads, the Andersons' next-door neighbors. The Anderson family is on an extended vacation in the Bahamas, thanks to an endless teachers' strike in the Andersons' home county. (Ralph insisted that his son Derek bring his books, which Derek termed "a grotesque bummer.") The Conrads have agreed to forward their mail until the Andersons return to Flint City, but printed on this envelope, in large letters, is DO NOT FORWARD HOLD FOR ARRIVAL. When Ralph opens the package, he finds a flash drive titled* If It Bleeds, *presumably referring to the old news trope which proclaims "If it bleeds, it leads." The drive holds two items. One is a folder containing photographs and audio spectrograms. The other is a kind of report, or spoken-word diary, from Holly Gibney, with whom the detective shared a case that began in Oklahoma and ended in a Texas cave. It was a case that changed Ralph Anderson's perception of reality forever. The final words of Holly's audio report are from an entry dated December 19th, 2020. She sounds out of breath.*

I have done the best I can, Ralph, but it may not be enough. In spite of all my planning there's a chance I won't come out of this alive. If that's the case, I need you to know how much your friendship has meant to me. If I do die, and you choose to continue what I've started, please be careful. You have a wife and son.

[*This is where the report ends.*]

*December 8–9, 2020*

## 1

Pineborough Township is a community not far from Pittsburgh. Although much of western Pennsylvania is farm country, Pineborough boasts a thriving downtown and just shy of 40,000 residents. As you enter the municipal city limits, you pass a gigantic bronze creation of dubious cultural merit (although the residents seem to like it). This is, according to the sign, THE WORLD'S LARGEST PINE CONE! There is a turnout for people who want to picnic and take pictures. Many do, some posing their younger children on the cone's scales. (A small sign reads "No children over 50 lbs on the Pine Cone, please.") On this day it's too cold for picnics, the Porta John has been taken away for the season, and the bronze creation of dubious cultural merit is decked out in blinking Christmas lights.

Not far beyond the giant cone, close to where the first traffic light marks the beginning of downtown Pineborough, is Albert Macready Middle School, where almost five hundred students attend grades seven, eight, and nine — no teachers' strike here.

At quarter to ten on the 8th, a Pennsy Speed Delivery truck pulls into the school's circular drive. The delivery guy gets out and stands in front of his truck for a minute or two, consulting his clipboard. Then he pushes his glasses up on the bridge of his narrow nose, gives his little mustache a stroke, and goes around to the back. He rummages and retrieves a square package about three feet on all sides. He carries it easily enough, so it can't be too heavy.

At the door is an admonishment reading ALL SCHOOL VISITORS MUST BE ANNOUNCED AND APPROVED. The driver pushes the button on the intercom below the sign and Mrs. Keller, the school secretary, asks him how she can help.

"Got a package here for something called . . ." He bends to look at the label. "Boy-howdy. Looks like Latin. It's for the Nemo . . . Nemo Impune . . . or maybe you say Impuny . . ."

Mrs. Keller helps him out. "The Nemo Me Impune Lacessit Society, right?"

On her video monitor, the delivery guy looks relieved. "If you say so. The last word is

230

*Society,* for sure. What does it mean?"

"Tell you inside."

Mrs. Keller is smiling as the delivery guy walks through the metal detector, enters the main office, and puts the package on the counter. It's plastered with stickers, a few of Christmas trees and holly and Santas, many more of Scottish guys in kilts and Black Watch caps honking on bagpipes.

"So," he says, taking his reader off his belt and aiming it at the address label. "What's Nemo Me Impuny when it's home with its shoes off?"

"The Scottish national motto," she says. "It means *No one provokes me with impunity.* Mr. Griswold's Current Affairs class has a partner school in Scotland, near Edinburgh. They email and Facebook and send pictures to each other and things like that. The Scottish kids root for the Pittsburgh Pirates, our kids for the Buckie Thistle Football Club. The Current Affairs kids watch the games on YouTube. Calling themselves the Nemo Me Impune Lacessit Society was probably Griswold's idea." She peers at the return address on the label. "Yup, Renhill Secondary School, that's the one. Customs stamp and everything."

"Christmas presents, I bet," the delivery guy says. "Gotta be. Because look here." He tips the box up, showing her DO NOT OPEN UNTIL 18 DECEMBER, carefully

231

printed and bookended by two more bagpipe-blowing Scots.

Mrs. Keller nods. "That's the last day of school before the Christmas break. God, I hope Griswold's kids sent *them* something."

"What kind of presents do Scottish kids send American kids, do you think?"

She laughs. "I just hope it's not haggis."

"What's that? More Latin?"

"Sheep's heart," Mrs. Keller says. "Also liver and lungs. I know because my husband took me to Scotland for our tenth wedding anniversary."

The delivery guy pulls a face that makes her laugh some more, then asks her to sign the window in his reader gadget. Which she does. He wishes her a good day and a merry Christmas. She wishes him the same. When he's gone, Mrs. Keller grabs a loitering kid (no hall pass, but Mrs. Keller lets it go this once) to take the box to the storage closet between the school library and the first-floor teachers' room. She tells Mr. Griswold about the package during the lunch break. He says he'll take it down to his classroom at three-thirty, after the last bell. Had he taken it at lunch, the carnage might have been even worse.

The American Club at Renhill Secondary did not send the kids at Albert Macready a Christmas box. There is no such company as Pennsy Speed Delivery. The truck, later discovered abandoned, was stolen from a mall parking lot shortly after Thanksgiving. Mrs. Keller will excoriate herself for not noticing that the delivery guy wasn't wearing a name tag, and when he aimed his reader at the package's address label, it didn't beep the way the ones used by the UPS and FedEx drivers did, because it was a fake. So was the customs stamp.

The police will tell her anyone might have missed these things, and she has no reason to feel responsible. She does, nevertheless. The school's security protocols — the cameras, the main door that's locked when school is in session, the metal detector — are good, but they're only machinery. She is (or was) the human part of the equation, the guardian at the gate, and she let the school down. She let the *kids* down.

Mrs. Keller feels that the arm she lost will only be the beginning of her atonement.

## 2

It's 2:45, and Holly Gibney is getting ready for an hour that always makes her happy. That may suggest certain low tastes, but she still enjoys her sixty minutes of weekday television viewing, and tries to insure that Finders Keepers (nice new digs for the detective agency, fifth floor of the Frederick Building downtown) is empty from three to four. Since she's the boss — a thing she still finds hard to believe — that isn't difficult.

Today Pete Huntley, her partner in the business since Bill Hodges died, is out trying to track down a runaway at the city's various homeless shelters. Jerome Robinson, taking a year off from Harvard while he tries to turn a forty-page sociology paper into what he hopes will be a book, is also working for Finders Keepers, although only part-time. This afternoon he's south of the city, looking for a dognapped golden retriever named Lucky who may have been dumped at a Youngstown, Akron, or Canton dog impound when Lucky's owners refused to pay the demanded ransom of ten thousand dollars. Of course the dog may just have been turned loose in the Ohio countryside — or killed — but maybe not. The dog's name is a good omen, she told Jerome. She said she was hopeful.

"You have Holly hope," Jerome said, grinning.

"That's right," she replied. "Now go on, Jerome. Fetch."

She's got a good chance of being alone until it's time to close the place up, but it's only the hour between three and four that she really cares about. With one eye on the clock, she writes a starchy email to Andrew Edwards, a client who was worried that his partner was trying to hide business assets. Turns out the partner wasn't, but Finders did the work and needs to be paid. *This is our third billing,* Holly writes. *Please clear your account so we don't have to turn this matter over to a collection agency.*

Holly finds she can be much more forceful when she can write "our" and "we" rather than "my" and "I." She's working on that, but as her grandfather was wont to say, "Rome wasn't built in a day, and neither was Philadelphia."

She sends off the email — *whoosh* — and shuts down her computer. She glances at the clock. Seven to three. She goes to the little fridge and takes out a can of Diet Pepsi. She puts it on one of the coasters the firm gives out (YOU LOSE, WE FIND, YOU WIN), then opens the top left drawer of her desk. In here, concealed by a pile of junk paperwork, is a bag of Snickers Bites. She takes out six, one for each commercial break during her show, unwraps them, and lines them up.

Five to three. She turns on the television but mutes it. Maury Povich is currently strutting around and inciting his studio audience. She may have low tastes, but not that low. She considers eating one of her Snickers and tells herself to wait. Just as she is congratulating herself on her forbearance, she hears the elevator and rolls her eyes. It must be Pete. Jerome is way down south.

It's Pete, all right, and smiling. "Oh, happy day," he says. "Somebody finally got Al to send a repairman —"

"Al did nothing," Holly said. "Jerome and I took care of it. It was just a glitch."

"How —"

"There was a small hack involved." She's still got one eye on the clock: three minutes to three. "Jerome did that, but I could have." Once more, honesty compels her. "At least I think so. Did you find the girl?"

Pete gives her two thumbs up. "At Sunrise House. My first stop. Good news, she wants to go home. She called her mom, who's coming to get her."

"Are you sure? Or is that what she told you?"

"I was there when she made the call. I saw the tears. This is a good resolution, Holly. I just hope Mom's not a deadbeat like that guy Edwards."

"Edwards will pay," she says. "My heart is set on it." On the TV, Maury has been replaced by a dancing bottle of diarrhea medicine. Which in Holly's opinion is actually an improvement. "Now be quiet, Pete, my show is coming on in one minute."

"Oh my God, are you still watching that guy?"

Holly gives him a forbidding look. "You are welcome to watch, Pete, but if you intend to make sarcastic remarks and spoil my enjoyment, I wish you would leave."

*Be assertive,* Allie Winters likes to tell her. Allie is her therapist. Holly saw another

236

therapist briefly, a man who has written three books and many scholarly articles. This was for reasons apart from the demons that have chased her out of her teens. She needed to talk about more recent demons with Dr. Carl Morton.

"No sarcastic remarks, roger that," Pete says. "Man, I can't believe you and Jerome bypassed Al. Took the bull by the horns, so to speak. You rock, Holly."

"I am trying to be more assertive."

"And you're succeeding. Is there a Coke in the fridge?"

"Only diet."

"Uck. That stuff tastes like —"

"Hush."

It's three o'clock. She unmutes the TV just as her show's theme song starts up. It's the Bobby Fuller Four singing "I Fought the Law." A courtroom comes on the screen. The spectators — actually a studio audience, like Maury's but less feral — are clapping along with the music, and the announcer intones, "Steer clear if you're a louse, because *John Law* is in the house!"

"All rise!" George the bailiff cries.

The spectators get up, still clapping and swaying, as Judge John Law comes out of his chambers. He's six-six (Holly knows this from *People* magazine, which she hides even better than her Snickers Bites) and bald as an eight-ball . . . although he's more dark

237

chocolate than black. He's wearing volumi-
nous robes that sway back and forth as he
boogies his way to the bench. He grabs the
gavel and tick-tocks it back and forth like a
metronome, flashing a full deck of white
teeth.

"Oh my dear Jesus in a motorized wheelchair," Pete says.

Holly gives him her most forbidding look.
Pete claps one hand over his mouth and
waves the other one in surrender.

"Siddown, siddown," says Judge Law —
actual name Gerald Lawson, Holly also
knows this from *People,* but it's close enough
— and the spectators all sit down. Holly likes
John Law because he's straight from the
shoulder, not all snarky and poopy like that
Judge Judy. He gets to the point, just as Bill
Hodges used to . . . although Judge John Law
is no substitute, and not just because he's a
fictional character on a TV show. It's been
years since Bill passed away, but Holly still
misses him. Everything she is, everything she
has, she owes to Bill. There's no one like him,
although Ralph Anderson, her police detective friend from Oklahoma, comes close.

"What have we got today, Georgie, my
brother from another mother?" The spectators chortle at this. "Civil or criminal?"

Holly knows it's unlikely the same judge
would handle both kinds of cases — and a
new one every afternoon — but she doesn't

238

mind; the cases are always interesting.

"Civil, Judge," Georgie the bailiff says. "The plaintiff is Mrs. Rhoda Daniels. The defendant is her ex-husband, Richard Daniels. At issue is custody of the family dog, Bad Boy."

"A dog case," Pete says. "Right up our alley."

Judge Law leans on his gavel, which is extra-long. "And is Bad Boy in the house, Georgie my man?"

"He's in a holding room, Judge."

"Very good, very good, and does Bad Boy bite, as his name might indicate?"

"According to security, he seems to have a very sweet nature, Judge Law."

"Excellent. Let's hear what the plaintiff has to say about Bad Boy."

At this point, the actor playing Rhoda Daniels enters the courtroom. In real life, Holly knows, the plaintiff and defendant would already be seated, but this is more dramatic. As Ms. Daniels sways down the center aisle in a dress that's too tight and heels that are too high, the announcer says, "We'll return to Judge Law's courtroom in just a minute."

An ad for death insurance comes on, and Holly pops her first Snickers Bite into her mouth.

"Don't suppose I could have one of those, could I?" Pete asks.

"Aren't you supposed to be on a diet?"

"I get low sugar at this time of day."

Holly opens her desk drawer — reluctantly — but before she can get to the candy bag, the old lady worrying about how she can pay her husband's funeral expenses is replaced by a graphic that says BREAKING NEWS. This is followed by Lester Holt, and Holly knows right away it's going to be serious. Lester Holt is the network's big gun. *Not another 9/11,* she thinks every time something like this happens. *Please God, not another 9/11 and not nuclear.*

Lester says, "We're interrupting your regularly scheduled programming to bring you news of a large explosion at a middle school in Pineborough, Pennsylvania, a town about forty miles southeast of Pittsburgh. There are reports of numerous casualties, many of them children."

"Oh my God," Holly says. She puts the hand that was in the drawer over her mouth.

"These reports are so far unconfirmed, I want to emphasize that. I think . . ." Lester puts a hand to his ear, listens. "Yes, okay. Chet Ondowsky, from our Pittsburgh affiliate, is on the scene. Chet, can you hear me?"

"Yes," a voice says. "Yes, I can, Lester."

"What can you tell us, Chet?"

The picture switches away from Lester Holt to a middle-aged guy with what Holly thinks

240

of as a local news face: not handsome enough to be a major market anchor, but presentable. Except the knot of his tie is crooked, there's no makeup to cover the mole beside his mouth, and his hair is mussy, as if he didn't have time to comb it.

"What's that he's standing beside?" Pete asks.

"I don't know," Holly says. "Hush."

"Looks sort of like a giant pine co—"

*"Hush!"* Holly could care less about the giant pine cone, or Chet Ondowsky's mole and mussed-up hair; her attention is fixed on the two ambulances that go screaming past behind him, nose to tail with their lights flashing. Casualties, she thinks. Numerous casualties, many of them children.

"Lester, what I can tell you is that there are almost certainly at least seventeen dead here at Albert Macready Middle School, and many more injured. This comes from a county sheriff's deputy who asked not to be identified by name. The explosive device may have been in the main office, or a nearby storage room. If you look over there . . ."

He points, and the camera obediently follows his finger. At first the picture is blurry, but when the cameraman steadies and zooms, Holly can see a large hole has been blown in the side of the building. Bricks scatter across the lawn in a corona. And as she's taking this in — with millions of others, probably — a man in a yellow vest emerges from the hole with something in his arms. A small something wearing sneakers. No, one sneaker. The other has apparently been torn off in the blast.

The camera returns to the correspondent and catches him straightening his tie. "The Sheriff's Department will undoubtedly be holding a press conference at some point, but right now informing the public is the least of their concerns. Parents have already started to gather . . . ma'am? Ma'am, can I speak to you for just a moment? Chet Ondowsky, WPEN, Channel 11."

The woman who comes into the shot is vastly overweight. She has arrived at the school without a coat, and her flower print housedress billows around her like a caftan. Her face is dead pale except for bright spots of red on her cheeks, her hair is disarrayed enough to make Ondowsky's mussy 'do look neat, her plump cheeks glisten with tears.

They shouldn't be showing this, Holly thinks, and I shouldn't be watching it. But they are, and I am.

"Ma'am, do you have a child who attends Albert Macready?"

"My son and daughter both do," she says, and grabs Ondowsky's arm. "Are they okay? Do you know that, sir? Irene and David Vernon. David's in the seventh grade. Irene's in the ninth. We call Irene Deenie. Do you know if they are okay?"

"I don't, Mrs. Vernon," Ondowsky says. "I think you should talk to one of the deputies, over where they're setting up those sawhorses."

"Thank you, sir, thank you. Pray for my kids!"

"I will," Ondowsky says as she rushes off, a woman who will be very lucky to survive the day without having some sort of cardiac episode . . . although Holly guesses that right now her heart is the least of her concerns. Right now her heart is with David and Irene, also known as Deenie.

Ondowsky turns back to the camera. "Everyone in America will be praying for the Vernon children, and all the children who were attending Albert Macready Middle School today. According to the information I have now — it's sketchy, and this could change — the explosion occurred at about two-fifteen, an hour ago, and was strong enough to shatter windows a mile away. The glass . . . Fred, can you get a shot of this pine cone?"

"There, I knew it was a pine cone," Pete says. He's leaning forward, eyes glued to the television.

Fred the camera guy moves in, and on the pine cone's petals, or leaves, or whatever you called them, Holly can see shards of broken glass. One actually appears to have blood on it, although she can hope it's just a passing reflection cast by the lights on one of the ambulances.

Lester Holt: "Chet, that's horrible. Just awful."

The camera pulls back and returns to Ondowsky. "Yes, it is. This is a horrible scene. Lester, I want to see if . . ."

A helicopter with a red cross and MERCY HOSPITAL stenciled on the side is landing in the street. Chet Ondowsky's hair swirls in the wash of the rotors, and he raises his voice to be heard.

*"I want to see if I can do anything to help! This is terrible, just a terrible tragedy! Back to you in New York!"*

Lester Holt returns, looking upset. "Be safe, Chet. Folks, we're going to return you to your regularly scheduled programming, but we'll continue to update you on this developing situation at NBC Breaking News on your —"

Holly uses the remote and kills the TV. She has lost her taste for make-believe justice, at least for today. She keeps thinking of that limp form in the arms of the man wearing the yellow vest. One shoe off, one shoe on, she thinks. Deedle-deedle-dumpling, my son John. Will she watch the news tonight? She supposes she will. Won't want to, but won't be able to help herself. She'll have to know how many casualties. And how many are children.

Pete surprises her by taking her hand. Usually she still doesn't like to be touched, but right now his hand feels good holding hers.

"I want you to remember something," he says.

She turns to him. Pete is grave.

"You and Bill stopped something much worse than this from happening," he says. "That crackpot fuck Brady Hartsfield could have killed hundreds at the rock concert he tried to blow up. Maybe thousands."

"And Jerome," she says in a low voice. "Jerome was there, too."

"Yep. You, Bill, and Jerome. The Three Musketeers. That you *could* stop. And did. But stopping this one —" Pete nods to the TV. "That was someone else's responsibility."

### 3

At seven o'clock Holly is still in the office, going over invoices that don't really need her attention. She managed to resist turning on the office TV and watching Lester Holt at six-thirty, but she doesn't want to go home just yet. That morning she had been looking forward to a nice veggie dinner from Mr. Chow, which she would eat while watching *Pretty Poison,* a vastly overlooked thriller from 1968 starring Anthony Perkins and Tuesday Weld, but tonight she doesn't want poison, pretty or otherwise. She has been poisoned by the news from Pennsylvania, and

245

still might not be able to resist turning on CNN. That would gift her with hours of tossing and turning until two or even three in the morning.

Like most people in the media-soaked twenty-first century, Holly has become inured to the violence men (it's still mostly men) do to each other in the name of religion or politics — those ghosts — but what happened at that suburban middle school is too much like what almost happened at the Midwest Culture and Arts Complex, where Brady Hartsfield tried to blow up a few thousand kids, and what did happen at City Center, where he plowed a Mercedes sedan into a crowd of job-seekers, killing . . . she doesn't remember how many. She doesn't want to remember.

She is putting away the files — she has to go home sometime, after all — when she hears the elevator again. She waits to see if it will go past the fifth floor, but it stops. Probably Jerome, but she still opens the second drawer of her desk and loosely grips the can there. It has two buttons. One blares an earsplitting horn. The other dispenses pepper spray.

It's him. She lets go of the IntruderGuard and closes the drawer. She marvels (and not for the first time since he came back from Harvard) at how tall and handsome he's become. She dislikes that fur around his mouth, what he calls "the goat," but would never tell him so. Tonight his usual energetic walk is slow and a little slumped. He gives her a perfunctory "Yo, Hollyberry," and drops into the chair that in business hours is reserved for clients.

Usually she would admonish him about how much she dislikes that childish nickname — it's their form of call-and-response — but not tonight. They are friends, and because she's a person who has never had many, Holly tries her best to deserve the ones she has. "You look very tired."

"Long drive. Heard the news about the school? It's all over the sat radio."

"I was watching *John Law* when they broke in. Since then I've been avoiding it. How bad?"

"They're saying twenty-seven dead so far, twenty-three of them kids between twelve and fourteen. But it'll go higher. There are still a few kids and two teachers they haven't been able to account for, and a dozen or so in critical condition. It's worse than Parkland. Make you think of Brady Hartsfield?"

"Of course."

"Yeah, me too. The ones he got at City Center and the ones he could have gotten if we'd been just a few minutes slower that night at the 'Round Here concert. I try not to think about that, tell myself we won that one, because when my mind goes to it I get the willies."

Holly knows all about the willies. She has them often.

Jerome rubs a hand slowly down one cheek and in the quiet she can hear the scritch-scritch of his fingers on the day's new bristles. "Sophomore year at Harvard I took a philosophy course. Did I ever mention that to you?"

Holly shakes her head.

"It was called —" Jerome makes finger-quotes. "— 'The Problem of Evil.' In it, we talked a lot about concepts called inside evil and outside evil. We . . . Holly, you okay?"

"Yes," she says, and she is . . . but at the mention of outside evil, her mind immediately turns to the monster she and Ralph tracked to his final lair. The monster had gone under many names and worn many faces, but she had always thought of him simply as the outsider, and the outsider had been as evil as they come. She's never told Jerome about what happened in the cave known as the Marysville Hole, although she supposes he knows something pretty dire went on there — a lot more than made it into the newspapers.

He's looking at her uncertainly. "Go on," she tells him. "This is very interesting to me." It's the truth.

"Well . . . the class consensus was there's outside evil if you believe in outside good —"

"God," Holly says.

"Yes. Then you can believe there really are demons, and exorcism is a valid response to them, there really are malevolent spirits —"

"Ghosts," Holly says.

"Right. Not to mention curses that really work, and witches, and *dybbuks,* and who knows what else. But in college, all that stuff pretty much gets laughed out of court. God Himself mostly gets laughed out of court."

"Or Herself," Holly says primly.

"Yeah, whatever, if God doesn't exist, I guess the pronouns don't matter. So that leaves inside evil. Moron stuff. Guys who beat their children to death, serial killers like Brady fucking Hartsfield, ethnic cleansing, genocide, 9/11, mass shootings, terrorist attacks like the one today."

"Is that what they're saying?" Holly asks. "A terrorist attack, maybe ISIS?"

"That's what they're *assuming,* but no one's claimed responsibility yet."

Now his other hand on his other cheek, scritch-scritch, and are those tears in Jerome's eyes? She thinks they are, and if he cries, she will, too, she won't be able to help it. Sadness is catching, and how poopy is that?

"But see, here's the deal about inside and outside evil, Holly — *I don't think there's any difference.* Do you?"

She considers everything she knows, and everything she's been through with this young man, and Bill, and Ralph Anderson. "No," she says. "I don't."

"I think it's a bird," Jerome says. "A big bird, all frowsy and frosty gray. It flies here, there, and everywhere. It flew into Brady Hartsfield's head. It flew into the head of the guy who shot all those people in Las Vegas. Eric Harris and Dylan Klebold, they got the bird. Hitler. Pol Pot. It flies into their heads, and when the wetwork's done, it flies away again. I'd like to catch that bird." He clenches his hands and looks at her and yes, those are tears. "Catch it and wring its fucking neck."

Holly comes around the desk, kneels beside him, and puts her arms around him. It's a clumsy hug with him sitting in the chair, but it does the job. The dam breaks. When he speaks against her cheek, she feels the scratch of his stubble.

"The dog's dead."

"What?" She can barely make out what he's saying through his sobs.

"Lucky. The golden. When whoever stole him didn't get the ransom, the bastard cut him open and threw him in a ditch. Some-body spotted him — still alive, barely — and took him to the Ebert Animal Hospital in Youngstown. Where he lived for maybe half an hour. Nothing they could do. Not so lucky after all, huh?"

"All right," Holly says, patting his back. Her own tears are flowing, and there's snot, too. She can feel it running out of her nose.

250

Oough. "All right, Jerome. It's okay."

"It's not. You know it's not." He pulls back and looks at her, cheeks wet and shining, goatee damp. "Cut that nice dog's belly open, and threw him in the ditch with his intestines hanging out, and you know what happened then?"

Holly knows but shakes her head.

"The bird flew away." He wipes his sleeve across his eyes. "Now it's in someone else's head, it's better than ever, and on we fucking go."

### 4

Just before ten o'clock, Holly gives up the book she's trying to read and turns on the TV. She takes a look at the talking heads on CNN, but can't bear their chatter. Hard news is what she wants. She switches to NBC, where a graphic, complete with grim music, reads SPECIAL REPORT: TRAGEDY IN PENNSYLVANIA. Andrea Mitchell is now anchoring in New York. She begins by telling America that the president has tweeted his "thoughts and prayers," as he does after each of these horror shows: Pulse, Las Vegas, Parkland. This meaningless twaddle is followed by the updated score: thirty-one dead, seventy-three (oh God, so many) wounded, nine in critical condition. If Jerome was right, that means at least three of the criticals have died.

251

"Two terrorist organizations, Houthi Jihad and the Liberation Tigers of Tamil Eelam, have claimed responsibility for the bombing," Mitchell says, "but sources in the State Department say neither claim is credible. They are leaning toward the idea that the bombing may have been a lone-wolf attack, similar to that perpetrated by Timothy McVeigh, who set off a huge blast at the Alfred P. Murrah Federal Building in Oklahoma City in 1995. That explosion took a hundred and sixty-eight lives."

Many of those also children, Holly thinks. Killing children for God, or ideology, or both — no hell could be hot enough for those who'd do such things. She thinks of Jerome's frosty gray bird.

"The man who delivered the bomb was photographed by a security camera when he buzzed for entry," Mitchell continues. "We are going to put his picture up for the next thirty seconds. Look closely, and if you recognize him, call the number on your screen. There is a reward of two hundred thousand dollars for his arrest and subsequent conviction."

The picture comes up. It's color, and clear as a bell. It's not perfect because the camera is positioned above the door and the man is looking straight ahead, but it's pretty good. Holly leans forward, all her formidable job skills — some that were always innate, some

honed during her work with Bill Hodges —
kicking in. The guy is either Caucasian with a
tan (not likely at this time of year but not
impossible), a light-skinned Latino, a Middle
Easterner, or possibly wearing makeup. Holly
opts for Caucasian and makeup. She puts his
age as mid-forties. He's wearing specs with
gold frames. His black mustache is small and
neatly trimmed. His hair, also black, is short.
She can see this because he's not wearing a
cap, which would have obscured more of his
face. Bold son of a gun, Holly thinks. He
knew there would be cameras, he knew there
would be pictures, and he didn't care.

"Not a son of a gun," she says, still staring.
Recording every feature. Not because this is
her case, but because it's her nature. "He's a
son of a *bitch,* is what he is."

Back to Andrea Mitchell. "If you know him,
call the number on the screen, and do it right
away. Now we're going to take you to the Macready Middle School and our man on the
scene. Chet, are you still there?"

He is, standing in a pool of bright light
thrown by the camera. More bright lights are
shining on the middle school's wounded side;
each tumbled brick casts its own sharp
shadow. Generators are roaring. People in
uniform rush here and there, shouting and
talking into mikes. Holly sees FBI on some
of the jackets, ATF on others. There's a crew
in white Tyvek body suits. Yellow crime scene

tape flutters. There is a sense of controlled chaos. At least Holly hopes it's controlled. Someone must be in charge, maybe in the Winnebago she can see at the far left of the shot.

Lester Holt is presumably at home, watching this in his pj's and slippers, but Chet Ondowsky is still going. A regular Energizer Bunny is Mr. Ondowsky, and Holly can understand that. This is probably the biggest story he'll ever cover, he was in on it almost from the start, and he's chasing it for all he's worth. He's still wearing his suit jacket, which was probably okay when he got to the site, but now the temperature has dropped. She can see his breath, and she's pretty sure he's shivering.

Someone give him something warmer, for heaven's sake, Holly thinks. A parka, or even a sweatshirt.

The suit jacket will have to be thrown out. It's smeared with brick dust and torn in a couple of places, sleeve and pocket. The hand holding the mike is also smeared with brick dust, and something else. Blood? Holly thinks it is. And the streak on his cheek, that's blood, too.

"Chet?" Andrea Mitchell's disembodied voice. "Are you there?"

The hand not holding the mike goes to his earpiece, and Holly sees there are Band-Aids on two of the fingers. "Yes, I'm here." He

254

faces the camera. "This is Chet Ondowsky, reporting from the bombing site at Albert Macready Middle School in Pineborough, Pennsylvania. This ordinarily peaceful school was rocked by an explosion of enormous strength sometime not long after two o'clock this afternoon —"

Andrea Mitchell appears on a split screen. "Chet, we understand from a source at Homeland Security that the explosion happened at two-nineteen P.M. I don't know how the authorities can pinpoint the time that exactly, but apparently they can."

"Yes," Chet says, sounding a little distracted, and Holly thinks how tired he must be. And will he be able to sleep tonight? She guesses not. "Yes, that sounds just about right. As you can see, Andrea, the search for victims is winding down, but the forensic work is just beginning. There will be more personnel on the scene by daybreak, and —"

"Excuse me, Chet, but you took part in the search yourself, is that right?"

"Yes, Andrea, we all pitched in. Townspeople, some of them parents. Also Alison Greer and Tim Witchick from KDKA, Donna Forbes from WPCW, and Bill Larson from —"

"Yes, but I'm hearing you pulled two children from the ruins yourself, Chet."

He doesn't bother looking falsely modest and aw-shucks; Holly awards him points for that. He keeps it on a reporting level. "That's correct, Andrea. I heard one of them moaning and saw the other. A girl and a boy. I know the boy's name, Norman Fredericks. The girl . . ." He wets his lips. The mike in his hand trembles, and Holly thinks not just from the cold. "The girl was in bad shape. She was . . . calling for her mother."

Andrea Mitchell looks stricken. "Chet, that's awful."

It is. Too awful for Holly. She picks up the remote to kill the feed — she has the salient facts, more than she has any use for — and then hesitates. It's the torn pocket she's looking at. Maybe torn while Ondowsky was searching for victims, but if he's Jewish, it might have been done on purpose. It might have been *keriah*, the rending of garments after a death and the symbolic exposure of a wounded heart. She guesses that is the truth of that torn pocket. It is what she wants to believe.

### 5

The sleeplessness she expected doesn't happen; Holly drops off within a matter of minutes. Perhaps crying with Jerome let out some of the poison the news from Pennsylvania had injected in her. Giving comfort and receiving it. As she slips away, she thinks she should talk about that with Allie Winters at their next session.

She wakes sometime deep in the early hours of December 9th, thinking about the correspondent, Ondowsky. Something about him — what? How tired he looked? The scratches and brick dust on his hands? The torn pocket?

That, she thinks. It must have been. Maybe I was dreaming about it.

She mutters briefly into the dark, a kind of prayer. "I miss you, Bill. I'm taking my Lexapro and I'm not smoking."

Then she's out and doesn't wake up until the alarm goes at 6 A.M.

*December 9–13, 2020*

## 1

Finders Keepers has been able to move to the new, pricier digs on the fifth floor of the Frederick Building downtown because business has been good, and the rest of that week is busy for Holly and Pete. There's no time for Holly to watch *John Law* and little to think about the school explosion in Pennsylvania, though the news reports continue and it never completely leaves her mind.

The agency has working relationships with two of the city's big law firms, the white-shoe kind with lots of names on the door. "Macintosh, Winesap, and Spy," Pete likes to joke. As retired police, he has no great love for lawyers, but he would be the second to admit (Holly would be the first) that subpoenas and process-serving pay very well. "Merry fucking Christmas to these guys," Pete says as he goes out on Thursday morning with a briefcase full of woe and annoyance.

In addition to serving papers, Finders Keepers is on speed-dial at several insurance companies — locals, not affiliated with the big boys — and Holly spends most of Friday investigating an arson claim. It's a pretty big one, the policy holder really needs the money, and she has been tasked with making sure that he was actually in Miami, as he claimed, when his warehouse went up in flames. Turns out he was, which is good for him but not so good for Lake Fidelity.

In addition to those things, which reliably pay the big bills, there's an absconding debtor to track (Holly does this on her computer and locates him quickly by checking his credit charges), bail-jumpers to put on the radar — what's known in the trade as skip-tracing — and lost kids and dogs. Pete usually goes after the kids, and when Jerome's working, he's great with the dogs.

She's not surprised that Lucky's death hit him so hard, not just because it was so extraordinarily cruel but because the Robinson family lost their beloved Odell to congestive heart failure the year before. There are no dogs on the docket, either lost or abducted, on that Thursday and Friday, which is good, because Holly is too busy and Jerome is at home, doing his own thing. The project that started as a school paper has now become a priority with him, if not an outright obsession. His folks are doubtful about their son's decision to take what he calls "a gap year." Holly isn't. She doesn't necessarily think Jerome is going to shock the world, but she has an idea he *will* make it sit up and take notice. She has faith in him. And Holly hope. That, too.

She can only follow developments on the middle school explosion out of the corner of her eye, and that's okay, because there haven't been many. Another victim has died — a teacher, not a student — and a number of kids with minor injuries have been released from various area hospitals. Mrs. Althea Keller, the only person who actually spoke to the delivery guy/bomber, has regained consciousness, but she had little to add, other than the fact that the package purported to be from a school in Scotland, and that cross-Atlantic relationship was in Pineborough's weekly newspaper, along with a group photo of the Nemo Me Impune Lacessit Society (perhaps ironic but probably not, all eleven of the Impunies, as they called themselves, survived the explosion uninjured). The van was found in a nearby barn, wiped clean of prints and bleach-cleaned of DNA. The police have been inundated with calls from people eager to identify the perp, but none of the calls has produced results. Hopes of an early capture are being replaced by fears that the guy may not be done but only getting started. Holly hopes this isn't so, but her experience with Brady Hartsfield makes her fear the worst. Best case scenario, she thinks (with a coldness that once would have been alien to her), he's killed himself.

On Friday afternoon, as she's finishing her report to Lake Fidelity, the phone rings. It's her mother, and with news Holly has been dreading. She listens, she says the appropriate things, and she allows her mother to treat her as the child she thinks Holly still is (even though the purpose of this call will involve Holly acting like a grownup), asking if Holly is remembering to brush after every meal, if she is remembering to take her medication with food, if she is limiting her movies to four a week, etc., etc. Holly tries to ignore the headache her mother's calls — and this call in particular — almost always bring on. She assures her mother that yes, she will be there on Sunday to help, and yes, she will be there by noon, so they can eat one more meal as a family.

My family, Holly thinks. My fracked-up family.

Because Jerome keeps his phone off when he's working, she calls Tanya Robinson, Jerome and Barbara's mom. Holly tells Tanya she won't be able to eat Sunday dinner with them because she needs to go upstate. Kind of a family emergency. She explains, and Tanya says, "Oh, Holly. I'm so sorry to hear that, sweetie. Are you going to be all right?"

"Yes," Holly says. It's what she always says when someone asks her that horrible loaded question. She's pretty sure she sounds okay, but as soon as she hangs up, she puts her hands over her face and begins to cry. It's that *sweetie* that does it. To have someone call her, who was known in high school as Jibba-Jibba, sweetie.

To have that, at least, to come back to.

**2**

On Saturday night Holly plans her drive using the Waze app on her computer, factoring in a stop to pee and gas up her Prius. To get there by noon, she will have to leave at seven-thirty, which will give her time for a cup of tea (decaf), toast, and a boiled egg. With this groundwork laid to a nicety, she lies awake for two hours as she didn't on the night after the Macready School blew up, and when she does sleep, she dreams of Chet Ondowsky. He is telling about the carnage he saw when he joined the first responders, and saying things he would never say on television. There was blood on the bricks, he says. There was a shoe with a foot still in it, he says. The little girl who cried for her mommy, he says, screamed in pain even though he tried to be gentle when he took her in his arms. He tells these things in his best just-the-facts voice, but as he talks he rends his clothes. Not just his suit coat pocket and sleeve, but first one lapel and then the other. He yanks off his tie and rips it in two. Then the shirt right down the front, popping off the buttons.

The dream either fades before he can go to work on the trousers of his suit, or her conscious mind refuses to remember it the next morning when her phone alarm goes off. In any case, she wakes feeling unrested, and she eats her egg and toast with no pleasure, just fueling up for what will be a trying day. She usually enjoys a road trip, but the prospect of this one sits on her shoulders like a physical weight.

Her little blue bag — what she thinks of as her notions bag — is by the door, packed with a clean change of clothes and her toiletries, in case she has to spend the night. She slides the strap onto her shoulder, takes the elevator down from her cozy little apartment, opens the door, and there is Jerome Robinson sitting on the front step. He's drinking a Coke and his backpack with its JERRY GARCIA LIVES sticker is resting beside him.

"Jerome? What are you doing here?" And because she can't help it: "And drinking Coke at seven-thirty in the morning, oough!"

"I'm going with you," he says, and the look he gives her says that arguing will do no good. That's okay, because she doesn't want to.

"Thanks, Jerome," Holly says. It's hard, but

she manages not to cry. "That's very good of you."

Jerome drives the first half of the journey, and at the gas-and-pee stop on the turnpike, they switch. Holly feels her sense of dread at what's awaiting her (*us,* she corrects herself) starting to close in as they get closer to the Cleveland suburb of Covington. To keep it at bay, she asks Jerome how his project is going. His book.

"Of course, if you don't want to talk about it, I know some authors don't —"

But Jerome is willing enough. It began as a required assignment for a class called Sociology in Black and White. Jerome decided to write about his great-great-grandfather, born of former slaves in 1878. Alton Robinson spent his childhood and early adulthood in Memphis, where a thriving black middle class existed in the latter years of the nineteenth century. When yellow fever and white vigilante gangs struck at that nicely balanced sub-economy, much of the black community simply pulled up stakes, leaving the white folks they'd worked for to cook their own food, dispose of their own garbage, and wipe their own babies' beshitted bottoms.

Alton settled in Chicago, where he worked in a meat-packing plant, saved his money, and opened a juke joint two years before

Prohibition. Rather than close down when "the biddies started busting the barrels" (this from a letter Alton wrote to his sister — Jerome has found a trove of letters and documents in storage), he changed locations and opened a South Side speakeasy that became known as the Black Owl.

The more Jerome discovered about Alton Robinson — his dealings with Alphonse Capone, his three escapes from assassination (the fourth did not go so well), his probable sideline in blackmail, his political kingmaking — the more his paper grew, and the more his work for other classes seemed insignificant in comparison. He turned the long essay in and received a laudatory grade.

"Which was sort of a joke," he tells Holly as they roll into the last fifty miles of their journey. "That paper was just, you know, the tip of the iceberg. Or like the first verse in one of those endless English ballads. But by then I was halfway through spring semester, and I had to pick up the slack in my other courses. Make the mater and pater proud, you know."

"That was very adult of you," says the woman who feels she never succeeded in making her mother and late father proud. "But it must have been hard."

"It *was* hard," Jerome says. "I was on fire, kiddo. Wanted to drop everything else and chase great-great-Grandpa Alton. That man had a fabulous life. Diamonds and pearl stickpins and a mink coat. But letting it age a little was the right thing to do. When I went back to it — this was last June — I saw how it had a theme, or could have, if I did the job right. Have you ever read *The Godfather?*"

"Read the book, saw the movie," Holly says promptly. "All three movies." She feels compelled to add, "The last one isn't very good."

"Do you remember the epigraph of the novel?"

She shakes her head.

"It's from Balzac. 'Behind every great fortune there is a crime.' That was the theme I saw, even though the fortune ran through his fingers long before he was shot down in Cicero."

"It really is like *The Godfather,*" Holly marvels, but Jerome shakes his head.

"It's not, because black people can never be American in the same way Italian and Irish people can. Black skin withstands the melting pot. I want to say . . ." He pauses. "I want to say that discrimination is the father of crime. I want to say that Alton Robinson's tragedy was that he thought that *through* crime he could achieve some sort of equality, and that turned out to be a chimera. In the end he wasn't killed because he got crossways with Paulie Ricca, who was Capone's successor, but because he was black. Because he was a *nigger.*"

Jerome, who used to irritate Bill Hodges (and scandalize Holly) by sometimes doing a minstrel show colored accent — all *yassuh boss* and *I sho do, suh!* — spits this last word.

"Do you have a title?" Holly asks quietly. They are nearing the Covington exit.

"I think so, yeah. But I didn't think it up." Jerome looks embarrassed. "Listen, Hollyberry, if I tell you something, do you promise to keep it secret? From Pete, and from Barb and my parents? Especially them."

"Of course. I can keep a secret."

Jerome knows this is true, but still hesitates for a moment before plunging. "My prof in that Black and White sociology class sent my paper to an agent in New York. Elizabeth Austin is her name. She was interested, so after Thanksgiving I sent her the hundred or so pages I've written since summer. Ms. Austin thinks it's publishable, and not just by an academic press, which was about as high as I was shooting. She thinks one of the majors might be interested. She suggested calling it by the name of great-great-Gramp's speakeasy. *Black Owl: The Rise and Fall of an American Gangster.*"

"Jerome, that's wonderful! I bet tons of people would be interested in a book with a title like that."

"Black people, you mean."

"No! All kinds! Do you think only white people liked *The Godfather?*" Then a thought strikes her. "Only how would your family feel about it?" She's thinking of her own family, which would be horrified to have such a skeleton dragged out of the closet.

"Well," Jerome says, "they both read the paper and loved it. Of course, that's different from a book, isn't it? One that might be read by a lot more people than a teacher. But it's four generations back, after all . . ."

Jerome sounds troubled. She sees him look at her, but only out of the corner of her eye; Holly always faces directly forward when she's driving. Those movie sequences where the driver looks at his passenger for seconds at a time while delivering dialogue drive her absolutely crazy. She always wants to shout, *Look at the road, dummy! Do you want to hit a kid while you're discussing your love life?*

"What do you think, Hols?"

She considers this carefully. "I think you should show your parents as much as you showed the agent," she says at last. "Listen to what they say. Get a read on their feelings and respect them. Then . . . push ahead. Write it all down — the good, the bad, and the ugly." They've come to the Covington exit. Holly puts on her blinker. "I've never written a book, so I can't say for sure, but I think it takes a certain amount of bravery. So that's what you should do, I think. Be brave."

And that's what I need to be now, she thinks. Home is only two miles away, and home is where the heartache is.

**4**

The Gibney house is in a development called Meadowbrook Estates. As Holly weaves her way through the spiderweb of streets (to the home of the spider, she thinks, and is immediately ashamed of thinking about her mother that way), Jerome says, "If I lived here and came home drunk, I'd probably spend at least an hour finding the right house."

He's right. They're New England saltboxes, only set apart from one another by different colors . . . which wouldn't be much help at night, even with the streetlights. There are probably different flowerbeds in the warm months, but now the yards of Meadowbrook Estates are covered in crusty scarves of old snow. Holly could tell Jerome that her mother likes the sameness, it makes her feel safe (Charlotte Gibney has her own issues), but doesn't. She's gearing up for what promises to be a stressful lunch and an even more stressful afternoon. Moving day, she thinks. Oh God.

She pulls into the driveway of 42 Lily Court, kills the engine, and turns to Jerome. "You need to be prepared. Mother says he's gotten a lot worse in the last few weeks. Sometimes she exaggerates, but I don't think she is this time."

"I understand the situation." He gives one of her hands a brief squeeze. "I'll be fine. You just take care of yourself, okay?"

Before she can reply, the door of Number 42 opens and Charlotte Gibney comes out, still in her good church clothes. Holly raises one hand in a tentative hello gesture, which Charlotte doesn't return.

"Come inside," she says. "You're late."

Holly knows she's late. By five minutes.

As they approach the door, Charlotte gives Jerome a what's-he-doing-here look.

"You know Jerome," Holly says. It's true; they've met half a dozen times, and Charlotte always favors him with that same look. "He came to keep me company, and lend moral support."

Jerome gives Charlotte his most charming smile. "Hello, Mrs. Gibney. I invited myself along. Hope you don't mind."

To this Charlotte simply says, "Come in, I'm freezing out here." As though it had been their idea for her to come out on the stoop rather than her own.

Number 42, where Charlotte has lived with her brother since her husband died, is overheated and smelling so strongly of potpourri that Holly hopes she won't begin coughing. Or gagging, which would be even worse. There are four side tables in the little hall, narrowing the passage to the living room

270

enough to make the trip perilous, especially since each table is crammed with the little china figurines that are Charlotte's passion: elves, gnomes, trolls, angels, clowns, bunnies, ballerinas, doggies, kitties, snowmen, Jack and Jill (with a bucket each), and the *pièce de la résistance,* a Pillsbury Doughboy.

"Lunch is on the table," Charlotte says. "Just fruit cup and cold chicken, I'm afraid — but there's cake for dessert — and . . . and . . ."

Her eyes fill with tears, and when Holly sees them, she feels — in spite of all the work she's done in therapy — a surge of resentment that's close to hate. Maybe it is hate. She thinks of all the times she cried in her mother's presence and was told to go to her room "until you get that out of your system." She feels an urge to throw those very words in her mother's face now, but gives Charlotte an awkward hug instead. As she does, she feels how close the bones lie under that thin and flabby flesh, and realizes her mother is old. How can she dislike an old woman who so obviously needs her help? The answer seems to be quite easily.

After a moment Charlotte pushes Holly away with a little grimace, as though she smelled something bad. "Go see your uncle and tell him lunch is ready. You know where he is."

Indeed Holly does. From the living room

271

comes the sound of professionally excited announcers doing a football pregame show. She and Jerome go single-file, so as not to risk upsetting any members of the china gallery.

"How many of these does she have?" Jerome murmurs.

Holly shakes her head. "I don't know. She always liked them, but it's gotten out of hand since my father died." Then, lifting her voice and making it artificially bright: "Hi, Uncle Henry! All ready for lunch?"

Uncle Henry clearly didn't make the run to church. He's slumped in his La-Z-Boy, wearing a Purdue sweatshirt with some of his breakfast egg on it, and a pair of jeans, the kind with the elasticized waist. They are riding low, showing a pair of boxer shorts with tiny blue pennants on them. He looks from the TV to his visitors. For a moment he's totally blank, then he smiles. "Janey! What are you doing here?"

That goes through Holly like a glass dagger, and her mind flashes momentarily to Chet Ondowsky, with his scratched hands and torn suit coat pocket. And why would it not? Janey was her cousin, bright and vivacious, all the things Holly could never be, and she was Bill Hodges's girlfriend for awhile, before she died in another explosion, victim of a bomb planted by Brady Hartsfield and meant for Bill himself.

"It's not Janey, Uncle Henry." Still with that

artificial brightness, the kind usually saved for cocktail parties. "It's Holly."

There's another of those blank pauses as rusty relays go about business they used to do lickety-split. Then he nods. "Sure. It's my eyes, I guess. From looking at the TV too long."

His eyes, Holly thinks, are hardly the point. Janey is years in her grave. *That's* the point.

"Come here, girl, and give me a hug."

She does so, as briefly as possible. When she pulls back, he's staring at Jerome. "Who's this . . ." For a terrible moment she thinks he's going to finish by saying *this black boy* or maybe even *this jigaboo,* but he doesn't. "This guy? I thought you were seeing that cop."

This time she doesn't bother to correct him about who she is. "It's Jerome. Jerome Robinson. You've met him before."

"Have I? Mind must be going." He says it not even as a joke, just as a kind of conversational placeholder, without realizing that's exactly the case.

Jerome shakes his hand. "How you doing, sir?"

"Not bad for an old fella," Uncle Henry says, and before he can say more, Charlotte calls — practically shrieks — from the kitchen that lunch is on.

"His master's voice," Henry says good-humoredly, and when he stands up, his pants

273

fall down. He doesn't seem to realize.

Jerome gives Holly a tiny jerk of the head toward the kitchen. She gives him a doubtful look in return, but goes.

"Let me just help you with those," Jerome says. Uncle Henry doesn't reply but only stares at the TV with his hands dangling at his sides while Jerome pulls up his pants. "There you go. Ready to eat?"

Uncle Henry looks at Jerome, startled, as if just registering his presence. Which is probably true. "I don't know about you, son," he says.

"Don't know what about me, sir?" Jerome asks, taking Uncle Henry by the shoulder and getting him turned toward the kitchen.

"The cop was too old for Janey, but you look too young." He shakes his head. "I just don't know."

## 5

They get through lunch, with Charlotte scolding Uncle Henry along and sometimes helping him with his food. Twice she leaves the table and comes back wiping her eyes. Through analysis and therapy, Holly has come to realize that her mother is almost as terrified of life as Holly herself used to be, and that her most unpleasant characteristics — her need to criticize, her need to control situations — arise from that fear. Here is a situation she can't control.

And she loves him, Holly thinks. That, too. He's her brother, she loves him, and now he's leaving. In more ways than one.

When lunch is finished, Charlotte banishes the men to the living room ("Watch your game, boys," she tells them) while she and Holly do up the few dishes. As soon as they are alone, Charlotte tells Holly to have her friend move her car so they can get Henry's out of the garage. "His things are in the trunk, all packed and ready to go." She's speaking out of the corner of her mouth like an actress in a bad spy movie.

"He thinks I'm Janey," Holly says.

"Of course he does, Janey was always his favorite," Charlotte says, and Holly feels another of those glass daggers go in.

## 6

Charlotte Gibney might not have been pleased to see Holly's friend turn up with her daughter, but she's more than willing to allow Jerome to pilot Uncle Henry's big old boat of a Buick (125,000 miles on the clock) to the Rolling Hills Elder Care Center, where a room has been waiting since the first of December. Charlotte was hoping her brother could remain at home through Christmas, but now he's begun to wet the bed, which is bad, and to wander the neighborhood, sometimes in his bedroom slippers, which is worse.

When they arrive, Holly doesn't see a single

rolling hill in the vicinity, just a Wawa store and a decrepit bowling alley across the street. A man and a woman in blue Care Center jackets are leading a line of six or eight golden oldies back from the bowling alley, the man holding up his hands to stop traffic until the group is safely across. The inmates (not the right word, but it's the one that occurs to her) are holding hands, making them look like prematurely aged children on a field trip.

"Is this the movies?" Uncle Henry asks as Jerome wheels the Buick into the turnaround in front of the Care Center entrance. "I thought we were going to the movies."

He's riding shotgun. At the house, he actually tried to get in behind the wheel until Charlotte and Holly got him turned around. No more driving for Uncle Henry. Charlotte filched her brother's driver's license from his wallet in June, during one of Henry's increasingly long naps. Then sat at the kitchen table and cried over it.

"I'm sure they'll have movies here," Charlotte says. She's smiling, and biting her lip as she does it.

They are met in the lobby by a Mrs. Braddock, who treats Uncle Henry like an old friend, grasping both of his hands and telling him how glad she is "to have you with us."

"With us for what?" Henry asks, looking around. "I have to go to work soon. The paperwork is all messed up. That Hellman is

276

worse than useless."

"Do you have his things?" Mrs. Braddock asks Charlotte.

"Yes," Charlotte says, still smiling and biting her lip. Soon she may be crying. Holly knows the signs.

"I'll get his suitcases," Jerome says quietly, but there's nothing wrong with Uncle Henry's ears.

"What suitcases? *What suitcases?*"

"We have a very nice room for you, Mr. Tibbs," Mrs. Braddock says. "Plenty of sunsh—"

"They call me *Mister* Tibbs!" Uncle Henry bellows in a very credible Sidney Poitier imitation that makes the young woman at the desk and a passing orderly look around, startled. Uncle Henry laughs and turns to his niece. "How many times did we watch that movie, Holly? Half a dozen?"

This time he got her name right, which makes her feel even worse. "More," Holly says, and knows she may soon cry herself. She and her uncle watched a lot of movies together. Janey may have been his favorite, but Holly was his movie-buddy, the two of them sitting on the couch with a bowl of popcorn between them.

"Yes," Uncle Henry says. "Yes indeed." But he's losing it again. "Where are we? Where are we really?"

The place where you're probably going to

die, Holly thinks. Unless they take you to the hospital to do it. Outside, she sees Jerome unloading a couple of tartan suitcases. Also a suit bag. Will her uncle ever wear a suit again? Yes, probably . . . but only once.

"Let's look at your room," Mrs. Braddock says. "You're going to like it, Henry!"

She takes his arm, but Henry resists. He looks at his sister. "What's going on here, Charlie?"

Don't cry now, Holly thinks, hold it in, don't you dare. But oh poop, here come the waterworks, and in full flow.

"Why are you crying, Charlie?" Then: "I don't want to be here!" It's not his stentorian "Mister Tibbs" bellow, more of a whine. Like a kid realizing he's about to get a shot. He turns from Charlotte's tears to see Jerome coming in with his luggage. "Here! Here! What are you doing with those traps? They're mine!"

"Well," Jerome says, but doesn't seem to know how to go on.

The oldies are filing in from their trip to the bowling alley, where Holly is sure a great many gutter balls were rolled. The employee who raised his hands to stop traffic joins a nurse who seems to have appeared from nowhere. She is broad of beam and thick of bicep.

These two close in on Henry and take him gently by the arms. "Let's go this way," says

278

the bowling alley guy. "Have a look at the new crib, brother. See what you think."

"Think of what?" Henry asks, but he begins to walk.

"You know something?" the nurse says. "The game's on in the common room, and we've got the biggest TV you've ever seen. You'll feel like you're on the fifty-yard line. We'll take a quick gander at your room, then you can watch it."

"Plenty of cookies, too," Mrs. Braddock says. "Fresh baked."

"Is it the Browns?" Henry asks. They are approaching double doors. He will soon disappear behind them. Where, Holly thinks, he'll begin living the dimmed-out remainder of his life.

The nurse laughs. "No, no, not the Browns, they're out of it. The Ravens. Peck 'em and deck 'em!"

"Good," Henry says, then adds something he never on God's earth would have said before his neural relays began to rust out. "Those Browns are all a bunch of cunts."

Then he is gone.

Mrs. Braddock reaches into the pocket of her dress and hands Charlotte a tissue. "It's perfectly natural for them to be upset on moving-in day. He'll settle down. I have some more paperwork for you if you feel up to it, Mrs. Gibney."

Charlotte nods. Over the sodden bouquet

of the tissue, her eyes are red and streaming. This is the woman who scolded me for crying in public, Holly marvels. The one who told me to stop trying to be the center of attention. This is payback, and I could have done without it.

Another orderly (the woods are full of them, Holly thinks) has materialized and is loading Uncle Henry's faded tartan bags and his Brooks Brothers suiter onto a trolley, as if this place were just another Holiday Inn or Motel 6. Holly is staring at this and holding back her own tears when Jerome takes her gently by the arm and leads her outside.

They sit on a bench in the cold. "I want a cigarette," Holly says. "First time in a long while."

"Pretend," he says, and exhales a plume of frosty air.

She inhales and blows out her own cloud of vapor. She pretends.

### 7

They don't stay overnight, although Charlotte assures them there's plenty of room. Holly doesn't like to think of her mother spending this first night alone, but she can't bear to stay. It isn't the house where Holly grew up, but the woman who lives here is the woman she grew up with. Holly is very different from the pale, chain-smoking, poetry-writing (bad poetry) girl who grew up in

Charlotte Gibney's shadow, but that's hard to remember in her presence, because her mother still sees her as the damaged child who went everywhere with her shoulders hunched and her eyes cast down.

It's Holly driving the first leg this time, and Jerome does the rest. It's long after dark when they see the lights of the city. Holly has been dozing in and out, thinking in a disconnected way about how Uncle Henry mistook her for Janey, the woman who was blown up in Bill Hodges's car. That leads her wandering mind back to the explosion at Macready Middle School, and the correspondent with the torn pocket and the brick dust on his hands. She remembers thinking that there was something different about him that night.

Well sure, she thinks as she drifts toward another doze. In between the first bulletin that afternoon and the special report that night, Ondowsky helped search the rubble, thus transitioning from reporting the story to becoming a part of it. That would change anyb—

Suddenly her eyes snap open and she sits bolt upright, startling Jerome. "What? Are you all ri—"

"The mole!"

He doesn't know what she's talking about and Holly doesn't care. It probably doesn't mean anything, anyway, but she knows Bill Hodges would have congratulated her on her observation. And on her memory, the thing Uncle Henry is now losing.

"Chet Ondowsky," she said. "The news correspondent who was first on the scene after the school blew up. In the afternoon he had a mole beside his mouth, but when the special report came on that night at ten, it was gone."

"Thank God for Max Factor, huh?" Jerome says as he leaves the expressway.

He's right, of course, it even occurred to her when the news bulletin came on: crooked tie, no time to cover the mole with makeup. Later on, when Ondowsky's support crew arrived, they took care of that. Still, it's a little strange. Holly is sure a makeup person would have left the scratches — they were good TV, made the correspondent look heroic — but wouldn't the makeup guy or gal have cleaned some of the brick dust from around Ondowsky's mouth in the process of covering the mole?

"Holly?" Jerome asks. "Are you overcranking again?"

"Yes," she says. "Too much stress, not enough rest."

"Let it go."

"Yes," she says. It's good advice. She intends to follow it.

*December 14, 2020*

### 1

Holly expected another night of tossing and turning, but she sleeps right through until her phone alarm ("Orinoco Flow") gently wakes her. She feels rested, fully herself again. She slips to her knees, does her few morning meditations, then settles into her tiny breakfast nook for a bowl of oatmeal, a cup of yogurt, and a big mug of Constant Comment.

As she enjoys her little repast, she reads the local paper on her iPad. News of the Macready School bombing has slipped from the front page (dominated, as usual, by the president's idiotic shenanigans) to the National News section. This is because there have been no fresh developments. More victims have been released from the hospital; two kids, one of them a talented basketball player, remain in critical condition; the police

283

claim to be following a number of leads. Holly doubts it. There is nothing about Chet Ondowsky, and he's the first person she thought of when Enya's high notes urged her back to wakefulness. Not her mother, not her uncle. Was she dreaming about Ondowsky? If she was, she can't remember.

She exits the newspaper, opens Safari, and types in Ondowsky's name. The first thing she learns is that his real first name is Charles, not Chester, and he's been with Pittsburgh's NBC affiliate for the last two years. His stated beat is charmingly alliterative: crime, community, and consumer fraud.

There are any number of videos. Holly clicks on the most recent, titled "WPEN Welcomes Chet and Fred Home." Ondowsky enters the newsroom (wearing a new suit), followed by a young man wearing a plaid shirt and khaki pants with big pockets on the sides. They are greeted by a wave of applause from the station's staff, both the on-air people and the studio crew. Looks like forty or fifty in all. The young man — Fred — grins. Ondowsky reacts with surprise, then pleasure of an appropriately modest sort. He even applauds them in return. A woman dressed to the nines, probably a news anchor, comes forward. "Chet, you're our hero," she says, and kisses him on the cheek. "You too, Freddy." No kiss for the young man though, just a quick pat on the shoulder.

"I'll rescue you anytime, Peggy," Ondowsky says, drawing laughter and more applause. That's where the clip ends.

Holly watches some more clips, choosing at random. In one, Chet stands outside a burning apartment building. In another, he's at the site of a multiple vehicle pileup on a bridge. In the third, he's reporting on the groundbreaking of a new YMCA, complete with ceremonial silver spade and a soundtrack featuring the Village People. A fourth, from just before Thanksgiving, shows him knocking repeatedly on the door of a so-called "pain clinic" in Sewickley, and getting nothing for *his* pains but a muffled "No questions, go away!"

Busy guy, busy guy, Holly thinks. And in none of these clips does Charles "Chet" Ondowsky have a mole. Because it's always covered with makeup, she tells herself as she rinses her few dishes in the sink. It was just that once, when he had to get on the air in a hurry, that it showed. And why are you worrying about this, anyway? It's like when some annoying pop song turns into an earworm.

Because she's up early, she has time for an episode of *The Good Place* before leaving for work. She goes into her television room, picks up the remote, then just holds it, staring at the blank screen. After a bit, she puts the remote down and goes back into the kitchen. She powers up her iPad and finds the clip of

Chet Ondowsky doing his investigative song and dance about the Sewickley pain clinic.

After the guy inside tells Chet to get lost, the story goes to Ondowsky in a medium close-up, holding the mike (WPEN logo prominently displayed) to his mouth and smiling grimly. "You heard it, self-identified 'pain doctor' Stefan Muller refusing to answer questions and telling us to go away. We did, but we'll keep coming back and asking questions until we get some answers. This is Chet Ondowsky, in Sewickley. Back to you, David."

Holly watches it again. On this run-through she freezes the picture just as Ondowsky is saying *we'll keep coming back.* The mike dips a bit at that point, giving her a good view of his mouth. She spreads her fingers to zoom the image until his mouth fills the screen. There is no mole there, she's sure of it. She'd see its ghost even if it was covered with foundation and powder.

Thoughts of *The Good Place* have left her mind.

Ondowsky's initial report from the scene of the explosion isn't on the WPEN site, but it is on the NBC News site. She goes to it and once more spreads her fingers, enlarging the image until the screen is filled with Chet Ondowsky's mouth. And guess what, that isn't a mole at all. Is it dirt? She doesn't think so. She thinks it's hair. A spot he missed shav-

286

ing, maybe.

Or maybe something else.

Maybe the remains of a fake mustache.

Now thoughts of getting in to the office early so she can check the answering machine and do some peaceful paperwork before Pete comes in have also left her mind. She gets up and walks twice around the kitchen, her heart beating hard in her chest. What she's thinking can't be true, it's totally stupid, but what if it is true?

She googles *Macready Middle School Explosion* and finds the still of the delivery guy/bomber. She uses her fingers to enlarge the picture, focusing on the guy's mustache. She's thinking about those cases you read about from time to time where some serial arsonist turns out to be a fireman, either from the responding department or from a volunteer crew. There was even a true crime book about that, *Fire Lover,* by Joseph Wambaugh. She read it when she was in high school. It's like some fracked-up Munchausen by proxy.

Too monstrous. Can't be.

But Holly finds herself wondering for the first time how Chet Ondowsky got to the scene of the explosion so fast, beating all the other reporters by . . . well, she doesn't know just how long, but he was there first. She knows that.

But wait, does she? She didn't see any other reporters doing stand-ups during that first bulletin, but can she be sure?

She rummages in her bag and finds her phone. Since the case she and Ralph Anderson shared — the one that ended in gunfire at the Marysville Hole — she and Ralph often talk, and it's usually early in the morning. Sometimes he calls her; sometimes she's the one who reaches out. Her finger hovers over his number but doesn't descend. Ralph is on an unexpected (and well deserved) vacation with his wife and son, and even if he's not still sleeping at seven in the morning, it's his family time. *Bonus* family time. Does she want to bother him with this on so little?

Maybe she can use her computer and figure it out for herself. Set her mind at rest. She learned from the best, after all.

Holly goes to her desktop, calls up the picture of the delivery guy/bomber, and prints it out. Then she selects several headshots of Chet Ondowsky — he's a news guy, so there are plenty — and prints them, as well. She takes all of them out to the kitchen, where the morning light is strongest. She arranges them in a square, the bomber's picture in the middle, the Ondowsky shots all around it. She studies them carefully for a full minute. Then she closes her eyes, counts to thirty, and studies them again. She lets out a sigh that's a little disappointed and exasperated, but mostly relieved.

She remembers a conversation she had with

Bill once, a month or two before the pancreatic cancer finished her ex-cop partner off. She asked if he read detective novels, and Bill said only Michael Connelly's Harry Bosch stories and the 87th Precinct novels by Ed McBain. He said those books were based on actual police work. Most of the others were "Agatha Christie bullshit."

He told her one thing about the 87th Precinct books that had stuck with her. "McBain said there are only two types of human faces, pig faces and fox faces. I'd add that sometimes you see a man or woman with a horse face, but they're rare. Mostly yeah, it's pigs and foxes."

Holly finds this a useful yardstick as she studies the headshots on her kitchen table. Both men are okay looking (wouldn't crack a mirror, her mother might have said), but in different ways. The delivery guy/bomber — Holly decides to call him George, just for the sake of convenience — has a fox face: rather narrow, the lips thin, the chin small and tight. The narrowness of the face is accentuated by the way George's black hair starts high on the temples, and how it's short and combed tight to the skull. Ondowsky, on the other hand, has a pig face. Not in any gross way, but it's round rather than narrow. His hair is light brown. His nose is broader, his lips fuller. Chet Ondowsky's eyes are round, and if he's wearing corrective lenses, they are contacts. George's eyes (what she can see of them behind his glasses) look like they might be tilted at the corners. The skin tones are different, too. Ondowsky is your textbook white guy, with ancestors probably hailing from Poland or Hungary or someplace like that. George the Bomber has a slight olive blush to his skin. To top it off, Ondowsky has a cleft chin, like Kirk Douglas. George does not.

They probably aren't even the same height, Holly thinks, although of course it's impossible to tell for sure.

Nevertheless, she grabs a Magic Marker from the mug on the kitchen counter and doodles a mustache on one of the Ondowsky headshots. She puts this one next to the security camera still of George. It doesn't change anything. These two can't possibly be the same guy.

Still . . . as long as she's here . . .

She returns again to her office computer (still in her pajamas) and begins searching for other early coverage that would have been fed from the affiliates to the networks — ABC, FOX, CBS. In two of them she can see the WPEN newsvan in the background. In the third, she sees Ondowsky's cameraman winding up electrical cable, getting ready to move to a new location. His head is bent but Holly recognizes him anyway, by the baggy khakis with the side pockets. It's Fred from the welcome home video. Ondowsky isn't in that one, so he's probably already helping in the rescue efforts.

She goes back to Google and finds another station, an independent, that was probably on the scene. She plugs *WPIT Breaking News Macready School* into her search engine and finds a video of a young woman who looks barely old enough to be out of high school. She's doing her stand-up beside the giant metal pine cone with its blinking Christmas lights. Her station's newsvan is there, parked in the turnout behind a Subaru sedan.

The young reporter is clearly horrified, stumbling over her words, doing a clumsy job of reporting that will never get her hired (or even noticed) by one of the bigger stations. Holly doesn't care. When the young woman's cameraman zooms in on the school's broken-out side, focusing on EMTs, police, and plain old civilians digging in the wreckage and carrying stretchers, she gleeps (Bill's word) Chet Ondowsky. He's digging like a dog, bent over and tossing bricks and broken boards between his spread legs. He came by those cuts on his hands honestly.

"He *was* there first," Holly says. "Maybe not before the first first responders, but before any of the other TV —"

Her phone rings. It's still in the bedroom, so she answers on her desktop, a little fillip Jerome added on one of his visits.

291

"Are you on your way?" Pete asks.

"To where?" Holly is honestly bewildered. She feels like she's been yanked out of a dream.

"Toomey Ford," he says. "Did you really forget? That's not like you, Holly."

It's not, but she has. Tom Toomey, who owns the dealership, is pretty sure one of his salesmen — Dick Ellis, a star performer — has been under-reporting his accounts, possibly to provide for a little dolly he's seeing on the side, possibly to support a drug habit. ("He sniffs a lot," Toomey said. "Claims it's the air conditioning. In December? Give me a break.") This is Ellis's day off, which means it's a perfect opportunity for Holly to run some numbers, do some comparisons, and see if something's wrong.

She could make an excuse to Pete, but the excuse would be a lie, and she doesn't do that. Unless she absolutely has to, anyway. "I did forget. I'm sorry."

"Want me to go out there?"

"No." If the numbers support Toomey's suspicions, Pete will have to go out later and confront Ellis. Being ex-police himself, he's good at that. Holly, not so much. "Tell Mr. Toomey I'll meet him for lunch, wherever he wants, and Finders will pick up the tab."

"Okay, but he'll pick someplace expensive." A pause. "Holly, are you chasing something?"

Is she? And why did she think of Ralph

Anderson so quickly? Is there something she's not telling herself?

"Holly? Still there?"

"Yes," she says, "I'm here. I just overslept."

So. Lying after all.

## 2

Holly takes a quick shower, then dresses in one of her fade-into-the-woodwork business suits. Chet Ondowsky stays on her mind all the while. It occurs to her that she might know a way to answer the major question that's nagging at her, so she goes back to her computer and opens Facebook. No sign that Chet Ondowsky does that one, or Instagram, either. Unusual for a TV personality. They usually love social media.

Holly tries Twitter, and bingo, there he is: **Chet Ondowsky @condowsky1**.

The school explosion happened at 2:19. Ondowsky's first tweet from the scene came over an hour later, and this doesn't surprise Holly: busy-busy-busy was **condowsky1**. The tweet reads, *Macready School. Horrible tragedy. 15 dead so far, maybe many more. Pray, Pittsburgh, pray.* It's heartrending, but Holly's heart isn't rent. She's gotten very tired of all the "thoughts and prayers" bullpoop, maybe because it seems too pat, somehow, probably because she's not interested in Ondowsky's aftermath tweets. They are not what she's looking for.

She becomes a time traveler, scrolling back along Ondowsky's feed to before the explosion happened, and at 1:46 P.M. she finds a photograph of a retro diner with a parking lot in the foreground. The neon sign in the window says WE'VE GOT HOME COOKIN', GOOD LOOKIN'! Ondowsky's tweet is below the picture. *Just time for coffee and pie at Clauson's before off to Eden. See my report on the World's Largest Garage Sale on PEN tonight at 6!*

Holly googles Clauson's Diner and finds it in Pierre Village, Pennsylvania. A further check on Google (what did we ever do without it, she wonders) shows her that Pierre Village is less than fifteen miles from Pineborough and the Macready School. Which explains how he and his cameraman got there first. He was on his way to cover the World's Largest Garage Sale in a town called Eden. A further check shows her that Eden Township is ten miles north of Pierre Village, and about the same distance from Pineborough. He just happened to be in the right place — near it, anyway — at the right time.

Besides, she's pretty sure the local police (or maybe the investigators from ATF) have already asked both Ondowsky and Fred the cameraman about their fortuitous arrival, not because either is an actual suspect but because the authorities will be crossing every *t* and dotting every *i* in a bombing situation where there have been multiple fatalities and casualties.

Her phone is now in her handbag. She takes it out, calls Tom Toomey, and asks if it's too late for her to come by the dealership and look at some figures. Maybe have a peek at the suspected salesman's computer?

"Absolutely," Toomey tells her. "But I had my face fixed for lunch at DeMasio's. Their fettuccini alfredo's amazing. Is that still part of the deal?"

"Absolutely," Holly says, inwardly wincing as she thinks of the expense slip she will be filling out later — DeMasio's isn't cheap. As she goes out, she tells herself to think of it as penance for lying to Pete. Lies are a slippery slope, each one usually leading to two more.

### 3

Tom Toomey devours his fettuccini alfredo with a napkin tucked into the collar of his shirt, eating and slurping with abandon, and follows it up with a mixed-nut panna cotta. Holly has an antipasto and refuses dessert, settling for a cup of decaf (she eschews caffeine after 8 A.M.).

"You really should have dessert," Toomey says. "It's a celebration. Looks like you saved me a bundle."

"*We* did," Holly says. "The firm. Pete will get Ellis to own up and there'll be at least some restitution. That should draw a line under it."

"There you go! So come on," he coaxes. Selling seems to be his default position. "Have something sweet. Treat yourself." As if she's the one who just got the scoop on a cheating employee.

Holly shakes her head and tells him she's full. The fact is she wasn't hungry when she sat down, although her oatmeal was hours ago. Her mind keeps returning to Chet Ondowsky. Her earworm.

"Watching your figure, I guess, huh?"

"Yes," Holly says, which isn't quite a lie; she watches her calorie intake, and her figure takes care of itself. Not that she has anyone to watch it for. Mr. Toomey should be watching his own figure, he's digging his grave with his fork and spoon, but it isn't her place to tell him that.

"You should bring in your lawyer and a forensic accountant if you plan to prosecute Mr. Ellis," she says. "My figures won't be enough in court."

"You betcha." Toomey concentrates on his panna cotta, demolishing what's left, then looks up. "I don't get it, Holly. I thought you'd be more pleased. You nailed a bad guy."

How bad the salesman is or isn't would depend on why he's been chipping away money on the side, but that isn't Holly's business. She only gives Toomey what Bill used to call her Mona Lisa smile.

"Something else on your mind?" Toomey asks. "Another case?"

"Not at all," Holly replies, which is also not a lie, not really; the Macready School explosion is also none of her business. She has no skin in the game, Jerome would say. But that mole that wasn't a mole stays on her mind. Everything about Chet Ondowsky seems legit except for the thing that got her wondering about him in the first place.

There is a reasonable explanation, she thinks as she motions for the waiter to bring the check. You're just not seeing it. Let it go.

Just let it go.

4

The office is empty when she gets back. Pete has left a note on her computer that says *Rattner spotted in a bar down by the lake. On my way. Call me if you need me.* Herbert Rattner is a bail-jumper with a long history of not appearing when his cases (there have been many) are called in court. Holly mentally wishes Pete luck and goes to the files, which she — and Jerome, when he gets a chance — have been digitizing. It will keep her mind off Ondowsky, she thinks, but it doesn't. After just fifteen minutes she gives up and goes to Twitter.

Curiosity killed the cat, she thinks, but satisfaction brought him back. I'll just check this one thing, then return to the scut work.

She finds Ondowsky's diner tweet. Before, she was concentrating on the words. Now it's the photograph that she studies. Silver retro diner. Cute neon sign in the window. Parking in front. The lot is only half full, and nowhere does she see the WPEN newsvan.

"They might have parked around back," she says. Maybe true — she has no way of knowing if there are more spaces behind the diner — but why do that when there were so many available spaces in front, just a few steps from the door?

She starts to exit the tweet, then stops and bends forward until her nose is almost touching the screen. Her eyes are wide. She feels the sense of satisfaction she gets when she finally thinks of the word that's been giving her fits in a crossword, or when she finally sees where a troublesome piece goes into a jigsaw puzzle.

She highlights Ondowsky's diner photo and slides it to one side. Then she finds the video of the inept young reporter doing her stand-up beside the giant pine cone. The indie station's van — older and humbler than those of the network affiliates — is parked in the turnout behind a forest green Subaru sedan. Which means the Subaru was almost certainly there first, or the positions would be reversed. Holly freezes the video and pulls the diner photo as close as she can, and yes, there's a forest green Subaru sedan in the diner parking lot. It's not conclusive, there are plenty of Subarus on the road, but Holly knows what she knows. It's the same one. It's Ondowsky's. He parked in the turnout and then hustled to the scene.

She's so deep in the center of her head that when her phone rings, she gives a little scream. It's Jerome. He wants to know if she has any lost dogs for him. Or lost kids — he says he feels ready to move up to the next rung on the ladder.

"No," she says, "but you could . . ."

She stops short of asking him if he can track down any information about a WPEN cameraman named Fred, perhaps by posing as a blogger or a magazine writer. She should be able to track down Fred herself, using her trusty computer. And there's something else. She doesn't want Jerome involved in this. She won't let herself think exactly why, but the feeling is strong.

"Could what?" he asks.

"I was going to say that if you wanted to go bar-hopping down by the lake, you could look for —"

"*Love* bar-hopping," Jerome says. "Love it."

"I'm sure you do, but you'd be looking for Pete, not drinking beer. See if he needs any help with a bail-jumper named Herbert Rattner. Rattner's white, about fifty . . ."

"Neck tattoo of a hawk or something,"

Jerome says. "Saw the photo on the bulletin board, Hollyberry."

"He's a non-violent offender, but be careful, just the same. If you see him, don't approach him without Pete."

"Got it, got it." Jerome sounds excited. His first real crook.

"Be careful, Jerome." She can't help reiterating this. If anything happened to Jerome, it would wreck her. "And please don't call me Hollyberry. It's worn very thin."

He promises, but she doubts if he means it.

Holly returns her attention to her computer, eyes ticking back and forth between the two forest green Subarus. It means nothing, she tells herself. You're only thinking what you're thinking because of what happened in Texas. Bill would call it Blue Ford Syndrome. If you bought a blue Ford, he said, you suddenly saw blue Fords everywhere. But this wasn't a blue Ford, it was a green Subaru. And she can't help what she is thinking.

There is no *John Law* for Holly that afternoon. By the time she leaves the office, she has more information, and she's troubled.

### 5

At home, Holly makes herself a little meal and fifteen minutes later has forgotten what it was. She calls her mother to ask if she's been to see Uncle Henry. Yes, Charlotte says. Holly asks how he's doing. He's confused,

Charlotte says, but he seems to be adjusting. Holly has no idea if this is true, because her mother has a way of jiggering her view of the world until she's seeing it the way she wants to see it.

"He'd like to see you," Charlotte says, and Holly promises she'll go as soon as she can — maybe this weekend. Knowing he'll call her Janey, because Janey is the one he wants. The one he loves best and always will, even though Janey has been dead for six years. This isn't self-pity, just the truth. You have to accept the truth.

"Have to accept the truth," she says. "Have to, like it or not."

With this in mind she picks up her phone, almost calls Ralph, and again keeps herself from doing it. Why spoil his time off just because the two of them bought a blue Ford down in Texas and now she's seeing them everywhere?

Then she realizes she doesn't *have* to talk to him, at least not in person. She gets her phone and a bottle of ginger ale and goes into the TV room. Here the walls are lined with books on one side and DVDs on the other, everything arranged in alphabetical order. She sits in her comfortable viewing chair, but instead of powering up the big-screen Samsung, she opens her phone's recording app. She just looks at it for a few moments, then pushes the big red button.

"Hello, Ralph, it's me. I'm recording this on December fourteenth. I don't know if you'll ever hear it, because if what I'm thinking turns out to be nothing, and it probably will, I'll just delete it, but saying it out loud might, um, clarify my thoughts."

She pauses the recording, thinking about how she should start.

"I know you remember what happened in that cave when we finally met the outsider face to face. He wasn't used to being found out, was he? He asked what made me able to believe. It was Brady that made me able to do that, Brady Hartsfield, but the outsider didn't know about Brady. He asked if it was because I'd seen another like him somewhere. Do you remember how he looked and sounded when he asked that? I do. Not just eager, *greedy.* He thought he was the only one. I thought so, too, I think we both did. But Ralph, I'm starting to wonder if there might be another one, after all. Not quite the same, but similar — the way dogs and wolves are similar, say. It might only be what my old friend Bill Hodges used to call Blue Ford Syndrome, but if I'm right, I need to do something about it. Don't I?"

The question sounds plaintive, lost. She pauses the recording again, thinks about deleting that last, and decides not to. Plaintive and lost is exactly how she feels right now, and besides — Ralph will probably never hear this.

She goes again.

"Our outsider needed time to transform. There was a period of hibernation, weeks or months, while he changed from looking like one person to looking like another. He wore a chain of faces going back years, maybe even centuries. This guy, though . . . if what I'm thinking is true, he can change much faster, and I'm having trouble believing that. Which is kind of ironic. Do you remember what I said to you the night before we went after our perp? That you had to set your lifelong concept of reality aside? It was okay for the others not to believe, but you had to. I said if you didn't believe we were probably going to die, and that would allow the outsider to keep moving along, wearing the faces of other men and leaving them to take the blame when more children died."

She shakes her head, even laughs a little.

"I was like one of those revival preachers exhorting unbelievers to come to Jesus, wasn't I? Only now *I'm* the one trying not to believe. Trying to tell myself it's just paranoid Holly Gibney, jumping at shadows the way I used to before Bill came along and taught me to be brave."

Holly takes a deep breath.

"The man I'm worried about is named Charles Ondowsky, although he goes by Chet. He's a TV reporter, and his beat is what he calls the three Cs: crime, community, and consumer fraud. He does cover community affairs, stuff like groundbreaking ceremonies and the World's Largest Garage Sale, and he covers consumer fraud — there's even a segment on his station's nightly news called *Chet on Guard* — but what he covers mostly is crime and disaster. Tragedy. Death. Pain. And if all that doesn't remind you of the outsider who killed the boy in Flint City and the two little girls in Ohio, I'd be very surprised. Shocked, in fact."

She pauses the recording long enough to take a big drink of her ginger ale — her throat is as dry as the desert — and lets out a resounding belch that makes her giggle. Feeling a little better, Holly pushes the record button and makes her report, just as she would when investigating any case — repo, lost dog, car salesman chipping six hundred dollars here, eight hundred there. Doing that is good. It's like disinfecting a wound that has begun to show some minor but still troubling redness.

*December 15, 2020*

When she wakes up the next morning, Holly feels brand new, ready to work and also ready to put Chet Ondowsky and her paranoid suspicions about him behind her. Was it Freud or Dorothy Parker who once said that sometimes a cigar is just a cigar? Whichever one it was, sometimes a dark spot beside a reporter's mouth is just hair or dirt that *looks* like hair. Ralph would tell her that if he ever heard her audio recording, which he almost certainly won't. But it did the job; talking it out cleared her head. In that way it was like her therapy sessions with Allie. Because if Ondowsky could somehow morph into George the Bomber, then morph back into himself again, why would he leave a little piece of George's mustache behind? The idea is ridiculous.

Or take the green Subaru. Yes, it belongs to Chet Ondowsky, she's sure of that. She took it for granted that he and his cameraman

(Fred Finkel is his name, finding that was a snap, no Jerome necessary) were traveling together in the station's newsvan, but that was an assumption rather than a deduction, and Holly believes the path to hell is paved with faulty assumptions.

Now that her mind is rested, she can see that Ondowsky's decision to travel alone is perfectly reasonable and perfectly innocent. He's a star reporter at a big metro TV station. He's Chet on Guard, for heaven's sake, and as such he can get up a little later than the hoi polloi, maybe drop by the station, and later enjoy coffee and pie at his favorite diner while Fred the faithful cameraman goes to Eden to do B-roll (as a film buff, Holly knows that's what they call it) and maybe even — if Fred has aspirations of rising in the news department hierarchy — pre-interview the people Ondowsky should talk to when he does his World's Largest Garage Sale stand-up for the six o'clock news.

Only Ondowsky gets the news flash, maybe on a police scanner, about the school explosion and beats feet to the location. Fred Finkel does the same, driving the newsvan. Ondowsky parks beside that ridiculous pine cone and that's where he and Finkel go to work. All perfectly explicable, no supernatural elements need apply. This is just a case of a private investigator hundreds of miles away who happens to be suffering from Blue Ford

306

Syndrome.

*Voilà.*

Holly has a good day at the office. Rattner, that master criminal, has been spotted by Jerome in a bar with the amazing (to Holly, at least) name of the Edmund Fitzgerald Taproom, and escorted to county lockup by Pete Huntley. Pete is currently at the Toomey dealership where he will confront Richard Ellis.

Barbara Robinson, Jerome's sister, drops by, telling Holly (rather smugly) that she has been excused from afternoon classes because she's doing a report called *Private Investigation: Fact vs. Fiction.* She asks Holly a few questions (recording the answers on her own phone), then helps Holly with the files. At three o'clock, they settle down to watch *John Law.*

"I love this guy, he's so jive," Barbara says as Judge Law boogies his way to the bench.

"Pete doesn't agree," Holly says.

"Yes, but Pete is white," Barbara says.

Holly looks at Barbara, wide-eyed. "*I'm* white."

Barbara giggles. "Well, there's white and there's *really* white. Which is what Mr. Huntley is."

They laugh together, then watch as Judge Law deals with a burglar who claims he didn't do anything, he's just a victim of racial profiling. Holly and Barbara give each other one of those telepathic looks — *as if.* Then they burst out laughing again.

A *very* good day, and Chet Ondowsky hardly crosses Holly's mind until her phone rings at six o'clock that evening, just as she's settling in to watch *Animal House*. That call, from Dr. Carl Morton, changes everything. When it finishes, Holly makes one of her own. An hour later, she receives another call. She takes notes on all three.

The next morning she's on her way to Portland, Maine.

*December 16, 2020*

## 1

Holly gets up at three o'clock in the morning. She's packed, she's printed out her Delta ticket, she doesn't have to be at the airport until seven and it's a short ride, but she can't sleep anymore. She would not, in fact, think she had slept at all except for her Fitbit, which registers two hours and thirty minutes. Shallow sleep and precious little of it, but she's made do on less.

She has coffee and a cup of yogurt. Her bag (overhead bin–sized, of course) is waiting by the door. She calls the office and leaves a message for Pete, telling him she won't be in the office today and maybe not for the rest of the week. It's a personal matter. She's about to end the call when something else occurs to her.

"Please have Jerome tell Barbara that she should watch *The Maltese Falcon, The Big*

*Sleep,* and *Harper* for the 'fiction' part of her private investigation report. All three movies are in my collection. Jerome knows where I keep the spare key to my apartment."

With that done, she opens the recording app on her phone and begins to add to the report she is making for Ralph Anderson. She's starting to believe she may have to send it to him, after all.

## 2

Although Allie Winters is Holly's regular therapist, and has been for years, Holly did some research and sought out Carl Morton after she returned from her dark adventures in Oklahoma and Texas. Dr. Morton has written two books of case histories, similar to those of Oliver Sacks but too clinical for best-sellerdom. Still, she thought he was the right man, he was relatively close, and so she sought him out.

She had two fifty-minute sessions with Morton, enough to recount the complete and unvarnished story of her dealings with the outsider. She didn't care if Dr. Morton believed all, some, or none. The important thing, as far as Holly was concerned, was getting it out before it could grow inside her like a malignant tumor. She didn't go to Allie because she thought it would poison the work the two of them were doing on Holly's other issues, and that was the last thing Holly wanted.

There was another reason for going to a secular confessor like Carl Morton. *Have you seen another one like me somewhere?* the outsider had asked. Holly hadn't; Ralph hadn't; but the legends of such creatures, known to Latinos on both sides of the Atlantic as *El Cuco,* had been around for centuries. So . . . maybe there *were* others.

Maybe there were.

## 3

Toward the end of their second and last session, Holly said, "May I tell you what I think *you* think? I know that's very impertinent, but may I?"

Morton gave her a smile probably meant to be encouraging but which Holly read as indulgent — he wasn't as hard to read as he perhaps liked to believe. "Go right ahead, Holly. This is your time."

"Thank you." She had folded her hands. "You must know that at least some of my story is true, because the events were well publicized, from the rape-murder of the Peterson boy in Oklahoma to the events — some of them, at least — that occurred at the Marysville Hole in Texas. The death of Detective Jack Hoskins, from Flint City, Oklahoma, for instance. Am I right?"

Morton had nodded.

"As for the rest of my story — the shape-changing outsider and what happened to him in that cave — you believe those are stress-induced delusions. Am I right about that?"

"Holly, I wouldn't characterize —"

Oh, spare me the jargon, Holly thought, and then had interrupted him — a thing of which she would have been incapable not so long ago.

"It doesn't matter how you characterize it. You're welcome to whatever you believe. But I want something from you, Dr. Morton. You attend lots of conferences and symposiums. I know this, because I researched you online."

"Holly, aren't we wandering a bit from the subject of your story? And your perceptions of that story?"

No, she thought, because that story is told. What matters is what comes next. I'm hoping it will be nothing, and it probably will be, but it never hurts to be sure. Being sure helps a person sleep better at night.

"When you go to those conferences and symposiums, I want you to talk about my case. I want you to describe it. Write it up if you like, that would be fine, too. I want you to be specific about my belief, which you're welcome to characterize as delusional, that I encountered a creature that renews itself by eating the pain of the dying. Will you do that? And if you ever — *ever* — meet or get an email from a fellow therapist who says he has

312

or had a patient suffering from that exact same delusion, will you give that therapist my name and telephone number?" And then, to be gender neutral (which she always strives to be): "Or her."

Morton had frowned. "That would hardly be ethical."

"You're wrong," Holly said. "I've checked the law. Talking to another therapist's *patient* would be unethical, but you can give the therapist my name and number if I give you permission to do so. And I do."

Holly waited for his response.

## 4

She pauses her recording long enough to check the time and get a second cup of coffee. It will give her the jitters and acid indigestion, but she needs it.

"I saw him thinking it over," Holly says into her phone. "I think what tipped the scales was knowing what a good story *my* story would make in his next book or article or compensated appearance. It did, too. I read one of the articles and looked at one of the conference videos. He changes the locations, and he calls me Carolyn H., but otherwise it's the whole *megillah.* He's especially good when talking about what happened to our perp when I hit him with the Happy Slapper — that brought gasps from the audience in the video. And I'll give him this, he always

313

ends my part of his lectures by saying he would like to hear from anyone with patients suffering similar delusional fantasies."

She pauses to think, then restarts the recording.

"Dr. Morton called last night. It's been awhile, but I knew who it was right away, and I knew it was going to lead back to Ondowsky. I remember something else you said once, Ralph: there's evil in the world, but there's also a force for good. You were thinking about the piece of menu you found, the one from a restaurant in Dayton. That fragment linked the murder in Flint City to two similar murders in Ohio. That's how I came to be involved, just a little scrap of paper that could have easily blown away. Maybe something *wanted* it to be found. I like to think so, anyway. And maybe that same thing, that force, has something more for me to do. Because I can believe the unbelievable. I don't want to, but I can."

She stops there and puts her phone in her purse. It's still way early to go to the airport, but she will, anyway. It's just how she rolls.

I'll be early to my own funeral, she thinks, and opens her iPad to find the nearest Uber.

### 5

At five in the morning, the cavernous airport terminal is almost completely deserted. When it's filled with travelers (sometimes absolutely bursting at the seams with their chattering bustle) the music floating down from the overhead speakers is barely noticeable, but at this hour, with nothing but the hum of a janitor's floor-buffer to compete with, Fleetwood Mac's "The Chain" sounds not just eerie but like a harbinger of doom.

Nothing is open on the concourse except for Au Bon Pain, but that's good enough for Holly. She resists the temptation to put another coffee on her tray, settles instead for a plastic cup of orange juice and a bagel, and takes the tray to a table at the back. After looking around to make sure no one is close (she is, in fact, the only current customer), she takes out her phone and resumes her report, speaking low and stopping every so often to marshal her thoughts. She still hopes Ralph will never get this. She still hopes that what she thinks may be a monster will only turn out to be a shadow. But if he does get it, she wants to make sure he gets *all* of it.

Especially if she's dead.

## 6

*From Holly Gibney's report to Detective Ralph Anderson:*

Still December 16th. I'm at the airport, got here early, so I have some time. Actually quite a bit.

[*Pause*]

I think I left off by telling you that I knew

315

Dr. Morton right away. Had him from hello, as the saying is. He said he'd checked with his lawyer after our last session — out of curiosity, he claimed — to find out if I was correct when I said that putting me in touch with another patient's therapist wouldn't be an ethical breach.

"It turned out to be a gray area," he said, "so I didn't do it, especially since you elected to stop therapy, at least with me. But the call I got yesterday from a Boston psychiatrist named Joel Lieberman made me reconsider."

Ralph, Carl Morton has actually had news of another possible outsider for over a year, but he didn't call me. He was timid. As a timid person myself I can understand that, but it still makes me mad. Probably it shouldn't, because Mr. Bell didn't know about Ondowsky then, but it still

[*Pause*]

I'm getting ahead of myself. Sorry. Let's see if I can keep this in order.

In 2018 and 2019, Dr. Joel Lieberman was seeing a patient living in Portland, Maine. This patient took the Downeaster — I assume that's a train — to keep his once-monthly appointments in Boston. The man, Dan Bell as it turns out, is an elderly gentleman who seemed perfectly rational to Dr. Lieberman except for his firm belief that he had discovered the existence of a supernatural creature, which he called a "psychic vampire."

316

Mr. Bell believed that this creature had been around for a long time, at least sixty years and perhaps much longer.

Lieberman attended a lecture Dr. Morton gave in Boston. Last summer, this was — 2019. During his lecture, Dr. Morton discussed the case of "Carolyn H." Me, in other words. He asked any attendees who had patients with similar delusions to get in touch with him, as I had asked. Lieberman did.

Have you got the picture? Morton talked about my case, as I asked him to. He inquired if there were doctors or therapists who'd had patients with similar neurotic convictions, *also* as I asked him to. But for sixteen months he didn't put me in touch with Lieberman, as I practically *implored* him to do. His ethical concerns held him back, but there was something more. I'll get to that.

Then, yesterday, Dr. Lieberman called Dr. Morton again. His patient from Portland had stopped coming in for sessions some time ago, and Lieberman assumed he had seen the last of him. But on the day after the Macready School explosion, the patient called out of the blue and asked if he could come in for an emergency session. He was extremely distraught, so Lieberman made room for him. The patient — Dan Bell, as I now know — claimed that the Macready School bombing was the work of this psychic vampire. He stated this unequivocally. He was so upset that Dr. Lieberman thought about an intervention and perhaps even a short involuntary committal. But then the man calmed down, and said he needed to discuss his ideas with someone he only knew of as Carolyn H.

I need to consult my notes here.

[*Pause*]

All right, I have them. Here I want to quote Carl Morton as exactly as I can, because it's the other reason he hesitated to call me.

He said, "It wasn't just ethical concerns that held me back, Holly. There is great danger in putting people with similar delusional ideations together. They have a tendency to reinforce each other, which can deepen neuroses into full-blown psychoses. This is well documented."

"Then why did you?" I asked.

"Because so much of your story was based on known facts," he said. "Because to some degree it challenged my established belief system. And because Lieberman's patient already knew about you, not from his therapist but from an article I wrote about your case in *Psychiatric Quarterly*. He said Carolyn H. would understand."

Do you see what I mean about a possible force for good, Ralph? Dan Bell was reaching out for me, just as I was reaching out for him, and before I could be sure that he even existed.

"I'll give you Dr. Lieberman's numbers, office and cell," Dr. Morton said. "He'll decide whether or not to put you in touch with his patient." Then he asked if I might also have concerns about the middle school explosion in Pennsylvania, concerns relating to our discussions in therapy. He was flattering himself on that, there *were* no discussions — I just talked and Morton listened. I thanked him for getting in touch with me, but I didn't answer his question. I suppose I was still mad that he waited so long to call.

[*Here there is an audible sigh.*]

Actually, there's no suppose about it. I still need to work on my anger issues.

I'll have to stop soon, but it shouldn't take long to finish bringing you up to date. I called Lieberman on his cell, because it was evening. I introduced myself as Carolyn H. and asked for his patient's name and contact number. He gave me both, but reluctantly.

He said, "Mr. Bell is anxious to talk to you, and after careful thought, I've decided to agree. He's very elderly now, and this is in the nature of a last wish. Although I should add that other than his fixation on this so-called psychic vampire, he's not suffering any of the cognitive decline we often see in the elderly."

That made me think of my Uncle Henry, Ralph, who has Alzheimer's. We had to put him in care last weekend. Thinking about that makes me very sad.

Lieberman said that Mr. Bell is ninety-one, and coming to his most recent appointment must have been very difficult for him, even though he had his grandson to assist him. He said that Mr. Bell is suffering from a number of physical ailments, the worst being congestive heart failure. He said that under other circumstances, he might worry that talking to me would reinforce his neurotic fixation and mar the rest of what might otherwise be a fruitful and productive life, but given Mr. Bell's current age and condition, he didn't feel that was much of an issue.

Ralph, it may be projection on my part, but I found Dr. Lieberman rather pompous. Still, he said one thing at the end of our conversation that moved me, and has stayed with me. He said, "This is an old man who is very frightened. Try not to frighten him more than he already is."

I don't know if I can do that, Ralph. I'm frightened myself.

[*Pause*]

This place is filling up, and I should go to my gate, so I'll make this quick. I called Mr. Bell, introducing myself as Carolyn H. He asked for my real name. That was my Rubicon, Ralph, and I crossed it. I said I was Holly Gibney and asked if I might come and see him. He said, "If it's about the school explosion, and the thing calling itself Ondowsky, as soon as possible."

With a change of planes in Boston, Holly arrives at the Portland Jetport just before noon. She checks into Embassy Suites and calls Dan Bell's number. The phone rings half a dozen times, long enough for Holly to wonder if the old man has died in the night, leaving her questions about Charles "Chet" Ondowsky unanswered. Assuming the old fellow actually has some answers.

As she's about to end the call, a man picks up. Not Dan Bell, a younger man. "Hello?"

"This is Holly," she says. "Holly Gibney. I was wondering when —"

"Oh, Ms. Gibney. Now would be fine. Grampa's having a good day. Actually slept through the night after talking to you, and I can't remember the last time he did that. Do you have the address?"

"19 Lafayette Street."

"That's right. I'm Brad Bell. How soon can you come?"

"As soon as I can get an Uber." And a sandwich, she thinks. A sandwich would also be good.

## 8

As she slips into the back seat of the Uber, her phone rings. It's Jerome, wanting to know where she is and what she's doing and if he can help. Holly says she's sorry, but it really is personal. She says she'll tell him later, if she can.

"Is it about Uncle Henry?" he asks. "Are you chasing down some kind of treatment option? That's what Pete thinks."

"No, not Uncle Henry." Another old man, she thinks. One who might or might not turn out to be compos mentis. "Jerome, I really can't talk about this."

"Okay. As long as you're all right."

It's really a question, and she supposes he's got a right to ask it, because he remembers when she wasn't.

"I'm fine." And, just to prove she hasn't lost the plot: "Don't forget to tell Barbara about those private detective movies."

"Already taken care of," he says.

"Tell her she may not be able to use them in her paper, but they will provide valuable background." Holly pauses and smiles. "Also, they're extremely entertaining."

"I'll tell her. And you're sure you're —"

"Fine," she says, but as she ends the call, she thinks about the man — the *thing* — she and Ralph confronted in the cave, and she shivers. She can barely stand to think of that creature, and if there's another, how can she possibly face it alone?

**9**

Certainly Holly won't be facing it with Dan Bell, who's all of eighty pounds and sitting in a wheelchair with an oxygen tank clipped to the side. He's a shadow-man, with a mostly bald skull and dark purple patches under his bright but exhausted eyes. He and his grandson live in a fine old brownstone full of fine old furniture. The living room is airy; the drapes are pulled back to allow in floods of cold December sunlight. Yet the smells under the air freshener (Glade Clean Linen, if she's not mistaken) remind her inevitably of the smells, stubborn and not to be denied, that she detected wafting into the lobby of the Rolling Hills Elder Care Center: Musterole, Bengay, talcum powder, pee, the approaching end of life.

She's shown into Bell's presence by the grandson, a man of about forty whose dress and mannerisms seem curiously old-fashioned, almost courtly. The hall is lined with half a dozen framed pencil drawings, full-face portraits of four men and two women, all good and all surely done by the same hand. They strike her as an odd introduction to the house; most of the subjects look rather skeevy. There's a much larger picture over the fireplace in the living room, where a small and cozy fire has been kindled. This one, an oil painting, shows a beautiful young woman with black, merry eyes.

"My wife," Bell says in his cracked voice. "Dead these many years, and how I miss her. Welcome to our home, Ms. Gibney."

He rolls his chair toward her, wheezing with the effort it takes, but when the grandson moves forward to help, Bell waves him off. He holds out a hand which arthritis has turned into a driftwood sculpture. She shakes it with care.

"Have you had lunch?" Brad Bell asks.

"Yes," Holly says. A hastily gobbled chicken salad sandwich on the short ride from her hotel to this fashionable neighborhood.

"Would you like tea or coffee? Oh, and we have pastries from Two Fat Cats. They are excellent."

"Tea would be wonderful," Holly says. "Decaf, if you have it. And I'd love a pastry."

"I want tea and a turnover," the old man says. "Apple or blueberry, doesn't matter which. And I want *real* tea."

"Coming right up," Brad says, and leaves them.

Dan Bell immediately leans forward, eyes fixed on Holly's, and says in a low conspiratorial voice, "Brad's terribly gay, you know."

"Oh," Holly says. She can think of nothing else to say except *I was pretty sure he was,* and that seems rude.

"*Terribly* gay. But he's a genius. He's helped me with my researches. I can be sure — I *have* been sure — but Brad's the one who provided the proof." He wags a finger at her, marking off each syllable. "*In . . . contro . . . vertible!*"

324

Holly nods and sits in a wing chair, knees together and purse on her lap. She's starting to think that Bell actually *is* in the grip of a neurotic fantasy and she's running up a blind alley. This doesn't irritate or exasperate her; on the contrary, it fills her with relief. Because if he is, she probably is, too.

"Tell me about *your* creature," Dan says, leaning even further forward. "In his article, Dr. Morton says you call it an outsider." Those bright, exhausted eyes are still fixed on hers. Holly thinks of a cartoon vulture sitting on a tree branch.

Although it once would have been difficult for Holly not to do what people asked her to do — almost impossible — she shakes her head.

He sits back in his wheelchair, disappointed. "No?"

"You already have most of my story from the article Dr. Morton published in *Psychiatric Quarterly,* and from videos you may have seen on the Internet. I came to hear *your* story. You called Ondowsky a thing, an *it.* I want to know how you can be so sure he's an outsider."

"Outsider is a good name for him. Very good." Bell straightens his cannula, which has come askew. "A very good name. I'll tell you over our tea and pastries. We'll have them upstairs, in Brad's workroom. I'll tell you everything. You'll be convinced. Oh yes."

325

"Brad —"

"Brad knows everything," Dan says, waving that driftwood hand dismissively. "A good boy, gay or not." Holly has time to muse that when you're in your nineties, even men twenty years older than Brad Bell must seem like boys. "A *smart* boy, too. And you don't have to tell me your story if you don't want to — although I would love for you to fill in certain details I'm curious about — but before I tell you what I know, I must insist that you tell me what caused you to suspect Ondowsky in the first place."

This is a reasonable request, and she runs down her reasoning . . . such as it is. "Mostly it was that little spot of hair beside his mouth that kept bugging me," she finishes. "It was as if he put on a false mustache and was in such a hurry when he peeled it off that he didn't get all of it. Only if he could change his whole physical appearance, why would he even *need* a false mustache?"

Bell waves his hand dismissively. "Did *your* outsider have facial hair?"

Holly thinks, frowning. The first person the outsider impersonated (that she knew of), an orderly named Heath Holmes, didn't. The second one didn't have face hair, either. His third target had a goatee, but when Holly and Ralph confronted the outsider in the Texas cave, his transformation hadn't been complete.

"I don't think so. What are you saying?"

"I don't think they can grow facial hair," Dan Bell says. "I think if you saw your outsider naked — I assume you never did?"

"No," Holly says, and because she can't help it: "Oough."

That makes Dan smile. "If you had, I think you would have seen no pubic hair. And clean armpits."

"The thing we met in that cave had hair on his head. So does Ondowsky. So did George."

"George?"

"What I call the man who delivered the package with the bomb in it to the Macready School."

"George. Ah, I see." Dan appears to meditate on this for a moment. A little smile touches the corners of his mouth. Then it fades. "Head hair is different, though, isn't it? Children have hair on their heads before puberty. Some are *born* with hair on their heads."

Holly sees his point, and hopes it really *is* a point and not just another facet of this old man's delusion.

"There are other things the bomber — George, if you like — can't change the way he changes his physical appearance," Dan says. "He needed to put on a fake uniform and wear fake glasses. He needed a fake truck and a fake package reader. And he needed a fake mustache."

"Ondowsky may also have fake eyebrows," Brad says, coming in with a tray. On it are two mugs of tea and a pile of turnovers. "But probably not. I've studied pictures of him until my eyes are practically rolling down my cheeks. I think he may have had implants to normalize what would otherwise have just been fuzz. The way baby eyebrows are just fuzz." He bends to put the tray on the coffee table.

"No, no, your workroom," Dan says. "Time to get this show on the road. Ms. Gibney — Holly — will you push me? I'm rather tired."

"Of course."

They pass a formal dining room and a cavernous kitchen. At the end of the hall is a stair-chair, which runs up to the second floor on a steel rail. Holly hopes it's more reliable than the elevator in the Frederick Building.

"Brad had this put in when I lost the use of my legs," Dan says. Brad hands Holly the tray and transfers the old man to the stair-chair with the ease of long practice. Dan pushes a button and begins to rise. Brad takes the tray back and he and Holly walk along beside the chair, which is slow but sure.

"This is a very nice house," Holly says. *Must have been expensive* is the unspoken corollary.

Dan, nevertheless, reads her mind. "Grandfather. Pulp and paper mills."

The penny drops for Holly. The supply

328

closet at Finders Keepers is stacked with Bell copier paper. Dan sees her face and smiles.

"Yes, that's right, Bell Paper Products, now part of an overseas conglomerate that kept the name. Until the nineteen-twenties, my grandfather owned mills all over western Maine — Lewiston, Lisbon Falls, Jay, Mechanic Falls. All shuttered now, or turned into shopping malls. He lost most of his fortune in the Crash of '29 and the Depression. That was the year I was born. No life of Riley for my father or me, we had to work for our beer and skittles. But we managed to keep the house."

On the second floor, Brad transfers Dan to another wheelchair and hooks him up to another bottle of oxygen. This floor seems to consist of one large room where the December sunlight has been forbidden to enter. The windows have been covered with blackout curtains. There are four computers on two work desks, several gaming consoles that look state-of-the-art to Holly, a ton of audio equipment, and a gigantic flatscreen TV. Several speakers have been mounted on the walls. Two more flank the TV on either side.

"Put the tray down, Brad, before you spill everything."

The table Dan indicates with one of his arthritic hands is covered with computing magazines (several of them copies of *Sound-Phile,* which Holly has never heard of), flash drives, external hard drives, and cables. Holly starts trying to clear a place.

"Oh, just put all that rickrack on the floor," Dan says.

She looks at Brad, who nods apologetically. "I'm a little messy," he says.

When the tray is safely in place, Brad puts pastries on three plates. They look delicious, but Holly no longer knows if she's hungry or not. She's starting to feel like Alice at the Mad Hatter's teaparty. Dan Bell takes a sip from his cup, smacks his lips, then grimaces and places a hand on the left side of his shirt. Brad is at his side immediately.

"Do you have your pills, Grampa?"

"Yes, yes," Dan says, and pats the side pocket of his wheelchair. "I'm all right, you can stop *hovering*. It's just the excitement of having someone in the house. Someone who *knows*. It's probably good for me."

"Not so sure about that, Grampa," Brad says. "Maybe you better take a pill."

"I'm fine, I said."

"Mr. Bell —" Holly begins.

"Dan," the old man says, once more wagging his finger, which is grotesquely bent with arthritis but still admonitory. "I'm Dan, he's Brad, you're Holly. We're all friends here." He laughs again. This time it sounds out of breath.

"You have to slow down," Brad says. "Un-

330

less you want another trip to the hospital, that is."

"Yes, Mother," Dan says. He cups a hand over his beak of a nose and takes several deep breaths of oxygen. "Now give me one of those turnovers. And we need napkins."

But there are no napkins. "I'll get some paper towels from the bathroom," Brad says, and off he goes.

Dan turns to Holly. "Terribly forgetful. *Terribly.* Where was I? Does it even matter?"

Does any of this? Holly wonders.

"I was telling you that my father and I had to work for a living. Did you see the pictures downstairs?"

"Yes," Holly says. "Yours, I assume."

"Yes, yes, all mine." He holds up his twisted hands. "Before *this* happened to me."

"They're very good," Holly says.

"Not so bad," he says, "although the ones in the hall aren't the best. Those were for work. Brad put them up. Insisted. I also did some paperback covers back in the fifties and sixties, for publishers like Gold Medal and Monarch. They were much better. Crime, mostly — half-dressed babes with smoking automatics. They brought in a little extra. Ironic, when you think about my full-time job. I was with the Portland PD. Retired at sixty-eight. Did my forty and four more."

Not just an artist but another cop, Holly thinks. First Bill, then Pete, then Ralph, and

331

now him. She once more thinks of how some force, invisible but strong, seems to be pulling her into this, quietly insisting on parallels and continuations.

"My grandfather was a mill-owning capitalist, but since then we've all been blue. Dad was police, and I followed in his footsteps. As my son followed in mine. Brad's father, I'm speaking of. He died in a crash while chasing a man, probably drunk, driving a stolen car. That man lived. May be living today, for all I know."

"I'm very sorry," Holly says.

Dan ignores her effort at condolence. "Even Brad's mother was in the family trade. Well, in a way. She was a court stenographer. When she died, I took the boy in. I don't care if he's gay or not, nor does the police department. Although he doesn't work for them full-time. With him it's more of a hobby. Mostly he does . . . this." He waves his deformed hand at the computer equipment.

"I design audio for games," Brad says quietly. "The music, the effects, the mix." He has returned with a whole roll of paper towels. Holly takes two and spreads them on her lap.

Dan goes on, seemingly lost in the past. "After my radio car days were over — I never rose to detective, never wanted to — I worked mostly in dispatch. Some cops don't like riding a desk, but I never minded, because I had another job as well, one that kept me busy long after retirement. You could say that's one side of the coin. What Brad does, when they call him in, is the other side. Between the two of us, Holly, we *nailed* this, pardon my French, this *shitbag*. He's been in our sights for years."

Holly has finally taken a bite of her turnover, but now opens her mouth, allowing an unsightly shower of crumbs to fall to the plate and paper towels in her lap. *"Years?"*

"Yes," Dan says. "Brad's known since he was in his twenties. He's worked on this with me since 2005 or so. Isn't that right, Brad?"

"A little later," Brad says, after swallowing a bite of his own turnover.

Dan shrugs. It looks painful. "It all starts to melt together when you're my age," he says, then turns what's almost a glare on Holly. His bushy eyebrows (no faking there) draw together. "But not with Ondowsky, as he's now calling himself. On him I'm crystal clear. Right back to the beginning . . . or at least to where I came in. We've arranged quite a show for you, Holly. Brad, is that first video cued up?"

"All ready, Grampa." Brad grabs his iPad and uses a remote to turn on the big TV. It's currently showing nothing but a bluescreen and the word READY.

Holly hopes *she* is.

## 10

"I was thirty-one when I first saw him," Dan says. "I know that because my wife and boy had a little birthday party for me just a week before. It seems like a long time ago and it seems like no time at all. I was still on radio cars then. Marcel Duchamp and I were parked just off Marginal Way, behind a snowbank and waiting for speeders, not very likely on a weekday morning. Eating crullers, drinking coffee. I remember Marcel was ribbing me about some paperback cover I'd done, asking how my wife liked me painting pictures of hot women in their undies. I think I was just telling him that his wife had posed for that one when the guy ran up to the car and knocked on the driver's side window." He pauses. Shakes his head. "You always remember where you were when you get bad news, don't you?"

Holly thinks of the day she found out that Bill Hodges was gone. Jerome made that call, and she was pretty sure he'd been choking back tears.

"Marcel rolled his window down and asked the guy if he needed help. He said no. He had a transistor radio — that was what we had instead of iPods and cell phones back in those days — and asked if we'd heard about what just happened in New York."

Dan pauses to straighten his cannula and adjust the flow of oxygen from the tank on the side of his chair.

"We hadn't heard anything except for what was on the police radio, so Marcel turned that off and turned on the regular one. Found the news. This is what the jogger was talking about. Go ahead and run the first one, Brad."

Dan's grandson has his electronic tablet on his lap. He pokes at it and says to Holly, "I'm going to mirror this to the big screen. One second . . . okay, here we go."

On the screen, to somber music, comes the title card of an old-time newsreel. WORST AIR CRASH IN HISTORY, it reads. What follows is crisp black-and-white footage of a city street that looks like a bomb hit it.

"The terrible aftermath of the worst air disaster in history!" the announcer intones. "In a Brooklyn street lies the shattered remnant of a jet transport that collided with another airliner in murky New York skies." On the tail of the plane — or what remains of it — Holly can read UNIT. "The United Airlines aircraft plummeted into a brownstone residential section, killing six on the ground as well as eighty-four passengers and the crew."

Now Holly sees firemen in old-fashioned helmets rushing through the wreckage. Some are carrying stretchers to which are strapped blanket-covered bodies.

"Normally," the announcer continues, "this United flight and the Trans World Airlines flight it collided with would have been separated by miles, but the TWA plane — Flight 266, carrying forty-four passengers and crew — was far off course. It crashed on Staten Island."

More covered bodies on more stretchers. A huge airplane wheel, the rubber shredded and still smoking. The camera pans the wreckage of 266, and Holly sees Christmas presents wrapped in gay paper scattered everywhere. The camera zooms in on one, to show a little Santa Claus attached to the bow. Santa is smoldering and blackened with soot.

"You can stop it there," Dan says. Brad pokes his tablet and the big TV returns to bluescreen.

Dan turns to Holly.

"A hundred and thirty-four dead in all. And when did it happen? December sixteenth, 1960. Sixty years ago to this very day."

Only a coincidence, Holly thinks, but a chill shivers through her just the same, and once again she thinks of how there may be forces in this world moving people as they will, like men (and women) on a chessboard. The confluence of dates could be a coincidence, but can she say that about all that's brought her here to this house in Portland, Maine? No. There's a chain going all the way back to another monster named Brady Hartsfield. Brady, who allowed her to believe in the first place.

"There was one survivor," Dan Bell says, startling her out of her reverie.

Holly points at the bluescreen, as if the newsreel were still playing there. "Someone survived *that?*"

"Only for a day," Brad says. "The newspapers called him the Boy Who Fell from the Sky."

"But it was someone else who coined the phrase," Dan says. "Back then in the New York metro area, there were three or four independent TV stations as well as the networks. One of them was WLPT. Long gone now, of course, but if something was filmed or taped, chances are good that you can find it on the Internet. Prepare yourself for a shock, young lady." He nods at Brad, who begins poking at his tablet again.

Holly learned at her mother's knee (and with her father's tacit approval) that overt displays of emotion weren't just embarrassing and unpleasant but shameful. Even after years of work with Allie Winters, she usually keeps her feelings bottled up and tightly capped, even among friends. These are strangers, but when the next clip starts on the big screen, she screams. She can't help it.

*"That's him! That's Ondowsky!"*

"I know," Dan Bell says.

## 11

Only most people would say it wasn't, and Holly knows this.

They'd say *Oh yes, there's a resemblance, just as there's a resemblance between Mr. Bell and his grandson, or between John Lennon and his son Julian, or between me and Aunt Elizabeth.* They'd say *I bet it's Chet Ondowsky's grandfather. Gosh, the apple sure doesn't fall far from the tree, does it?*

But Holly, like the old man in the wheelchair, knows.

The man holding the old-fashioned WLPT microphone is fuller in the face than Ondowsky, and the lines on that face suggest he's ten, maybe even twenty years older. His crewcut is salt-and-pepper, and it comes to a slight widow's peak that Ondowsky doesn't have. He has the beginning of jowls, and Ondowsky doesn't have those, either.

Behind him, some firefighters scurry about in the sooty snow, picking up packages and luggage, while others turn hoses on the remains of the United plane and two burning brownstones behind it. Just pulling away is a big old Cadillac of an ambulance with its lights flashing.

"This is Paul Freeman, reporting from the Brooklyn site of the worst air crash in American history," the reporter says, puffing out white vapor with every word. "All were killed onboard this United Airlines jet except for one boy." He points to the departing ambulance. "The boy, as yet unidentified, is in that ambulance. He is —" The reporter calling himself Paul Freeman pauses dramatically. "— The Boy Who Fell from the Sky! He was thrown from the rear section of the plane, still on fire, and landed in a snowbank. Horrified bystanders rolled him in the snow and put out the flames, but I saw him loaded into the ambulance, and I can tell you that his injuries looked severe. His clothes were almost entirely burned off, or melted into his skin."

"Stop it there," the old man commands. His grandson does so. Dan turns to Holly. His blue eyes are faded but still fierce. "Do you see it, Holly? Do you *hear* it? I'm sure to the viewing audience he just looked and sounded horrified, doing his job under difficult conditions, but —"

"He's not horrified," Holly said. She's thinking of Ondowsky's first report from the Macready School bombing. Now she sees that with clearer eyes. "He's *excited.*"

"Yes," Dan says, and nods. "Yes indeed. You understand. Good."

"Thank God someone else does," Brad says.

"The boy's name was Stephen Baltz," Dan says, "and this Paul Freeman saw the burned boy, perhaps heard his screams of pain — because witnesses said the boy *was* conscious, at least to begin with. And do you know what I think? What I have come to believe? That he was *feeding*."

"Of course he was," Holly says. Her lips feel numb. "On the boy's pain and on the horror of the bystanders. On the *death*."

"Yes. Get ready for the next one, Brad." Dan sits back in his chair, looking tired. Holly doesn't care. She needs to know the rest. She needs to know everything. The old fever is on her.

"When did you go looking for this? How did you find out?"

"I first saw the clip you just watched the evening of the crash, on *The Huntley-Brinkley Report*." He sees her puzzlement and smiles a little. "You're too young to remember Chet Huntley and David Brinkley. It's now called *NBC Nightly News*."

Brad says, "If an indie station arrived at some big news event first, and got good footage, they'd sell the report to one of the networks. That's what must have happened with this, and how Grampa got to see it."

"Freeman got there first," Holly muses. "Are you saying . . . do you think Freeman *caused* those planes to crash?"

Dan Bell shakes his head so emphatically that the cobwebby remains of his hair fly. "No, just struck lucky. Or played the odds. Because there are always tragedies in big cities, aren't there? Chances for a thing like him to feed. And who knows, a creature like him may be attuned to the approach of major disasters. Maybe he's like a mosquito — they can smell blood from miles away, you know. How can we know, when we don't even know what he is? Run the next one, Brad."

Brad starts the clip, and the man who comes on the big screen is once more Ondowsky . . . but he's different. Thinner. Younger than "Paul Freeman," and younger than the version of Ondowsky doing his report near the blown-out side of the Macready School. But it's *him.* The face is different, the face is the same. The microphone he's holding has the letters KTVT attached to it. Three women are standing with him. One of them is wearing a Kennedy political button. Another has a placard, crumpled and somehow forlorn, that reads ALL THE WAY WITH JFK IN '64!

"This is Dave Van Pelt, reporting from Dealey Plaza, across from the Texas School Book Depository, where —"

"Freeze it," Dan says, and Brad does. Dan turns to Holly. "It's him again, right?"

"Yes," Holly says. "I'm not sure anyone else would see it, I'm not sure how *you* saw it so long after the plane crash report, but it is. My father once told me something about cars. He said the companies — Ford, Chevrolet, Chrysler — offer lots of different models, and they change them from year to year, but they're all from the same template. He . . . Ondowsky . . ." But words fail her and she can only point to the black-and-white image on the screen. Her hand is trembling.

"Yes," Dan says softly. "Very well put. He's different models, but from the same template. Except there are at least two templates, maybe more."

"What do you mean?"

"I'll get to that." His voice is rustier than ever, and he drinks some more tea to lubricate it. "I only saw this report by chance, because I was a *Huntley-Brinkley* man when it came to the evening news. But after Kennedy was shot, everyone turned over to Walter Cronkite, including me. Because CBS had the best coverage. Kennedy was shot on a Friday. This report was on the *CBS Evening News* the following day, the Saturday. What news people call a backgrounder. Go ahead, Brad. But take it from the top."

The young reporter in the horrible plaid sport coat begins again. "This is Dave Van Pelt, reporting from Dealey Plaza, across from the Texas School Book Depository, where John F. Kennedy, the thirty-fifth President of the United States, was fatally shot yesterday. I'm here with Greta Dyson, Monica Kellogg, and Juanita Alvarez, Kennedy supporters who were right here where I'm standing when the shots were fired. Ladies, can you tell me what you saw? Miss

Dyson?"

"Shots . . . blood . . . there was blood from the back of his poor *head . . .*" Greta Dyson is weeping so hard she can barely be understood, which Holly supposes is sort of the point. Viewers at home are probably weeping right along with her, thinking that her grief stands for theirs. And for the grief of a nation. Only the reporter . . .

"He's eating it up," she says. "Just pretending to be concerned, and not doing a very good job of it, at that."

"Absolutely," Dan says. "Once you look at it the right way, it's impossible to miss. And look at the other two ladies. They're crying, too. Hell, a lot of people were crying that Saturday. And in the weeks that followed. You're right. He's eating it up."

"And you think he knew it was going to happen? Like a mosquito smelling blood?"

"I don't know," Dan says. "I just don't know."

"We do know he only started working at KTVT that summer," Brad says. "I wasn't able to find out much about him, but that much I did get. From a history of the station on the Internet. And he was gone by the spring of 1964."

"The next time he turns up — that I know about, anyway — is in Detroit," Dan says. "1967. During what was known at the time as the Detroit Rebellion, or the 12th Street

343

Riot. It started when the police raided an after-hours bar, a so-called blind pig, and spread city-wide. Forty-three killed, twelve hundred injured. It was the top news story for five days, which was how long the violence went on. This is from another independent station, but it got picked up by NBC and ran on the nightly news. Go ahead, Brad."

A reporter is standing in front of a burning storefront, interviewing a black man with blood running down his face. The man is almost incoherent with grief. He says that's his dry-cleaning business burning down across the way, and he doesn't know where his wife and daughter are. They have disappeared into the city-wide melee. "I have lost everything," he says. *"Everything."*

And the reporter, this time calling himself Jim Avery? He's a small-city TV guy for sure. Stouter than "Paul Freeman," verging on fat, and short (his interviewee towers over him), and balding. Different model, same template. It's Chet Ondowsky buried in that fat face. It's also Paul Freeman. And Dave Van Pelt.

"How did you tip to this, Mr. Bell? How in heaven's name —"

"Dan, remember? It's Dan."

"How could you see the resemblance wasn't just a resemblance?"

Dan and his grandson look at each other and exchange a smile. Holly, watching this momentary byplay, thinks again, Different models, same template.

"You noticed the pictures in the hall, right?" Brad asks. "That was Grampa's other job when he was on the cops. He was a natural for it."

Once again, the penny drops. Holly turns to Dan. "You were a sketch artist. That was your other police job!"

"Yes, although I did a lot more than sketch. I was no cartoonist. I did *portraits.*" He thinks, then adds, "You've heard people say they never forget a face? Mostly they're exaggerating or outright lying. I'm not." The old man speaks matter-of-factly. If it's a gift, Holly thinks, it's as old as he is. Maybe once it blew his mind. Now he takes it for granted.

"I've seen him work," Brad says. "If not for the arthritis in his hands, he could turn around, face the wall, and do you in twenty minutes, Holly, and every detail would be right. Those pictures in the hall? All people who were caught based on Grampa's portraits."

"Still —" she begins doubtfully.

"To remember faces is only part of it," Dan says. "It doesn't help when it comes to getting a likeness of a perpetrator, because *I'm* not the one who saw him. You understand?"

"Yes," Holly says. She's interested in this for reasons other than his ID of Ondowsky in his many different guises. She's interested in it because in her own work as an investigator, she is still learning.

"The witness comes in. In some cases — like a carjacking or a robbery — several witnesses come in. They describe the doer. Only it's like the blind men with the elephant. You know that story?"

Holly does. The blind man who grabs the tail says it's a vine. The one who grabs the trunk thinks it's a python. The one who grabs the leg is sure it's the bole of a big old palm tree. Eventually the blind men get into a brawl about who is right.

"Every witness sees the guy in a slightly different way," Dan says. "And if it's one witness, he or she sees him in different ways on different days. No, no, they say, I was wrong, the face is too fat. It's too thin. He had a goatee. No, it was a mustache. His eyes were blue. No, I slept on it and I guess they were actually gray."

He takes another long pull of O2. Looking more tired than ever. Except for the eyes in their purple pouches. They are bright. Focused. Holly thinks that if the Ondowsky-thing saw those eyes, he might be afraid. Might want to shut them before they saw too much.

"My job is to look past all the variations and see the similarities. That's the real gift and what I put in my pictures. It's what I put in my first pictures of this guy. Look."

From the side pocket of his chair he takes a

346

small folder and hands it to her. Inside are half a dozen pieces of thin drawing paper going brittle with age. There's a different version of Charles "Chet" Ondowsky on each one. They are not as detailed as his rogue's gallery in the front hall, but they are still extraordinary. In the first three she's looking at Paul Freeman, Dave Van Pelt, and Jim Avery.

"Did you draw these from memory?" she asks.

"Yes," Dan says. Again not boasting, just stating a fact. "Those first three were drawn soon after I saw Avery. Summer of '67. I've made copies, but those are the originals."

Brad says, "Remember the time-frame, Holly. Grampa saw these men on TV before VCRs, DVRs, or the Internet. For ordinary viewers, you saw what you saw and then it was gone. He had to rely on memory."

"And these others?" She's spread out the other three like a fan of cards. Faces with different hairlines, different eyes and mouths, different lines, different ages. All different models from the same template. All Ondowsky. She can see it because she's seen the elephant. That Dan Bell saw it back in the day is amazing. Genius, really.

He points to the drawings she's holding, one after another. "That one's Reginald Holder. He reported from Westfield, New Jersey, after John List killed his whole family.

Interviewed sobbing friends and neighbors. The next one is Harry Vail, reporting from Cal State Fullerton after a janitor named Edward Allaway shot and killed six people. Vail was on the scene before the blood was dry, interviewing survivors. The last one, his name escapes me —"

"Fred Liebermanenbach," Brad says. "Correspondent for WKS, Chicago. He covered the Tylenol poisonings in 1982. Seven people died. Talked to grieving relatives. I have all these video clips, if you want to see them."

"He's got plenty of clips, we've uncovered seventeen different versions of your Chet Ondowsky," Dan says.

"*Seventeen?*" Holly is flabbergasted.

"Those are just the ones we know of. No need to look at all of them. Slide those first three drawings together and hold them up to the TV, Holly. It's not a lightbox, but it should do."

She holds them in front of the bluescreen, knowing what she'll see. It's one face.

Ondowsky's face.

An outsider.

## 12

When they go downstairs, Dan Bell isn't exactly sitting in the stair-chair; it's more like lolling. No longer just tired, exhausted. Holly really doesn't want to trouble him further, but will have to.

348

Dan Bell also knows they're not done. He asks Brad to bring him a knock of whiskey.

"Grampa, the doctor said —"

"Fuck the doctor and the horse he rode in on," Dan says. "It'll brighten me up. We'll finish, you show Holly that last . . . thing . . . and then I'll lie down. I slept through last night, and I bet I will again tonight. This is such a weight off my shoulders."

But now it's on mine, Holly thinks. I wish Ralph was here. I wish for Bill even more.

Brad brings his gramps a Flintstone jelly glass with barely enough whiskey in it to cover the bottom. Dan gives it a sour look but accepts it without comment. From the side pocket of his wheelchair he takes a bottle of pills with a geriatric-friendly screw-off cap. He shakes out a pill and half a dozen others spill onto the floor.

"Balls," says the old man. "Pick those up, Brad."

"I'll get them," Holly says, and does. Dan, meanwhile, puts the pill in his mouth and swallows it with the whiskey.

"Now I know *that's* not a good idea, Grampa," Brad says, sounding prissy.

"At my funeral, no one will say I died young and handsome," Dan replies. Some color has come into his cheeks, and he's sitting up straight in his chair again. "Holly, I have perhaps twenty minutes before that almost useless dram of whiskey wears off. Half an hour at most. I know you have more questions, and we have one more thing for you to look at, but let's try to be brief."

"Joel Lieberman," she says. "The psychiatrist you saw in Boston starting in 2018."

"What about him?"

"You didn't go to him because you thought you were crazy, did you?"

"Of course not. I went for the same reasons I imagine you went to see Carl Morton, with his books and lectures about people with weird neuroses. I went to tell everything I knew to someone who was paid to listen. And to find someone else who had reasons to believe the unbelievable. I was looking for you, Holly. Just as you were looking for me."

Yes. It's true. Still, she thinks, it's a miracle we got together. Or fate. Or God.

"Although Morton changed all the names and locations for his article, it was easy for Brad to track you down. The thing calling itself Ondowsky wasn't there reporting from the Texas cave, by the way. Brad and I looked at all the news footage."

Holly says, "My outsider didn't show up on tape or film. There was footage where he should have been part of a crowd, but he wasn't there." She taps the drawings of Ondowsky in his various guises. "*This* perp is on TV *all* the time."

"Then he's different," the old man says, and shrugs. "The way housecats and bobcats are different but similar — same template, different models. As for you, Holly, you were barely mentioned in the news reports, and never by name. Only as a private citizen who helped with the investigation."

"I asked to be kept out of it," Holly mutters.

"By then I'd read about Carolyn H. in Dr. Morton's articles. I tried to reach out to you with Dr. Lieberman — made a trip to Boston to see him, which wasn't easy. I knew that even if you hadn't recognized Ondowsky for what he was, you would have good reason to believe my story if you heard it. Lieberman called your guy Morton and here you are."

One thing troubles Holly, and very much. She says, "Why now? You've known about this thing for years, you've been *hunting* it —"

"Not hunting," Dan says. "*Keeping track* would be a more accurate way to put it. Since 2005 or so, Brad has been monitoring the Internet. In every tragedy, in every mass shooting, we look for him. Don't we, Brad?"

"Yes," Brad says. "He's not always there, he wasn't at Sandy Hook or in Las Vegas when Stephen Paddock killed all those concert-goers, but he was working at WFTV in Orlando in 2016. He interviewed survivors from the Pulse nightclub shooting the next day. He always picks the ones who are most upset, the ones who were inside or lost friends who were."

Of course he does, Holly thinks. Of course. Their grief is tasty.

"But we didn't know he was at the nightclub until after the school bombing last week," Brad says. "Did we, Grampa?"

"No," Dan agrees. "Even though we checked all the Pulse news footage as a matter of course during the aftermath."

"How did you miss him?" Holly asks. "Pulse was over four years ago! You said you never forget a face, and by then you knew Ondowsky's, even with the changes it's always the same, a pig face."

They look at her with identical frowns, so Holly explains what Bill told her about most people having either pig faces or fox faces. In every version she's seen here, Ondowsky's face is rounded. Sometimes a little, sometimes a lot, but it's always a pig face.

Brad still looks puzzled, but his grandfather smiles. "That's good. I like it. Although there are exceptions, some people have —"

"Horse faces," Holly finishes for him.

"Just what I was going to say. And some people have weasel faces . . . although I suppose you could say weasels have a certain foxy aspect, don't they? Certainly Philip Hannigan . . ." He trails off. "Yes. And in *that* aspect, I bet he always has a fox face."

"I don't understand you."

"But you will," Dan says. "Show her the

352

Pulse clip, Brad."

Brad starts the clip and turns the iPad to face Holly. Again, it's a reporter doing a stand-up, this time in front of a huge pile of flowers and heart balloons and signs saying things like MORE LOVE AND LESS HATE. The reporter is beginning to interview a sobbing young man with the remains of either dirt or mascara smudging his cheeks. Holly doesn't listen, and this time she doesn't scream because she doesn't have the breath to do it. The reporter — Philip Hannigan — is young, blond, skinny. He looks like he stepped into the job right out of high school, and yes, he has what Bill Hodges would have called a fox face. He is looking at his interview subject with what could be concern . . . empathy . . . sympathy . . . or barely masked greed.

"Freeze it," Dan says to Brad. And to Holly: "Are you all right?"

"That's not Ondowsky," she whispers. "That's *George.* That's the man who delivered the bomb to the Macready School."

"Oh, but it *is* Ondowsky," Dan says. He speaks gently. Almost kindly. "I already told you. This creature doesn't have just one template. He has two. At *least* two."

### 13

Holly turned off her phone before knocking on the Bells' door and doesn't think to turn

353

it on again until she's back in her room at the Embassy Suites. Her thoughts are swirling like leaves in a strong wind. When she does power up, to continue her report to Ralph, she sees that she has four texts, five missed calls, and five voicemail messages. The missed calls and voicemails are all from her mother. Charlotte knows how to text — Holly showed her — but she never bothers, at least when it comes to her daughter. Holly thinks her mother has found texting insufficient when it comes to crafting a really effective guilt trip.

She opens the texts first.

Pete: **All okay, H? I'm minding the store, so do your thing. If you need something, ask.**

Holly smiles at that.

Barbara: **I got the movies. They look good. Thanx, will return.** ☺

Jerome: **Maybe have a line on that chocolate Lab. In Parma Heights. Going to check. If you need something, I'm on my cell. Don't hesitate.**

The last one, also from Jerome: **Hollyberry.** ☺

In spite of all she's learned at the house on Lafayette Street, she has to laugh. And she has to tear up a little, too. They all care for her, and she cares for them. It's amazing. She'll try to hold onto that while she deals with her mother. She already knows how each of Charlotte's voicemails will end.

"Holly, where are you? Call me." That's the first.

"Holly, I need to speak to you about going to see your uncle this weekend. Call me." The second.

"Where are you? Why is your phone off? It's very inconsiderate. What if there was an emergency? Call me!" The third.

"That woman from Rolling Hills, Mrs. Braddock, I didn't like her, she seemed very full of herself, she called and said Uncle Henry is *very upset*! Why aren't you returning my calls? Call me!" Big number four.

The fifth is simplicity itself: "Call me!"

Holly goes into the bathroom, opens her notions bag, and takes an aspirin. Then she gets down on her knees and folds her hands on the edge of the tub. "God, this is Holly. I need to call my mother now. Help me to remember I can stand up for myself without being all nasty and poopy and getting into an argument. Help me to finish another day without smoking, I still miss cigarettes, especially at times like this. I still miss Bill, too, but I'm glad Jerome and Barbara are in my life. Pete, too, even though he can be a little slow on the uptake sometimes." She starts to stand, then resumes the position. "I also miss Ralph, and hope he's having a nice vacation with his wife and son."

Thus armored (or so she hopes), Holly calls

her mother. Charlotte does most of the talking. That Holly won't tell her where she is, what she's doing, or when she'll be back makes Charlotte very angry. Beneath the anger Holly senses fear, because Holly has escaped. Holly has a life of her own. That was not supposed to happen.

"Whatever you're doing, you *have* to be back this weekend," Charlotte says. "We need to go see Henry together. We're his *family.* All he's got."

"I may not be able to do that, Mom."

"Why? I want to know why!"

"Because . . ." *Because I'm chasing the case.* That's what Bill would have said. "Because I'm working."

Charlotte begins to cry. For the last five years or so it has always been her last resort when it comes to bringing Holly to heel. It no longer works, but it's still her default position and it still hurts.

"I love you, Mom," Holly says, and ends the call.

Is that true? Yes. It's liking that got lost, and love without liking is like a chain with a manacle at each end. Could she break the chain? Strike off the manacle? Perhaps. She's discussed that possibility with Allie Winters many times, especially after her mother told her — proudly — that she voted for Donald Trump (oough). Will she do it? Not now, maybe never. When Holly was growing up,

Charlotte Gibney taught her — patiently, perhaps even with good intentions — that she was thoughtless, helpless, hapless, careless. That she was *less.* Holly believed that until she met Bill Hodges, who thought she was more. Now she has a life, and it is more often than not a happy one. If she broke with her mother, it would lessen her.

I don't want to be less, Holly thinks as she sits on the bed in her Embassy Suites room. Been there, done that. "And got the tee-shirt," she adds.

She takes a Coke from the bar refrigerator (damn the caffeine). Then she opens her phone's recording app and continues her report to Ralph. Like praying to a God she can't quite believe in, it clears her head, and by the time she finishes, she knows how she'll go forward.

## 14

*From Holly Gibney's report to Detective Ralph Anderson:*

From here on, Ralph, I'll try to give you my conversation with Dan and Brad Bell verbatim, while it's still fresh in my mind. It won't be completely accurate, but it will be close. I should have recorded our talk, but never thought of it. I still have a lot to learn about this job. I only hope I get the chance.

I could see that Mr. Bell — the old Mr. Bell — wanted to go on, but once that little

357

bit of whiskey wore off, he couldn't. He said he needed to lie down and rest. The last thing he said to Brad was something about the sound recordings. I didn't understand that. Now I do.

His grandson wheeled him away to his bedroom, but first he gave me his iPad and opened a photo stream for me. I looked at the pictures while he was gone, then I looked at them again, and I was still looking at them when Brad came back. Seventeen photos, all taken from videos on the Internet, all of Chet Ondowsky in his various

[*Pause*]

His various incarnations, I guess you'd say. And an eighteenth. The one of Philip Hannigan outside the Pulse nightclub four years ago. No mustache, blond hair instead of dark, younger than in the security camera photo of George in his fake delivery uniform, but it was him, all right. Same face underneath. Same fox face. But not the same as Ondowsky. No way was he.

Brad came back with a bottle and two more jelly glasses. "Grampa's whiskey," he said. "Maker's Mark. Do you want a little?" When I said no, he poured quite a bit into one of the glasses. "Well, I need some," he said. "Did Grampa tell you I was gay? *Terribly* gay?"

I said he had, and Brad smiled.

"That's how he starts every conversation about me," he said. "He wants to get it right out front, on the record, to show he doesn't mind. But of course he does. He loves me, but he does."

When I said I felt sort of the same way about my mother, he smiled and said that we had something in common. I guess we do.

He said his grandfather had always been interested in what he called "the second world." Stories about telepathy, ghosts, strange disappearances, lights in the sky. He said, "Some people collect stamps. My grampa collects stories about the second world. I had my doubts about all that stuff until this."

He pointed at the iPad, where the picture of George was still on the screen. George with his package full of explosives, waiting to be buzzed into the Macready School office.

Brad said, "Now I think I could believe in anything from flying saucers to killer clowns. Because there really is a second world. It exists because people refuse to believe it's there."

I know that's true, Ralph. And so do you. It's how the thing we killed in Texas survived as long as it did.

I asked Brad to explain why his grandfather waited so long, although by then I had a pretty good idea.

He said his grandfather thought it was basically harmless. A kind of exotic chameleon, and if not the last of its species, then one of the last. It lives off grief and pain, maybe not a nice thing, but not so different from maggots living off decaying flesh or buzzards and vultures living off roadkill.

"Coyotes and hyenas live that way, too," Brad said. "They're the janitors of the animal kingdom. And are we really any better? Don't people slow down for a good long look at an accident on the turnpike? That's roadkill, too."

I said that I always looked away. And said a prayer that the people involved in the accident would be all right.

He said if that was true, I was an exception. He said that most people *like* pain, as long as it's not theirs. Then he said, "I suppose you don't watch horror movies, either?"

Well, I do, Ralph, but those movies are make-believe. When the director calls cut, the girl who had her throat slashed by Jason or Freddy gets up and grabs a cup of coffee. But still, after this I may not . . .

[*Pause*]

Never mind, I don't have time to ramble off the subject. Brad said, "For every clip of killings or disasters that Grampa and I have collected, there are hundreds more. Maybe thousands. News people have a saying: If it bleeds, it leads. That's because the stories people are most interested in are bad news stories. Murders. Explosions. Car crashes. Earthquakes. Tidal waves. People like that

360

stuff, and they like it even more now that there's cell phone video. The security footage recorded inside Pulse, when Omar Mateen was still rampaging? That has millions of hits. *Millions.*"

He said Mr. Bell thought this rare creature was only doing what all the people who watch the news do: feeding on tragedy. The monster — he didn't call it an outsider — was just fortunate enough to live longer by doing it. Mr. Bell was content to watch and marvel until he saw the security camera still of the Macready School bomber. He has that memory for faces, and he knew he'd seen a version of that face at some act of violence, not that long ago. It took Brad less than an hour to isolate Philip Hannigan.

"I've found the Macready School bomber three more times so far," Brad said, and showed me pictures of the fox-faced man — always different but always George underneath — doing three different stand-ups. Hurricane Katrina in 2005. Illinois tornadoes in 2004. And the World Trade Center in 2001. "I'm sure there are more, but I haven't had time enough to hunt them out."

"Maybe it's a different man," I said. "Or creature." I was thinking that if there were two — Ondowsky, and the one we killed in Texas — there might be three. Or four. Or a dozen. I remembered a show I saw on PBS about endangered species. Only sixty black rhinos left in the world, only seventy Amur leopards, but that's a lot more than three.

"No," Brad said. "It's the same guy."

I asked him how he could be so sure.

"Grampa used to do sketches for the police," he said. "I sometimes do court-ordered wiretaps for them, and a few times I've miked up UCs. You know what those are?"

I did, of course. Undercovers.

"No more mikes under shirts," Brad said. "We use bogus cufflinks or shirt buttons these days. I once put a mike in the B logo of a Red Sox hat. B for bug, get it? But that's only part of what I do. Watch this."

He pulled his chair close to mine so we could both see his iPad. He opened an app called VocaKnow. There were several files inside it. One was labeled *Paul Freeman*. He was the version of Ondowsky who reported the plane crash in 1960, you remember.

Brad pushed PLAY, and I heard Freeman's voice, only crisper and clearer. Brad said he had cleaned the audio and dropped out the background noise. He called that sweetening the track. The voice came from the iPad's speaker. On the screen, I could *see* the voice, the way you can see soundwaves at the bottom of your phone or tablet when you tap the little microphone icon to send an audio text message. Brad called that a spectrogram voiceprint, and he claims to be a certified voiceprint examiner. Has given testimony in court.

Can you see that force we talked about at work here, Ralph? I can. Grandfather and grandson. One good with pictures, the other good with voices. Without both, this thing, their outsider, would still be wearing his different faces and hiding in plain sight. Some people would call it chance, or coincidence, like picking the winning numbers in a lottery, but I don't believe it. I can't, and I don't want to.

Brad put Freeman's plane-crash audio on repeat. Next he opened the sound file for Ondowsky, reporting from the Macready School, and also put that one on repeat. The two voices overlapped each other, turning everything into meaningless gabble. Brad muted the sound and used his finger to separate the two spectrograms, Freeman on the top half of his iPad and Ondowsky on the bottom half.

"You see, don't you?" he asked, and of course I did. The same peaks and valleys were running across both, almost in sync. There were a few minor differences, but it was basically the same voice, although the recordings had been made sixty years apart. I asked Brad how the two wave-forms could look so similar when Freeman and Ondowsky were saying different things.

"His face changes, and his body changes," Brad said, "but his voice never does. It's called vocal uniqueness. He *tries* to change it — sometimes he raises the pitch, sometimes he lowers it, sometimes he even tries a little bit of an accent — but he doesn't try very hard."

I said, "Because he's confident the physical changes are enough, along with the changes in location."

"I think so," Brad said. "Here's something else. Everyone also has a unique delivery. A certain rhythm that's determined by breath units. Look at the peaks. That's Freeman punching certain words. Look at the valleys where he takes a breath. Now look at Ondowsky."

They were the same, Ralph.

"There's one other thing," Brad said. "Both voices pause on certain words, always with *s* or *th* sounds in them. I think at some point, God knows how long ago, this thing talked with a lisp, but of course a TV news reporter can't lisp. He's taught himself to correct it by touching his tongue to the roof of his mouth, keeping it away from his teeth, because that's where a lisp happens. It's faint, but it's there. Listen."

He played me a sound bite of Ondowsky at the middle school, the part where he says "The explosive device may have been in the main office."

Brad asked if I heard it. I asked him to play it again, to make sure it wasn't just my imagination trying to hear what Brad said was there. It wasn't imagination. Ondowsky says, "The explo . . . sive device may have been in the main of . . . fice."

Next, he played a sound bite of Paul Freeman at the 1960 crash site. Freeman says, "He was thrown from the rear section of the plane, still on fire." And I heard it again, Ralph. Those tiny pauses on *section* and *still.* The tongue touching the roof of the mouth to stop the lisp.

Brad put a third spectrogram on his tablet. It was Philip Hannigan interviewing the young man from Pulse, the kid with the smudged mascara on his cheeks. I couldn't hear the young man, because Brad scrubbed his voice out along with all the background noises, like sirens and people talking. It was just Hannigan, just *George,* and he could have been right in the room with us. "What was it like in there, Rodney? And how did you escape?"

Brad played it for me three times. The peaks and valleys on the spectrogram matched the ones still running above it — Freeman and Ondowsky. That was the technical part, Ralph, and I could appreciate it, but what really got to me, what gave me the chills, were those tiny pauses. Short on *what was it like,* longer on *escape,* which must be especially hard for lispers to conquer.

Brad asked me if I was satisfied, and I said

I was. Nobody who hasn't been through what we've been through would have been, but I was. He isn't the same as our outsider, who had to hibernate during his transformations and couldn't be seen on video, but he's certainly that being's first or second cousin. There's so much about these things we don't know, and I suppose we never will.

I need to stop now, Ralph. I haven't had anything to eat today but a bagel and a chicken sandwich and a little bit of a turn-over. If I don't get something soon, I'll probably pass out.

More later.

## 15

Holly orders out to Domino's — a small veggie pizza and a large Coke. When the young man shows up, she tips according to Bill Hodges's rule of thumb: fifteen per cent of the bill if the service is fair, twenty per cent if the service is good. This young man is prompt, so she tips the full amount.

She sits at the little table by the window, munching away and watching as dusk begins to steal over the Embassy Suites parking lot. A Christmas tree is blinking its lights on and off down there, but Holly has never had less Christmas spirit in her life. Today the thing she's investigating was only pictures on a TV screen and spectrograms on an iPad. Tomorrow, if all goes as she hopes it will (she has

Holly hope), she'll be face to face with it. That will be scary.

It has to be done; she has no choice. Dan Bell is too old and Brad Bell is too scared. He flat-out refused, even after Holly explained that what she planned to do in Pittsburgh couldn't possibly put him at risk.

"You don't know that," Brad said. "For all you know, the thing's telepathic."

"I've been face to face with one," Holly had replied. "If it was telepathic, Brad, I'd be dead and it would still be alive."

"I'm not going," Brad said. His lips were trembling. "My grampa needs me. He's got a very bad heart. Don't you have friends?"

She does, and one is a very good cop, but even if Ralph was in Oklahoma, would she risk him? He's got a family. She doesn't. As for Jerome . . . no. No way. The Pittsburgh part of her budding plan really shouldn't be dangerous, but Jerome would want to be all in, and that *would* be dangerous. There's Pete, but her partner has almost zero imagination. He'd do it, but treat the whole thing as a joke, and if there's one thing Chet Ondowsky isn't, it's a joke.

Dan Bell might have taken the shape-shifter on when he was younger, but in those years he was content to just watch, fascinated, when it popped up from time to time, a Where's Waldo of disaster. Feeling almost sorry for it, maybe. But now things have changed. Now it is no longer content to live on the aftermath of tragedy, gobbling grief and pain before the blood dries.

This time it *brought* the carnage, and if it gets away with it once, it will do it again. Next time the death toll may be much higher, and Holly will not allow that.

She opens her laptop on the room's chintzy excuse for a desk and finds the email from Brad Bell she was expecting.

*Attached is what you requested. Please use the materials wisely, and please keep us out of it. We have done what we can.*

Well, Holly thinks, not quite. She downloads the attachment and then calls Dan Bell's phone. She expects Brad to answer again, but it's the old man, sounding relatively rejuvenated. There's nothing like a nap to do that; Holly takes one whenever she can, but these days the opportunity doesn't come around as often as she'd like.

"Dan, it's Holly. Can I ask you one more question?"

"Shoot."

"How does he move from job to job without being discovered? This is the age of social media. I don't understand how that works."

For a few seconds there's only the sound of his heavy, oxygen-assisted breathing. Then he says, "We've talked about that, Brad and I. We have some ideas. He . . . *it* . . . wait, Brad wants the damn phone."

There's a smatter of talk she can't pick up, but Holly gets the gist: the old guy doesn't like being co-opted. Then Brad is on. "You want to know how he keeps getting jobs on TV?"

"Yes."

"It's a good question. Really good. We can't be sure, but we think he jimmies his way in."

"Jimmies?"

"It's a broadcast term. Jimmying is how radio personalities and TV reporters move up in big markets. In those places there's always at least one local TV station. Small. Unaffiliated. Pays peanuts. They mostly do community affairs. Everything from opening a new bridge to charity drives to city council meetings. This guy gets on the air there, does a few months, then applies at one of the big stations, using audition tapes from the little local station. Anybody seeing those tapes would get right away that he's good at the job. A pro." Brad gives a short laugh. "He'd have to be, wouldn't he? He's been doing it for at least sixty damn years. Practice makes perf—"

The old man interrupts with something. Brad says he'll tell her, but that isn't good enough for Holly. She's suddenly impatient with both of them. It's been a long day.

"Brad, put the phone on speaker."

"Huh? Oh, okay, good idea."

*"I think he was doing it on radio, too!"* Dan

bawls. It's as if he thinks they're communicating with tin cans on a waxed string. Holly winces and holds the phone away from her ear.

"Grampa, you don't have to talk so loud."

Dan lowers his voice, but only slightly. "On the radio, Holly! Even before there was TV! And before there was radio, he might have been covering bloodshed for the newspapers! God knows how long he — *it* — has been alive."

"Also," Brad says, "he must have a rolling file of references. Probably the aspect you call George writes some for Ondowsky, and the one you call Ondowsky has written some for George. You understand?"

Holly does . . . sort of. It makes her think of a joke Bill told her once, about brokers marooned on a desert island getting rich trading each other's clothes.

"Let me talk, goddammit," Dan says. "I understand as well as you do, Bradley. I'm not stupid."

Brad sighs. Living with Dan Bell can't be easy, Holly thinks. On the other hand, living with Brad Bell is probably no bed of roses, either.

"Holly, it works because TV talent is a seller's market at big local affiliates. People move up, some quit the business . . . and he's good at the job."

"*It*," Brad says. "*It's* good at the job."

She hears coughing and Brad tells his grandfather to take one of his pills.

"Jesus, will you stop being such an old woman?"

Felix and Oscar, yelling at each other across the generation gap, Holly thinks. It might make a good sitcom, but when it comes to getting information it's extremely poopy.

"Dan? Brad? Will you stop . . ." *Bickering* is the word that comes to mind, but Holly can't quite bring herself to say it, even though she's wound tight. "Stop your discussion for a minute?"

They are blessedly quiet.

"I understand what you're saying, and it makes sense as far as it goes, but what about his work history? Where he went to broadcasting school? Don't they wonder? Ask questions?"

Dan says gruffly, "He probably tells them he's been out of the business for awhile and decided to get back in."

"But we don't really know," Brad says. He sounds pissed, either because he can't answer Holly's question to her satisfaction (or to his own), or because he's smarting over being called an old woman. "Listen, there was a kid in Colorado who posed as a doctor for almost four years. Prescribed drugs, even did operations. Maybe you read about it. He was seventeen passing for twenty-five, and didn't have a college degree in *anything,* let alone medicine. If he could slip through the cracks, this outsider could."

"Are you done?" Dan asks.

"Yes, Grampa." And sighs.

"Good. Because *I* have a question. Are you going to meet him, Holly?"

"Yes." Along with the pictures, Brad has included a spectrograph screen grab of Freeman, Ondowsky, and Philip Hannigan — aka George the Bomber. To Holly's eye, all three look identical.

"When?"

"I hope tomorrow, and I'd like you both to keep completely quiet about this, please. Will you do that?"

"We will," Brad says. "Of course we will. Won't we, Grampa?"

"As long as you tell us what happens," Dan says. "If you can, that is. I used to be a cop, Holly, and Brad works with the cops. We probably don't have to tell you that meeting him could be dangerous. *Will* be dangerous."

"I know," Holly says in a small voice. "I work with an ex-cop myself." And worked with an even better one before him, she thinks.

"Will you be careful?"

"I'll try," Holly says, but she knows there always comes a point when you have to stop being careful. Jerome talked about a bird that carried evil like a virus. All frowsy and frosty gray, he said. If you wanted to catch it and

372

wring its fracking neck, there came a time when you had to stop being careful. She doesn't think that will happen tomorrow, but it will soon.

Soon.

## 16

Jerome has turned the space over the Robinsons' garage into a writing room and is using it to work on his book about great-great-Gramps Alton, also known as the Black Owl. He's beavering away on it this evening when Barbara lets herself in and asks Jerome if she's interrupting. Jerome tells her he can use a break. They get Cokes from the small refrigerator nestled beneath one sloping eave.

"Where is she?" Barbara asks.

Jerome sighs. "*No how's your book going, J? No did you find that chocolate Lab, J?* Which I did, by the way. Safe and sound."

"Good for you. And how's your book going, J?"

"Up to page 93," he says, and sweeps a hand through the air. "I'm *sailing.*"

"That's good, too. Now where is she?"

Jerome takes his phone out of his pocket and touches an app called WebWatcher. "See for yourself."

Barbara studies the screen. "The airport in Portland? Portland, *Maine?* What's she doing there?"

"Why don't you call her and ask?" Jerome

says. "Just say 'Jerome snuck a tracker on your phone, Hollyberry, because we're worried about you, so what are you up to? Spill it, girl.' Think she'd like that?"

"Don't joke," Barbara says. "She'd be super-pissed. That would be bad, but she'd also be hurt, and that would be worse. Besides, we know what it's about. Don't we?"

Jerome had suggested — just suggested — that Barbara could peek at the history on Holly's home computer when she went to pick up those movies for her school report. If, that was, Holly's password at home was the same as the one she used at work.

That turned out to be the case, and while Barbara had felt extremely creepy and stalkerish about looking at her friend's search history, she had done it. Because Holly hadn't been the same after her trip to Oklahoma and subsequent trip to Texas, where she had nearly been killed by an off-the-rails cop named Jack Hoskins. There was a great deal more to that story than her near miss that day, and both of them knew it, but Holly refused to talk about it. And at first that seemed okay, because little by little the haunted look had left her eyes. She had returned to normal . . . Holly-normal, at least. But now she was gone, doing something she'd refused to talk about.

So Jerome had decided to track Holly's location with the WebWatcher app.

And Barbara had looked at Holly's search history.

And Holly — trusting soul that she was, at least when it came to her friends — had not wiped it.

Barbara discovered Holly had looked at many trailers for upcoming movies, had visited Rotten Tomatoes and Huffington Post, and had several times visited a dating site called Hearts & Friends (who knew?), but many of her current searches had to do with the terrorist bombing at the Albert Macready Middle School. There were also searches for Chet Ondowsky, a TV reporter at WPEN in Pittsburgh, a place called Clauson's Diner in Pierre, Pennsylvania, and someone named Fred Finkel, who turned out to be a cameraman at WPEN.

Barbara took all this to Jerome and asked if he thought Holly might be on the verge of some sort of weirdo breakdown, maybe kicked off by the Macready School bombing. "Maybe she's like, flashing back to when her cousin Janey got blown up by Brady Hartsfield."

Based on her searches, it certainly crossed Jerome's mind that Holly had caught the scent of another really bad man, but there's something else that seemed — to him, at least — equally plausible.

"Hearts & Friends," he says to his sister now.

"What about it?"

"Has it not occurred to you that Holly might be, don't gasp, hooking up? Or at least meeting a guy she's exchanged emails with?"

Barbara stares at him with her mouth open. Almost laughs, then doesn't. What she says is, "Hmmm."

"Meaning what?" Jerome says. "Give me some insight here. You spend girl-time with her —"

"Sexist, J."

He ignores that. "Does she have a friend of the male persuasion? Now or ever?"

Barbara considers this carefully. "You know what, I don't think so. I think she might still be a virgin."

*What about you, Barb?* is the thought that immediately jumps into Jerome's mind, but some questions should not be asked of eighteen-year-old girls by their big brothers.

"She's not *gay,* or anything," Barbara hastens on. "She never misses a Josh Brolin flick, and when we saw that stupid shark movie a couple of years ago, she actually *moaned* when she saw Jason Statham with his shirt off. Do you really think she'd go all the way to *Maine* for a date?"

"The plot thickens," he says, peering into his phone. "She's not at the airport. If you zoom in, you'll see it's Embassy Suites. She's probably drinking champagne with some guy who likes frozen daiquiris, strolling in the moonlight, and discussing classic films."

Barbara makes as if to punch him in the face, only springing her hand open at the last second.

"Tell you what," Jerome says. "I think we better leave this alone."

"For real?"

"I think so, yeah. We need to remember that she survived Brady Hartsfield. *Twice.* Whatever happened in Texas, she got through that, too. She's a little shaky on top, but down deep . . . solid steel."

"Got that right," Barbara says. "Looking at her browser . . . that made me feel skeevy."

"*This* makes me feel skeevy," he says, and taps the blinking dot on his phone that marks the Embassy Suites. "I'm going to sleep on it, but if I feel the same in the morning, I'm gonna dump it. She's a good woman. Brave. Lonely, too."

"And her mother's a witch," Barbara adds.

Jerome doesn't disagree. "Maybe we should just let her alone. Work it out, whatever it is."

"Maybe we should." But Barbara looks unhappy about it.

Jerome leans forward. "One thing I know for sure, Barb. She's never going to find out that we tracked her at all. Is she?"

"Never," Barbara says. "Or that I peeked at her searches."

"Good. We have that straight. Now can I go

back to work? I want to get another two pages before I knock off."

## 17

Holly isn't even close to knocking off. In fact, she's just about to get started on the evening's real work. She thinks about kneeling for a little more prayer first and decides she would only be procrastinating. She reminds herself that God helps those who help themselves.

Chet Ondowsky's *Chet on Guard* segment has its own webpage, where folks who feel they have been burned can call in on an 800 number. This line is manned (or womaned) twenty-four hours a day, and the page claims all calls will be kept absolutely confidential.

Holly takes a deep breath and makes the call. It rings just a single time. "*Chet on Guard,* this is Monica speaking, how may I help?"

"Monica, I need to speak to Mr. Ondowsky. It's quite urgent."

The woman responds smoothly and with no hesitation. Holly's sure she's got a script, complete with possible variations, on the screen in front of her, "I'm sorry, ma'am, but Chet has either left for the day or is on assignment. I'll be happy to take your contact information and pass it on to him. Some information on the nature of your consumer complaint would also be helpful."

"This isn't exactly a consumer complaint," she says, "but it *is* about consuming. Will you

378

tell him that, please?"

"Ma'am?" Monica is clearly puzzled.

"I need to speak to him tonight, and before nine P.M. Tell him it concerns Paul Freeman and the plane crash. Have you got that?"

"Yes, ma'am." Holly can hear the clitter-clitter-clitter of the woman typing.

"Tell him it also concerns Dave Van Pelt in Dallas and Jim Avery in Detroit. And tell him — this is very important — that it concerns Philip Hannigan and the Pulse nightclub."

This startles Monica out of her previously smooth delivery. "Isn't that where the man shot —"

"Yes," Holly says. "Tell him to call by nine, or I will take my information elsewhere. And don't forget to tell him it's not about consumers, but it *is* about consuming. He'll know what that means."

"Ma'am, I can pass the message on, but I can't guarantee —"

"If you pass it on, he'll call," Holly says, and hopes she's right. Because she doesn't have a Plan B.

"I need your contact information, ma'am."

"You have my number on your screen," Holly says. "I'll wait for Mr. Ondowsky's call to give my name. Please have a pleasant evening."

Holly ends the call, wipes sweat from her brow, and checks her Fitbit. Heart rate is 89. Not bad. There was a time when a call like that would have rammed it up over 150. She looks at the clock. Quarter of seven. She takes her book out of her travel bag and immediately puts it back. She's too tense to read. So she paces.

At quarter to eight she's in the bathroom with her shirt off, washing her armpits (she doesn't use deodorant; aluminum chlorohydrate is supposed to be safe but she has her doubts), when her phone rings. She takes two deep breaths, sends up the briefest of prayers — *God help me not to frack up* — and answers.

## 18

Her phone's screen says UNKNOWN. Holly isn't surprised. He's calling on his personal phone or maybe a burner.

"This is Chet Ondowsky, to whom am I speaking?" The voice is smooth, friendly, and controlled. A veteran TV reporter's voice.

"My name is Holly. That's all you need to know for now." She thinks she sounds okay so far. She punches her Fitbit. Pulse is 98.

"What's this about, Holly?" Interested. Inviting confidences. This isn't the man who reported on the bloody horror in Pineborough Township; this is Chet on Guard, wanting to know how the guy who paved your driveway shafted you on the price or how much the power company stiffed you for kilowatts you didn't burn.

"I think you know," she says, "but let's

make sure. I'm going to send you some pictures. Give me your email address."

"If you check the *Chet on Guard* webpage, Holly, you'll find —"

"Your *personal* email address. Because you don't want anyone seeing this. You really don't."

There's a pause, long enough for Holly to think she might have lost him, but then he gives her the address. She jots it on a sheet of Embassy Suites notepaper.

"I'm sending it right away," she says. "Pay special attention to the spectrographic analysis and the picture of Philip Hannigan. Call me back in fifteen minutes."

"Holly, this is very unusu—"

"*You're* very unusual, Mr. Ondowsky. Aren't you? Call me back in fifteen minutes, or I'll take what I know public. Your time starts as soon as my email goes through."

"Holly —"

She ends the call, drops the phone on the rug, and bends over, head between her knees and face in her hands. Don't faint, she tells herself. Don't you fracking do it.

When she feels okay again — as okay as she can be under the circumstances, which are very stressful — she opens her laptop and sends off the material Brad Bell gave her. She doesn't bother adding a message. The pictures *are* the message.

Then she waits.

Eleven minutes later her phone lights up. She grabs it at once but lets it ring four times before taking the call.

He doesn't bother with hello. "These prove nothing." It's still the perfectly modulated tone of the veteran TV personality, but all the warmth has gone out of it. "You know that, right?"

Holly says, "Wait until people compare the picture of you as Philip Hannigan with the one of you standing outside the school with that package in your hands. The false mustache will fool nobody. Wait until they compare the spectrogram of Philip Hannigan's voice to the spectrogram of Chet Ondowsky's voice."

"Who is this *they* you're referring to, Holly? The police? They'd laugh you right out of the station."

"Oh no, not the police," Holly said. "I can do better than that. If TMZ isn't interested, Gossip Glutton will be. Or DeepDive. And the Drudge Report, they always like the strange stuff. On TV there's *Inside Edition* and *Celeb.* But do you know where I'd go first?"

Silence from the other end. But she can hear him breathing.

*It* breathing.

*"Inside View,"* she says. "They ran with the Night Flier story for over a year, Slender Man for two. They wrung those stories dry. They've

still got a circulation of over three million, and they'll eat this up."

"Nobody believes that shit."

This isn't true, and they both know it.

"They'll believe this. I've got a lot of information, Mr. Ondowsky, what I believe you reporters call deep background, and when it comes out — if it comes out — people will start digging into your past. *All* your pasts. Your cover won't just come apart, it will explode." Like the bomb you planted to kill those children, she thinks.

Nothing.

Holly chews on her knuckles and waits him out. It's very hard, but she does it.

At last he asks, "Where did you get those pictures? Who gave them to you?"

Holly knew this was coming, and knows she has to give him something. "A man who's been onto you for a long time. You don't know him and you'll never find him, but you also don't have to worry about him. He's very old. What you have to worry about is me."

There's another long pause. Now one of Holly's knuckles is bleeding. At last the question she's been waiting for arrives: "What do you want?"

"I'll tell you tomorrow. You're going to meet me at noon."

"I have an assignment —"

"Cancel it," commands the woman who once scuttled through life with her head down and her shoulders hunched. "This is your assignment now, and I don't think you want to blow it."

"Where?"

Holly is ready for this. She's done her research. "The food court of the Monroeville Mall. That's less than fifteen miles from your TV station, so it should be convenient for you and safe for me. Go to Sbarro, look around, you'll see me. I'll be wearing a brown leather jacket open over a pink sweater with a turtleneck collar. I'll have a slice of pizza and coffee in a Starbucks cup. If you're not there by five past noon, I'll leave and start shopping my merchandise."

"You're a kook and no one will believe you." He doesn't sound confident, but he doesn't sound afraid, either. He sounds angry. That's all right, Holly thinks, I can work with that.

"Who are you trying to convince, Mr. Ondowsky? Me, or yourself?"

"You're a piece of work, lady. You know that?"

"I'll have a friend watching," she says. Not true, but Ondowsky won't know that. "He doesn't know what it's about, don't worry about that, but he'll be keeping an eye on me." She pauses. "And on you."

"What do you want?" he asks again.

"Tomorrow," Holly says, and ends the call.

Later, after she's made arrangements to fly

to Pittsburgh the following morning, she lies in bed, hoping for sleep but not expecting much. She wonders — as she did when she conceived this plan — if she really needs to meet him face to face. She thinks she does. She thinks she's convinced him that she's got the goods on him (as Bill would say). Now she has to look him in the eye and give him a way out. Has to convince him that she's willing to make a deal. And what kind of deal? Her first wild idea was to tell him she wants to be like him, that she wants to live . . . maybe not forever, that seems too extreme, but for hundreds of years. Would he believe that, or would he think she was conning him? Too risky.

Money, then. Has to be.

That he will believe, because he has been watching the human parade for a long time. And looking down on it. Ondowsky believes that for lesser beings, for the herd he sometimes thins, it always comes down to money.

Sometime after midnight, Holly finally drops off. She dreams of a cave in Texas. She dreams of a thing that looked like a man until she hit it with a sock loaded with ball bearings and the head collapsed like the false front it was.

She cries in her sleep.

*December 17, 2020*

1

As an honor roll senior at Houghton High, Barbara Robinson is pretty much free to go as she lists during her free period, which runs from 9:00 to 9:50. When the bell rings releasing her from her Early English Writers class, she wanders down to the art room, which is deserted at this hour. She takes her phone from her hip pocket and calls Jerome. From the sound of his voice, she's pretty sure she woke him up. Oh for the life of a writer, she thinks.

Barbara doesn't waste time. "Where is she this morning, J?"

"Don't know," he says. "I dumped the tracker."

"True?"

"True."

"Well . . . okay."

"Can I go back to sleep now?"

"No," she says. Barbara has been up since 6:45, and misery loves company. "Time to get up and grab the world by the balls."

"Mouth, sister," he says, and boom, he's gone.

Barbara stands by some kid's really bad watercolor of the lake, staring at her phone and frowning. Jerome is probably right, Holly went off to meet some guy she met on that dating website. Not to fuck him, that's not Holly, but to make a human connection? To reach out, as her therapist has no doubt been telling her she must do? That Barbara can believe. Portland has got to be at least five hundred miles from the site of that bombing she was so interested in, after all. Maybe more.

Put yourself in her shoes, Barbara tells herself. Wouldn't you want your privacy? And wouldn't you be mad if you ever found out that your friends — your *so-called* friends — were spying on you?

Holly *wasn't* going to find out, but did that change the basic equation?

No.

Was she still worried (a *little* worried)?

Yes. But some worries had to be lived with.

She slips her phone back into her pocket and decides to go down to the music room and practice her guitar until 20th Century American History. She's trying to learn the old Wilson Pickett soul shouter, "In the

Midnight Hour." The bar chords in the bridge are a bitch, but she's getting there.

On her way out, she almost runs into Justin Freilander, a junior who's a founding member of Houghton's geek squad, and who has — according to rumor — a major crush on her. She smiles at him and Justin immediately turns that alarming shade of red of which only white boys are capable. Rumor confirmed. It suddenly occurs to Barbara that this might be fate.

She says, "Hey Justin. I wonder if you could help me with something?"

And takes her phone out of her pocket.

## 2

While Justin Freilander is examining Barbara's phone (which is still, oh God, warm from being in her back pocket), Holly is landing at Pittsburgh International. Ten minutes later she's in line at the Avis counter. Uber would be cheaper, but having her own ride is wiser. A year or so after Pete Huntley came onboard at Finders Keepers, the two of them took a driving course meant to teach surveillance and evasion — a refresher for him, new for her. She doesn't expect to need the former today, but recourse to the latter isn't out of the question. She is meeting a dangerous man.

She parks in the lot of an airport hotel to kill some time (early to my own funeral, she thinks again). She calls her mother. Charlotte doesn't answer, which doesn't mean she's not there; direct-to-voicemail is one of her old punishing techniques for when she feels her daughter has stepped out of line. Holly next calls Pete, who asks again what she's doing and when she'll be back. Thinking of Dan Bell and his *terribly* gay grandson, she tells him she's visiting friends in New England and will be in the office bright and early on Monday morning.

"You better be," Pete says. "You have a depo on Tuesday. And the office Christmas party is on Wednesday. I plan to kiss you under the mistletoe."

"Oough," Holly says, but she's smiling.

She arrives at the Monroeville Mall at quarter past eleven and makes herself sit in the car for another fifteen minutes, alternately punching her Fitbit (pulse running just over 100) and praying for strength and calm. Also to be convincing.

At eleven-thirty she enters the mall and takes a slow stroll past some of the shops — Jimmy Jazz, Clutch, Boobaloo strollers — looking in the windows not to scope out the merchandise but to catch a reflected glimpse of Chet Ondowsky, should he be watching her. And it *will* be Chet. His other self, the one she thinks of as George, is the most wanted man in America just now. Holly supposes he might have a third template, but she thinks it unlikely; he's got a pig-self and a fox-self, why would he think he'd need more?

At ten minutes of twelve, she gets in line at Starbucks for a cup of coffee, then queues at Sbarro for a slice of pizza she doesn't want. She unzips her jacket so the pink turtleneck shows, then finds an unoccupied table in the food court. Although it's lunchtime, there are quite a few of those — more than she expected, and that makes her uneasy. The mall itself is low on foot traffic, especially for the Christmas shopping season. Seems to have fallen on hard times, everybody buys from Amazon these days.

Noon comes. A young man wearing cool sunglasses and a quilted jacket (a couple of ski-lift tags dangle jauntily from the zipper) slows, as if he means to chat her up, then moves on. Holly is relieved. She has little in the way of brush-off skills, never having had much reason to develop them.

At five past noon she starts to think Ondowsky isn't coming. Then, at seven past, a man speaks from behind her, and in the warm, we're-all-pals-here voice of a TV regular. "Hello, Holly."

She jumps and almost spills her coffee. It's the young man with the cool sunglasses. At first she thinks this is a third template after all, but when he takes them off she sees it's Ondowsky, all right. His face is slightly more angular, the creases around his mouth are gone, and his eyes are closer together (not a good look for TV), but it's him. And not young at all. She can't see any lines and wrinkles on his face, but she senses them, and thinks there may be a lot. The masquerade is a good one, but up this close it's like Botox or plastic surgery.

Because I know, she thinks. I know what he is.

"I thought it would be best if I looked just a bit different," he says. "When I'm Chet, I tend to get recognized. TV journalists aren't exactly Tom Cruise, but . . ." A modest shrug finishes the thought.

With his sunglasses off, she sees something else: his eyes have a shimmery quality, as if they're underwater . . . or not there at all. And isn't there something similar going on with his mouth? Holly thinks of how the picture looks when you're at a 3-D movie and take off the glasses.

"You see it, don't you?" The voice is still warm and friendly. It goes well with the small smile dimpling the corners of his mouth. "Most people don't. It's the transition. It will be gone in five minutes, ten at most. I had to come here directly from the station. You've caused me some problems, Holly."

She realizes she can hear the small pause when he occasionally puts his tongue to the roof of his mouth to stop the lisp.

"That makes me think of an old country

song by Travis Tritt." She sounds calm enough but she can't take her eyes from his, where the sclera shimmers into the iris and the iris shimmers into the pupil. For the time being, they're countries with unstable borders. "It's called 'Here's a Quarter, Call Someone Who Cares.' "

He smiles, the lips seeming to spread too far, and then, snap! The minute shivers in his eyes remain, but his mouth is solid again. He looks to her left, where an old gent in a parka and tweed cap is reading a magazine. "Is that your friend? Or is it the woman over there who's been looking into the window of Forever 21 a suspiciously long time?"

"Maybe it's both of them," Holly says. Now that the confrontation is here, she feels okay. Or almost; those eyes are disturbing and disorienting. Looking into them too long will give her a headache, but he would take looking away as a sign of weakness. And it would be.

"You know me, but all I have is your given name. What's the rest of it?"

"Gibney. Holly Gibney."

"And what is it you want, Holly Gibney?"

"Three hundred thousand dollars."

"Blackmail," he says, and gives his head a small shake, as if he's disappointed in her. "Do you know what blackmail is, Holly?"

She remembers one of the late Bill Hodges's old maxims (there were many): You

392

don't answer a perp's questions; the perp answers yours. So she simply sits and waits with her small hands folded beside her unwanted slice of pizza.

"Blackmail is rent," he says. "Not even rent-to-buy, a scam Chet on Guard knows well. Let's suppose I had three hundred thousand dollars, which I don't — there's a big difference between what a TV reporter makes and what a TV actor makes. But let's suppose."

"Let's suppose you've been around for a long, long time," Holly says, "and putting money away all the while. Let's suppose that's how you finance your . . ." Your what, exactly? "Your lifestyle. And your background. Bogus IDs and all."

He smiles. It's charming. "All right, Holly Gibney, let's suppose that. The central problem for me remains: blackmail is rent. When the three hundred K is gone, you'll come back with your Photoshopped pictures and your electronically altered voiceprints and threaten me with exposure all over again."

Holly is ready for this. She didn't need Bill to tell her that the best confabulation is the one containing the most truth. "No," she says. "Three hundred thousand is all I want, because it's all I need." She pauses. "Although there *is* one other thing."

"And what would that be?" The pleasant TV-trained tones have become condescending.

"Let's stick with the money for now. Recently my Uncle Henry was diagnosed with Alzheimer's. He's in an elder care facility that specializes in housing and treating people like him. It's very expensive, but that's really beside the point because he hates it there, he's very *upset,* and my mother wants to bring him back home. Only she can't care for him. She thinks she can, but she can't. She's getting old, she has medical problems of her own, and the house would have to be retrofitted for an invalid." She thinks of Dan Bell. "Ramps, a stair-chair, and a bed-hoist to start with, but those things are minor. I'd want to hire round-the-clock care for him, including an RN in the daytime."

"Such expensive plans, Holly Gibney. You must love the old dear very much."

"I do," Holly says.

It's the truth even though Uncle Henry is a pain in the ass. Love is a gift; love is also a chain with a manacle at each end.

"His general health is bad. Congestive heart failure is the main physical problem." Again she has Dan Bell to draw on. "He's in a wheelchair and on oxygen. He might live another two years. It's possible he could live three. I've run the numbers and three hundred thousand dollars would keep him for five."

"And if he lives six, you'd come back."

She finds herself thinking of young Frank

Peterson, murdered by that other outsider in Flint City. Murdered in the most gruesome and painful way. She's suddenly furious with Ondowsky. Him with his trained TV reporter's voice and his condescending smile. He's a piece of poop. Except *poop* is too mild. She leans forward, fixing her gaze on those eyes (which have finally, thankfully, begun to settle).

"Listen to me, you child-murdering piece of shit. I don't want to ask you for more money. I didn't even want to ask you for *this* money. I never want to see you again. I can't believe I'm actually planning to let you go, and if you don't wipe that fracking smile off your face, I just may change my mind."

Ondowsky recoils as if slapped, and the smile does indeed disappear. Has he ever been spoken to like this? Maybe, but not for a long time. He's a respected TV journalist! When he's Chet on Guard, cheating contractors and pill-mill proprietors quail at his approach! His eyebrows (they are very thin, she notices, as if hair really doesn't want to grow there) draw together. "You can't —"

"Shut up and listen to me," Holly says in a low, intense voice. She leans even further forward, not just invading his space but threatening it. This is a Holly her mother has never seen, although Charlotte's seen enough in these last five or six years to consider her daughter a stranger, maybe even a changeling.

"Are you listening? You better be, or I'll call this off and walk away. I won't get three hundred thousand from *Inside View,* but I'll bet I can get fifty, and that's a start."

"I'm listening." *Listening* has one of those pauses in the middle. This one is longer. Because he's upset, Holly surmises. Good. Upset is just how she wants him.

"Three hundred thousand dollars. Cash. Fifties and hundreds. Put it in a box like the one you took to the Macready School, although you don't have to bother with the Christmas stickers and the fake uniform. Bring it to my place of business on Saturday evening at six P.M. That gives you the rest of today and all of tomorrow to put the cash together. Be on time, not late like you were today. If you're late, your goose is cooked. You want to remember how close I am to pulling the plug on this. You make me sick." Also the truth, and she guesses that if she pushed the button on the side of her Fitbit now, her pulse would be up around 170.

"Just for the sake of discussion, what *is* your place of business? And what business do you do there?"

Answering those questions may be signing her death warrant if she fracks up, Holly knows this, but it's too late to turn back now. "The Frederick Building." She names the city. "On Saturday at six, and just before Christmas, we'll have the whole place to ourselves. Fifth floor. Finders Keepers."

"What is Finders Keepers, exactly? Some kind of collection agency?" He wrinkles his nose, as if at a bad smell.

"We do a few collections," Holly admits. "Mostly other things. We're an investigative agency."

"Oh my God, are you an actual *private eye*?" He has regained enough of his *sang-froid* to sarcastically pat his chest in the vicinity of his heart (if he has one, Holly bets it's black).

Holly has no intention of chasing that. "Six o'clock, fifth floor. Three hundred thousand. Fifties and hundreds in a box. Use the side door. Phone me when you arrive and I'll give you the lock code by text."

"Is there a camera?"

The question doesn't surprise Holly in the least. He's a TV reporter. Unlike the outsider who killed Frank Peterson, cameras are his life.

"There is, but it's broken. From the ice storm early this month. It hasn't been fixed yet."

She can see he doesn't believe that, but it happens to be the truth. Al Jordan, the building super, is a lazybones who should have been fired (in Holly's humble opinion, and Pete's) long since. It's not just the side entrance camera; if not for Jerome, people with offices on the eighth floor would still be trudging up the stairs all the way to the top of the building.

"There's a metal detector inside the door, and that *does* work. It's built into the walls; there's no way to dodge around it. If you come early, I'll know. If you try to bring a gun, I'll know that. Following me?"

"Yes." No smile now. She doesn't have to be telepathic to know he's thinking she's a meddlesome, troublesome cunt. That's fine with Holly; it beats being a wimp scared of her own shadow.

"Take the elevator. I'll hear it, it's noisy. When it opens, I'll be waiting for you in the hall. We'll make the exchange there. Everything's on a flash drive."

"And how will the exchange work?"

"Never mind for now. Just believe it's going to work so we both walk away."

"And I'm supposed to trust you on that?"

Another question she has no intention of answering. "Let's talk about the other thing I need from you." This is where she either seals the deal . . . or doesn't.

"What is it?" Now he sounds almost sullen.

"The old man I told you about, the one who spotted you —"

"How? How did he do that?"

"Never mind that, either. The thing is, he's been keeping an eye on you for years. *Decades.*"

She watches his face closely and is satisfied with what she sees there: shock.

"He left you alone because he thought you were a hyena. Or a crow. Something that lives on roadkill. Not nice, but part of the . . . I don't know, the ecosystem, I guess. But then you decided that wasn't enough, didn't you? You thought why wait around for some tragedy, some *massacre,* when I can make my own. DIY, right?"

Nothing from Ondowsky. He simply watches her, and even though his eyes are now still, they're awful. It's her death warrant, all right, and she's not just signing it. She's writing it herself.

"Have you done it before?"

A long pause. Just when Holly has decided he isn't going to answer — which will *be* an answer — he does. "No. But I was hungry." And he smiles. It makes her feel like screaming. "You look frightened, Holly Gibney."

No use lying about that. "I am. But I'm also determined." She leans forward into his space again. It's one of the hardest things she's ever done. "So here is the other thing. I'll give you a pass this time, but *never do it again.* If you do, I'll know."

"And then what? You'll come after me?"

It's Holly's turn not to speak.

"How many copies of this material do you actually have, Holly Gibney?"

"Only one," Holly says. "Everything's on

the flash drive, and I'll give it to you on Saturday evening. *But.*" She points a finger at him, and is pleased to see it doesn't tremble. "I know your face. I know *both* your faces. I know your voice, things about it you may not know yourself." She's thinking of the pauses to defeat the lisp. "Go your way, eat your rotten food, but if I even *suspect* you've caused another tragedy — another Macready School — then yes, I'll come after you. I'll hunt you down. I'll blow up your life."

Ondowsky looks around at the nearly empty food court. Both the old man in the tweed cap and the woman who was staring at the mannequins in the window of Forever 21 are gone. There are people queuing at the fast food franchises, but their backs are turned. "I don't think *anyone's* watching us, Holly Gibney. I think you're on your own. I think I could reach across this table and snap your scrawny neck and be gone before anyone realized what happened. I'm very fast."

If he sees she's terrified — and she is, because she knows he's both desperate and furious to find himself in this position — he may do it. *Probably* will do it. So once more she forces herself to lean forward. "You might not be fast enough to keep me from screaming your name, which I believe everyone in the Pittsburgh metro area knows. I'm quite speedy myself. Would you like to take that chance?"

There's a moment when he's either deciding or pretending to. Then he says, "Saturday
evening at six, Frederick Building, fifth floor.
I bring the money, you give me the thumb
drive. That's the deal?"

"That's the deal."

"And you'll keep your silence."

"Unless there's another Macready School,
yes. If there is, I'll start shouting what I know
from the rooftops. And I'll go on shouting
until someone believes me."

"All right."

He sticks out his hand, but doesn't seem
surprised when Holly declines to shake it. Or
even touch it. He gets to his feet and smiles
again. It's the one that makes her feel like
screaming.

"The school was a mistake. I see that now."

He puts on his sunglasses and is halfway
across the food court almost before Holly
has time to register his departure. He wasn't
lying about being fast. Maybe she could have
avoided his hands if he'd reached across the
small table, but she has her doubts. One
quick twist and he'd've been gone, leaving a
woman with her chin on her chest, as if she's
dozed off over her little lunch. But it's only a
temporary reprieve.

*All right,* he said. Just that. No hesitation,
no asking for assurances. No questions about
how she could be sure some future explosion
resulting in multiple casualties — a bus, a

train, a shopping center like this one —
wasn't his doing.

*The school was a mistake,* he said. *I see that
now.*

But *she* was the mistake, one that needed
to be corrected.

He doesn't mean to pay me, he means to
kill me, she thinks as she takes her untouched
slice and her Starbucks cup to the nearest
trash receptacle. Then she almost laughs.

Like I didn't know that all along?

## 3

The mall parking lot is cold and windswept.
At the height of the holiday buying season it
should be full, but it's only at half capacity, if
that. Holly is exquisitely aware that she's on
her own. There are large empty spaces where
the wind can really do its work, numbing her
face and sometimes almost making her stag-
ger, but there are also clusters of parked cars.
Ondowsky could be hiding behind any one of
them, ready to leap out (*I'm very fast*) and
grab her.

She runs the last ten steps to the rental,
and once she's inside, she pushes the button
that locks all the doors. She sits there for half
a minute, getting herself under control. She
doesn't check her Fitbit because she wouldn't
like its news.

Holly drives away from the mall, checking
her rearview mirror every few seconds. She

402

doesn't believe she's being followed, but goes into evasive driving mode anyway. Better safe than sorry.

She knows Ondowsky might expect her to take a commuter flight back home, so she plans to spend the night in Pittsburgh and take an Amtrak tomorrow. She pulls into a Holiday Inn Express and turns on her phone to check for messages before going inside. There's one from her mother.

"Holly, I don't know where you are, but Uncle Henry's had an accident at that damn Rolling Hills place. He may have a broken arm. Please call me. *Please.*" Holly hears both her mother's distress and the old accusation: I needed you and you've disappointed me. Again.

The pad of her finger comes within a millimeter of returning her mother's call. Old habits are hard to break and default positions are hard to change. The flush of shame is already heating her forehead, cheeks, and throat, and the words she'll say when her mother answers are already in her mouth: *I'm sorry.* And why not? All her life she's been apologizing to her mother, who always forgives her with that expression on her face that says *Oh Holly, you never change. You are such a reliable disappointer.* Because Charlotte Gibney also has her default positions.

This time Holly stays her finger, thinking.

Why, exactly, should she be sorry? What would she be apologizing for? That she wasn't there to save poor addled Uncle Henry from breaking his arm? That she didn't answer the phone the minute, the very *second,* that her mother called, as if Charlotte's life is the important life, the real life, and Holly's only her mother's cast shadow?

Facing Ondowsky was hard. Refusing to immediately answer her mother's *cri de coeur* is just as hard, maybe even harder, but she does. Although it makes her feel like a bad daughter, she calls the Rolling Hills Elder Care Center instead. She identifies herself and asks for Mrs. Braddock. She's put on hold and suffers "The Little Drummer Boy" until Mrs. Braddock comes on. Holly thinks it's music to commit suicide by.

"Ms. Gibney!" Mrs. Braddock says. "Is it too early to wish you happy holidays?"

"Not at all. Thank you. Mrs. Braddock, my mother called and said my uncle has had an accident."

Mrs. Braddock laughs. "*Saved* one, more like it! I called your mother and told her. Your uncle's mental state may have deteriorated somewhat, but there's certainly nothing wrong with his reflexes."

"What happened?"

"The first day or so he didn't want to come out of his room," Mrs. Braddock says, "but that's not unusual. Our new arrivals are always disoriented, and often in distress. Sometimes in great distress, in which case we give them something to calm them down a bit. Your uncle didn't need that, and yesterday he came out all on his own and sat in the dayroom. He even helped Mrs. Hatfield with her jigsaw puzzle. He watched that crazy judge show he likes —"

*John Law*, Holly thinks, and smiles. She's hardly aware that she is constantly checking her mirrors to make sure Chet Ondowsky (*I'm very fast*) isn't lurking.

"— afternoon snacks."

"Beg pardon?" Holly says. "I lost you for a second."

"I said that when the show was over, some of them headed into the dining hall, where there are afternoon snacks. Your uncle was walking with Mrs. Hatfield, who is eighty-two and rather unsteady. Anyway, she tripped and might have taken quite a bad fall, only Henry grabbed her. Sarah Whitlock — she's one of our nurses' aides — said he reacted very quickly. 'Like lightning' were her actual words. Anyway, he took her weight and fell against the wall, where there's a fire extinguisher. State law, you know. He has quite the bruise, but he may have saved Mrs. Hatfield from a concussion or even worse. She's very frail."

"Uncle Henry didn't break anything? When he hit the fire extinguisher?"

Mrs. Braddock laughs again. "Oh, heavens no!"

"That's good. Tell my uncle he's my hero."

"I will. And once again, happy holidays."

"I'm Holly and therefore must be jolly," she says, a creaky witticism she's been using at this time of year since she was twelve. She ends the call on Mrs. Braddock's laughter, then looks at the dull brick side of the Holiday Inn Express for awhile, arms crossed over her scant bosom, brow furrowed in thought. She comes to a decision and calls her mother.

"Oh, Holly, at last! Where have you been? Isn't it bad enough I have my brother to worry about without having to worry about you, too?"

The urge to say *I'm sorry* once more arises, and she reminds herself again that she has nothing to apologize for.

"I'm fine, Mom. I'm in Pittsburgh —"

*"Pittsburgh!"*

"— but I can be home in a little over two hours, if the traffic isn't bad and Avis will let me return their car down there. Is my room made up?"

"It's *always* made up," Charlotte says.

Of course it is, Holly thinks. Because eventually I'll come to my senses and return to it.

"Great," Holly says. "I'll be there in time for supper. We can watch some television and go see Uncle Henry tomorrow, if that would be —"

"I'm so worried about him!" Charlotte cries.

But not worried enough to jump in your car and go there, Holly thinks. Because Mrs. Braddock called you and you know. This isn't about your brother; it's about bringing your daughter to heel. It's too late for that, and I think in your heart you know it, but you won't stop trying. That's also a default position.

"I'm sure he's all right, Mom."

"They say he is, but of course they would, wouldn't they? Those places always have their guard up in case of lawsuits."

"We'll visit and see for ourselves," Holly says. "Right?"

"Oh, I guess so." A pause. "I suppose you'll leave after we visit him, won't you. Go back to that city." Subtext: that Sodom, that Gomorrah, that pit of sin and degradation. "I'll be having Christmas by myself while you have Christmas dinner with your friends." Including that young black man who looks like he might take drugs.

"Mom." Sometimes Holly feels like screaming. "The Robinsons invited me weeks ago. Right after Thanksgiving. I told you, and you said it was fine." What Charlotte had actually said was *Well I suppose, if you feel you have to.*

407

"That was when I thought Henry would still be here."

"Well, how about if I stay Friday night, too?" She can do that for her mother, and she can also do it for herself. She's sure Ondowsky is perfectly capable of finding out where she lives in the city and showing up there, twenty-four hours early and with murder on his mind. "We could have Christmas early."

"That would be wonderful," Charlotte says, brightening up. "I can roast a chicken. And asparagus! You love asparagus!"

Holly hates asparagus, but telling her mother that would be useless. "Sounds good, Mom."

4

Holly seals the deal with Avis (at an additional fee, of course) and gets on the road, stopping only once to gas up, grab a Filet-O-Fish at Mickey D's, and make a couple of calls. Yes, she tells Jerome and Pete, she's finished her personal business. She'll be spending most of the weekend with her mother and visiting her uncle in his new residence. Back at work on Monday.

"Barbara is digging the movies," Jerome tells her, "but she says they're totally vanilla. She says that watching them, you'd think there was no such thing as black people."

"Tell her to put it in her report," Holly says.

"I'll give her *Shaft* when I get a chance. Now I have to get back on the road. The traffic is very heavy, although I don't know where they're all going. I went to a mall and it was half-empty."

"They're visiting relatives, just like you," Jerome says. "Relatives are the one thing Amazon can't deliver."

As she merges back onto I-76, it occurs to Holly that her mother will undoubtedly have Christmas presents for her, and she has nothing for Charlotte. She can already see her mother's martyred look when she turns up emptyhanded.

So she stops at the next shopping center, even though it means she won't be at *casa* Gibney until after dark (she hates driving at night), and buys her mother some slippers and a nice bathrobe. She makes sure to keep the sales slip for when Charlotte tells her that Holly has bought the wrong sizes.

Once she's on the road again, and safe inside her rental car, Holly draws in a deep breath and lets it out in a scream.

It helps.

### 5

Charlotte embraces her daughter on the doorstep, then draws her inside. Holly knows what comes next.

"You've lost weight."

"Actually I'm just the same," Holly says,

and her mother gives her The Look, the one that says *once an anorexic, always an anorexic.*

Dinner is take-out from the Italian place down the road, and as they eat Charlotte talks about how hard things have been without Henry. It's as if her brother has been gone five years instead of five days, and not to a nearby elder care facility but to spend his old age doing stupid stuff far away — running a bicycle shop in Australia or painting sunsets in the tropic isles. She does not ask Holly about her life, her work, or what she was doing in Pittsburgh. By nine o'clock, when Holly can reasonably plead tiredness and go to bed, she's started to feel as if she's growing younger and smaller, diminishing to the sad, lonely, and anorexic girl — yes, it was true, at least during her nightmare freshman year of high school, when she was known as Jibba-Jibba Gibba-Gibba — who lived in this house.

Her bedroom is just the same, with the dark pink walls that always made her think of half-cooked flesh. Her stuffed animals are still on the shelf above her narrow bed, with Mr. Rabbit Trick holding pride of place. Mr. Rabbit Trick's ears are ragged, because she used to nibble on them when she couldn't sleep. The Sylvia Plath poster still hangs on the wall above the desk where Holly wrote her bad poetry and sometimes imagined committing suicide in the manner of her idol. As she undresses, she thinks she might have done it, or at least tried it, if their oven had been gas instead of electric.

It would be easy — much too easy — to think this childhood room has been waiting for her, like a monster in a horror story. She's slept here several times in the sane (*relatively* sane) years of her adulthood, and it has never eaten her. Her mother has never eaten her, either. There *is* a monster, but it's not in this room or in this house. Holly knows she would do well to remember that, and to remember who she is. Not the child who nibbled Mr. Rabbit Trick's ears. Not the adolescent who threw up her breakfast most days before school. She is the woman who, along with Bill and Jerome, saved those children at the Midwest Culture and Arts Complex. She is the woman who survived Brady Hartsfield. The one who faced another monster in a Texas cave. The girl who hid in this room and never wanted to come out is gone.

She kneels, says her nightly prayer, and gets into bed.

## 1

Charlotte, Holly, and Uncle Henry sit in one corner of the Rolling Hills common room, which has been decorated for the season. There are ribbons of tinsel and sweet-smelling swags of fir that almost overcome the more permanent aroma of pee and bleach. There's a tree hung with lights and candy canes. Christmas music spills down from the speakers, tired tunes Holly could live happily without for the rest of her life.

The residents don't seem exactly bursting with holiday spirit; most of them are watching an infomercial for something called the Ab Lounge, featuring a hot chick in an orange leotard. A few others are turned away from the tube, some silent, some holding conversations with each other, some talking to themselves. A wisp of an old lady in a

412

green housecoat is bent over a huge jigsaw puzzle.

"That's Mrs. Hatfield," Uncle Henry says. "I don't recall her first name."

"Mrs. Braddock says you saved her from a bad fall," Holly says.

"No, that was Julia," Uncle Henry says. "Back at the *ohhhh-ld* swimmin hole." He laughs as people do when they are remembering days of yore. Charlotte rolls her eyes. "I was sixteen, and I believe Julia was . . ." He trails off.

"Let me see your arm," Charlotte commands.

Uncle Henry cocks his head. "My arm? Why?"

"Just let me see it." She seizes it and pushes up his shirtsleeve. There's a good-sized but not especially remarkable bruise there. To Holly it looks like a tattoo gone bad.

"If this is how they take care of people, we should sue them instead of paying them," Charlotte says.

"Sue who?" Uncle Henry says. Then, with a laugh: "*Horton Hears a Who!* The kids loved that one!"

Charlotte stands. "I'm going to get a coffee. Maybe one of those little tart things, as well. Holly?"

Holly shakes her head.

"You're not eating again," Charlotte says, and leaves before Holly can reply.

Henry watches her go. "She never lets up, does she?"

This time it's Holly who laughs. She can't help it. "No. She doesn't."

"No, never does. You're not Janey."

"No." And waits.

"You're . . ." She can almost hear rusty gears turning. "Holly."

"That's right." She pats his hand.

"I'd like to go back to my room, but I don't remember where it is."

"I know the way," Holly says. "I'll take you." They walk slowly down the hall together.

"Who was Julia?" Holly asks.

"Pretty as the dawn," Uncle Henry says. Holly decides that's answer enough. Certainly a better line of poetry than she ever wrote.

In his room, she tries to guide him to the chair by the window, but he disengages his hand from hers and goes to the bed, where he sits with his hands clasped between his thighs. He looks like an elderly child. "I think I'll lie down, sweetie. I'm tired. Charlotte makes me tired."

"Sometimes she makes me tired, too," Holly says. In the old days she never would have admitted this to Uncle Henry, who was all too often her mother's co-conspirator, but this is a different man. In some ways a much gentler man. Besides, in five minutes he'll forget she said it. In ten, he'll forget she was here.

414

She bends to kiss his cheek, then stops with her lips just above his skin when he says, "What's wrong? Why are you afraid?"

"I'm not —"

"Oh, you are. You are."

"All right," she says. "I am. I'm afraid." Such a relief to admit it. To say it out loud.

"Your mother . . . my sister . . . it's on the tip of my tongue . . ."

"Charlotte."

"Yes. Charlie's a coward. Always was, even when we were children. Wouldn't go in the water at . . . the place . . . I can't remember. *You* were a coward, but you grew out of it."

She looks at him, amazed. Speechless.

"Grew out of it," he repeats, then pushes off his slippers and swings his feet onto the bed. "I'm going to have a nap, Janey. This isn't such a bad place, but I wish I had that thing . . . that thing you twist . . ." He closes his eyes.

Holly goes to the door with her head down. There are tears on her face. She takes a tissue from her pocket and wipes them away. She doesn't want Charlotte to see them. "I wish you could remember saving that woman from falling down," she says. "The nurses' aide said you moved like lightning."

But Uncle Henry doesn't hear. Uncle Henry has gone to sleep.

## 2

*From Holly Gibney's report to Detective Ralph Anderson:*

I expected to finish this last night in a Pennsylvania motel, but a family matter came up and I drove to my mother's house instead. Being here is difficult. There are memories, many of them not so good. I will stay tonight, though. It's better that I do. Mom is out now, buying things for an early Christmas dinner that will probably not be tasty. Cooking has never been one of her talents.

I hope to finish my business with Chet Ondowsky — the thing that calls itself that, anyway — tomorrow evening. I'm scared, no sense lying about that. He promised to never do anything again like the Macready School, promised it right away, without even thinking it over, and I don't believe it. Bill wouldn't, and I am sure you wouldn't, either. He has a taste for it now. He may also have a taste for being the heroic rescuer, although he must know that calling attention to himself is a bad idea.

I phoned Dan Bell and told him I intended to put an end to Ondowsky. I felt that as ex-police himself he would understand and approve. He did, but told me to be careful. I will try to do that, but I'd be lying if I didn't say that I have a very bad feeling about this. I also called my friend Barbara Robinson and told her I will be staying over at my mother's on Saturday night. I need to make sure that she and her brother Jerome think I won't be in the city tomorrow. No matter what happens to me, I need to know they will not be at risk.

Ondowsky is worried about what I may do with the information I've gotten, but he's also confident. He'll kill me if he can. I know this. What he *doesn't* know is that I have been in these situations before, and won't underestimate him.

Bill Hodges, my friend and sometime partner, remembered me in his will. There was the death benefit from his insurance policy, but there were other keepsakes that mean even more to me. One was his service weapon, a .38 Smith & Wesson Military and Police revolver. Bill told me that most city police now carry the Glock 22, which holds fifteen rounds instead of six, but that he himself was old-school, and proud of it.

I don't like guns — hate them, in fact — but I will use Bill's tomorrow, and I won't hesitate. There will be no discussion. I had one conversation with Ondowsky, and that was enough. I will shoot him in the chest, and not just because the best shot is always the center mass shot, a thing I learned in the shooting class I took two years ago.

The real reason is

[*Pause*]

You remember what happened in the cave,

when I hit the thing we found there in the head? Of course you do. We dream about it, and we'll never forget it. I believe the force — the *physical* force — that animates these things is a kind of alien brain that has replaced the human brain which might have existed before being taken over. I don't know where it originated, and I don't care. Shooting this thing in the chest may not kill it. In fact, Ralph, I'm sort of counting on that. I believe there is another way to get rid of it for good. You see there's been a glitch.

My mother just drove in. I'll try to finish this later today or tomorrow.

## 3

Charlotte won't let Holly help with the cooking; every time her daughter comes into the kitchen, Charlotte shoos her out. It makes for a long day, but the dinner hour finally arrives. Charlotte has put on the green dress she wears every Christmas (proud of the fact that she can still get into it). Her Christmas pin — holly and holly berries — is in its accustomed place over her left breast.

"An authentic Christmas dinner, just like in the old days!" she exclaims as she leads Holly into the dining room by the elbow. Like a prisoner being led into an interrogation room, Holly thinks. "I've made all your favorites!"

They sit across from each other. Charlotte

has lit her aromatherapy candles, which give off a lemongrass scent that makes Holly want to sneeze. They toast each other with thimble glasses of Mogen David wine (an authentic oough if ever there was one) and wish each other a merry Christmas. Then comes a salad already dressed with the snot-like ranch dressing Holly hates (Charlotte thinks she loves it), and the dry-as-papyrus turkey, which can only be swallowed with lots of gravy to grease its passage. The mashed potatoes are lumpy. The overcooked asparagus is as limp and hateful as ever. Only the carrot cake (store-bought) is tasty.

Holly eats everything on her plate and compliments her mother. Who beams.

After the dishes are done (Holly dries, as always; her mother claims she never gets all the "smutch" off the pots), they repair to the living room, where Charlotte hunts out the DVD of *It's a Wonderful Life.* How many Christmas seasons have they watched it? A dozen at least, and probably more. Uncle Henry used to be able to quote every line. Maybe, Holly thinks, he still can. She's googled Alzheimer's and found out there's no way of telling what areas of the mind remain bright as the circuits shut down, one by one.

Before the film begins, Charlotte hands Holly a Santa hat . . . and with great ceremony. "You always wear it when we watch this," she says. "Ever since you were a little girl. It's a *tradition.*"

Holly has been a movie buff all her life and has found things to enjoy even in films the critics have roasted (she believes, for example, that Stallone's *Cobra* is woefully underestimated), but *It's a Wonderful Life* has always made her uneasy. She can relate to George Bailey at the beginning of the film, but by the end he strikes her as someone with a serious bipolar condition who's arrived at the manic part of his cycle. She has even wondered if, after the movie ends, he creeps out of bed and murders his whole family.

They watch the movie, Charlotte in her Christmas dress and Holly in her Santa hat. Holly thinks, I am moving somewhere else now. I feel myself going. It's a sad place, full of shadows. This is the place where you know death is very close.

On the screen, Janie Bailey says, "Please, God, something's the matter with Daddy."

That night when she sleeps, Holly dreams that Chet Ondowsky comes out of the Frederick Building elevator with his jacket torn at the sleeve and the pocket. His hands are smeared with brick dust and blood. His eyes are shimmering, and when his lips spread in a wide grin, squirming red bugs spill from his mouth and stream down his chin.

## 1

Holly sits in four lanes of unmoving south-
bound traffic, still fifty miles from the city,
thinking if this miles-long jam-up doesn't let
go, she might be late to her own funeral
instead of early.

Like many people who struggle with insecurity, she's a compulsive planner-aheader, and
consequently almost always early. She expected to be at the Finders Keepers office by
one o'clock on this Saturday at the latest, but
now even three is starting to look optimistic.
The cars around her (and a big old
dumptruck ahead of her, its dirty butt loom-
ing like a steel cliff) make her feel claustro-
phobic, buried alive (*my own funeral*). If she
had cigarettes in the car, she would be smoking them one after the other. She resorts to
cough drops instead, what she calls her anti-
smoking devices, but she only stashed half a

dozen in her coat pocket and soon they will be gone. That would leave her fingernails, had they not been clipped too short to get a good grip.

I'm late for a very important date.

It wasn't because of the gift-giving, which came after her mother's traditional Christmas breakfast of waffles and bacon (it's not Christmas for almost a week, but Holly was willing to pretend along with Charlotte). Charlotte gave Holly a frilly silk blouse she'll never wear (even if she lives), a pair of medium heels (ditto), and two books: *The Power of Now* and *Anxious for Nothing: Finding Calm in a Chaotic World.* Holly hadn't had the opportunity to wrap her presents, but she did buy a Christmassy gift bag to put them in. Charlotte oohed over the fur-lined slippers and shook her head indulgently over the bathrobe, a $79.50 purchase.

"This is at least two sizes too big. I don't suppose you saved the sales slip, honey."

Holly, who knew damn well she did, said, "I think it's in my coat pocket."

So far so good. But then, out of the blue, Charlotte suggested that they go and see Henry and wish him a merry-merry, since Holly wasn't going to be there on the actual big day. Holly glanced at the clock. Quarter of nine. She'd hoped to be on the road and headed south by nine, but there was such a thing as carrying obsessional behavior too far — why, exactly, did she want to arrive five hours early? Plus, if things went badly with Ondowsky this would be her last chance to see Henry, and she was curious about what he'd said: *Why are you afraid?*

How did he know that? He had certainly never seemed particularly sensitive to the feelings of others before. More the opposite, actually.

So Holly agreed, and they went, and Charlotte insisted on driving, and there was a fender-bender at a four-way stop sign. No airbags deployed, no one was hurt, no police were summoned, but it did involve certain predictable justifications on Charlotte's part. She invoked a mythical patch of ice, ignoring the fact that she only slowed rather than stopped at the four-way, as she always did; all of her driving life, Charlotte Gibney had assumed she had the right-of-way.

The man in the other vehicle was nice enough about it, nodding and agreeing with everything Charlotte said, but it involved an exchange of insurance cards, and by the time they were on their way again (Holly was quite sure the man whose fender they'd bumped dropped her a wink before getting back into his own vehicle), it was ten o'clock, and the visit turned out to be a total bust, anyway. Henry had no idea who either of them were. He said he had to get dressed for work and told them to stop bothering him. When Holly kissed him goodbye, he looked at her suspiciously and asked if that was a Jehovah's Witnesses thing.

"You drive back," Charlotte said when they were outside. "I'm far too upset."

Holly was more than happy to do that.

She had left her traveling bag in the front hall. As she slung it over her shoulder and turned to her mother for their usual parting salute — two dry pecks on the cheek — Charlotte flung her arms around the daughter she had denigrated and belittled her whole life (not always unknowingly) and burst into tears.

"Don't go. Please stay another day. If you can't stay until Christmas, at least stay through the weekend. I can't stand to be on my own. Not yet. Maybe after Christmas, but not yet."

Her mother was clutching her like a drowning woman and Holly had to suppress a panicky urge not just to push her away but to actually fight her off. She endured the hug as long as she could, then wriggled free.

"I have to go, Mom. I have an appointment."

"A date, you mean?" Charlotte smiled. Not a nice one. There were too many teeth in it. Holly had thought she was done being shocked by her mother, but it seemed that wasn't the case. "Really? *You?*"

Remember this could be the last time you see her, Holly thought. If it is, you don't want to leave with angry words. You can be angry at her again if you live through this.

"It's something else," she said. "But let's have some tea. I have time for that."

So they had tea and the date-filled cookies Holly had always hated (they tasted *dark,* somehow), and it was almost eleven before she was finally able to escape her mother's house, where the scent of the lemongrass candles still lingered. She kissed Charlotte on the cheek as they stood on the stoop. "I love you, Mom."

"I love you, too."

Holly got as far as the door of her rental car, was actually touching the handle, when Charlotte called to her. Holly turned, almost expecting her mother to come leaping down the steps, arms spread, fingers hooked into claws, screaming *Stay! You must stay! I command it!*

But Charlotte was still on the stoop with her arms wrapped around her middle. Shivering. She looked old and unhappy. "I made a mistake about the bathrobe," she said. "It *is* my size. I must have read the tag wrong."

Holly smiled. "That's good, Mom. I'm glad."

She backed down the driveway, checked for traffic, and turned toward the turnpike. Ten past eleven. Plenty of time.

That's what she thought then.

## 2

Her inability to discover the cause of the holdup only adds to Holly's anxiety. The local AM and FM stations tell her nothing, including the one that's supposed to have turnpike traffic info. Her Waze app, usually so reliable, is totally useless. The screen shows a smiling little man digging a hole with a shovel above the message WE'RE CURRENTLY UNDER CONSTRUCTION BUT WE'LL BE BACK SOON!

Frack.

If she can make it another ten miles, she can get off at Exit 56 and take Highway 73, but right now Highway 73 might as well be on Jupiter. She feels around in her coat pocket, finds the last cough drop, and unwraps it while staring at the rear end of the dumptruck where a bumper sticker reads HOW'S MY DRIVING?

All these people should be at malls, Holly thinks. They should be shopping at malls and downtown small businesses and helping the local economy instead of giving their money to Amazon and UPS and Federal Express. All of you should get off this fracking highway so people with really important business could . . .

The traffic starts to move. Holly gives a cry

426

of triumph that's hardly out of her mouth before the dumptruck stops again. On her left, a man is chatting on his phone. On her right, a woman is freshening her lipstick. Her rental car's digital clock tells her she now cannot expect to arrive at the Frederick Building until four o'clock. Four at the earliest.

That still would leave me two hours, Holly thinks. Please God, please let me be there in time to get ready for him. For *it*. For the monster.

## 3

Barbara Robinson puts aside her copy of the college catalogue she has been perusing, turns on her phone, and goes to the Web-Watcher app Justin Freilander has put on her phone.

"You know that tracking someone without their permission isn't exactly kosher, right?" Justin had said. "I'm not sure it's even, like, totally legal."

"I just want to make sure my friend is okay," Barbara had said, and gave him a radiant smile that melted any reservations he might have had.

God knows Barbara has her own reservations; just looking at the little green dot on the map makes her feel guilty, especially since Jerome dumped his own tracker. But what Jerome doesn't know (and Barbara won't tell

427

him) is that after Portland, Holly went to Pittsburgh. That, combined with the web searches Barbara looked at on Holly's home computer, makes her think Holly's interested in the Macready School bombing after all, and that interest seems to focus on either Charles "Chet" Ondowsky, the reporter from WPEN who was first on the scene, or Fred Finkel, his cameraman. Barbara thinks it's almost certainly Ondowsky Holly is interested in, because there are more searches for him. Holly has even jotted his name on the pad beside her computer . . . with two question marks after it.

Barbara doesn't want to think her friend is having some kind of mindfuck, maybe even a nervous breakdown, nor does she want to believe Holly might have somehow stumbled on the trail of the school bomber . . . but she knows that's not beyond the realm, as they say. Holly is insecure, Holly spends *way* too much time doubting herself, but Holly is also smart. Is it possible that Ondowsky and Finkel (a pairing that inevitably reminds her of Simon & Garfunkel) somehow stumbled across a clue to the bomber without knowing it, or even realizing it?

This idea makes Barbara think of a film she watched with Holly. *Blow-Up,* it was called. In it, a photographer taking pictures of lovers in a park accidentally photographs a man hiding in the bushes with a pistol. What if something like that happened at the Macready School? What if the bomber had returned to the scene of the crime to gloat over his handiwork, and the TV guys had filmed him as he watched (or even pretended to help)? What if Holly had somehow realized that? Barbara knew and accepted that the idea was farfetched, but didn't life sometimes imitate art? Maybe Holly had gone to Pittsburgh to interview Ondowsky and Finkel. That would be safe enough, Barbara supposes, but what if the bomber was still in the area, and Holly went after him?

What if the *bomber* went after *her*?

All of this is probably bullshit, but Barbara is nevertheless relieved when the WebWatcher app tracks Holly leaving Pittsburgh and driving to her mother's house. She almost deleted the tracker then, certainly doing so would have eased her conscience, but then Holly had called her yesterday, apparently for no reason other than to tell her she'd be staying over at her mom's on Saturday night. And then, at the end of the call, Holly had said, "I love you."

Well, of course she does, and Barbara loves her, but that was understood, not the kind of thing you had to say out loud. Except maybe on special occasions. Like if you'd had a fight with your friend and were making up. Or if you were going on a long trip. Or going off to fight in a war. Barbara is sure it was the last thing men and women said to their parents or partners before leaving to do that.

And there had been a certain *tone* to the way she'd said it that Barbara didn't like. Sad, almost. And now the green dot tells Barbara that Holly isn't staying the night at her mother's after all. She's apparently headed back to the city. Change of plans? Maybe a fight with her mother?

Or had she flat-out lied?

Barbara glances at her desk and sees the DVDs she's borrowed from Holly for her report: *The Maltese Falcon, The Big Sleep,* and *Harper.* She thinks they'll be the perfect excuse to talk to Holly when Holly gets back. She'll affect surprise to find Holly at home, then try to find out what was so important in Portland and Pittsburgh. She may even confess to the tracker — that will depend on how things go.

She checks Holly's location on her phone again. Still the turnpike. Barbara guesses that the traffic might be jammed up by construction or an accident. She looks at her watch, then back at the green dot. She thinks that Holly will be lucky to get back much before five o'clock.

And I'll be at her apartment by five-thirty, Barbara thinks. I hope nothing's wrong with her . . . but I think maybe there is.

# 4

The traffic crawls . . . then stops.

Crawls . . . and stops.

Stops.

I'm going to lose my mind, Holly thinks. It's just going to snap while I sit here looking at the back of that dumptruck. I'll probably hear the sound when it goes. Like a breaking branch.

The light has begun to drain out of this December day, just two calendar squares away from the shortest day of the year. The dashboard clock tells her that the earliest she can now hope to arrive at the Frederick Building is five o'clock, and that will only happen if the traffic starts to move again soon . . . and if she doesn't run out of gas. She's down to just over a quarter of a tank.

I could miss him, she thinks. He could show up, and call me to text him the door code, and get no answer. He'll think I lost my nerve and chickened out.

The idea that coincidence, or some malign force (Jerome's bird, all frowsy and frosty gray), may have decreed that her second face to face with Ondowsky should not happen brings her no relief. Because she's not just on his personal hit parade now, she's number one with a bullet. Facing him on her home ground, and with a plan, was to be her advantage. If she loses it, he'll try to blind-side her. And he could succeed.

Once she reaches for her phone to call Pete, to tell him that a dangerous man is going to show up at the side door of their building, and he should approach with caution, but Ondowsky would talk his way out of it. Easily. He talks for a living. Even if he didn't, Pete is getting on in years and at least twenty pounds over what he weighed when he retired from the police. Pete is slow. The thing pretending to be a TV reporter is fast. She will not risk Pete. She's the one who let the genie out of the bottle.

Ahead of her, the dumptruck's taillights go out. It rolls ahead fifty feet or so and stops again. This time, however, the stop is briefer and the next forward advance is longer. Is it possible that the jam is breaking? She hardly dares to believe it, but she has Holly hope.

Which turns out to be justified. In five minutes she's doing forty. After seven, she's up to fifty-five. After eleven, Holly puts her foot down and takes possession of the passing lane. When she shoots by the three-car pileup that caused the jam, she barely gives the wrecks that have been pulled over to the median strip a glance.

If she can keep her speed to seventy until she leaves the turnpike at midtown, and if she catches most of the traffic lights, she estimates she can be at her building by five-twenty.

Holly actually arrives in the vicinity of her building at five minutes past five. Unlike the weirdly underpopulated Monroeville Mall, downtown is busy-busy-busy. This is both good and bad. Her chances of spotting On-dowsky in the bustle of bundled-up shoppers on Buell Street are small, but his chances of grabbing her (if he means to do that, and she wouldn't put it past him) are equally small. It's what Bill would call a push.

As if to make up for her bad luck on the turnpike, she spots a car pulling out of a parking space almost directly across from the Frederick Building. She waits until it's gone, then backs carefully into the space, trying to ignore the poophead behind her laying on his horn. Under less fraught circumstances that constant blare might have induced her to let the space go, but she doesn't see another space on the whole block. That would leave her with the parking garage, probably on one of the upper levels, and Holly has seen too many movies where bad things happen to women in parking garages. Especially after dark, and it's dark now.

The horn-blower rolls past as soon as the front end of Holly's rental car has cleared enough space, but the poophead — not a he but a she — slows long enough to wish Holly a little Christmas cheer with her middle fin-ger.

There's a break in the traffic when Holly exits the car. She could jaywalk to the other side of the street — jay-*trot,* anyway — but she joins a crowd of shoppers waiting for the walk light at the next corner instead. Safety in numbers. She has her key to the building's front door in her hand. She has no intention of going around to the side entrance. It's in a service alley where she'd be an easy target.

As she slips the key into the lock, a man with a muffler over his lower face and a Russian hat jammed down to his eyebrows passes her almost close enough to jostle. Ondowsky? No. At least *probably* no. How can she be sure?

The shoebox of a lobby is empty. The lights are low. Shadows stretch everywhere. She hurries to the elevator. This is one of downtown's older buildings, only eight floors, Midwest to the core, and there's only the one for passengers. Roomy and supposedly state-of-the-art, but one is one. Tenants have been known to grumble about this, and those in a hurry often take the stairs, especially those with offices on the lower floors. Holly knows there's also a freight elevator, but that one will be locked off for the weekend. She pushes the call button, suddenly sure the elevator will once more be out of order and her plan will collapse. But the doors open immediately and a female robo-voice welcomes her in. "Hello. Welcome to the Frederick Building." With the lobby empty, it sounds to Holly like a disembodied voice in a horror movie.

The doors close and she pushes for 5. There's a TV screen that shows news items and ads during the week, but now it's off. No Christmas music either, thank heaven.

"Going up," the robo-voice says.

He'll be waiting for me, she thinks. He's gotten in somehow, he'll be waiting for me when the elevator doors open, and I'll have nowhere to run.

But the doors open on an empty hall. She walks past the mail-drop (as old-fashioned as the talking elevator is newfangled), past the women's and men's, and stops at a door marked STAIRS. Everybody complains about Al Jordan, and with cause; the building's superintendent is both incompetent and lazy. But he must be connected somehow, because he keeps his job in spite of the way the trash piles up in the basement, the broken side entrance camera, and the slow — almost whimsical — delivery of packages. Then there's the matter of the fancy Japanese elevator, which pissed *everybody* off.

This afternoon Holly is actively hoping for more of Al's carelessness, so she doesn't have to waste time getting a chair to stand on from the office. She opens the door to the stairs, and she's in luck. Clustered there on the landing — and blocking the way to the sixth floor, probably a fire code violation — is a cache of cleaning supplies which include a mop leaning against the stair rail and a squeegee bucket half-filled with wash water.

Holly considers dumping the bucket's murky contents down the stairs — it would serve Al right — but in the end she can't bring herself to do it. She pushes it into the women's, removes the squeegee attachment, and dumps the filthy water down one of the sinks. She then rolls it to the elevator with her satchel of a purse hanging awkwardly from the crook of her arm. She pushes the call button. The doors open and the robo-voice tells her (just in case she's forgotten), "This is five." Holly remembers the day when Pete came puffing into the office and said, "Can you program that thing to say 'Tell Al to fix me, then kill him'?"

Holly turns the bucket over. If she keeps her feet together (and is careful), there's just room for her to stand on it between the rollers. From her purse she takes out a Scotch tape dispenser and a small package wrapped in brown paper. Standing on tiptoe, stretching until the bottom of her shirt pulls free of her pants, she tapes the package in the far left corner of the elevator car's ceiling. It's thus high above eye level, where (according to the late Bill Hodges) people tend not to look. Ondowsky better not. If he does, she's hung.

She takes her phone out of her pocket, holds it up, and snaps a picture of the package. If things go as she hopes, Ondowsky will never see this photo, which isn't much of an insurance policy in any case.

The elevator's doors have closed again. Holly pushes the open button and rolls the mop bucket back up the hall, returning it to where she found it on the stair landing. Then she goes past Brilliancy Beauty Products (where no one seems to work except for one middle-aged man who reminds Holly of an old cartoon character named Droopy Dog) to Finders Keepers, at the end. She unlocks the door and lets herself in with a sigh of relief. She looks at her watch. Nearly five-thirty. Time is now very tight, indeed.

She goes to the office safe and runs the combination. She takes out the late Bill Hodges's Smith & Wesson revolver. Although she knows it's loaded — an unloaded handgun is useless even as a club, another of her mentor's dictums — she rolls the chamber to make sure, then snaps it closed.

Center mass, she thinks. As soon as he comes out of the elevator. Don't worry about the box with the money; if it's cardboard, the slug will go right through, even if he's holding it in front of his chest. If it's steel, I'll have to go for a headshot. The range will be short. It could be messy, but —

She surprises herself with a little laugh.

But Al has left cleaning supplies.

Holly looks at her watch. 5:34. That leaves her twenty-six minutes before Ondowsky shows up, assuming he's on time. She still has things to do. All are important. Deciding which is the *most* important is a no-brainer, because if she doesn't survive this, someone has to know about the thing that bombed the Macready School in order to eat the pain of the survivors and the bereaved, and there is one person who will believe her.

She turns on her phone, opens the recording app, and begins to speak.

## 6

The Robinsons gave their daughter a nifty little Ford Focus for her eighteenth birthday, and as Holly is parking downtown on Buell Street, Barbara is three blocks from Holly's apartment building, stopped at a red light. She takes the opportunity to glance at the WebWatcher app on her phone and murmurs "Shit." Holly hasn't gone home. She's at the office, although Barbara can't understand why she'd go there on a Saturday evening this close to Christmas.

Holly's building is straight ahead, but when the light turns green, Barbara turns right, toward downtown. It won't take her long to get there. The front door of the Frederick Building will be locked, but she knows the code for the side door in the service alley.

She's been at Finders Keepers with her brother many times, and sometimes they go in that way.

I'll just surprise her, Barbara thinks. Take her out for coffee and find out what the hell's going on. Maybe we can even grab a quick bite and hit a movie.

The thought makes her smile.

## 7

*From Holly Gibney's report to Detective Ralph Anderson:*

I don't know if I've told you everything, Ralph, and I don't have time to go back and check, but you know the most important thing: I've stumbled across another outsider, not the same as the one we dealt with in Texas, but related. A new and improved model, let's say.

I'm in the little reception area of Finders, waiting for him. My plan is to shoot him as soon as he steps out of the elevator with the blackmail money, and I think that's how this is going to go. I think he has come to pay me off rather than kill me, because I think I convinced him that I only want money, along with his promise never to commit another mass killing. Which he probably doesn't mean to keep.

I've tried to think as logically about this as I can, because my life depends on it. If I were him, I'd pay off once, then see what happens.

439

Would I plan to leave my job at the Pittsburgh station afterwards? I might, but I might stay. To test the blackmailer's good faith. If the woman were to come back, try double-dipping, *then* I'd kill her and disappear. Wait a year or two, then resume my old pattern. Maybe in San Francisco, maybe in Seattle, maybe in Honolulu. Start working at a local indie, then move up. He'll get new ID and new references. God knows how they can stand up in this age of computers and social media, Ralph, but somehow they do. Or have so far.

Would he worry about me passing on what I know to someone else? Maybe to his TV station? No, because once I blackmail him, I become complicit in his crime. What I'm counting on most is his confidence. His *arrogance.* Why wouldn't he be confident and arrogant? He's been getting away with this for a long, long time.

But my friend Bill taught me to always have a backup plan. "Belt and suspenders, Holly," he'd say. "Belt and suspenders."

*If* he suspects I mean to kill him instead of blackmail him out of three hundred thousand dollars, he'll try to take precautions. What precautions? I don't know. Surely he must know I have a firearm, but I don't think he can get one in because he has to assume the metal detector would alert me. He may use the stairs, and that could be a problem even

440

if I hear him coming. If that happens, I'll have to play it by ear.

[*Pause*]

Bill's .38 is my belt; the package I taped to the elevator ceiling is my suspenders. My insurance. I have a picture of it. He'll want it, but there's nothing in that package but a tube of lipstick.

I have done the best I can, Ralph, but it may not be enough. In spite of all my planning there's a chance I won't come out of this alive. If that's the case, I need you to know how much your friendship has meant to me. If I do die, and you choose to continue what I've started, please be careful. You have a wife and son.

## 8

It's 5:43. Time is racing, racing.

That fracking traffic jam! If he comes early, before I'm ready . . .

If that happens I'll make something up to keep him downstairs for a few minutes. I don't know what, but I'll think of something.

Holly powers up the reception area's desktop. She has her own office, but this is the computer she prefers, because she likes to be right out front instead of buried in the back. It's also the computer she and Jerome used when they got tired of listening to Pete complain about having to climb to the fifth floor. What they did certainly wasn't legal, but it solved the problem and that information should still be in this computer's memory. It better be. If it's not, she's fracked. She may be fracked anyway, if Ondowsky uses the stairs. If he does that, she'll be ninety per cent sure that he's come to kill her rather than pay her.

The desktop is a state-of-the-art iMac Pro, very fast, but today it seems to take forever booting up. While she waits, she uses her phone to email the sound file containing her report to herself. She takes a flash drive from her purse — this is the one containing the various photos Dan Bell has amassed, plus Brad Bell's spectrograms — and as she plugs it into the back of the computer, she thinks she hears the elevator moving. Which is impossible, unless someone else is in the building.

Someone like Ondowsky.

Holly flies to the office door with the gun in her hand. She throws the door open, sticks her head out. Hears nothing. The elevator is quiet. Still on five. It was her imagination.

She leaves the door open and hurries back to the desk to finish up. She has fifteen minutes. That should be enough, assuming she can remove the fix Jerome figured out and reinstate the computer glitch that had everyone climbing the stairs.

I'll know, she thinks. If the elevator goes down after Ondowsky gets off, I'm okay.

Golden. If it doesn't . . .

But it's no good thinking about that.

**9**

The stores are open late because of the Christmas season — the sacred time when we honor the birth of Jesus by maxing out our credit cards, Barbara thinks — and she sees at once that she won't find parking on Buell. She takes a ticket at the entrance to the parking garage across from the Frederick Building and finally finds a space on the fourth level, just below the roof. She hurries to the elevator, looking around constantly, one hand in her purse. Barbara has also seen too many movies where bad things happen to women in parking garages.

When she arrives safely on the street, she hurries to the corner just in time to catch the walk light. On the other side she looks up and sees a light on the fifth floor of the Frederick Building. At the next corner, she turns right. A little way down the block is an alley marked with signs reading NO THROUGH TRAFFIC and SERVICE VEHICLES ONLY. Barbara turns down it and stops at the side entrance. She's bending to tap in the door code when a hand grips her shoulder.

**10**

Holly opens the email she's sent herself and moves the attachment to the flash drive. She hesitates for a moment, looking at the blank title strip below the drive's icon. Then she types IF IT BLEEDS. A good enough name. It's the story of that thing's fracking life, after all, she thinks, it's what keeps it alive. Blood and pain.

She ejects the drive. The desk in the reception area is where they do all their mailing, and there are plenty of envelopes, all different sizes. She takes a small padded one, slips the flash drive into it, seals it, then has a moment of panic when she remembers that Ralph's mail is going to some neighbor's house. She knows Ralph's address by heart and could send it there, but what if some mailbox pirate grabbed it? The thought is nightmarish. What was the neighbor's name? Colson? Carver? Coates? None of those are right.

Time, racing away from her.

She's about to address the envelope to *Ralph Anderson's Next Door Neighbor* when the name comes to her: Conrad. She slaps on stamps willy-nilly and jots quickly on the front of the envelope:

Detective Ralph Anderson
619 Acacia Street
Flint City, Oklahoma 74012

Below this she adds **C/O CONRADS (Next Door)** and **DO NOT FORWARD**

**HOLD FOR ARRIVAL**. It will have to do. She takes the envelope, runs flat-out to the mail-drop near the elevator, and tosses it in. She knows that Al is as lazy about collecting the mail as he is about everything else, and it may lie at the bottom of the chute (which, to be fair, few people use in this day and age) for a week, or — given the holiday season — even longer. But there is really no hurry. Eventually it will go.

Just to be sure she was imagining things, she punches the elevator call button. The doors open; the car is there and the car is empty. So it really was her imagination. She runs back to Finders Keepers, not exactly gasping but breathing hard. Some of it's the sprint; most of it is stress.

Now the last thing. She goes to the Mac's finder and types in what Jerome titled their fix: EREBETA. It's the brand name of their troublesome elevator; it's also the Japanese word for elevator . . . or so Jerome claimed.

Al Jordan adamantly refused to call a local company to fix the glitch, insisting that it had to be done by an accredited Erebeta repairperson. He invoked dire possibilities should anything else be done and there was an accident: criminal liability, million-dollar lawsuits. Better to just close the elevator's eight floor-stops off with yellow OUT OF ORDER tape and wait for the proper repairperson to show up. It won't be long, Al assured his irate tenants. A week at most. Sorry for the inconvenience. But the weeks had stretched into almost a month.

"No inconvenience for him," Pete grumbled. "His office is in the basement, where he sits on his ass all day watching TV and eating doughnuts."

Finally Jerome stepped in, telling Holly something that she — a computer whiz herself — already knew: if you could use the Internet, you could find a fix for every glitch. Which they had done, by mating this very computer to the much simpler one controlling the elevator.

"Here it is," Jerome had said, pointing at the screen. He and Holly had been by themselves, Pete out making the rounds of bailbondsmen, drumming up trade. "Do you see what's happening?"

She did. The elevator's computer had stopped "seeing" the floor stops. All it saw were its terminal points.

Now all she has to do is pull off the Band-Aid they put on the elevator's program. And hope. Because there will be no time to test it. Time is too tight. It's four minutes of six. She calls up the floor menu, which shows a real-time representation of the elevator shaft. The stops are marked, B through 8. The car is stopped on 5. At the top of the screen, in green, is the word READY.

Not yet you're not, Holly thinks, but you

will be. I hope.

Her phone rings two minutes later, just as she's finishing.

## 11

Barbara utters a small scream and whirls around, back against the side entrance, looking up at the dark shape of the man who has grabbed her.

"Jerome!" She pats her hand against her chest. "You scared the bejesus out of me! What are you doing here?"

"I was just about to ask you the same question," Jerome says. "As a rule, girls and dark alleys don't mix."

"You lied about taking the tracker off your phone, didn't you?"

"Well, yes," Jerome admits. "But since you obviously put on one of your own, I don't think you can exactly claim the moral high grou—"

That's when another dark shape looms up behind Jerome . . . only it's not entirely dark. The shape's eyes are glaring like the eyes of a cat caught in a flashlight beam. Before Barbara can shout at Jerome to look out, the shape swings something at her brother's head. There's a terrible dull crunch and Jerome collapses to the pavement.

The shape grabs her, shoves her against the door, and pins her there with one gloved hand wrapped around her neck. From the other he drops a chunk of broken brick. Or maybe it's concrete. All Barbara knows for sure is that it's dripping with her brother's blood.

He bends toward her close enough for her to see a round, unremarkable face below one of those furry Russian hats. That weird glare is gone from his eyes. "Don't scream, girlfriend. You don't want to do that."

"You killed him!" It comes out in a wheeze. He hasn't choked off all her air, at least not yet, but he's cut off most of it. "You killed my brother!"

"No, he's still alive," the man says. He smiles, showing two rows of teeth that are orthodontic perfection. "I'd know if he was dead, believe me. But I can *make* him dead. Scream, try to get away — annoy me, in other words — and I'll hit him until his brains spurt like Old Faithful. Are you going to scream?"

Barbara shakes her head.

The man's smile widens into a grin. "That's a good girlfriend, girlfriend. You're afraid, aren't you? I like that." He breathes deeply, as if inhaling her terror. "You should be afraid. You don't belong here, but on the whole I'm glad you came."

He leans closer. She can smell his cologne and feel the meat of his lips as he whispers in her ear.

*"You're tasty."*

## 12

Holly reaches for her phone with her eyes fixed on the computer. The elevator's floor menu is still on the screen, but below the diagram of the shaft there's now a choice box offering EXECUTE or CANCEL. She only wishes she could be completely sure that selecting EXECUTE will cause something to happen. And that it will be the right something.

She picks up the phone, ready to text Ondowsky the code for the side door, and freezes. It's not ONDOWSKY in the window of her phone, and it's not UNKNOWN CALLER. It's the smiling face of her young friend Barbara Robinson.

Oh dear God no, Holly thinks. Please God no.

"Barbara?"

"There's a man, Holly!" Barbara is crying, barely understandable. "He hit Jerome with something and knocked him out, I think it was a brick and he's bleeding so *bad* —"

Then she's gone, and the thing masquerading as Ondowsky is there, speaking to Holly in his trained TV voice. "Hi, Holly, Chet here."

Holly freezes. Not for long in the outside world, probably less than five seconds, but inside her head it feels much longer. This is her fault. She tried to keep her friends away, but they came anyway. They came because they were worried about her, and that *makes* it her fault.

"Holly? Are you still there?" There's a smile in his voice. Because things have broken his way, and he's enjoying himself. "This changes things, wouldn't you say?"

Can't panic, Holly thinks. I can and will give up my life if it will save theirs, but I can't panic. If I do that we're *all* going to die.

"Have they?" she says. "I still have what you want. Hurt that girl, do anything more to her brother, and I'll blow up your life. I won't stop."

"Have you also got a gun?" He doesn't give her a chance to answer. "Of course you do. *I* don't, but I did bring a ceramic knife. Very sharp. Remember I'll have the girl when I come to our little *tête-à-tête.* I won't kill her if I see you with a gun in your hand, that would be the waste of a good hostage, but I'll disfigure her while you watch."

"There won't be a gun."

"I think I'll trust you on that." Still amused. Relaxed and confident. "But I don't think we'll be exchanging money for the flash drive, after all. Instead of money, you can have my little girlfriend. How does that sound?"

Like a lie, Holly thinks.

"It sounds like a deal. Let me talk to Barbara again."

"No."

"Then I won't give you the code."

He actually laughs. "She knows it, she was getting ready to tap it in when her brother accosted her. I was watching from behind the Dumpster. I'm sure I could persuade her to tell me. Do you want me to persuade her? Like this?"

Barbara screams, a sound that makes Holly cover her mouth. Her fault, her fault, all her fault.

"Stop. Stop hurting her. I just want to know if Jerome is still alive."

"For the time being. He's making weird little snuffling sounds. May have a brain injury. I hit him hard, felt I had to. He's a big one."

He's trying to freak me out. He doesn't want me thinking, just reacting.

"He's bleeding quite a bit," Ondowsky continues. "Head-wounds, you know. But it's pretty cold, and I'm sure that will aid the clotting. Speaking of cold, let's stop fucking around. Give me the code unless you want me to twist her arm again, and this time I'll dislocate it."

"Four-seven-five-three," Holly says. What choice?

## 13

The man does indeed have a knife: black handle, long white blade. Holding Barbara by one arm — the one he hurt — he points the tip of the knife at the lock pad. "Do the

451

honors, girlfriend."

Barbara pushes the numbers, waits for the green light, then opens the door. "Can we put Jerome inside? I can drag him."

"I'm sure you could," the man says, "but no. He looks like a chill dude. We'll just let him chill a little more."

"He'll freeze to death!"

"Girlfriend, you'll *bleed* to death if you don't get a move on."

No, you won't kill me, Barbara thinks. At least not until you get what you want.

But he could hurt her. Put out one of her eyes. Flay her cheek open. Cut off an ear. His knife looks very sharp.

She goes in.

**14**

Holly stands in the open door of the Finders Keepers office, looking down the hall. Her muscles thrum with adrenaline; her mouth is as dry as a desert stone. She holds her position when she hears the elevator start down. She can't hit execute on the program she has running until it comes back up.

I have to save Barbara, she thinks. Jerome too, unless he's beyond help.

She hears the elevator stop on the ground floor. Then, after an eternity, it starts up again. Holly steps backward, her eyes not leaving the closed elevator doors at the end of the hall. Her phone is lying beside the computer's mousepad. She slips it into the left front pocket of her pants, then looks down just long enough to position the cursor over EXECUTE.

She hears a scream. It's muffled by the rising elevator car, but it's a girl's scream. It's Barbara.

My fault.

All my fault.

## 15

The man who hurt Jerome takes Barbara by the arm, like a guy escorting his best girl into the ballroom where the big dance is going on. He hasn't relieved her of her purse (or ignored it, more likely), and the metal detector gives a feeble beep when they pass through, probably from her phone. Her captor ignores it. They pass the stairwell that until lately was used every day by the Frederick Building's resentful residents, then enter the lobby. Outside the door, in another world, Christmas shoppers are passing to and fro with their bags and packages.

I was out there, Barbara marvels. Just five minutes ago, when things were still all right. When I still foolishly believed I had a life ahead of me.

The man pushes the elevator button. They hear the sound of the descending car.

"How much money were you supposed to pay her?" Barbara asks. Beneath her fear, she feels a dull disappointment that Holly would deal with this man at all.

"Doesn't matter now," he says, "because I've got you. Girlfriend."

The elevator stops. The doors open. The robo-voice welcomes them to the Frederick Building. "Going up," it says. The doors shut. The car begins to rise.

The man lets go of Barbara, takes off his furry Russian hat, drops it between his shoes, and lifts his hands in a magician's flourish. "Watch this. I think you'll like it, and our Ms. Gibney certainly deserves to see it, since it's what made all this trouble in the first place."

What happens next is horrible beyond Barbara's previous understanding of the word. In a movie it could be dismissed as no more than a cool special effect, but this is real life. A ripple runs up the round middle-aged face. It starts at the chin and rises not past the mouth but *through* it. The nose wavers, the cheeks stretch, the eyes shimmer, the forehead contracts. Then, suddenly, the whole head turns to semi-transparent jelly. It quivers and shimmies and sags and pulses. Inside it are confused tangles of writhing red stuff. Not blood; that red stuff is full of flocking black specks. Barbara shrieks and falls back against the wall of the elevator. Her legs fail her. Her purse slips off her shoulder and thumps to the floor. She slides down the wall of the elevator with her eyes bulging from their sockets. Her bowels and bladder let go.

Then the jelly head solidifies, but the face that appears is entirely different from that of the man who knocked Jerome unconscious and forcibly escorted her to the elevator. It's narrower, and the skin is two or three shades darker. The eyes are tilted at the corners instead of round. The nose is sharper and longer than the blunt beak of the man who hauled her into the elevator. The mouth is thinner.

This man looks ten years younger than the one who grabbed her.

"Good trick, wouldn't you say?" Even his voice is different.

*What are you?* Barbara tries to say this, but no words will come out of her mouth.

He bends down and gently places the strap of her purse back on her shoulder. Barbara shrinks from the touch of his fingers but can't entirely avoid them. "Don't want to lose your wallet and credit cards, do you? They'll help the police to identify you, in case . . . well, in case." He makes a burlesque of holding his new nose. "Dear me, did we have a little accident? Oh well, you know what they say, shit happens." He titters.

The elevator stops. The doors slide open on the fifth-floor hall.

## 16

When the elevator stops, Holly takes one more quick glance at the screen of the computer, then clicks the mouse. She doesn't wait to see if the floor-stops, B through 8, gray out as they were when she and Jerome did their repair-job, following the steps Jerome found at a webpage titled *Erebeta Bugs and How to Fix Them.* She doesn't need to. She'll know one way or the other.

She walks back to the office door and looks down the twenty-five yards of hallway to the elevator. Ondowsky has Barbara by the arm . . . only when he looks up, she sees it's no longer him. Now it's George, minus the mustache and the delivery man's brown uniform.

"Come on, girlfriend," he says. "Move those feet."

Barbara comes stumbling out. Her eyes are huge and blank and wet with tears. Her beautiful dark skin has gone the color of clay. Spittle runs from one side of her mouth. She looks almost catatonic, and Holly knows why: she saw Ondowsky change.

This terrorized girl is her responsibility, but Holly can't think about that now. She has to stay in the moment, has to listen, has to have Holly hope . . . although that has never seemed so distant.

The elevator doors slide closed. With Bill's gun removed from the equation, any chance

Holly has depends on what happens next. At first there's nothing and her heart turns to lead. Then, instead of staying put, as Erebeta elevators are programmed to do until they are called, she hears it descending. Thank God, she hears it descending.

"Here's my little girlfriend," George the killer of children says. "She's kind of a bad girlfriend. I believe she's gone pee-pee and poo-poo in her pants. Come closer, Holly. You'll smell it for yourself."

Holly doesn't move from the doorway. "I'm curious," she says. "Did you actually bring any money?"

George grins, showing teeth that are a lot less TV-ready than those of his alter-ego. "Actually, no. There's a cardboard box behind the Dumpster where I hid when I saw this one and her brother coming, but there's nothing in there but catalogues. You know, the kind that come addressed to Current Resident."

"So you never intended to pay me," Holly says. She takes a dozen steps down the hall, stopping when they're fifteen yards apart. If this was football, she'd be in the red zone. "Did you?"

"No more than you ever intended to give me that flash drive and let me go," he says. "I can't read minds, but I have a long history of reading body language. And faces. Yours is completely open, although I'm sure you think otherwise. Now pull your shirt out of your pants and lift it. Not all the way, those bumps on your chest hold no interest for me, just enough so I can make sure you're not armed."

Holly lifts her shirt and does a complete turn without being asked.

"Now pull up your pantslegs."

She does this, too.

"No throwdown," George says. "Good." He cocks his head, looking at her the way an art critic might study a painting. "Gosh, you're an ugly little thing, aren't you?"

Holly makes no reply.

"Have you ever in your life had so much as a single date?"

Holly makes no reply.

"Ugly little waif, no more than thirty-five but already going gray. Not bothering to cover it up, either, and if that isn't waving the white flag, I don't know what is. Do you send your dildo a card on Valentine's Day?"

Holly makes no reply.

"My guess is you compensate for your looks and insecurity with a sense of . . ." He breaks off and looks down at Barbara. "Jesus Christ, you're heavy! And you *stink*!"

He lets go of Barbara's arm and she collapses in front of the women's room door with her hands spread, her bottom raised, and her forehead on the tiles. She looks like a Muslim woman about to begin Isha'a. Her sobs are low, but Holly can hear them. Oh yes, she can hear them very well.

George's face changes. Not back to Chet Ondowsky's, but into a feral sneer that shows Holly the real creature inside him. Ondowsky has a pig face, George has a fox face, but this is the face of a jackal. Of a hyena. Of Jerome's gray bird. He kicks Barbara's bluejeaned butt. She wails in pain and surprise.

"Get in there!" he shouts. "Get in there, clean yourself up, let the grownups finish their business!"

Holly wants to run those last fifteen yards, shouting at him to stop kicking her, but of course that's what he wants. And if he really means to stash his hostage in the women's bathroom, it may give her the chance she needs. At the very least it opens the playing field. So she holds her ground.

"Get . . . *in there*!" He kicks her again. "I'll deal with you after I deal with this meddling bitch. You want to pray she plays straight with me."

Sobbing, Barbara pushes the door to the women's bathroom open with her head and crawls inside. Not, however, before George administers another kick to her backside. Then he looks at Holly. The sneer is gone. The smile is back. Holly guesses it's supposed to look charming, and on Ondowsky's face it might. Not on George's.

"Well, Holly. Girlfriend's in the shithouse and now it's just us. I can go in and open up

459

her guts with this . . ." He holds up the knife.
". . . or you can give me what I came for and I'll leave her alone. I'll leave you both alone."

I know better, Holly thinks. Once you get what you came for, no one is walking away, including Jerome. If he isn't dead already.

She tries to project both doubt and hope. "I don't know if I can believe you."

"You can. Once I have the drive, I'll fade away. From your life and from the world of Pittsburgh broadcasting. It's time to move along. I knew that even before this guy —" He draws the hand not holding the knife slowly down the length of his face, as if drawing down a veil. "— planted the bomb. I think maybe that's *why* he planted it. So yes, Holly, you can believe me."

"Maybe I should run back to the office and lock the door," she says, and hopes her face shows she's actually considering this. "Call 911."

"And leave the girl to my tender mercies?" George points his long knife at the door to the women's room and smiles. "I don't think so. I saw how you looked at her. Besides, I'd have you before you took three steps. As I told you in the mall, I'm fast. Enough talk. Give me what I want and I'll go away."

"Do I have a choice?"

"What do you think?"

She pauses, sighs, wets her lips, finally nods. "You win. Just leave us alive."

"I will." As at the mall, the response is too fast. Too glib. She doesn't believe him. He knows and doesn't care.

"I'm going to take my cell phone out of my pocket," Holly says. "I have to show you a picture."

He says nothing, so she takes it out, very slowly. She opens her photo stream, selects the picture she took in the elevator, and holds the phone out to him.

Now tell me, she thinks. I don't want to do it myself, so tell me, you bastard.

And he does. "I can't see it. Come closer."

Holly steps toward him, still holding the phone out. Two steps. Three. Twelve yards away, then ten. He's squinting at the phone. Eight yards now, and see how reluctant I am?

"Closer, Holly. My eyes are a little wonky for a few minutes after I change."

You're a black liar, she thinks but takes another step, still holding the phone out. He'll almost certainly take her with him when he goes down. If he goes down. And that's okay.

"You see it, right? It's in the elevator. Taped to the roof. Just take it and g—"

Even in her hyper-alert state, Holly barely sees George move. At one moment he's standing outside the women's, squinting at the picture on her phone. At the next, he's got one arm around her waist and the other gripping her outstretched hand. He wasn't kidding about being fast. Her phone tumbles to the floor as he drags her toward the elevator. Once inside, he'll kill her and take the package taped to the ceiling. Then he'll go into the bathroom and kill Barbara.

That, at least, is his plan. Holly has another one.

"What are you doing?" Holly cries — not because she doesn't know, but because this is now the required line.

He doesn't answer, only pushes the call button. It doesn't light, but Holly hears the elevator hum into life. It's coming up. She will try to break free of him at the last second. Likewise he'll try to break free of *her* when he understands what's happening. She cannot let that happen.

George's narrow fox face breaks into a smile. "You know what, I think this is all going to work out just fi—"

He stops because the elevator doesn't. It passes the fifth floor — they can see a brief shutter of light from inside as it goes by — and keeps rising. His hands loosen in surprise. Only for a moment, but it's long enough for Holly to break his grip and step back.

What happens next takes no more than ten seconds, but in her current amped-up state, Holly sees it all.

The door to the stairwell bangs open and Jerome lurches out. His eyes stare from a mask of caked blood. In his hands is the mop that was on the stairwell, the wooden shaft leveled. He sees George and charges at him, yelling as he comes: *"Where's Barbara? Where's my sister?"*

George sweeps Holly aside. She strikes the wall with a bone-rattling thud. Black dots swarm across her vision. George reaches for the mop's shaft and yanks it easily out of Jerome's hands. He pulls it back, meaning to strike Jerome with it, but that is when the women's room door bangs open.

Barbara runs out with the pepper spray from her purse in her hand. George turns his head in time to catch a faceful. He screams and covers his eyes.

The elevator reaches the eighth floor. The hum of the machinery stops.

Jerome is going for George. Holly screams *"Jerome, no!"* and drives her shoulder into his midsection. He collides with his sister and the two of them hit the wall between the two bathroom doors.

The elevator alarm goes off, an amplified bray that screams *panic panic panic.*

George turns his red and streaming eyes toward the sound just as the elevator doors open. Not just the doors on five, but on all the floors. This is the glitch that caused the elevator to be shut down.

Holly runs at George with her arms outstretched. Her scream of fury merges with the bellowing alarm. Her outstretched hands connect with his chest and she pushes him into the shaft. For a moment he seems to hang there, eyes and mouth wide with terror and surprise. The face starts to sag and change, but before George can become Ondowsky again (if that is what's happening), he's gone. Holly is hardly aware of the strong brown hand — Jerome's — that grabs the back of her shirt and saves her from following George down the shaft.

The outsider screams as he goes.

Holly, who considers herself a pacifist, is savagely delighted by the sound.

Before she can hear the thud of his body at the bottom, the elevator doors slide shut. On this floor and all the other floors. The alarm stops and the car starts down, on the way to the basement, its other terminal point. The three of them watch the brief flash of light from between the doors as the car passes five.

"*You* did that," Jerome says.

"Damn right," Holly says.

## 17

Barbara's knees fold and she goes down in a half-faint. The can of pepper spray falls from her relaxing hand and rolls to a stop against the elevator doors.

Jerome kneels beside his sister. Holly pushes him gently away and takes Barbara's hand. She brushes back the sleeve of Barbara's coat, but before she can even begin to take a pulse, Barbara is trying to sit up.

"Who . . . what was he?"

Holly shakes her head. "No one." This might actually be the truth.

"Is he gone? Holly, *is he gone?*"

"He's gone."

"Down the elevator shaft?"

"Yes."

"Good. *Good.*" She starts to get up.

"Just lie still for a minute, Barb. You only grayed out. It's Jerome I'm worried about."

"I'm okay," Jerome says. "Hard head. That was the TV guy, wasn't it? Kozlowski, or whatever."

"Yes." And no. "You look like you've lost at least a pint of blood, Mr. Hard Head. Look at me."

He looks at her. His pupils are the same size, and that's good news.

"Can you remember the name of your book?"

He gives her an impatient look through his raccoon mask of congealing blood. *"Black Owl: The Rise and Fall of an American Gangster."* He actually laughs. "Holly, if he'd scrambled my brains, I never could have remembered the code for the side door. Who *was* he?"

"The man who blew up that school in Pennsylvania. Not that we're ever going to tell anyone that. It would raise too many

465

questions. Lower your head, Jerome."

"It hurts to move it," he says. "My neck feels sprung."

"Do it anyway," Barbara says.

"Sis, don't mean to get personal and all, but you don't smell so good."

Holly says, "I've got this, Barbara. There's a pair of pants and some tee-shirts in my closet. They'll fit you, I think. Take something to change into. Clean yourself up in the bathroom."

It's clear that Barbara wants to do just that, but she lingers. "You sure you're all right, J?"

"Yes," he says. "Go on."

Barbara goes down the hall to Finders Keepers. Holly feels the back of Jerome's neck, finds no swelling, and tells him again to lower his head. She sees a minor laceration at the crown and a much deeper gash lower down, but the occipital bone must have caught (and withstood) the brunt of the blow. She thinks Jerome got lucky.

She thinks they all did.

"I need to clean myself up, too," Jerome says, looking at the men's room.

"No, don't do that. I probably shouldn't have let Barbara do it, either, but I don't want her meeting the cops with her . . . in her current state of disarray."

"I sense a woman with a plan," Jerome says, then wraps his hands around himself. "God, I'm cold."

466

"That's shock. You probably need a hot drink. I'd make you tea, but there's no time for that." She is struck by a sudden, horrible thought: if Jerome had taken the elevator, her whole plan — rickety thing that it was — could have fallen apart. "Why did you take the stairs?"

"So he wouldn't hear me coming. Even with the world's worst headache, I knew where he'd be. You were the only one in the building." He pauses. "Not Kozlowski. *On-dowsky.*"

Barbara returns with the clean clothes bundled in her arms. She has begun crying again. "Holly . . . I saw him change. His head turned to *jelly.* It . . . it . . ."

"What in God's name is she talking about?" Jerome asks.

"Never mind now. Maybe later." Holly gives her a brief hug. "Clean up, change your clothes. And Barbara? Whatever it was, it's dead now. Okay?"

"Okay," she whispers, and goes into the bathroom.

Holly turns back to Jerome. "Were you tracking my phone, Jerome Robinson? Was Barbara? Were *both* of you?"

The bloody young man standing in front of her smiles. "If I promise to never, *ever,* call you Hollyberry again, do I have to answer those questions?"

**18**

In the lobby, fifteen minutes later.

Holly's pants are too tight for Barbara, and they're highwater, but she managed to get them buttoned. The ashy look is fading from her cheeks and forehead. She'll survive this, Holly thinks. There will be bad dreams, but she'll come through.

The blood on Jerome's face is drying to a crack-glaze. He says he has a bitch of a headache but no, he's not dizzy. Not nauseous. Holly isn't surprised about the headache. She has Tylenol in her purse, but she doesn't dare give him any. He'll get stitches — and an X-ray, no doubt — at the ER, but right now she has to make sure their stories are straight. Once that's taken care of, she has to finish cleaning up her own mess.

"You two came here because I wasn't at home," she says. "You thought I must be at the office, catching up, because I'd spent a few days with my mother. Right?"

They nod, willing to be led.

"You went to the side door in the service alley."

"Because we know the code," Barbara says.

"Yes. And there was a mugger. Right?"

More nods.

"He hit you, Jerome, and tried to grab Barbara. She got him with the pepper spray in her purse. Full face. Jerome, you jumped up and grappled with him. He ran off. Then you two came inside to the lobby and called 911."

Jerome asks, "Why did we come to see you in the first place?"

Holly is stumped. She remembered to reinstate the elevator fix (did it while Barbara was in the bathroom cleaning up and changing, easy-peasy), and she dropped Bill's gun into her handbag (just in case), but she hasn't even considered the thing Jerome is asking about.

"Christmas shopping," Barbara says. "We wanted to pry you out of the office to go Christmas shopping with us. Didn't we, Jerome?"

"Oh yeah, that's right," Jerome says. "We were going to surprise you. Were you here, Holly?"

"No," she says. "I was gone. In fact, I *am* gone. Christmas shopping on the other side of town. That's where I am right now. You didn't call me right after the attack because . . . well . . ."

"Because we didn't want to upset you," Barbara says. "Right, Jerome?"

"Right."

"Good," Holly says. "Can you both remember that story?"

They say they can.

"Then it's time for Jerome to call 911."

Barbara says, "What are you going to do, Hols?"

"Clean up." Holly points at the elevator.

"Oh, Christ," Jerome says. "I forgot there's a body down there. I clean forgot."

"*I* didn't," Barbara says, and shudders. "Jesus, Holly, how can you ever explain a dead guy at the bottom of the elevator shaft?"

Holly is remembering what happened to the other outsider. "I don't think it will be an issue."

"What if he's still alive?"

"He fell five stories, Barb. Six, counting the basement. And then the elevator . . ." Holly turns one hand palm up and brings the other down on it, making a sandwich.

"Oh," Barbara says. Her voice is faint. "Right."

"Call 911, Jerome. I think you're basically okay, but I'm no doctor."

While he does that, she goes to the elevator and brings it up to the first floor. With the fix in place again, it works fine.

When the doors open, Holly spies a furry hat, the kind the Russians call an ushanka. She remembers the man who passed by her as she was opening the lobby door.

She returns to her two friends, holding the hat in one hand. "Tell me the story again."

"Mugger," Barbara says, and Holly decides that's good enough. They're smart, and the rest of the story is simple. If everything works out the way she thinks it will, the cops aren't going to care about where she was, anyway.

**19**

Holly leaves them and takes the stairs to the basement, which stinks of old cigarette smoke and what she's afraid is mold. The lights are off and she has to use her phone to look for the switches. Shadows leap as she shines it around, making it all too easy to imagine the Ondowsky-thing in the dark, waiting to spring out at her and fasten its hands around her neck. Her skin is lightly sheened with sweat, but her face is cold. She has to consciously stop her teeth from chattering. I'm in shock myself, she thinks.

At last she finds a double row of switches. She flips them all, and banks of fluorescents light up with a hive buzzing. The basement is a filthy labyrinth of stacked bins and boxes. She thinks again that their building superintendent — whose salary they pay — is your basic man-slut.

She orients herself and goes to the elevator. The doors (the ones down here are filthy and the paint is chipped) are firmly shut. Holly puts her bag on the floor and takes out Bill's revolver. Then she removes the elevator drop-key from its hook on the wall and jams it into the hole on the lefthand door. The key hasn't been used for a long time, and it's balky. She has to put the gun in the waistband of her slacks and use both hands before it will turn. Gun once more in hand, she pushes one of the doors. Both of them slide open.

A smell of mingled oil, grease, and dust wafts out. In the center of the shaft is a long piston-like thing which she'll later learn is called the plunger. Scattered around it, among a litter of cigarette butts and fast food bags, are the clothes Ondowsky was wearing when he went on his final trip. A short one, but lethal.

Of Ondowsky himself, also known as Chet on Guard, there is no sign.

The fluorescents down here are bright, but the bottom of the shaft is still too shadowy for Holly's liking. She finds a flashlight on Al Jordan's cluttered worktable and shines it carefully around, making sure to check behind the plunger. She's not looking for Ondowsky — he's gone — but for bugs of a certain exotic type. Dangerous bugs that may be looking for a new host. She sees none. Whatever infested Ondowsky may have outlived him, but not for long. She spies a burlap sack in one corner of the cluttered, filthy basement, and stuffs Ondowsky's clothes into it, along with the fur hat. His undershorts go last. Holly picks them up between two tweezed fingers, revulsion pulling her mouth down at the corners. She drops the shorts into the sack with a shudder and a little cry (*"Oough!"*) and then uses the flats of her hands to run the elevator doors closed. She relocks them with the drop-key, then hangs the key back on its hook.

She sits and waits. Once she's sure Jerome, Barbara, and the 911 responders must be gone, she shoulders her purse and carries the bag containing Ondowsky's clothes upstairs. She leaves by the side door. She thinks about tossing the clothes into the Dumpster, but that would be a little too close for comfort. She takes the bag with her instead, which is perfectly okay. Once she's on the street, she's just one more person carrying a parcel.

She's barely started her car when she gets a call from Jerome, telling her that he and Barbara were victims of a mugging just as they were about to let themselves into the Frederick Building by the side door. They're at Kiner Memorial, he says.

"Oh my God, that's terrible," Holly says. "You should have called me sooner."

"Didn't want to worry you," Jerome says. "We're basically okay, and he didn't get anything."

"I'll be there as soon as I can."

Holly dumps the burlap bag containing Ondowsky's clothes in a trashcan on her way to John M. Kiner Memorial Hospital. It's starting to snow.

She turns on the radio, gets Burl Ives bellowing "Holly Jolly Christmas" at the top of his fracking voice, and turns it off again. She hates that song above all others. For obvious reasons.

You can't have everything, she thinks; into every life a little poop must fall. But sometimes you *do* get what you need. Which is really all a sane person can ask for.

And she is.

Sane.

*December 22, 2020*

Holly has to give a deposition at the offices of McIntyre and Curtis at ten o'clock. It's one of her least favorite things, but she's just a minor witness in this custody case, which is good. It's a Samoyed at issue, rather than a child, and that lowers the stress level a bit. There are a few nasty questions from one of the lawyers, but after what she's been through with Chet Ondowsky — and George — the interrogation seems pretty tame. She's done in fifteen minutes. She turns on her phone once she's in the corridor, and sees she's missed a call from Dan Bell.

But it isn't Dan who answers when she calls back; it's the grandson.

"Grampa had a heart attack," Brad says. "*Another* heart attack. It's actually his fourth. He's in the hospital, and this time he won't be coming out."

There's a long, watery intake of breath. Holly waits.

474

"He wants to know how things went with you. What happened with the reporter. The *thing.* If I could give him good news, I think it would make it easier for him to go."

Holly looks around to make sure she's alone. She is, but she lowers her voice anyway. "It's dead. Tell him it's dead."

"Are you sure?"

She thinks of that final look of surprise and fear. She thinks of the scream as he — it — went down. And she thinks of the abandoned clothes at the bottom of the shaft.

"Oh yes," she says. "I'm sure."

"We helped? Grampa, *he* helped?"

"Couldn't have done it without either of you. Tell him he may have saved a lot of lives. Tell him Holly says thanks."

"I will." Another watery intake of breath. "Do you think there are more like him?"

After Texas, Holly would have said no. Now she cannot be sure. One is a unique number. When you have two, you may be seeing the beginning of a pattern. She pauses, then gives an answer she doesn't necessarily believe . . . but *wants* to believe. The old man watched for years. For decades. He deserves to go out with a win under his belt.

"I don't think so."

"Good," Brad says. "That's good. God bless, Holly. You have a merry Christmas."

Under the circumstances she can't wish him the same, so she simply thanks him.

*Are* there more?

She takes the stairs rather than the elevator.

*December 25, 2020*

## 1

Holly spends thirty minutes of her Christmas morning drinking tea in her bathrobe and talking to her mother. Only it's mostly listening, as Charlotte Gibney goes through her usual litany of passive-aggressive complaints (Christmas alone, achy knees, bad back, etc., etc.), punctuated by long-suffering sighs. Finally Holly feels able, in good conscience, to end the call by telling Charlotte she will be there in a few days, and they'll go see Uncle Henry together. She tells her mother that she loves her.

"I love you, too, Holly." After another sigh that indicates such loving is hard, hard, she wishes her daughter a merry Christmas, and that part of the day is over.

The rest is more cheerful. She spends it with the Robinson family, happy to fall in with their traditions. There's a light brunch at ten, followed by the exchange of gifts. Holly gives Mr. and Mrs. Robinson certificates for wine and books. For their children, she was happy to splurge a little more: a spa day (mani-pedi included) for Barbara, and wireless earbuds for Jerome.

She, in turn, is given not only a $300 gift card for the AMC 12 cinemas close to her, but a year's subscription to Netflix. Like many deeply committed cineastes, Holly is conflicted about Netflix and has so far resisted it. (She loves her DVDs but firmly believes movies should first be seen on the big screen.) Still, she has to admit she's been sorely tempted by Netflix and all the other streaming platforms. So many new things, and all the time!

The Robinson household is normally gender-neutral and everyone-is-equal, but on Christmas afternoon there's a reversion (perhaps out of nostalgia) to the sexual roles of the previous century. Which is to say, the women cook while the men watch basketball (with occasional trips to the kitchen for tastes of this and that). As they sit down to an equally traditional holiday dinner — turkey with all the trimmings and two kinds of pie for dessert — it begins to snow.

"Could we join hands?" Mr. Robinson asks.

They do.

"Lord, bless the food we are about to receive from your bounty. Thank you for this time together. Thank you for family and friends. Amen."

"Wait," Tanya Robinson says. "That's not enough. Lord, thank you so much that neither of my beautiful children was badly hurt by the man who attacked them. It would break my heart if they weren't at this table with us. Amen."

Holly feels Barbara's hand tighten on hers, and hears a faint sound from the girl's throat. Something that might have been a cry, had it been set free.

"Now everyone has to tell one thing they're grateful for," Mr. Robinson says.

They go around the table. When it's Holly's turn, she says she's grateful to be with the Robinsons.

## 2

Barbara and Holly try to help with the washing-up, but Tanya shoos them out of the kitchen, telling them to "do something Christmassy."

Holly suggests a walk. Maybe to the bottom of the hill, maybe all the way around the block. "It will be pretty in the snow," she says.

Barbara's up for it. Mrs. Robinson tells them to get back by seven, because they're going to watch *A Christmas Carol*. Holly hopes it will be the one with Alastair Sim, which in her opinion is the only one worth watching.

It's not just pretty outside; it's beautiful. They are the only ones on the sidewalk, their boots crunching in two inches of new-fallen powder. Streetlights and Christmas lights are surrounded by swirling halos. Holly sticks out her tongue to catch some flakes, and Barbara does the same. It makes them both laugh, but when they reach the bottom of the hill and Barbara turns to her, she's solemn.

"All right," she says. "It's just the two of us. Why are we out here, Hols? What did you want to ask?"

"Just how you're doing with it," Holly says. "Jerome I don't worry about. He got clobbered, but he didn't see what you did."

Barbara takes a shuddering breath. Because of the snow melting on her cheeks, Holly can't tell if she's crying. Crying might be good. Tears can be healing.

"It's not that so much," she says at last. "The way he changed, I mean. The way his head seemed to turn to jelly. It was horrible, sure, and it opens the gates . . . you know . . ." She puts her mittened hands to her temples. "The gates in here?"

Holly nods.

"You realize *anything* could be out there."

"See ye devils, then shall ye not see angels?" Holly says.

"Is that the Bible?"

"It doesn't matter. If what you saw isn't troubling you, Barb, then what is?"

480

"Mom and Dad could have *buried* us!" Barbara bursts out. "They could have been at that table alone! Not eating turkey and stuffing, they wouldn't want anything like that, maybe just S-Sp-Spam —"

Holly laughs. She can't help it. And Barbara can't help joining in. Snow is gathering on her knitted cap. To Holly she looks very young. Of course she *is* young, but more like a twelve-year-old than a young woman who will be going to Brown or Princeton next year.

"Do you see what I mean?" Barbara takes Holly's gloved hands. "It was *close.* It was really, really *close.*"

Yes, Holly thinks, and it was your regard for me that put you there.

She embraces her friend in the falling snow. "Sweetheart," she says, "we're all close. All the time."

### 3

Barbara starts up the steps to the house. Inside, there will be cocoa and popcorn and Scrooge trumpeting that the spirits have done it all in one night. But there's a final bit of business that needs to be done out here, so Holly takes Barbara's arm for a moment in the thickening snow. She holds out a card she put in her coat pocket before leaving for the Robinsons', in case it might be needed. There's nothing on it but a name and a number.

481

Barbara takes it and reads it. "Who's Carl Morton?"

"A therapist I saw after I came back from Texas. I only saw him twice. That was all the time I needed to tell my story."

"Which was what? Was it like . . ." She doesn't finish. She doesn't have to.

"I might tell you someday, you and Jerome both, but not on Christmas. Just know that if you need to talk to someone, he'll listen." She smiles. "And because he's heard my story, he might even believe yours. Not that that matters. Telling it is what helps. At least it did me."

"Getting it out there."

"Yes."

"Would he tell my parents?"

"Absolutely not."

"I'll think about it," Barbara says, and puts the card in her pocket. "Thank you." She hugs Holly. And Holly, who once upon a time feared to be touched, hugs back. Hard.

**4**

It *is* the Alastair Sim version, and when Holly drives slowly home through the blowing snow, she can't remember a happier Christmas. Before going to bed, she uses her tablet to send Ralph Anderson a text message.

There will be a package from me when you get back. I have had quite an adventure, but all is well. We'll talk, but it can wait. Hope you & yours had a merry (tropical) Christmas. Much love.

She says her prayers before turning in, finishing as she always does, by saying that she's not smoking, she's taking her Lexapro, and she misses Bill Hodges.

"God bless us every one," she says. "Amen."

She gets in bed. Turns out the light.

Sleeps.

*February 15, 2021*

Uncle Henry's mental decline has been rapid. Mrs. Braddock has told them (regretfully) that it's often the case once patients are in care.

Now, as Holly sits beside him on one of the couches facing the big-screen TV in the Rolling Hills common room, she finally gives up trying to make conversation with him. Charlotte already has; she's at a table across the room, helping Mrs. Hatfield with her current jigsaw puzzle. Jerome has come with them today, and is also helping. He's got Mrs. Hatfield laughing, and even Charlotte can't help smiling at some of J's amiable chatter. He's a charming young man, and he's finally won Charlotte over. Not an easy thing to do.

Uncle Henry sits with his eyes wide and his mouth agape, the hands that once fixed Holly's bicycle after she crashed it into the Wilsons' picket fence now lying slack between his splayed legs. His pants bulge with the continence pants beneath. Once he was a ruddy man. Now he's pale. Once he was a stout man. Now his clothes hang on his body and his flesh sags like an old sock that's lost its elastic.

Holly takes one of his hands. It's just meat with fingers. She laces her own fingers through his and squeezes, hoping for a return, but no. Soon it will be time to go, and she's glad. It makes her feel guilty, but there it is. This isn't her uncle; he's been replaced by an oversized ventriloquist's dummy with no ventriloquist to lend it speech. The ventriloquist has left town and isn't coming back.

An ad for Otezla, urging these wrinkled, balding oldsters to "Show more of you!" ends, and is replaced by the Bobby Fuller Four: "I Fought the Law." Uncle Henry's chin has been sinking toward his chest, but now it comes up. And a light — low-wattage, to be sure — comes into his eyes.

The courtroom appears and the announcer intones, "Steer clear if you're a louse, because *John Law* is in the house!"

As the bailiff comes forward, Holly suddenly realizes why she gave the Macready School bomber the name she did. The mind is always at work, making connections and making sense . . . or at least trying to.

Uncle Henry finally speaks, his voice low and rusty from disuse. "All rise."

"All rise!" George the bailiff bellows.

The spectators don't just rise; they *get on up,* clapping and swaying. John Law jives his way in from his chambers. He grabs his gavel and tick-tocks it back and forth to the music. His bald head gleams. His white teeth flash. "What have we got today, Georgie, my brother from another mother?"

"I love this guy," Uncle Henry says in his rusty voice.

"So do I," she says, and puts an arm around him.

Uncle Henry turns to look at her.

And smiles.

"Hello, Holly," he says.

■ ■ ■ ■

# RAT

■ ■ ■ ■

# 1

Ordinarily, Drew Larson's story ideas came — on the increasingly rare occasions when they came at all — a little at a time, like dribbles of water drawn from a well that was almost dry. And there was always a chain of associations he could trace back to something he'd seen or heard: a real-world flashpoint.

In the case of his most recent short, the genesis had come when he'd seen a man changing a tire on the Falmouth entrance ramp to I-295, the guy down in an effortful squat while people honked and swerved around him. That had led to "Blowout," labored over for almost three months and published (after half a dozen rejections at larger magazines) in *Prairie Schooner*.

"Skip Jack," his one published story in *The New Yorker*, had been written while he was a grad student at BU. The seed of that one had been planted while listening to the college radio station in his apartment one night. The student DJ had attempted to play "Whole Lotta Love," by Zep, and the record had begun to skip. The skip went on for nearly forty-five seconds until the breathless kid killed the tune and blurted, "Sorry, guys, I was taking a shit."

"Skip Jack" was twenty years ago. "Blowout" had been published three years ago. In between, he had managed four others. They were all in the three-thousand-word range. All had taken months of labor and revision. There had never been a novel. He had tried, but no. He had pretty much given that ambition up. The first two efforts at long-form fiction had given him problems. The last try had caused *serious* problems. He had burned the manuscript, and had come close to burning the house, as well.

Now this idea, arriving complete. Arriving like a long overdue engine pulling a train of many splendid cars.

Lucy had asked him if he'd drive down to Speck's Deli and pick up sandwiches for lunch. It was a pretty September day, and he told her he'd walk instead. She nodded approvingly and said it would be good for his waistline. He wondered later how different his life might have been if he'd taken the Suburban or the Volvo. He might never have had the idea. He might never have been at his father's cabin. He almost certainly would never have seen the rat.

He was halfway to Speck's, waiting at the corner of Main and Spring for the light to change, when the engine arrived. The engine was an image, one as brilliant as reality. Drew stood transfixed and staring at it through the sky. A student gave him a nudge. "Sign says you can walk, man."

Drew ignored him. The student threw him an odd look and crossed the street. Drew continued to stand on the curb as WALK became DON'T WALK and then WALK again.

Although he avoided western novels (with the exceptions of *The Ox-Bow Incident* and Doctorow's brilliant *Welcome to Hard Times*) and hadn't seen many western movies since his teenage years, what he saw as he stood on the corner of Main and Spring was a western saloon. A wagon-wheel chandelier with kerosene lanterns mounted on the spokes hung from the ceiling. Drew could smell the oil. The floor was plank. At the back of the room were three or four gaming tables. There was a piano. The man playing it wore a derby hat. Only he wasn't playing it now. He had turned to stare at what was happening at the bar. Standing next to the piano player, also staring, was a tall drink of water with an accordion strapped to his narrow chest. And at the bar, a young man in an expensive western suit was holding a gun to the temple of a girl in a red dress so low-cut that only a ruffle of

491

lace hid her nipples. Drew could see these two twice, once where they stood and once reflected in the backbar mirror.

This was the engine. The whole train was behind it. He saw the inhabitants of every car: the limping sheriff (shot at Antietam and still carrying the ball in his leg), the arrogant father willing to lay siege to an entire town to keep his son from being taken to the county seat where he would be tried and hung, the father's hired men on the roofs with their rifles. Everything was there.

When he came home, Lucy took one look at him and said, "You're either coming down with something or you've had an idea."

"It's an idea," Drew said. "A good idea. Maybe the best one I've ever had."

"Short story?"

He guessed that was what she was hoping for. What she wasn't hoping for was another visit from the fire department while she and the kids stood on the lawn in their nightclothes.

"Novel."

She put her ham and cheese on rye down. "Oh boy."

They didn't call what happened following the fire that almost took their house a nervous breakdown, but that's what it was. Not as bad as it could have been, but he'd missed half a semester of school (thank God for tenure) and had only regained his equilibrium thanks to twice-weekly therapy sessions, some magic pills, and Lucy's unfailing confidence that he *would* recover. Plus the kids, of course. The kids needed a father who wasn't caught in an unending loop of *must finish* and *can't finish.*

"This one is different. It's all there, Lucy. Practically gift-wrapped. It's going to be like taking dictation!"

She just looked at him, a slight frown creasing her brow. "If you say so."

"Listen, we didn't rent out Dad's cabin this year, did we?"

Now she looked not just worried but alarmed. "We haven't rented it out for two years. Not since Old Bill died." Old Bill Colson had been their caretaker, and Drew's mom and pop's caretaker before that. "You're not thinking —"

"I am, but only for a couple of weeks. Three at most. To get started. You can get Alice to help with the kids, you know she loves to come and the kids love their auntie. I'll be back in time to help you pass out the Halloween candy."

"You can't write it here?"

"Of course I can. Once I get a running start." He put his hands to his head like a man with a splitting headache. "The first forty pages at the cabin, that's all. Or maybe it'll be a hundred and forty, it might go that fast. I see it! I see it all!" He repeated, "It'll be like taking dictation."

"I need to think about it," she said. "And you do, too."

"All right, I will. Now eat your sandwich."

"All of a sudden I'm not that hungry," she said.

Drew was. He ate the rest of his, then most of hers.

## 2

That afternoon he went to see his old department head. Al Stamper had abruptly retired at the end of the spring semester, allowing Arlene Upton, also known as the Wicked Witch of Elizabethan Drama, to finally achieve the position of authority she had so long desired. Nay, lusted for.

Nadine Stamper told Drew that Al was on the back patio, drinking iced tea and taking in the sun. She looked as worried as Lucy had when Drew sprang his idea of going up to the camp in TR-90 for a month or so, and when he went out to the patio, Drew saw why. He also understood why Al Stamper — who had ruled the English Department like a benevolent despot for the last fifteen years — had abruptly stepped down.

"Stop gawking and have some tea. You know you want some." Al always believed he knew what people wanted. Arlene Upton loathed him in large part because Al usually *did* know what people wanted.

Drew sat down and took the glass. "How much weight have you lost, Al?"

"Thirty pounds. I know it looks like more, but that's because I wasn't carrying any extra to start with. It's pancreatic." He saw Drew's expression and raised the finger he used to quell arguments in faculty meetings. "No need for you or Nadie or anyone else to go crafting any obituaries just yet. The docs caught it relatively early. Confidence is high."

Drew didn't think his old friend looked especially confident, but held his tongue.

"Let's not talk about me. Let's talk about why you came. Have you decided how you're going to spend your sabbatical?"

Drew told him he wanted to take another stab at a novel. This time, he said, he was pretty sure he could bring it off. Positive, actually.

"That's what you said about *The Village on the Hill,*" Al said, "and you almost lost the wheels off your little red wagon when that one went south."

"You sound like Lucy," Drew said. "I didn't expect that."

Al leaned forward. "Listen to me, Drew. You're an excellent teacher, and you've written some fine short stories —"

"Half a dozen," Drew said. "Call the *Guinness Book of World Records.*"

Al waved this off. " 'Skip Jack' was in *Best*

"Yes," Drew said. "The one edited by Doctorow. Who's been dead lo these many years."

"Many fine writers have produced almost nothing but short stories," Al persisted. "Poe. Chekhov. Carver. And although I know you tend to steer clear of popular fiction, there's Saki and O. Henry on that side of things. Harlan Ellison in the modern age."

"Those guys did a lot better than half a dozen. And Al, this is a great idea. It really is."

"Would you care to tell me a little about it? A drone's eye view, so to speak?" He eyed Drew. "You don't. I can see that you don't."

Drew, who longed to do exactly that — because it was beautiful! damn near perfect! — shook his head. "Better to keep it in, I think. I'm going up to my father's old cabin for awhile. Long enough to get this thing rolling."

"Ah. TR-90, correct? The back of beyond, in other words. What does Lucy say about this idea?"

"Not crazy about it, but she'll have her sister to help with the kids."

"It's not the kids she's worried about, Drew. I think you know that."

Drew said nothing. He thought about the saloon. He thought about the sheriff. He already knew the sheriff's name. It was James Averill.

496

Al sipped his tea, then put the glass down beside a well-thumbed copy of Fowles's *The Magus.* Drew guessed there were underlinings on every page: green for character, blue for theme, red for phrases Al found remarkable. His blue eyes were still bright, but they were also a trifle watery now, and red around the rims. Drew didn't like to think he saw approaching death in those eyes, but thought maybe he did.

Al leaned forward, hands clasped between his thighs. "Tell me something, Drew. Tell me why this is so important to you."

## 3

That night, after making love, Lucy asked him if he really had to go.

Drew thought about it. Really did. She deserved that much. Oh, and so much more. She had stood by him, and when he'd gone through the bad time, he had leaned on her. He kept it simple. "Luce, this might be my last chance."

There was a long silence from her side of the bed. He waited, knowing if she told him she didn't want him to go, he would give in to her wishes. At last she said, "All right. I want this for you, but I'm a little bit scared. Can't lie about that. What's it going to be about? Or don't you want to say?"

"I do. I'm dying to spill it, but it's better to let the pressure build. I told Al the same thing when he asked."

"Just as long as it's not about academics screwing each other's spouses and drinking too much and having midlife crises."

"Not like *The Village on the Hill,* in other words."

She poked him with her elbow. "You said it, Mister, not me."

"It's nothing like that."

"Can you wait, honey? A week? Just to make sure it's real?" And in a smaller voice: "For me?"

He didn't want to; he wanted to go north tomorrow and start the day after. But . . . *just to make sure it's real.* That was not such a bad idea, maybe.

"I can do that."

"All right. Good. And if you do go up there, you'll be all right? You swear?"

"I'll be fine."

He saw the momentary gleam of her teeth as she smiled. "That's what men always say, isn't it?"

"If it doesn't work, I'll come back. If it starts to be like . . . you know."

To this she made no reply, either because she believed him or because she didn't. It was okay either way. They weren't going to have an argument about it, that was the important thing.

He thought she had gone to sleep, or was going, when she asked Al Stamper's ques-

498

tion. She had never asked before, not during his first two stabs at writing long form, not even during the ongoing clusterfuck that had been *The Village on the Hill.*

"Why is writing a novel so important to you? Is it the money? Because we're doing all right with your salary and the accounting work I'm picking up. Or is it the cachet?"

"Neither of those things, since there's no guarantee it would be published at all. And if it ended up in a desk drawer, like bad novels all over this round world of ours, I'd be okay with that." As these words came out of his mouth, he realized they were actually true.

"Then what?"

To Al, he'd spoken about completion. And about the excitement of exploring uncharted territory. (He didn't know if he actually believed that one, but knew it would appeal to Al, who was a closet romantic.) Such bullshit wouldn't do for Lucy.

"I have the tools," he said at last. "And I have the talent. So it might be good. It might even be commercial, if I understand the meaning of that word when it comes to fiction. Good matters to me, but that isn't the main thing. Not the big thing." He turned to her, took her hands, and put his forehead against hers. "*I need to finish.* That's all. That's the whole deal. After that I can either do it again, and with a lot less *sturm und drang,* or let go. Either would be fine with me."

"Closure, in other words."

"No." He had used the word with Al, but only because it was a word Al could understand and would accept. "It's something different. Something almost physical. Do you remember when Brandon got that cherry tomato stuck in his throat?"

"I'll never forget it."

Bran had been four. They were having a meal out at Country Kitchen in Gates Falls. Brandon began making a strangled gagging sound and clutching at his throat. Drew grabbed him, turned him around, and gave him the Heimlich. The tomato had popped out whole, and with an audible *thorp* sound, like a cork from a bottle. No damage done, but Drew would never forget their son's supplicatory eyes when he realized he couldn't breathe, and guessed Lucy never would, either.

"This is like that," he said. "Only stuck in my brain instead of my throat. I'm not choking, exactly, but I'm not getting enough air, either. *I need to finish.*"

"All right," she said, and patted his cheek.

"Do you understand?"

"No," she said. "But you do, and I guess that's enough. Going to sleep now." She turned on her side.

Drew lay awake for awhile, thinking of a

little town out west, a part of the country where he had never been. Not that it mattered. His imagination would carry him, he was sure of it. Any necessary research could be done later. Assuming the idea didn't turn into a mirage in the next week, that was.

Eventually he fell asleep and dreamed of a limping sheriff. A wastrel good-for-nothing son locked in a tiny crackerbox of a jail. Men on rooftops. A standoff that wouldn't — *couldn't* — last long.

He dreamed of Bitter River, Wyoming.

## 4

The idea didn't turn into a mirage. It grew stronger, brighter, and a week later, on a warm October morning, Drew loaded three boxes of supplies — mostly canned food — into the back of the old Suburban they used as a second vehicle. This was followed by a duffel bag full of clothes and toiletries. The duffel was followed by his laptop and the scuffed case containing his pop's old Olympia portable typewriter, which he wanted as a backup. He didn't trust the power in the TR; the lines had a tendency to come down when the wind blew, and the unincorporated townships were the last places where power was restored after a blow.

He had kissed the kids goodbye before they left for school; Lucy's sister would be there to welcome them when they got home. Now

501

Lucy stood in the driveway in a sleeveless blouse and her faded jeans. She looked slim and desirable, but her brow was furrowed as if she had one of her premenstrual migraines coming on.

"You need to be careful," she said, "and not just about your work. The north country empties out between Labor Day and hunting season, and cell phone coverage stops dead forty miles out of Presque Isle. If you break a leg walking in the woods . . . or get lost . . ."

"Honey, I don't do woods. When I walk — *if* I walk — I'll stick to the road." He took a closer look at her and didn't care for what he saw. It wasn't just the furrowed brow; her eyes had picked up a suspicious sheen. "If you need me to stay, I'll stay. Just say the word."

"Would you really?"

"Try me." Praying she wouldn't.

She was looking down at her sneakers. Now she raised her head and gave it a shake. "No. I understand this is important to you. So do Stacey and Bran. I heard what he said when he kissed you goodbye."

Brandon, their twelve-year-old, had said, "Bring back a big one, Dad."

"I want you to call me every day, Mister. No later than five, even if you're really rolling. Your cell won't work, but the landline does. We get a bill for it every month, and I called this morning just to be sure. Not only

502

did it ring, I got your pop's old answering machine message. Gave me a little bit of a chill. Like a voice from the grave."

"I bet." Drew's father had been dead for ten years. They had kept the cabin, using it a few times themselves, then renting it out to hunting parties until Old Bill, the caretaker, died. After that they stopped bothering. One group of hunters hadn't paid in full and another group had pretty well trashed the place. It hardly seemed worth the hassle.

"You should record a new message."

"I will."

"And fair warning, Drew — if I don't hear from you, I'll come up."

"Wouldn't be a good idea, honey. Those last fifteen miles on Shithouse Road would tear the exhaust right out from under the Volvo. Probably the transmission, too."

"Don't care. Because . . . I'm just going to say this, okay? When stuff goes wrong with one of the short stories, you can put it aside. There's a week or two of moping around the house, then you're yourself again. *Village on the Hill* was a whole different thing, and the next year was very scary for me and the kids."

"This one is —"

"Different, I know, you've said so half a dozen times, and I believe you, even though the only thing I know about it is that it's not a bunch of randy teachers having key parties in Updike country. Just . . ." She took him by the forearms, looking up at him earnestly. "If it starts to go wrong, if you start to lose the words like you did with *Village,* come home. Do you understand me? *Come home.*"

"I promise."

"Now kiss me like you mean it."

He did, gently parting her lips with his tongue and sliding one hand into the back pocket of her jeans. When he pulled back from her, Lucy was flushed. "Yes," she said. "Like that."

He got into the Suburban and had made it to the foot of the driveway when Lucy shouted "Wait! Wait!" and came running after him. She was going to tell him she'd changed her mind, she wanted him to stay and try writing the book in his upstairs office, he was sure of it, and he had to battle a desire to step on the gas and go powering down Sycamore Street without looking in the rearview mirror. Instead, he stopped with the Suburban's back end in the street and rolled down the window.

"Paper!" she said. She was out of breath and her hair was in her eyes. She pooched out her lower lip and blew it back. "Do you have paper? Because I doubt like hell if there's any up there."

He grinned and touched her cheek. "Two reams. Think that'll be enough?"

"Unless you're planning to write *The Lord of the Rings,* it should be." She gave him a

504

level gaze. The furrow had left her brow, at least for the time being. "Go on, Drew. Get out of here and bring back a big one."

## 5

As he turned onto the I-295 entrance ramp where he'd once upon a time seen a man changing a flat tire, Drew felt a lightening. His real life — kids, running errands, chores around the house, picking up Stacey and Brandon from their after-school activities — was behind him. He would come back to it in two weeks, three at the outside, and he supposed he would still have the bulk of the book to write amid the clanging round of that real life, but what was ahead of him was another life, one he would live in his imagination. He had never been able to fully inhabit that life while working on the other three novels, had never quite been able to get over. This time he felt he would. His body might be sitting in your basic no-frills cabin in the Maine woods, but the rest of him would be in the town of Bitter River, Wyoming, where a limping sheriff and three frightened deputies were faced with protecting a young man who'd killed an even younger woman in cold blood in front of at least forty witnesses. Protecting him from angry townspeople was only half of the lawmen's job. The rest was getting him to the county seat where he would be tried (if Wyoming even *had* coun-

505

ties in the 1880s; he would find that out later). Drew didn't know where old man Prescott had gotten the small army of gun thugs he was counting on to keep that move from happening, but he was sure it would come to him eventually.

Everything was eventual.

He merged onto I-95 at Gardiner. The Suburban — 120K on the clock — shimmied at sixty, but once he goosed it up to seventy, the shimmy disappeared and the old girl ran smooth as silk. He still had a four-hour run ahead of him, the last hour over increasingly narrow roads culminating in the one TR locals called the Shithouse Road.

He was looking forward to the drive, but not as much as he was looking forward to opening his laptop, connecting it up to the little Hewlett-Packard printer, and creating a document he would call BITTER RIVER #1. For once, thinking about the chasm of white space under the blinking cursor didn't fill him with a mixture of hope and fear. As he passed the Augusta town line, all he felt was impatience. This time was going to be okay. Better than okay. This time everything would come right.

He turned on the radio and began to sing along with the Who.

## 6

Late that afternoon Drew pulled up in front of TR-90's only business, a shambling, slump-roofed establishment called the Big 90 General Store (as if somewhere there was a Small 90). He gassed the Suburban, which was almost dry, at a rusty old rotary pump where a sign announced CASH ONLY and REGULAR ONLY and "DASH-AWAYS" WILL BE PERSECUTED and GOD BLESS AMERICA. The price was $3.90 a gallon. In the north country, you paid premium prices even for regular. Drew paused on the store's porch to lift the receiver of the bug-splattered pay phone that had been here when he was a kid, along with what he would swear was the same message, now faded almost to illegibility: DO NOT DEPOSIT COINS UNTIL YOUR PARTY ANSWERS. Drew heard the buzz of the open line, nodded, replaced the receiver in its rusty cradle, and went inside.

"Ayuh, ayuh, still works," said the refugee from *Jurassic Park* sitting behind the counter. "Amazin, ain't it." His eyes were red, and Drew wondered if he had perhaps been smoking a little Aroostook County Gold. Then the old fella pulled a snot-clotted bandanna from his back pocket and sneezed into it. "Goddam allergies, I get em every fall."

"Mike DeWitt, isn't it?" Drew asked.

"Nawp, Mike was my father. He passed on in Feberary. Ninety-seven fuckin years old, and the last ten he didn't know if he was afoot or on hossback. I'm Roy." He stuck his hand out over the counter. Drew didn't want to shake it — that was the one that had been manipulating the snotrag — but he had been raised to be polite, so he gave it a single pump.

DeWitt hooked his glasses down to the end of his beaky nose and studied Drew over them. "I know I look like m'dad, worse luck, and you look like yours. You *are* Buzzy Larson's boy, ain'tcha? Not Ricky, t'other one."

"That's right. Ricky lives in Maryland now. I'm Drew."

"Sure, that's right. Been up with the wife and kiddies, but not for awhile. Teacher, ain'tcha?"

"Yes." He passed DeWitt three twenties. DeWitt put them in the till and returned six limp singles.

"I heard Buzzy died."

"He did. My mom, too." One less question to answer.

"Sorry to hear it. What are you doing up here this time of year?"

"I'm on sabbatical. Thought I'd do a little writing."

"Oh, ayuh? At Buzzy's cabin?"

"If the road's passable." Only saying it so he wouldn't sound like a complete flatlander.

508

Even if the road was in bad shape, he'd find a way to bull the Suburban through. He hadn't come this far just to turn around.

DeWitt paused to snorkel back phlegm, then said, "Well, they don't call it Shithouse Road for nothin, you know, and there's probably a culvert or two washed out from the spring runoff, but you got your four-wheel drive, so you should be all right. Course you know Old Bill died."

"Yes. One of his sons dropped me a card. We couldn't make it to the funeral. Was it his heart?"

"Head. Put a bullet through it." Roy De-Witt said this with palpable relish. "He was comin down with the Alzheimer's, see? Constable found a notebook in his glovebox with all kinds of stuff written down in it. Directions, phone numbers, his wife's name. Even the fuckin dog's name. Couldn't take it, don'tcha see."

"Jesus," Drew said. "That's terrible." And it was. Bill Colson had been a nice man, soft-spoken, always combed and tucked in and smelling of Old Spice, always careful to tell Drew's pop — and later, Drew himself — when something needed repairs, and just how much it would cost.

"Ayuh, ayuh, and if you didn't know that, I don't s'pose you know he done it in the dooryard of your cabin."

Drew stared. "Are you kidding?"

"Wouldn't kid about . . . ." The bandanna appeared, more damp and bedraggled than ever. DeWitt sneezed into it. ". . . about a thing like that. Yessir. Parked his pickup, put the barrel of his .30-30 under his chin, and pulled the trigger. Bullet went right through and broke the back winda. Constable Griggs was standin right where you are now when he told me."

"Christ," Drew said, and in his mind, something changed. Instead of holding his pistol to the dancehall girl's temple, Andy Prescott — the wastrel son — was now holding it beneath her chin . . . and when he pulled the trigger, the bullet would exit the back of her skull and break the mirror behind the bar. Using this elderly gore-crow's story of Old Bill's death in his own story had an undoubted element of expediency, even strip-mining, but that wouldn't stop him. It was too good.

"Lousy thing, all right," DeWitt said. He was trying to sound sad, maybe even philo-sophical, but there was an unmistakable twinkle in his voice. He also knew when something was too good, Drew thought. "But you know he was Old Bill right to the very end."

"Meaning what?"

"Meaning he made his mess in the truck, not in Buzzy's cabin. He'd never do a thing like that, at least not while he still had some

510

of his right mind left." He began to hitch and snort again, and scrambled for the bandanna, but this time was a little late to catch all of the sneeze. Which was a juicy one. "He *care-took* that place, don'tcha see?"

<h1 style="text-align:center">7</h1>

Five miles north of the Big 90, the tar gave out. After five more miles on oiled hardpan, Drew came to a fork in the road. He bore left, onto rough gravel that thumped and pinged off the Suburban's undercarriage. This was Shithouse Road, unchanged, so far as he could tell, since his childhood. Twice he had to slow to two or three miles an hour in order to waddle the Suburban across washouts where culverts had indeed been plugged in the spring runoffs. Twice more he had to stop, get out, and move fallen trees off the road. Luckily they were birches, and light. One broke apart in his hands.

He came to the Cullum camp — deserted, boarded up, the driveway chained off — and then began counting phone-and-power poles, just as he and Ricky had as kids. A few were leaning drunkenly to starboard or port, but there were still exactly sixty-six between the Cullum camp and the overgrown driveway — also chained off — with the sign out front that Lucy had made when the kids were small: CHEZ LARSON. Beyond this driveway, he knew, were seventeen more poles, ending at the Farrington camp on the shore of Agelbemoo Lake.

Beyond the Farringtons' place lay a huge swath of unelectrified wilderness, at least a hundred miles on either side of the Canadian border. Sometimes he and Ricky had gone up to look at what they called Last Pole. It held a kind of fascination for them. Beyond that one there was nothing to hold back the night. Drew had once taken Stacey and Brandon to look at Last Pole, and Drew had not missed the *so what* expression that passed between them. They assumed electricity — not to mention Wi-Fi — went on forever.

He got out of the Suburban and unlocked the chain, having to push and diddle the key before it would finally turn. He should have gotten some 3-in-1 at the store, but you couldn't think of everything.

The driveway was almost a quarter of a mile long, with branches brushing at the sides and roof of the Suburban the whole way. Overhead were the two lines for the electric and the phone. He remembered them being taut back in the old days, but now they sagged along the diagonal Northern Maine Power cut running in from the road.

He came to the cabin. It looked desolate, forgotten. The green paint was peeling away with no Bill Colson to refresh it, the galvanized steel roof was drifted with fir needles and fallen leaves, and the satellite dish on the roof (its cup also filled with leaves and needles) looked like a joke out here in the woods. He wondered if Luce had been paying the monthly charge on the dish as well as the phone. If so, it was probably money for nothing, because he doubted if it still worked. He also doubted that DirecTV would send the check back with a note saying *whoops, we are returning your payment because your dish has shit the bed.* The porch was weatherbeaten but appeared sturdy enough (although it wouldn't do to take that for granted). Beneath it he could see a faded green tarp covering what Drew assumed was a cord or two of wood — maybe the last wood Old Bill had ever brought in.

He got out and stood by the Suburban, one hand on the warm hood. Somewhere a crow cawed. Distant, another crow answered. Other than the babble of Godfrey Brook on its way to the lake, those were the only sounds.

Drew wondered if he was parked on the very spot where Bill Colson had parked his own four-wheel drive and blown his brains out. Wasn't there a school of thought — maybe back in medieval England — that the ghosts of suicides were forced to remain in the places where they had ended their lives?

He started for the cabin, telling himself (scolding himself) that he was too old for campfire stories, when he heard something blundering toward him. What emerged from the screening pines between the cabin's clearing and the brook wasn't a ghost or a zombie apparition but a moose calf tottering on absurdly long legs. It came as far as the little equipment shed beside the house, then saw him and stopped. They stared at each other, Drew thinking that moose — whether young or full-grown — were among God's ugliest and most unlikely creatures, the calf thinking who knew what.

"No harm here, bud," Drew said softly, and the calf pricked its ears.

Now came more crashing and blundering, much louder, and the calf's mother shouldered her way through the trees. A branch fell on her neck and she shook it away. She stared at Drew, lowered her head, and pawed at the ground. Her ears went back and lay flat against her head.

*It means to charge me,* Drew thought. *It sees me as a threat to her baby, and it means to charge me.*

He thought of running for the Suburban, but it might be — probably was — too far. And running, even away from the calf, might set the mother off. So he simply stood where he was, trying to send soothing thoughts to the thousand-pound creature no more than thirty yards away. *Nothing to worry about here, moms, I'm harmless.*

She considered him for maybe fifteen seconds, head lowered and one hoof pawing the ground. It seemed longer. Then she went to her calf (never taking her eyes from the interloper) and put herself between it and Drew. She gave him another long look, seeming to debate her next move. Drew stood motionless. He was badly frightened, but also weirdly exalted. He thought, *If she charges me from this distance, I'm either going to be dead or so badly hurt I'll probably die anyway. If she doesn't, I'm going to do brilliant work here. Brilliant.*

He knew it was a false equivalency even at this moment, with his life at risk — he might as well have been a child believing he would get a bike for his birthday if a certain cloud blotted out the sun — but at the same time he felt it was absolutely true.

Moose Mom suddenly swung her head, butting the calf in the hindquarters. It gave an almost sheeplike cry, nothing like the hoarse blat of Pop's old moose-call, and trotted toward the woods. The mom followed, pausing to give Drew one final, baleful look: *follow me and die.*

Drew let out a breath he hadn't known he was holding (a hoary suspense novel cliché that turned out to be true) and started for the porch. The hand holding the keys was shaking slightly. He was already telling himself that he hadn't been in any danger, not really; if you didn't bother a moose — even a protective Moose Mom — it wouldn't bother you.

Besides, it could have been worse. It could have been a bear.

## 8

He let himself in, expecting a mess, but the cabin was spick and span. Old Bill's work, surely; it was even possible Bill had given it one last putting-to-rights on the day he killed himself. Aggie Larson's old rag rug still lay in the center of the room, threadbare around the edges but otherwise whole. There was a Ranger woodstove up on bricks and waiting to be loaded, its isinglass window as clean as the floor. To the left was a rudimentary kitchen. To the right, overlooking the woods sloping down to the brook, was an oak dining table. At the far end of the room were a swaybacked sofa, a couple of chairs, and a fireplace Drew felt dubious about lighting. God knew how much creosote might have collected in the chimney, not to mention wildlife: mice, squirrels, bats.

The cookstove was a Hotpoint that had probably been new back in the days when the only satellite circling the earth was the moon. Next to it, standing open and somehow corpselike, was an unplugged refrigerator. It was empty except for a box of Arm &

Hammer baking soda. The television in the living room area was a portable on a rolling cart. He remembered the four of them sitting in front of it, watching *M*A*S*H* reruns and eating TV dinners.

Plank stairs ran up the west wall of the cabin. There was a kind of gallery up there, lined with bookcases that mostly held paperbacks — what Lucy had called rainy-day camp reading. Two small bedrooms opened off the gallery. Drew and Lucy had slept in one, the kids in the other. Did they stop coming here when Stacey began to bitch about needing her privacy? Was that why? Or did they just get too busy for summer weeks at camp? Drew couldn't remember. He was just glad to be here, and glad none of their renters had made off with his mom's rag rug . . . although why would they? It had once been pretty damn gorgeous, but was now fit only to be walked over by people in woods-muddy shoes or bare feet wet from wading in the brook.

"I can work here," Drew said. "Yeah." He jumped at the sound of his own voice — still nerved up from his stare-down with Moose Mom, he supposed — and then laughed.

He didn't need to check the electricity, because he could see the red lamp flashing on Pop's old answering machine, but he flipped the switch for the overhead lights anyway, because the afternoon was starting

517

to thin out. He went over to the answering machine and hit PLAY.

"It's Lucy, Drew." She sounded wavery, as if her voice were coming from twenty thousand leagues under the sea, and Drew remembered this old answering gadget was basically a cassette deck. It was sort of amazing that it worked at all. "It's ten past three, and I'm a little worried. Are you there yet? Call me as soon as you can."

Drew was amused but also annoyed. He had come up here to avoid distractions, and the last thing he needed was Lucy looking over his shoulder for the next three weeks. Still, he supposed she had valid reasons to be concerned. He could have had an accident on the way up, or broken down on the Shithouse Road. She certainly couldn't be worried that he was going mental over a book he hadn't even started to write.

Thinking that brought back a memory of a lecture the English Department had sponsored five or six years before, Jonathan Franzen speaking to a full house on the art and craft of the novel. He had said that the peak of the novel-writing experience actually came before the writer began, while everything was still in his or her imagination. "Even the clearest part of what was in your mind gets lost in translation," Franzen had said. Drew remembered thinking that it was rather self-centered of the guy to assume that his experience was the general case.

Drew picked up the phone (the receiver was the old dumbbell shape, basic black and amazingly heavy), heard a good strong dial tone, and called Lucy's cell. "I'm here," he said. "No problems."

"Oh, good. How's the road? How's the cabin?"

They talked for awhile, then he talked to Stacey, who had just come in from school and demanded the phone. Lucy came back and reminded him to change the answering machine message because it was giving her the creeps.

"All I can promise is to try. This gadget was probably state-of-the-art in the seventies, but that was half a century ago."

"Do your best. Have you seen any wildlife?"

He thought of Moose Mom, her head lowered as she decided whether or not to charge and trample him to death.

"A few crows, that's about it. Hey, Luce, I want to haul my crap in before the sun goes down. I'll call later."

"Around seven-thirty would be good. You can talk to Brandon, he'll be back by then. He's eating dinner at Randy's house."

"Roger that."

"Anything else to report?" There might have been worry in her voice, or that might only have been his imagination.

"Nope. All quiet on the Western Front.

Love you, hon."

"Love you, too."

He placed the funny old-fashioned receiver back in its cradle and spoke to the empty cabin. "Oh wait, one other thing, honeybunch. Old Bill blew his head off right out front."

And shocked himself by laughing.

## 9

By the time he had his luggage and supplies in, it was past six o'clock and he was hungry. He tried the kitchen faucet, and after a few chugs and thumps in the pipes, began to get splurts of cloudy water that eventually ran cold, clear, and steady. He filled a pot, turned on the Hotpoint (the low hum of the big burner brought back memories of other meals here), and waited for the water to boil so he could add spaghetti. There was sauce, too. Lucy had thrown a bottle of Ragu into one of his boxes of supplies. He would have forgotten.

He considered heating up a can of peas, and decided not to. He was at camp and would eat camp style. No alcohol, though; he had brought none with him and hadn't bought any at the Big 90. If the work went well, as he expected, he might reward himself with a rack of Bud the next time he went down to the store. He might even find some salad stuff, although he had an idea that when it came to stocking vegetables, Roy De-Witt kept plenty of popcorn and hotdog relish on hand, and called it good. Maybe the odd bottle of sauerkraut for those with exotic tastes.

While he waited for the water to boil and the sauce to simmer, Drew turned on the TV, expecting nothing but snow. What he got instead was a bluescreen and a message that read DIRECTV CONNECTING. Drew had his doubts about that but left the TV alone to do its thing. Assuming it was doing anything.

He was rooting through one of the lower cabinets when Lester Holt's voice blared into the cabin, startling him so badly that he gave a yell and dropped the colander he'd just found. When he turned around, he saw NBC's nightly newscast, clear as a bell. Lester was reporting on the latest Trump farrago, and as he turned the story over to Chuck Todd for the dirty details, Drew grabbed the remote and killed the set. It was nice to know it worked, but he had no intention of junking up his mind with Trump, terrorism, or taxes.

He cooked a whole box of spaghetti and ate most of it. In his mind, Lucy waved a tut-tutting finger and mentioned — again — his growing middle-aged spread. Drew reminded her he had skipped lunch. He washed his few dishes, thinking about Moose Mom and suicide. Was there a place for either of them in *Bitter River*? Moose Mom, probably not. Suicide, maybe.

He supposed Franzen had had a point about the time before writing a novel actually began. It *was* a good time, because everything you saw and heard was possible grist for the mill. Everything was malleable. The mind could build a city, remodel it, then raze it, all while you were taking a shower or shaving or having a piss. Once you began, however, that changed. Every scene you wrote, every *word* you wrote, limited your options a little more. Eventually you were like a cow trotting down a narrow chute with no exit, trotting toward the —

"No, no, it's not like that at all," he said, once again startled by the sound of his own voice. "Not like that at all."

### 10

Dark came fast in the deep woods. Drew went around turning on the lamps (there were four of them, each shade more awful than the last), and then tackled the answering machine. He listened to his dead father's message twice, his good old pop who had never, so far as he could recall, said a mean word or raised a hand to his sons (mean words and raised hands had been their mother's province). It seemed wrong to erase it, but because there was no spare answering machine tape in Pop's desk, his marching orders from Lucy left him no choice. His recording was brief and to the point: "This is Drew. Please leave a message."

With that done, he put on his light jacket and went outside to sit on the steps and look at the stars. He was always stunned by how many you could see once you got away from the light pollution of even such a relatively small town as Falmouth. God had spilled a jug of light up there, and beyond the spill was eternity. The mystery of such an extended reality beggared comprehension. A breeze gusted, making the pines sigh in their sorrowful way, and suddenly Drew felt very alone and very small. A shiver went through him and he went back inside, deciding he'd light a small test fire in the stove, just to make sure it wasn't going to fill the cabin with smoke.

There was a crate flanking each side of the fireplace. One held kindling, probably brought in by Old Bill when he stored his last load of wood under the porch. The other contained toys.

Drew dropped to one knee and rummaged through them. A Wham-O Frisbee, which he vaguely remembered: he, Lucy, and the kids playing four-way out front, laughing it up every time someone skimmed the Frizz into the puckerbrush and had to go get it. A Stretch Armstrong doll he was pretty sure had been Brandon's, and a Barbie (indecently topless) that had positively been Stacey's.

Other things, though, he either didn't remember or had never seen before. A one-eyed teddy bear. A deck of Uno cards. A scatter of baseball cards. A game called Pass the Pigs. A top decorated with a circle of monkeys wearing baseball gloves — when he pumped the handle and set it loose, it wobbled drunkenly across the floor and whistled "Take Me Out to the Ball Game." He didn't care for this last. The monkeys seemed to wave their gloves up and down as the top spun, as if seeking help, and the tune began to sound vaguely sinister as it wound down.

He looked at his watch before reaching the bottom of the crate, saw it was quarter past eight, and called Lucy back. He apologized for being tardy, saying he'd gotten sidetracked by a box of toys. "I think I recognized Bran's old Stretch Armstrong —"

Lucy groaned. "Oh God, I used to hate that thing. It smelled so *weird.*"

"I remember. And a few other things, too, but there's stuff I could swear I never saw before. Pass the Pigs?"

"Pass the *what*?" She was laughing.

"It's a kids' game. What about a top with monkeys on it? Plays 'Take Me Out to the Ball Game.' "

"Nope . . . oh wait a minute. Three or four years ago we rented out the cabin to a family called the Pearsons, remember?"

"Vaguely." He didn't at all. If it had been

three years ago, he had probably been wrapped up in *The Village on the Hill. Tied* up, more like it. Bound and gagged. Literary S&M.

"They had a little boy, six or seven. Some of the toys must be his."

"Surprised he didn't miss them," Drew said. He was eyeing the teddy bear, which had the piebald look of a toy that had been hugged often and fervently.

"Want to talk to Brandon? He's here."

"Sure."

"Hi, Dad!" Bran said. "You finish your book yet?"

"Very funny. Starting tomorrow."

"How is it up there? Is it good?"

Drew looked around. The big downstairs room looked mellow in the light of the overheads and the lamps. Even the horrible shades looked okay. And if the stovepipe wasn't plugged, a little fire would take care of the mild chill.

"Yeah," he said. "It's good."

It was. He felt safe. And he felt pregnant, ready to pop. There was no fear about starting the book tomorrow, only anticipation. The words would pour out, he felt sure of it.

The stove was fine, the pipe open and drawing well. As his little fire burned down to embers, he made up the bed in the master bedroom (a joke; the room was hardly big enough to turn around in) with sheets and blankets that smelled only a trifle stale. At ten o'clock he turned in and lay looking up into the dark, listening to the wind sigh around the eaves. He thought of Old Bill committing suicide in the dooryard, but only briefly, and not with fear or horror. What he felt when he considered the old caretaker's final moments — the round circle of steel pressing into the underside of his chin, the last sights and heartbeats and thoughts — was not much different than he'd felt looking up at the complex and extravagant sprawl of the Milky Way. Reality was deep, and it was far. It held many secrets and went on forever.

## 11

He was up early the next morning. He ate breakfast, then called Lucy. She was getting the kids off to school — scolding Stacey because she hadn't finished her homework, telling Bran he'd left his backpack in the living room — so their conversation was necessarily brief. After the goodbyes, Drew pulled on his jacket and walked down to the brook. The trees on the far side had been logged at some point, opening up a million-dollar view of woods undulating into the distance. The sky was a steadily deepening blue. He stood there for almost ten minutes, enjoying the unassuming beauty of the world around him and trying to empty his mind. To make it ready.

526

Each semester he taught a bloc of Modern American and Modern British Literature, but because he had been published (and in *The New Yorker,* no less), his main job was teaching creative writing. He began each class and seminar by talking about the creative process. He told his students that just as most people had a certain routine they followed when they got ready for bed, it was important to have a routine as they prepared for each day's work session. It was like the series of passes a hypnotist makes as he prepares his subject for the trance state.

"The act of writing fiction or poetry has been compared to dreaming," he told his students, "but I don't think that's entirely accurate. I think it's more akin to hypnosis. The more you ritualize the preparation, the easier you'll find it to enter that state."

He practiced what he preached. When he returned to the cabin, he put on coffee. In the course of his morning, he would drink two cups, strong and black. While he waited for it to brew, he took his vitamin pills and brushed his teeth. One of the renters had shoved his pop's old desk under the stairs, and Drew decided to leave it there. An odd place to work, perhaps, but strangely cozy. Almost womblike. In his study at home, his last ritualized act before getting to work would have been to straighten his papers into neat piles, leaving an empty space at the left of his printer for fresh copy, but there was nothing on this desk to straighten.

He powered up his laptop and created a blank document. What followed was also part of the ritual, he supposed: naming the doc (BITTER RIVER #1), formatting the doc, and picking a font for the doc. He had used Book Antiqua while writing *Village,* but had no intention of using it on *Bitter River;* that would be bad mojo indeed. Aware that there might be power outages, causing him to resort to the Olympia portable, he picked the American Typewriter font.

Was that everything? No, one more thing. He clicked on Autosave. Even if there was an outage, he'd be unlikely to lose his copy, the laptop had a full battery, but it was better to be safe than sorry.

The coffee was ready. He poured himself a cup and sat down.

*Do you really want to do this? Do you really* intend *to do this*?

The answer to both was yes, so he centered the blinking cursor and typed

Chapter 1

He hit return and sat very still for a moment. Hundreds of miles south of here he supposed Lucy was sitting with her own cup of coffee in front of her own open laptop, where she kept the records of her current accounting clients. Soon she would fall into her own hypnotic trance — numbers instead of words — but right now she was thinking of him. He was quite sure of that. Thinking of him and hoping, maybe even praying, that he didn't . . . how had Al Stamper put it? . . . lose the wheels off his little red wagon.

"Not going to happen," he said. "It's going to be like taking dictation."

He looked at the blinking cursor a moment longer, then typed:

```
When the girl screamed, a sound
shrill enough to shatter glass,
Herk stopped playing the piano
and turned around.
```

After that, Drew was lost.

## 12

He had arranged his teaching schedule to start late in the day from the very start, because when he was working on his fiction, he liked to begin at eight. He always made himself go until eleven even though on many days he found himself struggling by ten-thirty. He often thought of a story — probably apocryphal — he had read about James Joyce. A friend had come into Joyce's house and found the famous writer at his desk with his head in his arms, a picture of abject despair. When the friend asked what was wrong, Joyce told him he'd only managed seven words all morning. "Ah, but James, that's good for you," the friend said. To which Joyce replied, "Perhaps, but I don't know what *order* they go in!"

Drew could relate to that story, apocryphal or not. It was the way he usually felt during that torturous last half hour. That was when the fear of losing his words set in. Of course during the last month or so of *The Village on the Hill,* he had felt that way every rotten second.

There was none of that nonsense this morning. A door in his head opened directly into the smoky, kerosene-smelling saloon known as the Buffalo Head Tavern, and he stepped through it. He saw every detail, heard every word. He was there, looking through the eyes of Herkimer Belasco, the piano player, when the Prescott kid put the muzzle of his .45 (the one with the fancy pearl-handle grips) under the chin of the young dancehall girl and began to harangue her. The accordion player covered his eyes when Andy Prescott pulled the trigger, but Herkimer kept his wide open and Drew saw it all: the sudden eruption of hair and blood, the bottle of Old Dandy shattered by the bullet, the crack in the mirror behind which the whiskey bottle had stood.

It was like no writing experience Drew had ever had in his life, and when hunger pangs finally pulled him from his trance (his breakfast had consisted of a bowl of Quaker Oats), he looked at the info strip on his laptop and saw it was almost two in the afternoon. His back ached, his eyes burned, and he felt exalted. Almost drunk. He printed his work (eighteen pages, fucking incredible) but left them in the output tray. He would go over them tonight with a pen — that was also part of his routine — but he already knew he would find precious little to correct. A dropped word or two, the occasional unintended repetition, maybe a simile that was working too hard or not hard enough. Otherwise it would be clean. He knew it.

"Like taking dictation," he murmured, then got up to make himself a sandwich.

## 13

Over the next three days he fell into a clockwork routine. It was as if he had been working at the cabin all his life — the creative part of it, anyway. He wrote from seven-thirty or so until almost two. He ate. He napped or walked along the road, counting power poles as he went. In the evening, he lit a fire in the woodstove, heated up something from a can on the Hotpoint, then called home to talk to Lucy and the kids. When the call was done, he would edit his pages, then read, choosing from the paperbacks in the upstairs bookcase. Before bed, he damped the fire in the woodstove and went out to look at the stars.

The story rolled. The pile of pages sitting next to the printer grew. There was no dread as he made his coffee, took his vitamins, and brushed his teeth, only anticipation. Once he sat down, the words were there. He felt that each of those days was Christmas, with new presents to unwrap. He barely noticed that he was sneezing quite a lot on the third day, or the slight roughness in his throat.

"What have you been eating?" Lucy asked him when he called that night. "Be honest, Mister."

"Mostly the stuff I brought, but —"

*"Drew!"* Dragging it out so it was *Drooo.*

"But I'm going to buy some fresh stuff tomorrow, after I finish working."

"Good. Go to the market in St. Christopher. It's not much, but it's better than that nasty little store down the road."

"Okay," he said, although he had no intention of going all the way to St. Christopher; that was a ninety-mile roundtrip, and he wouldn't be back until almost dark. It didn't occur to him until after he'd hung up that he had lied to her. Something he hadn't done since the last few weeks of working on *Village,* when everything started to go wrong. When he had sometimes sat for twenty minutes in front of the same laptop he was using now, debating between *a grove of wil-*

*lows* and *a copse of trees.* Both seemed right, neither seemed right. Sitting hunched over the laptop, sweating, resisting the urge to pound his forehead until he jarred the right descriptive phrase loose. And when Lucy asked him how it was going — with that *I'm worried* furrow in her brow — he had replied with that same single word, that same simple lie: *Okay.*

Undressing for bed, he told himself it didn't matter. If it was a lie it was a white one, just a device to short-circuit an argument before it could be born. Husbands and wives did it all the time. It was the way marriages survived.

He lay down, turned off the lamp, sneezed twice, and went to sleep.

## 14

On his fourth day of work, Drew woke up to plugged sinuses and a moderately sore throat, but no fever he could detect. He could work through a cold, had done so many times in his teaching career; prided himself, in fact, on his ability to bull through while Lucy had a tendency to take to her bed with tissues and NyQuil and magazines at the first sniffle. Drew never scolded her about this, although his mother's word for such behavior — "spleeny" — often came to mind. Lucy was allowed to pamper herself through her twice- or thrice-yearly colds, because she was a freelance accountant, and thus her own boss. In his sabbatical year that was technically true of him, as well . . . except it wasn't. In *The Paris Review* some writer — he couldn't remember who — had said, "When you're writing, the book is the boss," and it was true. If you slowed down the story began to fade, as dreams did on waking.

He spent the morning in the town of Bitter River, but with a box of Kleenex near at hand. When he finished for the day (another eighteen pages, he was absolutely killing it), he was amazed to see he'd used up half the tissues. The wastebasket beside Pop's old desk was drifted with them. There was a bright side to this; while struggling with *Village,* he had regularly filled the wastebasket beside his desk with discarded pages of copy: grove or copse? moose or bear? was the sun brilliant or blazing? There was none of that bullshit in the town of Bitter River, which he was increasingly reluctant to leave.

But leave he must. He was down to a few cans of corned beef hash and Beefaroni. The milk was gone, ditto orange juice. He needed eggs, hamburger, maybe some chicken, and for sure half a dozen frozen dinners. Also, he could use a bag of cough drops and a bottle of NyQuil, Lucy's old standby. The Big 90 would probably have all that stuff. If it didn't, he'd bite the bullet and drive to St. Christopher. Turn the white lie he'd told Lucy into the truth.

He made his slow, bumping way out Shithouse Road and pulled in at the Big 90. By then he was coughing as well as sneezing, his throat was a little worse, one ear felt stuffed up, and he thought maybe he had a touch of fever, after all. Reminding himself to add a bottle of Aleve or Tylenol to his shopping basket, he went inside.

Roy DeWitt had been replaced behind the counter by a scrawny young woman with purple hair, a nose ring, and what looked like a chrome stud in her lower lip. She was chewing gum. Drew, his mind still turned on from his morning's work (and maybe, who knew, that little touch of fever), saw her going home to a trailer up on cement blocks and two or three kids with dirty faces and home haircuts, the youngest a toddler dressed in a saggy diaper and a food-stained tee-shirt saying MOMMY'S L'IL MONSTER. That was a meanly vicious stereotype, and elitist as hell, but that didn't necessarily make it untrue.

Drew grabbed a market basket. "Do you have any fresh meat or produce?"

"Hamburgers and hotdogs in the cooler. Couple of pork chops, maybe. And we got coleslaw."

Well, he supposed that was produce of a sort. "What about chicken?"

"Nope. Got eggs, though. Might be able to

raise a chicken or two from those, would you keep em in a warm place." She laughed at this sally, exposing brown teeth. Not gum after all. Chaw.

Drew ended up filling two baskets. There was no NyQuil, but there was something called Dr. King's Cough & Cold Remedy, also Anacin and Goody's Headache Powder. He topped off his shopping spree with a few cans of chicken noodle soup (Jewish penicillin, his nana had called it), a tub of Shedd's Spread margarine, and two loaves of bread. It was the spongy white stuff, pretty industrial, but beggars couldn't be choosers. He saw soup and a toasted cheese sandwich in his not-too-distant future. Good grub for a man with a sore throat.

The counter woman rang him up, chewing away as she did it. Drew was fascinated by the rise and fall of the stud in her lip. How old would Mommy's l'il monster be before she had one just like it? Fifteen? Eleven, maybe? He told himself again that he was being an elitist, an elitist asshole, in fact, but his overstimulated mind kept running along a trail of associations just the same. Welcome Walmart shoppers. Pampers, inspired by babies. I love a man with a Skoal ring. Each day is a page in your fashion diary. Lock her up send her b—

"Hundred and eight-seventy," she said, snapping the flow of his thoughts.

"Holy crow, really?"

She smiled, revealing teeth he could have done without seeing again. "You want to shop out here in the willies, Mr. . . . Larson, is it?"

"Yes. Drew Larson."

"You want to shop out here in the willies, Mr. Larson, you gotta be prepared to pay the price."

"Where's Roy today?"

She rolled her eyes. "Dad's in the hospital, over St. Christopher. Got the flu, wouldn't go see the doctor, had to be a man about it, and it went pneumonia. My sister's sittin my kids so I can mind his business and lemme tell you, she *ain't* happy about it."

"I'm sorry to hear that." In truth, he didn't care much one way or the other about Roy DeWitt. What he cared about, what he was thinking about, was DeWitt's snot-clotted bandanna. And how he, Drew, had shaken the hand that had been using it.

"Not as sorry as I am. We'll be busy tomorrow with that storm comin in over the weekend." She pointed two spread fingers at his baskets. "I hope you c'n pay cash for that, the credit machine's busted and Dad keeps forgettin to get it fixed."

"I can do that. What storm?"

"A norther, that's what they're sayin on the Rivière-du-Loup. Quebec radio station, you know." She pronounced it *Kwa-beck.* "Lots of wind and rain. Comin in day after tomorrow. You're out there on the Shithouse, ain'tcha?"

"Yes."

"Well, if you don't want to be out there for the next month or so, you might want to pack up your groceries and your luggage and head back down south."

Drew was familiar with this attitude. Up here on the TR, it didn't matter if you were a Maine native; if you didn't come from Aroostook County, you were considered a namby-pamby flatlander who couldn't tell a spruce from a pine. And if you lived south of Augusta, you might as well be just another Masshole, by gorry.

"I think I'll be okay," he said, taking out his wallet. "I live on the coast. We've seen our share of nor'easters."

She looked at him with what might have been pity. "Not talking about a nor'easter, Mr. Larson. Talking about a *norther,* comin straight across O Canador from the Arctic Circle. Temperature's gonna fall off the table, they say. Goodbye sixty-five, hello thirty-eight. Could go lower. Then you got your sleet flyin horizontal at thirty miles per. You get stuck out there on Shithouse Road, you *stuck.*"

"I'll be okay," Drew said. "It'll be —" He stopped. He had been about to say *It'll be like taking dictation.*

"What?"

538

"Fine. It'll be fine."

"You better hope so."

## 15

On his way back to the cabin — the sun flaring in his eyes and kicking off a headache to go with his other symptoms — Drew brooded on that snotty bandanna. Also on how Roy DeWitt had tried to man through it and wound up in the hospital.

He glanced into the rearview mirror and briefly regarded his red, watery eyes. "I am *not* getting the fucking flu. Not when I'm on a roll." Okay, but why in God's name had he shaken that son of a bitch's hand, when it had undoubtedly been crawling with germs? Ones so big you'd hardly need a microscope to see them? And since he had, why hadn't he asked for the bathroom so he could wash them? Christ, his *kids* knew about hand-washing. He'd taught them himself.

"I am *not* getting the fucking flu," he repeated, then dropped the visor to keep the sun out of his eyes. To keep it from flaring in his eyes.

Flaring? Or glaring? Was *glaring* better, or was it too much?

He mused on this as he drove back to the cabin. He brought his groceries in and saw the message light was flashing. It was Lucy, asking that he call back as soon as possible. He felt that tug of annoyance again, the sense that she was looking over his shoulder, but then he realized it might not be about him. After all, not everything was. One of the kids might have gotten sick or had an accident.

He called, and for the first time in a long time — since *The Village on the Hill,* probably — they argued. Not as bad as some of the arguments they'd had in the first years of their marriage, when the kids had been small and money tight, those had been doozies, but bad enough. She had also heard about the storm (of course she had, she was a Weather Channel addict), and she wanted him to pack up and come home.

Drew told her that was a bad idea. Terrible, in fact. He had established a good working rhythm and was getting awesome stuff. A one-day break in that rhythm (and it would probably end up being two, or even three) might not put the book in jeopardy, but a change in his writing environment could. He would have thought she understood the delicacy of creative work — at least for him — after all these years, but it seemed she didn't.

"What you don't understand is how bad this storm is supposed to be. Haven't you been watching the news?"

"No." And then, lying for no good reason (unless it was because he felt spiteful toward her just now): "I have no reception. The dish doesn't work."

"Well, it's going to be bad, especially up north in those unincorporated townships near the border. That's where *you* are, in case you didn't notice. They're expecting widespread power outages because of the wind —"

"Good thing I brought Pop's type —"

"Drew, will you let me finish? Just this once?"

He fell silent, his head throbbing and his throat aching. In that moment he didn't like his wife very much. Loved her, sure, always would, but didn't like her. *Now she'll say thank you,* he thought.

"Thank you," she said. "I *know* you took your father's portable, but you'd be down to candlelight and cold food for days, maybe much longer."

*I can cook on the woodstove.* It was on the tip of his tongue to say that, but if he broke in on her again, the argument would veer onto a new subject, the one about how he didn't take her seriously, so on and so on and yada-yada-yada.

"I suppose you could cook on the wood-stove," she said, in a slightly more reasonable tone, "but if the wind blows like they say it's going to — gale-force sustained, hurricane-force gusts — a lot of trees are going to fall down and you'll be stuck out there."

*I planned to be out here, anyway,* he thought, but again held his tongue.

"I know you were planning to be out there

for two or three weeks, anyway," she said, "but a tree could also knock a hole in the roof and the phone line is going to come down with the power line, and you'll be cut off! What if something happened to you?"

"Nothing's going to —"

"Maybe not, but what if something happened to *us*?"

"Then you'd take care of it," he said. "I wouldn't have gone haring off to the middle of nowhere if I didn't think you could do that. And you have your sis. Besides, they exaggerate the weather reports, you know that. They turn six inches of fresh powder into the storm of the century. It's all about ratings. This will be the same. You'll see."

"Thank you for mansplaining that," Lucy said. Her tone was flat.

So here they were, going to that sore place he'd hoped to avoid. Especially with his throat, sinuses, and ear throbbing. Not to mention his head. Unless he was very diplomatic, they would be mired in the time-honored (or was *dishonored* more accurate?) argument about who knew better. From there they — no, *she* — could move onto the horrors of the paternalistic society. This was a subject upon which Lucy could expatiate endlessly.

"You want to know what I think, Drew? I think when a man says 'You know that,' which they do all the time, what they mean is

'*I* know that, but you're too *dumb* to know that. Hence, I must mansplain.' "

He sighed, and when the sigh threatened to turn into a cough, he stifled it. "Really? You want to go there?"

"Drew . . . we *are* there."

The weariness in her tone, as if he were a stupid child that could not seem to get even the simplest lesson, infuriated him. "Okay, here's a little more mansplaining, Luce. For most of my adult life, I've been trying to write a novel. Do I know why? No. I only know it's the missing piece in my life. *I need to do this,* and I am doing it. It's very, very important. You're asking me to risk that."

"Is it as important as me and the kids?"

"Of course not, but does it have to be a choice?"

"I think it is a choice, and you just made it."

He laughed, and the laugh turned into a cough. "That's pretty melodramatic."

She didn't chase that one; she had something else to chase. "Drew, are you okay? Not coming down with something, are you?"

In his mind he heard the scrawny woman with the stud in her lip saying *had to be a man about it, and it went pneumonia.*

"No," he said. "Allergies."

"Will you think about coming back, at least? Will you do that?"

"Yes." Another lie. He already had thought

about it.

"Call tonight, okay? Talk to the kids."

"Can I talk to you, too? If I promise not to mansplain anything?"

She laughed. Well, actually more of a chuckle, but still a good sign. "Fine."

"I love you, Luce."

"I love you, too," she said, and as he hung up, he had an idea — what English teachers liked to call an epiphany, he supposed — that her feelings were probably not much different from his. Yes, she loved him, he was sure of it, but on this afternoon in early October, she didn't like him much.

He was sure of that, too.

## 16

According to the label, Dr. King's Cough & Cold Remedy was twenty-six per cent alcohol, but after a healthy knock from the bottle that made Drew's eyes water and brought on a serious coughing fit, he guessed the manufacturer might have lowballed the content. Maybe just enough to keep it off the Big 90's liquor shelf with the coffee brandy, the apricot schnapps, and the Fireball Nips. But it cleared his sinuses most righteously, and when he spoke to Brandon that evening, his boy detected nothing out of the ordinary. It was Stacey who asked him if he was okay. Allergies, he told her, and repeated the same lie to Lucy when she took back her phone. At least there was no argument with her tonight, just the unmistakable trace of chill in her voice that he knew well.

It was chilly outside, as well. Indian summer seemed to be over. Drew had an attack of the shivers, and built up a good fire in the woodstove. He sat close to it in Pop's rocker, had another knock of Dr. King's, and read an old John D. MacDonald. From the credit page at the front, it looked like MacDonald had written sixty or seventy books. No problem finding the right word or phrase there, it seemed, and by the end of his life, he had even attained some critical cred. Lucky him.

Drew read a couple of chapters, then went to bed, hoping his cold would be better in the morning and also hoping he wouldn't have a cough syrup hangover. His sleep was uneasy and dream-haunted. He couldn't remember much of those dreams the next morning. Only that in one of them he had been in a seemingly endless hallway lined with doors on both sides. One of them, he felt sure, led to a way out, but he couldn't decide which one to try, and before he could pick one, he woke up to a cold, clear morning, a full bladder, and aching joints. He made his way to the bathroom at the end of the gallery, cursing Roy DeWitt and his besnotted bandanna.

## 17

His fever was still there, but it seemed to be lower, and the combination of Goody's Headache Powder and Dr. King's helped with his other symptoms. The work went pretty well, only ten pages instead of eighteen, but still amazing for him. It was true that he had to pause every now and then, looking for the right word or phrase, but he chalked that up to the infection running around in his body. And those words and phrases always came after a few seconds, clicking neatly into place.

The story was getting good. Sheriff Jim Averill had the killer in jail, but the gun thugs had showed up on an unscheduled train, a midnight special paid for by Andy Prescott's rich rancher daddy, and now they were laying siege to the town. Unlike *Village,* this book was more about plot than character and situation. That had worried Drew a little to begin with; as a teacher and reader (they weren't the same, but surely first cousins) he had a tendency to concentrate on theme, language, and symbolism rather than story, but the pieces also seemed to be clicking into place, almost of their own accord. Best of all, there was a strange bond beginning to form between Averill and the Prescott kid, which gave his story a resonance as unexpected as that midnight train.

Instead of going for an afternoon walk, he

turned on the TV and after a lengthy hunt through the DirecTV onscreen guide, found the Weather Channel. Having access to such a bewildering array of video input up here in the williwags might have amused him on another day, but not on this one. His long session at the laptop had left him wrung out, almost *hollowed* out, instead of energized. Why in God's name had he shaken DeWitt's hand? Common politeness, of course, and completely understandable, but why in God's name hadn't he washed afterwards?

*Been through all that,* he thought.

Yes, and here it was again, gnawing away. It sort of reminded him of his catastrophic last try at novel-writing, when he would lie awake long after Lucy had gone to sleep, mentally deconstructing and reconstructing the few paragraphs he'd managed that day, picking at the work until it bled.

*Stop. That's the past. This is now. Watch the goddam weather report.*

But it wasn't a report; the Weather Channel would never be so minimalist. This was a fucking opera of doom and gloom. Drew hadn't been able to understand his wife's love affair with the Weather Channel, which seemed populated solely by meteorological geeks. As if to underline this, they now gave names to even non-hurricane storms. The one the store clerk had warned him about, the one his wife was so worried about, had been dubbed Pierre. Drew could not conceive of a stupider name for a storm. It was swooping down from Saskatchewan on a northeast track (which made the woman with the lip stud full of shit, it *was* a nor'easter) that would bring it to TR-90 either tomorrow afternoon or evening. It was packing forty-mile-an-hour sustained winds, with gusts up to sixty-five.

"You might think that doesn't sound too bad," said the current weather geek, a young man with a fashionable beard scruff that made Drew's eyes hurt. Mr. Scruffy was a poet of the Pierre Apocalypse, not quite speaking in iambic pentameter, but close. "What you need to remember, though, is that temperatures are going to fall *radically* when this front comes through, I mean they're gonna *drop* off the *table.* Rain could turn to *sleet,* and you drivers up there in northern New England can't discount the possibility of *black ice.*"

*Maybe I* should *go home,* Drew thought.

But it was no longer just the book that was keeping him. The idea of that long drive out Shithouse Road feeling as drained as he did today made him even more tired. And when he finally made it to something approximating civilization, was he supposed to go tooling down I-95 sipping away at alcohol-laced cold medicine?

"The major thing, though," the scruffy

weather geek was saying, "is that this baby is going to meet a *ridge* of high *pressure* coming in from *east* — a very *unusual* phenomenon. That means our friends north of *Boston* could be in for what the old Yankees called *a three-day blow.*"

*Blow on this,* Drew thought, and grabbed his crotch.

Later, after an unsuccessful try at napping — all he did was toss and turn — Lucy called. "Listen to me, Mister." He hated when she called him that, it was like fingers dragged down a blackboard. "The forecast is only getting worse. You need to come home."

"Lucy, it's a storm, what my Pop used to call a cap of wind. Not nuclear war."

"You need to come home while you still can."

He had had enough of this, and enough of her. "No. I need to be here."

"You're a fool," she said. Then, for the first time he could remember, she hung up on him.

### 18

Drew turned on the Weather Channel as soon as he got up the following morning, thinking *As a dog returneth to its vomit, so a fool repeateth his folly.*

He was hoping to hear that Autumn Storm Pierre had changed course. It had not. Nor had his cold changed course. It didn't seem worse, but it didn't seem better, either. He called Lucy and got her voicemail. Possibly she was running errands; possibly she just didn't want to talk with him. That was okay with Drew either way. She was pissed at him, but she would get over it; no one trashed fifteen years of marriage over a storm, did they? Especially not one named Pierre.

Drew scrambled a couple of eggs and managed to eat half of them before his stomach warned him that stuffing down more might lead to a forcible ejection. He scraped his plate into the garbage, sat down in front of the laptop, and called up the current document (BITTER RIVER #3). He scrolled to where he had left off, looked at the white space beneath the blinking cursor, and started to fill it. The work went all right for the first hour or so, and then the trouble began. It started with the rocking chairs Sheriff Averill and his three deputies were meant to sit in outside the Bitter River jail.

They had to be sitting out front, in full view of the townsfolk and Dick Prescott's gun thugs, because that was the basis of the clever plan Averill had hatched to get Prescott's son out of town under the very noses of the hard men who were supposed to keep it from happening. The lawmen had to be seen, especially the deputy named Cal Hunt, who happened to be about the same height and build as the Prescott boy.

Hunt was wearing a colorful Mexican serape and a ten-gallon hat decorated with silver conchos. The hat's extravagant brim obscured his face. That was important. The serape and hat weren't Deputy Hunt's; he said he felt like a fool in a hat like that. Sheriff Averill didn't care. He wanted Prescott's men to be looking at the clothes, and not the man inside them.

All fine. Good storytelling. Then the trouble came.

"All right," Sheriff Averill told his deputies. "It's time we took a little night air. Be seen by whoever wants to look at us. Hank, bring that jug. I want to be sure those boys on the rooftops get a good look at the dumb sheriff getting drunk with his even dumber deputies."

"Do I have to wear this hat?" Cal Hunt almost moaned. "I'll never live it down!"

"What you ought to be concerned about is living through the night," Averill said. "Now come on. Let's just get these rocking chairs outside and

That was where Drew stopped, transfixed by the image of the tiny Bitter River sheriff's office containing three rocking chairs. No, *four* rocking chairs, because you had to add one for Averill himself. That was a lot more absurd than the ten-gallon, face-obscuring Stetson Cal Hunt was wearing, and not only because four rockers would fill the whole damn room. The whole *idea* of rocking chairs was antithetical to law enforcement, even in a small western town like Bitter River. People would laugh. Drew deleted most of the sentence and looked at what was left.

```
Let's just get these
```

These what? Chairs? Would the sheriff's office even *have* four chairs? It seemed unlikely. "Not like there's a fucking waiting room," Drew said, and wiped his forehead. "Not in a —" A sneeze surprised him and he let go before he could cover his mouth, spattering the laptop's screen with a fine spray of spittle, distorting the words.

"Fuck! Goddam *fuck!*"

He grabbed for tissues to wipe the screen, but the Kleenex box was empty. He got a dishtowel instead, and when he'd finished cleaning the screen, he thought of how much the soggy dishtowel looked like Roy DeWitt's bandanna. His besnotted bandanna.

```
Let's just get these
```

Was his fever worse? Drew didn't want to

believe that, wanted to believe the growing heat he felt (plus the increased throbbing in his head) was just the pressure of trying to solve this idiotic rocking chair problem so he could move on, but it certainly seemed like —

This time he managed to turn aside before the sneezing started. Not just one this time but half a dozen. He seemed to feel his sinuses bulging with each one. Like overinflated tires. His throat was throbbing, and so was his ear.

Let's just get these

It came to him then. A bench! There might be a bench in the sheriff's office where people could sit while they waited to do their little bits of business. He grinned and gave himself a thumbs up. Sick or not, the pieces were still falling into place, and was that really surprising? Creativity often seemed to run on its own clean circuit, regardless of the body's ills. Flannery O'Connor had lupus. Stanley Elkin had multiple sclerosis. Fyodor Dostoyevsky had epilepsy, and Octavia Butler suffered from dyslexia. What was a lousy cold, maybe even the flu, compared to things like that? He could work through this. The bench proved it, the bench was genius.

"Let's just get this bench outside and have a few drinks."

"But we're not really gonna drink, are we, Sheriff?" Jep Leonard asked. The plan had been explained to him carefully, but Jep was not exactly the brightest bulb in the

Brightest bulb in the chandelier? God no, that was an anachronism. Or was it? The bulb part for sure, no lightbulbs in the 1880s, but there *were* chandeliers back then, of course there were. There was one in the saloon! If he'd had an Internet connection he could have looked at any number of old-time examples of them, but he didn't. Just two hundred channels of TV, most of it total junk.

Better to use a different metaphor. If it even *was* a metaphor; Drew wasn't completely sure. Maybe it was just a comparative . . . comparative *something.* No, it was a metaphor. He was sure of it. Almost.

Never mind, that wasn't the point and this wasn't a classroom exercise, it was a book, it was *his* book, so stick to the writing. Eyes on the prize.

Not the ripest melon in the patch? Not the fastest horse in the race? No, those were awful, but —

Then he got it. Magic! He bent and typed rapidly.

The plan had been explained to

554

him carefully, but Jep was not exactly the smartest kid in the classroom.

Satisfied (well, *relatively* satisfied), Drew got up, had a knock of Dr. King's, then chased it with a glass of water to wash the taste out of his mouth: a slimy mixture of snot and cold medicine.

*This is like before. This is like what happened with* Village.

He could tell himself that wasn't true, that this time was entirely different, that the clean circuit wasn't so clean after all because he was running a fever, a pretty high one from the way it felt, and it was all because he'd handled that bandanna.

*No you didn't, you handled his hand. You handled the hand that handled the bandanna.*

"Handled the hand that handled the bandanna, right."

He turned on the cold tap and splashed his face. That made him feel a little better. He mixed Goody's Headache Powder with more water, drank it off, then went to the door and threw it open. He felt quite sure that Moose Mom would be there, so sure that for a moment (thank you, fever) he actually thought he *did* see her over there by the equipment shed, but it was only shadows moving in a slight breeze.

He took a number of deep breaths. *In goes*

*the good air, out goes the bad, when I shook
his hand I must have been mad.*

Drew went back inside and sat down at the
laptop. Pushing on seemed like a bad idea,
but not pushing on seemed even worse. So
he began to write, trying to recapture the
wind that had filled his sails and brought him
this far. At first it seemed to be working, but
by lunchtime (not that he had any interest in
eating) his interior sails had gone slack. Probably it was being sick, but it was still too
much like before.

*I seem to be losing my words.*

That was what he'd told Lucy, what he'd
told Al Stamper, but that wasn't the truth; it
was just what he could give them so they
could dismiss it as writer's block, something
he would eventually find his way through. Or
it might dissolve on its own. In truth, it was
the opposite. It was having too many words.
Was it a copse or a grove? Was it flaring or
glaring? Or maybe staring? Was a character
sunken eyed or hollow-eyed? Oh, and if
*hollow-eyed* was hyphenated, what about
*sunken eyed?*

He shut down at one o'clock. He had written two pages, and the feeling that he was
reverting to the nervous and neurotic man
who'd almost burned down his house three
years ago was getting harder to dismiss. He
could tell himself to let go of the small stuff
like rocking chairs versus bench, to let the

story carry him, but when he looked at the screen, every word there seemed wrong. Every word seemed to have a better one hiding behind it, just out of sight.

Was it possible that he was coming down with Alzheimer's? Could that be it?

"Don't be dumb," he said, and was dismayed at how nasal he sounded. Also hoarse. Pretty soon he'd lose his voice entirely. Not that there was anyone out here to talk to except himself.

*Get your ass home. You've got a wife and two fine kids to talk to.*

But if he did that, he would lose the book. He knew that as well as he knew his own name. After four or five days, when he was back in Falmouth and feeling better, he would open the *Bitter River* documents and the prose there would look like something someone else had written, an alien story he would have no idea how to finish. Leaving now would be like throwing away a precious gift, one that might never be given again.

*Had to be a man about it, and it went pneumonia,* Roy DeWitt's daughter had said, the subtext being *just another damn fool.* And was he going to do the same?

The lady or the tiger. The book or your life. Was the choice really that stark and melodramatic? Surely not, but he surely felt like ten pounds of shit in a five-pound bag, there was no doubt about that.

*Nap. I need a nap. When I wake up, I'll be able to decide.*

So he took another knock of Dr. King's Magic Elixir — or whatever it was called — and climbed the stairs to the bedroom he and Lucy had shared on other trips out here. He went to sleep, and when he woke up, the rain and wind had arrived and the choice was made for him. He had a call to make. While he still could.

## 19

"Hey, honey, it's me. I'm sorry I pissed you off. Really."

She ignored this completely. "It doesn't sound like allergies to me, Mister. It sounds like you're sick."

"It's just a cold." He cleared his throat, or tried to. "A pretty bad one, I guess."

The throat-clearing provoked coughing. He covered the mouthpiece of the old-fashioned phone, but he supposed she heard it anyway. The wind gusted, rain slapped against the windows, and the lights flickered.

"So now what? You just hole up?"

"I think I have to," he said, then rushed on. "It's not the book, not now. I'd come back if I thought it was safe, but that storm is here already. The lights just flickered. I'm going to lose the power and the phone before dark, practically guaranteed. Here I'll pause so you can say I told you so."

"I told you so," she said. "And now that we've got that out of the way, how bad are you?"

"Not that bad," he said, which was a far bigger lie than telling her the satellite dish didn't work. He thought he was quite bad indeed, but if he said that, it was hard to gauge how she might react. Would she call the Presque Isle cops and request a rescue? Even in his current condition, that seemed like an overreaction. Not to mention embarrassing.

"I hate this, Drew. I hate you being up there and cut off. Are you sure you can't drive out?"

"I might have been able to earlier, but I took some cold medicine before I laid down for a nap and overslept. Now I don't dare chance it. There are still washouts and plugged culverts from last winter. A hard rain like this is apt to put long stretches of the road underwater. The Suburban *might* make it, but if it didn't, I could be stranded six miles from the cabin and nine miles from the Big 90."

There was a pause, and in it Drew fancied he could hear what she was thinking: *Had to be a man about it, didn't you, just another damn fool.* Because sometimes *I told you so* was just not enough.

The wind gusted and the lights flickered again. (Or maybe they stuttered.) The phone gave a cicada buzz, then cleared.

"Drew? Are you still there?"

"I'm here."

"The phone made a funny sound."

"I heard it."

"You have food?"

"Plenty." Not that he felt like eating.

She sighed. "Then hunker down. Call me tonight if the phone still works."

"I will. And when the weather breaks, I'll come home."

"Not if there are trees down, you won't. Not until somebody decides to come in and clear the road."

"I'll clear them myself," Drew said. "Pop's chainsaw is in the equipment shed, unless one of the renters decided to take it. Any gas that was in the tank will have evaporated, but I can siphon some out of the Suburban."

"If you don't get sicker."

"I won't —"

"I'm going to tell the kids you're fine." Talking to herself more than him now. "No sense worrying them, too."

"That's a good —"

"This is fucked up, Drew." She hated it when he interrupted her, but had never had any qualms about doing it herself. "I want you to know that. When you put yourself in this position, you put us in it, too."

"I'm sorry."

"Is the book still going well? It better be. It better be worth all the worry."

"It's going fine." He was no longer sure of this, but what else could he tell her? *The shit's starting again, Lucy, and now I'm sick as well?* Would that ease her mind?

"All right." She sighed. "You're an idiot, but I love you."

"Love you, t—" The wind whooped, and suddenly the only light in the cabin was the dim and watery stuff coming in through the windows. "Lucy, I just lost the lights." He sounded calm, and that was good.

"Look in the equipment shed," she said. "There might be a Coleman lantern —"

There was another of those cicada buzzes, and then nothing but silence. He replaced the old-fashioned phone in its cradle. He was on his own.

## 20

He grabbed a musty old jacket from one of the hooks by the door and fought his way to the equipment shed through the late light, raising his arm once to fend off a flying branch. Maybe it was being sick, but the wind felt like it was already blowing forty per. He fumbled through the keys, cold water trickling down the back of his neck in spite of the jacket's turned-up collar, and had to try three before he found the one that fit the padlock on the door. Once again he had to diddle it back and forth to get it to turn, and by the time it did, he was soaked and coughing.

The shed was dark and full of shadows even with the door wide open, but there was enough light to see Pop's chainsaw sitting on a table at the back. There were also a couple of other saws, one a two-handed buck, and probably that was good, because the chainsaw looked useless. The yellow paint of the body was almost obscured by ancient grease, the cutting chain was badly rusted, and he couldn't imagine mustering the energy to yank the starter cord, anyway.

Lucy was right about the Coleman lantern, though. There were actually two of them sitting on a shelf to the left of the door, along with a gallon can of fuel, but one of them was clearly useless, the globe shattered and the handle gone. The other one looked okay. The silk mantles were attached to the gas jets, which was good; with his hands shaking the way they were, he doubted if he would have been able to tie them down. *Should have thought of this sooner,* he scolded himself. *Of course I should have gone home sooner. When I still could.*

When Drew tipped the can of fuel to the dimming afternoon light, he saw Pop's back-slanted printing on a strip of adhesive: USE THIS NOT UNLEADED GAS! He shook the can. It was half full. Not great, but maybe enough to last a three-day blow if he rationed his use.

He took the can and unbroken lantern back to the house, started to put them on the dining room table, then thought better of it. His hands were shaking, and he was bound to spill at least some of the fuel. He put the lantern in the sink instead, then shucked the sodden jacket. Before he could think about fueling the lantern, the coughing started again. He collapsed into one of the dining room chairs, hacking away until he felt he might pass out. The wind was howling, and something thudded on the roof. A much bigger branch than the one he'd fended off, from the sound.

When the coughing passed, he unscrewed the tap on the lantern's reservoir and went looking for a funnel. He didn't find one, so he tore off a strip of aluminum foil and fashioned a half-assed funnel from that. The fumes wanted to start the coughing again, but he controlled it until he got the lantern's little tank filled. When it was, he let go and bent over the counter with his burning forehead on one arm, hacking and choking and gasping for breath.

The fit eventually passed, but the fever was worse than ever. *Getting soaked probably didn't help,* he thought. Once he got the Coleman lit — *if* he got it lit — he'd take some more aspirin. Add a shot of headache powder and a knock of Dr. King's for good measure.

He pumped the little gadget on the side to

build pressure, opened the tap, then struck a kitchen match and slipped it through the ignition hole. For a moment there was nothing, but then the mantles lit up, the light so bright and concentrated it made him wince. He took the Coleman to the cabin's single closet, looking for a flashlight. He found clothes, orange vests for hunting season, and an old pair of ice skates (he vaguely remembered skating on the brook with his brother on the few occasions they'd been up here in the winter). He found hats and gloves and an elderly Electrolux vacuum cleaner that looked about as useful as the rusty chainsaw in the equipment shed. There was no flashlight.

The wind rose to a shriek around the eaves, making his head hurt. Rain lashed the windows. The last of the daylight continued to drain away, and he thought this was going to be a very long night. His expedition to the shed and his struggle to get the lamp lit had occupied him, but now that those chores were done, he had time to be afraid. He was stuck here because of a book that was (he could admit it now) starting to unravel like the others. He was stuck, he was sick, and he was apt to get sicker.

"I could die out here," he said in his new hoarse voice. "I really could."

Best not to think of that. Best to load up the woodstove and get it cranking, because the night was going to be cold as well as long.

*Temperatures are going to fall* radically *when this front comes through,* wasn't that what the scruffy weather geek had said? And the counter woman with the lip stud had said the same thing. Right down to the same metaphor (if it *was* a metaphor), which likened temperature to a physical object that could roll off a table.

That brought him back to Deputy Jep, who was not the smartest kid in the classroom. Really? Had he actually thought that would do? It was a shitty metaphor (if it even *was* a metaphor). Not just weak, dead on arrival. As he loaded the stove, his feverish mind seemed to open a secret door and he thought, *A sandwich short of a picnic.*

Better.

*All foam and no beer.*

Better still, because of the story's western milieu.

*Dumber than a bag of hammers. About as smart as a rock. Sharp as a marb—*

"Stop it," he almost begged. That was the problem. That secret door was the problem, because . . .

"I have no control over it," he said in his croaky voice, and thought, *Dumb as a frog with brain damage.*

Drew struck the side of his head with the heel of his hand. His headache flared. He did it again. And again. When he'd had enough

565

of that, he stuffed crumpled sheets of magazine under some kindling, scratched a match on the stovetop, and watched the flames lick up.

Still holding the lit match, he looked at the pages of *Bitter River* stacked beside the printer, and thought about what would happen if he touched them alight. He hadn't quite managed to burn down the house when he'd lit up *The Village on the Hill,* the fire trucks had arrived before the flames could do much more than scorch the walls of his study, but there would be no fire trucks out here on Shithouse Road, and the storm wouldn't stop the fire once it took hold, because the cabin was old and dry. Old as dirt, dry as your grandmother's —

The flame guttering along the matchstick reached his fingers. Drew shook it out, tossed it into the blazing stove, and slammed the grate shut.

"It's not a bad book and I'm not going to die out here," he said. "Not going to happen."

He turned off the Coleman to conserve the fuel, then sat down in the wing chair he spent his evenings in, reading paperbacks by John D. MacDonald and Elmore Leonard. There wasn't enough light to read by now, not with the Coleman off. Night had almost come, and the only light in the cabin was the shifting red eye of the fire seen through the woodstove's isinglass window. Drew pulled his chair a bit closer to the stove and wrapped his arms around himself to quell the shivers. He should change out of his damp shirt and pants, and do it right away if he didn't want to get even sicker. He was still thinking this when he fell asleep.

## 21

What woke him was a splintering crack from outside. It was followed by a second, even louder crack, and a thud that shook the floor. A tree had fallen, and it must have been a big one.

The fire in the woodstove had burned down to a bed of bright red embers that waxed and waned. Along with the wind, he could now hear a sandy rattling against the windows. The cabin's big downstairs room was stuporously hot, at least for the time being, but the temperature outside must have fallen (*off the table*) as predicted, because the rain had turned to sleet.

Drew tried to check the time, but his wrist was bare. He supposed he'd left his watch on the nighttable beside the bed, although he couldn't remember for sure. He could always check the time and date strip on his laptop, he supposed, but what would be the point? It was nighttime in the north woods. Did he need any other information?

He decided he did. He needed to find out

if the tree had fallen on his trusty Suburban and smashed the shit out of it. Of course *need* was the wrong word, *need* was for something you had to have, subtext being that if you could get it you might be able to change the overall situation for the better, and nothing in *this* situation would change either way, and was *situation* the right word, or was it too general? It was more of a *fix* than a situation, *fix* in this context meaning not to repair but —

"Stop it," he said. "Do you want to drive yourself crazy?"

He was pretty sure a part of him wanted exactly that. Somewhere inside his head, control panels were smoking and circuit breakers were fusing and some mad scientist was shaking his fists in exultation. He could tell himself it was the fever, but he had been in fine fettle when *Village* had gone bad. Same with the other two. Physically, at least.

He got up, wincing at the aches that now seemed to be afflicting all of his joints, and went to the door, trying not to hobble. The wind tore it from his grasp and bounced it off the wall. He grabbed it and held on, his clothes plastered against his body and his hair streaming back from his forehead. The night was black — black as the devil's riding boots, black as a black cat in a coalmine, black as a woodchuck's asshole — but he could make out the bulk of his Suburban and (maybe) tree branches waving above it on the far side. Although he couldn't be sure, he thought the tree had spared his Suburban and landed on the equipment shed, no doubt bashing in the roof.

He shouldered the door shut and turned the deadbolt. He didn't expect intruders on such a dirty night, but he didn't want it blowing open after he went to bed. And he *was* going to bed. He made his way to the kitchen counter by the shifting, chancy light of the embers and lit the Coleman lantern. In its glare the cabin looked surreal, caught by a flashbulb that didn't go out but just went on and on. Holding it in front of him, he crossed to the stairs. That was when he heard a scratching at the door.

*A branch,* he told himself. *Blown there by the wind and caught somehow, maybe on the welcome mat. It's nothing. Go to bed.*

The scratching came again, so soft he never would have heard it if the wind hadn't chosen those few moments to lull. It didn't sound like a branch; it sounded like a person. Like some orphan of the storm too weak or badly hurt to even knock and could only scratch. Only no one had been out there . . . or had there been? Could he be absolutely sure? It had been so dark. Black as the devil's riding boots.

Drew went to the door, freed the deadbolt, and opened it. He held up the Coleman lamp. No one there. Then, as he was about to shut the door again, he looked down and saw a rat. Probably a Norway, not huge but pretty big. It was lying on the threadbare welcome mat, one of its paws — pink, strangely human, like a baby's hand — outstretched and still scratching at the air. Its brown-black fur was littered with tiny bits of leaf, twig, and beads of blood. Its bulging black eyes were looking up at him. Its side heaved. That pink paw continued to scratch at the air, just as it had scratched at the door. A minuscule sound.

Lucy hated rodents, screeched her head off if she saw so much as a fieldmouse scuttering along the baseboard, and it did no good to tell her the wee sleekit cowerin beastie was undoubtedly a lot more terrified of her than she was of it. Drew didn't care much for rodents himself, and understood they carried diseases — hantavirus, rat bite fever, and those were only the two most common — but he'd never had Lucy's almost instinctive loathing of them. What he mostly felt for this one was pity. Probably it was that tiny pink paw, which continued scratching at nothing. Or maybe the pinpricks of white light from the Coleman lantern he saw in its dark eyes. It lay there panting and looking up at him with blood on its fur and in its whiskers. Broken up inside and probably dying.

Drew bent, one hand on his upper thigh, the other holding down the lantern for a better look. "You were in the equipment shed, weren't you?"

Almost surely. Then the tree had come down, smashing through the roof, destroying Mr. Rat's happy home. Had he been hit by a tree branch or a piece of the roof as he scuttled for safety? Maybe by a bucket of congealed paint? Had Pop's useless old Mc-Culloch chainsaw tumbled off the table and fallen on him? It didn't matter. Whatever it was had squashed him and maybe broken his back. He'd had just enough gas left in his ratty little tank to crawl here.

The wind picked up again, throwing sleet into Drew's hot face. Spicules of ice struck the globe of the lantern, hissed, melted, and ran down the glass. The rat panted. *The rat on the mat needs help stat,* Drew thought. Except the rat on the mat was beyond help. You didn't need to be a rocket scientist.

Except, of course, he *could* help.

Drew walked to the dead socket of the fireplace, pausing once for a coughing fit, and bent over the stand containing the little collection of fireplace tools. He considered the poker, but the idea of skewering the rat with it made him wince. He took the ash shovel instead. One hard hit ought to be enough to put it out of its misery. Then he could use the shovel to sweep it off the side of the porch. If he lived through tonight, he had no wish to start tomorrow by stepping on the

571

corpse of a dead rodent.

*Here is something interesting,* he thought. *When I first saw it, I thought "he." Now that I've decided to kill the damn thing, it's "it."*

The rat was still on the mat. Sleet had begun crusting on its fur. That one pink paw (so human, so human) continued to paw at the air, although now it was slowing down.

"I'm going to make it better," Drew said. He raised the shovel . . . held it at shoulder height for the strike . . . then lowered it. And why? The slowly groping paw? The beady black eyes?

A tree had crashed the rat's home and crushed him (*back to him now*), he had somehow dragged himself to the cabin, God knew how much effort it had taken, and was this to be his reward? Another crushing, this one final? Drew was feeling rather crushed himself these days and, ridiculous or not (probably it was), he felt a degree of empathy.

Meanwhile, the wind was chilling him, sleet was smacking him in the face, and he was shivering again. He had to close the door and he wasn't going to leave the rat to die slowly in the dark. And on a fucking welcome mat, to boot.

Drew set down the lantern and used the shovel to scoop it up (funny how liquid that pronoun was). He went to the stove and tilted the shovel so the rat slid onto the floor. That one pink paw kept scratching. Drew put his hands on his knees and coughed until he dry-retched and spots danced in front of his eyes. When the fit passed, he took the lantern back to his reading chair and sat down.

"Go ahead and die now," he said. "At least you're out of the weather and can do it where you're warm."

He turned off the lantern. Now there was just the faint red glow of the dying embers. The way they waxed and waned reminded him of the way that tiny pink paw had scratched . . . and scratched . . . and scratched. It was doing it still, he saw.

*I should build up the fire before I go up to bed,* he thought. *If I don't, this place is going to be as cold as Grant's Tomb in the morning.*

But the coughing, which had temporarily subsided, would no doubt begin again if he got up and started moving the phlegm around. And he was tired.

*Also, you put the rat down pretty close to the stove. I think you brought it in to die a natural death, didn't you? Not to broil it alive. Build the fire up in the morning.*

The wind droned around the cabin, occasionally rising to a womanish screech, then subsiding to that drone again. The sleet slatted against the windows. As he listened to these sounds, they seemed to merge. He closed his eyes, then opened them again. Had the rat died? At first he thought it had, but

573

then that tiny paw made another short slow stroke. So not quite yet.

Drew closed his eyes.

And slept.

## 22

He awoke with a start when another branch thudded down on the roof. He had no idea how long he had been out. It could have been fifteen minutes, it could have been two hours, but one thing was sure: there was no rat in front of the stove. Apparently Monsieur Rat hadn't been as badly hurt as Drew had thought; it had come around and was now somewhere in the house with him. He didn't much care for that idea, but it was his own fault. He had invited it in, after all.

*You have to invite them in,* Drew thought. *Vampires. Wargs. The devil in his black riding boots. You have to invite —*

"Drew."

He started so strongly at the sound of that voice that he almost kicked over the lantern. He looked around and by the light of the dying fire in the stove, saw the rat. He was on Pop's desk under the stairs, sitting on his back paws between the laptop and the portable printer. Sitting, in fact, on the manuscript of *Bitter River.*

Drew tried to speak, but at first could only manage a croak. He cleared his throat — which was painful — and tried again. "I

574

thought you just said something."

"I did." The rat's mouth didn't move, but the voice was coming from him, all right; it wasn't in Drew's head.

"This is a dream," Drew said. "Or delirium. Maybe both."

"No, it's real enough," the rat said. "You're awake and you're not delirious. Your fever's going down. Check for yourself."

Drew put a hand on his forehead. He did feel cooler, but that wasn't exactly trust-worthy, was it? He was conversing with a rat, after all. He felt in his pocket for the kitchen matches he'd left there, struck one, and lit the lantern. He held it up, expecting the rat to be gone, but he was still there, sitting on his back paws with his tail curled around his haunches and holding his weird pink hands to his chest.

"If you're real, get off my manuscript," Drew said. "I worked too hard on it for you to leave a bunch of ratshit on the title page."

"You did work hard," the rat agreed (but showing no signs of relocating). He scratched behind one ear, now seeming perfectly lively.

*Whatever fell on him must have just stunned him,* Drew thought. *If he's there at all, that is. If he was* ever *there.*

"You worked hard and at first you worked well. You were totally on the rails, running fast and hot. Then it started to go wrong, didn't it? Just like the other ones. Don't feel bad; wannabe novelists all over the world hit the same wall. Do you know how many half-finished novels are stuck in desk drawers or filing cabinets? *Millions.*"

"Getting sick fucked me up."

"Think back, think honestly. It was starting to happen even before that."

Drew didn't want to think back.

"You lose your selective perception," the rat said. "It happens to you every time. On the novels, at least. Doesn't happen at once, but as the book grows and begins to breathe, more choices need to be made and your selective perception erodes."

The rat went to all fours, trotted to the edge of Pop's desk, and sat up again, like a dog begging for a treat.

"Writers have different habits, different ways of getting in the groove, and they work at different speeds, but to produce a long work, there must always come extended periods of focused narration."

*I've heard that before,* Drew thought. *Almost word for word. Where?*

"At every single moment during those focused periods — those *flights of fancy* — the writer is faced with at least seven choices of word and expression and detail. Talented ones make the right choices with almost no conscious consideration; they are pro basketball players of the mind, hitting from all over the court."

*Where? Who?*

"A constant winnowing process is going on which is the basis of what we call creative wri—"

*"Franzen!"* Drew bellowed, sitting upright and sending a bolt of pain through his head. "That was part of the Franzen lecture! Almost word for word!"

The rat ignored this interruption. "You are capable of that winnowing process, but only in short bursts. When you try to write a novel — the difference between a sprint and a marathon — it always breaks down. You see all the choices of expression and detail, but the consequent winnowing begins to fail you. You don't lose the words, you lose the ability to choose the *correct* words. They look all right; they look all wrong. It's very sad. You're like a car with a powerful engine and a broken transmission."

Drew closed his eyes tight enough to make spots flare, and then sprang them open. His orphan of the storm was still there.

"I can help you," the rat announced. "If you want me to, that is."

"And you'd do this because?"

The rat cocked his head, as if unable to believe a supposedly smart man — a college English teacher who had been published in *The New Yorker*! — could be so stupid. "You were going to kill me with a shovel, and why not? I'm just a lowly rat, after all. But you

577

took me in instead. You saved me."

"So as a reward you give me three wishes." Drew said it with a smile. This was familiar ground: Hans Christian Andersen, Marie-Catherine d'Aulnoy, the Brothers Grimm.

"Just one," the rat said. "A very specific one. You can wish to finish your book." He lifted his tail and slapped it down on the manuscript of *Bitter River* for emphasis. "But it comes with a condition."

"And that would be?"

"Someone you care for will have to die."

More familiar ground. This turned out to be a dream where he was replaying his argument with Lucy. He had explained (not very well, but he had given it the old college try) that he *needed* to write the book. That it was very important. She had asked if it was as important as she and the kids. He had told her no, of course not, then asked if it had to be a choice.

*I think it is a choice,* she'd said. *And you just made it.*

"This isn't actually a magic wish situation at all," he said. "More of a business deal. Or a Faustian bargain. It's sure not like any of the fairy tales I read as a kid."

The rat scratched behind one ear, somehow keeping his balance while he did it. Admirable. "All the wishes in fairy tales come at a price. Then there's 'The Monkey's Paw.' Remember that one?"

"Even in a dream," Drew said, "I would not trade my wife or either of my kids for an oat opera with no literary pretensions."

As the words came out of his mouth, he realized that was why he had seized the idea of *Bitter River* so unquestioningly; his plot-driven western would never be stacked up against the next Rushdie or Atwood or Chabon. Not to mention the next Franzen.

"I would never ask you to," the rat said. "Actually, I was thinking of Al Stamper. Your old department head."

That silenced Drew. He just looked at the rat, which looked back with those beady black eyes. The wind blew around the cabin, sometimes gusting hard enough to shake the walls; the sleet rattled.

*Pancreatic,* Al had said when Drew commented on his startling weight loss. But, he had added, there was no need for anyone to be crafting obituaries just yet. *The docs caught it relatively early. Confidence is high.*

Looking at him, though — sallow skin, sunken eyes, lifeless hair — Drew had felt no confidence whatsoever. The key word in what Al had said was *relatively.* Pancreatic cancer was sly; it hid. The diagnosis was almost always a death sentence. And if he did die? There would be mourning, of course, and Nadine Stamper would be the chief mourner — they had been married for something like forty-five years. The members of the English

Department would wear black armbands for a month or so. The obituary would be long, noting Al's many accomplishments and awards. His books on Dickens and Hardy would be mentioned. But he was seventy-two at least, maybe even seventy-four, and nobody would say he died young, or with his promise unfulfilled.

Meanwhile, the rat was looking at him, its pink paws now curled against its furry chest.

*What the hell?* Drew thought. *It's only a hypothetical question. And one inside a dream, at that.*

"I guess I'd take the deal and make the wish," Drew said. Dream or no dream, hypothetical question or not, he felt uneasy saying it. "He's dying, anyway."

"You finish your book and Stamper dies," the rat said, as if to make sure Drew understood.

Drew gave the rat a cunning sideways look. "Will the book be published?"

"I'm authorized to grant the wish if you make it," the rat said. "I'm *not* authorized to predict the future of your literary endeavor. Were I to guess . . ." The rat cocked his head. "I'd guess it will be. As I said, you *are* talented."

"Okay," Drew said. "I finish the book, Al dies. Since he's going to die anyway, that seems okay to me." Only it didn't, not really. "Do you think he'll live long enough to read it, at least?"

"I just told you —"

Drew raised a hand. "Not authorized to predict the future of my literary endeavor, right. Are we done here?"

"There's one more thing I need."

"If it's my signature in blood on a contract, you can forget the whole deal."

"It's not all about you, Mister," the rat said. "I'm hungry." He jumped onto the desk's chair, and from the chair to the floor. He sped across to the kitchen table and picked up an oyster cracker, one Drew must have dropped on the day he had the grilled cheese and tomato soup. The rat sat up, grasping the oyster cracker in its paws, and went to work. The cracker was gone in seconds.

"Good talking to you," the rat said. It disappeared almost as quickly as the oyster cracker, zipping across the floor and into the dead fireplace.

"Goddam," Drew said.

He closed his eyes, then sprang them open. It didn't *feel* like a dream. He closed them again, opened them again. The third time he closed them, they stayed closed.

## 23

He awoke in his bed, with no memory of how he'd gotten there . . . or had he been here all night? That was more than likely, considering how fucked up he'd been thanks to Roy De-

Witt and his snotty bandanna. The whole previous day seemed like a dream, his conversation with the rat only the most vivid part of it.

The wind was still blowing and the sleet was still sleeting, but he felt better. There was no question of it. The fever was either going or entirely gone. His joints still ached and his throat was still sore, but neither was as bad as they had been last night, when part of him had been convinced he was going to die out here. *Died of pneumonia on Shithouse Road* — what an obituary that would have been.

He was in his boxers, the rest of his clothes heaped on the floor. He had no memory of undressing, either. He put them back on and went downstairs. He scrambled four eggs and this time ate them all, chasing each bite with orange juice. It was concentrate, all the Big 90 carried, but cold and delicious.

He looked across the room at Pop's desk and thought about trying to work, maybe switching from the laptop to the portable typewriter to save the laptop's battery. But after putting his dishes in the sink, he trudged up the stairs and went back to bed, where he slept until the middle of the afternoon.

The storm was still pounding away when he got up the second time, but Drew didn't care. He felt almost like himself again. He wanted a sandwich — there was bologna and cheese — and then he wanted to go to work.

Sheriff Averill was about to fool the gun thugs with his big abracadabra, and now that Drew felt rested and well, he couldn't wait to write it.

Halfway down the stairs, he noticed that the toybox by the fireplace was lying on its side with the toys that had been inside spilling out onto the rag rug. Drew thought he must have kicked it over on his sleepwalk to bed the previous night. He went to it and knelt, meaning to put the toys back in the box before starting work. He had the Frisbee in one hand and the old Stretch Armstrong in the other, when he froze. Lying on its side near Stacey's topless Barbie doll was a stuffed rat.

Drew felt his pulse throbbing in his head as he picked it up, so maybe he wasn't completely well, after all. He squeezed the rat and it gave a tired squeak. Just a toy, but sort of creepy, all things considered. Who gave their kid a stuffed rat to sleep with, when there was a perfectly good teddy bear (only one eye, but still) in the same box?

*No accounting for tastes,* he thought, and finished his mother's old maxim out loud: "Said the old maid as she kissed the cow."

Maybe he'd seen the stuffed rat at the height of his fever and it had kicked off the dream. Make that probably, or almost certainly. That he couldn't remember searching all the way to the bottom of the toybox didn't signify; hell, he couldn't even remember taking off his clothes and going to bed.

He piled the toys back into the box, made himself a cup of tea, and went to work. He was doubtful at first, hesitant, a little scared, but after a few initial missteps, he caught hold and wrote until it was too dark to see without using the lantern. Nine pages, and he thought they were good.

*Damn* good.

## 24

It wasn't a three-day blow; Pierre actually lasted four. Sometimes the wind and rain slackened and then the storm would crank up again. Sometimes a tree fell, but none as close as the one that had smashed the shed. That part hadn't been a dream; he'd seen it with his own eyes. And although the tree — a huge old pine — had largely spared his Suburban, it had fallen close enough to tear off the passenger side mirror.

Drew barely noticed these things. He wrote, he ate, he slept in the afternoon, he wrote again. Every now and then he had a sneezing fit, and every now and then he thought about Lucy and the kids, anxiously waiting for some word. Mostly he didn't think about them. That was selfish and he knew it and didn't care. He was living in Bitter River now.

Every now and then he had to pause for the right word to come to him (like messages floating up in the window of the Magic 8 Ball he'd had as a kid), and every now and then he had to get up and walk around the room as he tried to think of how to make a smooth transition from one scene to the next, but there was no panic. No frustration. He knew the words would come, and they did. He was hitting from all over the court, hitting from way downtown. He wrote on Pop's old portable now, pounding the keys til his fingers hurt. He didn't care about that, either. He had carried this book, this idea that had come to him out of nowhere while standing on a street corner; now it was carrying him.

What a fine ride it was.

## 25

They sat in the dank cellar with no light but the kerosene lantern the sheriff had found upstairs, Jim Averill on one side and Andy Prescott on the other. In the lantern's reddish-orange light, the kid looked no older than fourteen. He certainly didn't look like the half-drunk, half-mad young tough who had blown off that girl's head. Averill thought that evil was a very strange thing. Strange, and sly. It found a way in, as a rat finds its way into a house, it ate whatever you had been too stupid or lazy to put away, and when it was done it disappeared, its belly full. And what had been left behind when the murder-rat left Prescott? This. A frightened boy. He said he couldn't remember what he had done, and Averill believed him. He would hang for it just the same.

"What time is it?" Prescott asked.

Averill consulted his pocket watch. "Going on six. Five minutes later than the last time you asked me."

"And the stage is at eight?"

"Yes. When it's a mile or so out of town, one of my deputies will

Drew stopped, staring at the page in the typewriter. A bar of sun had just struck across it. He got up and went to the window. There was blue up there. Just enough to make a pair of overalls, Pop would have said, but it was growing. And he heard something, faint but unmistakable: the *rrrrrr* of a chainsaw.

He put on the musty jacket and went outside. The sound was still some distance away. He walked across the yard, which was littered with branches, to the remains of the equipment shed. Pop's bucksaw was lying beneath part of a fallen wall, and Drew was able to wiggle it out. It was a two-hander, but he'd be all right with it as long as any downed tree he came to wasn't too thick. *And take it easy,* he told himself. *Unless you want a relapse.*

For a moment he thought about just going back inside and resuming work instead of trying to meet whoever was down the road, cutting a path through the storm's leavings. A day or two before he would have done just that. But things had changed. An image rose in his mind (they came all the time now, unbidden), one that made him smile: a gambler on a losing streak, abjuring the dealer to hurry up and spin those fucking cards. He wasn't that guy anymore, and thank God. The book would still be there when he got back. Whether he resumed out here in the woods or back in Falmouth, it would be there.

He tossed the saw in the back of the Suburban and began rolling slowly up Shithouse Road, pausing every now and then to throw fallen branches out of his way before going on. He went almost a mile before he came to the first tree down across the road, but it was a birch, and he made quick work of it.

The chainsaw was very loud now, not *rrrrr* but *RRRRRRR*. Each time it ceased Drew would hear a big engine revving as his rescuer came closer, and then the saw would start up again. Drew was trying to cut his way through a much bigger tree and not having much luck when a Chevy 4×4, customized for woods work, came lumbering around the next bend.

The driver pulled up and got out. He was a big man with an even bigger belly, dressed in green overalls and a camo coat that flapped around his knees. The chainsaw he carried was industrial-sized, but looked almost like a toy in the guy's gloved hand. Drew knew who he was at once. The resemblance was unmistakable. So was the whiff of Old Spice that went with the smells of sawdust and chainsaw gasoline. "Hey there! You must be Old Bill's boy."

The big man smiled. "Ayuh. And you must be Buzzy Larson's."

"That's right." Drew hadn't known how much he needed to see another human being until this moment. It was like not knowing how thirsty you were until someone handed you a glass of cold water. He stuck out his hand. They shook over the downed tree.

"Your name's Johnny, right? Johnny Colson."

"Close. Jackie. Stand back and let me cut that tree for you, Mr. Larson. Take you all day with that buck."

Drew stood aside and watched as Jackie

cranked up his Stihl and zipped it through the tree, leaving a neat pile of sawdust on the leaf- and twig-littered road. Between the two of them, they shifted the smaller half into the ditch.

"How is it the rest of the way?" Drew asked, puffing a little.

"Not terrible, but there's one bad washout." He squinted one eye closed and sized up Drew's Suburban with the other. "That might getcha through, it's pretty high-sprung. If it don't, I could tow you, although it might ding up your exhaust system a dight."

"How did you know to come out here?"

"Your wife had Dad's number in her old address book. She talked to my ma, and Ma called me. Your wife is some worried about you."

"Yes, I suppose she is. And thinks I'm a damned fool."

This time Old Bill's boy — call him Young Jackie — did his squinting at the tall pines to one side of the road and said nothing. Yankees did not, as a rule, comment on other folks' marital situations.

"Well, I'll tell you what," Drew said. "How about you follow me back to my dad's cabin? Have you got time to do that?"

"Ayuh, got the day."

"I'll pack up my stuff — won't take long — and we can caravan back to the store. There's no cell coverage, but I can use the pay phone.

589

If the storm didn't knock it out, that is."

"Nah, it's okay. I called Ma from there. You probably don't know about DeWitt, do you?"

"Only that he was sick."

"Not anymore," Jackie said. "Died." He hawked, spat, and looked at the sky. "Gonna miss a pretty nice day, by the look. Jump in your truck, Mr. Larson. Follow me half a mile up to the Patterson place. You can turn around there."

## 26

Drew found the sign and picture in the window of the Big 90 both sad and amusing. Amusement was a fairly shitty way to feel, given the circumstances, but a person's interior landscape was sometimes — often, even — fairly shitty. CLOSED FOR FUNNERAL, the sign said. The picture was of Roy DeWitt next to a plastic backyard pool. He was wearing flip-flops and a pair of low-riding Bermuda shorts beneath the considerable overhang of his belly. He was holding a can of beer in one hand and appeared to have been caught in the middle of a dance step.

"Roy liked his Bud-burgers, all right," Jackie Colson observed. "You be okay from here, Mr. Larson?"

"Sure," Drew said. "And thank you." He held out his hand. Jackie Colson gave it a shake, jumped into his 4×4, and headed down the road.

Drew mounted the porch, put a handful of change on the ledge beneath the pay phone, and called home. Lucy answered.

"It's me," Drew said. "I'm at the store, and headed home. Still mad?"

"Get here and find out for yourself." Then: "You sound better."

"I am better."

"Can you make it tonight?"

Drew looked at his wrist and realized he'd brought the manuscript (of course!) but left his watch in the bedroom at Pop's cabin. Where it would stay until next year. He gauged the sun. "Not sure."

"If you get tired, don't try. Stop in Island Falls or Derry. We can wait another night."

"All right, but if you hear someone coming in around midnight, don't shoot."

"I won't. Did you get any work done?" He could hear hesitance in her voice. "I mean, getting sick and all?"

"I did. And it's good, I think."

"No problems with the . . . you know . . ."

"The words? No. No problems." At least not after that weird dream. "I think this one's a keeper. I love you, Luce."

The pause after he said it seemed very long. Then she sighed and said, "I love you, too."

He didn't like the sigh but would take the sentiment. There had been a bump in the road — not the first, and it wouldn't be the last — but they were past it. That was fine.

He racked the phone and got rolling.

As the day was winding down (a pretty nice one, just as Jackie Colson had predicted), he began seeing signs for the Island Falls Motor Lodge. He was tempted, but decided to press on. The Suburban was running well — some of the thumps and bumps on Shithouse Road actually seemed to have knocked the front end back into line — and if he shaded the speed limit a little and didn't get stopped by a state cop, he might be able to get home by eleven. Sleep in his own bed.

And work the next morning. That, too.

## 27

He came into their bedroom at just past eleven-thirty. He'd taken his muddy shoes off downstairs, and was trying to be quiet, but he heard the rustle of bedclothes in the dark and knew she was awake.

"Get in here, Mister."

For once that word didn't sting. He was glad to be home, and even gladder to be with her. Once he was in bed she put her arms around him, gave him a hug (brief, but strong), then turned over and went back to sleep. As Drew was drowsing toward sleep himself — those borderline transition moments when the mind becomes plastic — an odd thought came.

What if the rat had followed him? What if it

was under the bed right now?

*There* was *no rat,* he thought, and slept.

## 28

"Wow," Brandon said. His tone was respectful and a little awed. He and his sister were in the driveway waiting for the bus, their backpacks shouldered.

"What did you *do* to it, Dad?" Stacey asked.

They were looking at the Suburban, which was splattered with dried mud all the way up to the doorhandles. The windshield was opaque except for the crescents that had been cut by the windshield wipers. And there was the missing passenger side mirror, of course.

"There was a storm," Drew said. He was wearing pajama bottoms, bedroom slippers, and a Boston College tee. "And that road out there isn't in very good shape."

"Shithouse Road," Stacey said, clearly relishing the name.

Now Lucy came out as well. She stood looking at the hapless Suburban with her hands on her hips. "Holy crow."

"I'll get it washed this afternoon," Drew said.

"I like it that way," Brandon said. "It's cool. You must have done some crazy driving, Dad."

"Oh, he's crazy, all right," Lucy said. "Your crazy daddy. No doubt about that."

The schoolbus appeared then, sparing him

593

a comeback.

"Come inside," Lucy said after they'd watched the kids get on. "I'll fix you some pancakes or something. You look like you've lost weight."

As she turned away, he caught her hand. "Have you heard anything about Al Stamper? Talked to Nadine, maybe?"

"I talked to her the day you left for the cabin, because you told me he was sick. Pancreatic, that's so awful. She said he was doing pretty well."

"You haven't talked to her since?"

Lucy frowned. "No, why would I?"

"No reason," he said, and that was true. Dreams were dreams, and the only rat he'd seen at the cabin was the stuffed one in the toybox. "Just concerned about him."

"Call him yourself, then. Cut out the middle man. Now do you want some pancakes or not?"

What he wanted to do was work. But pancakes first. Keep things quiet on the home front.

## 29

After pancakes, he went upstairs to his little study, plugged in his laptop, and looked at the hard copy he'd done on Pop's typewriter. Start by keyboarding it in, or just press on? He decided on the latter. Best to find out right away if the magic spell that had been over *Bitter River* still held, or if it had departed when he left the cabin.

It did hold. For the first ten minutes or so he was in the upstairs study, vaguely aware of reggae from downstairs, which meant that Lucy was in *her* study, crunching numbers. Then the music was gone, the walls dissolved, and moonlight was shining down on DeWitt Road, the rutted, potholed track running between Bitter River and the county seat. The stagecoach was coming. Sheriff Averill would hold his badge high and flag it down. Pretty soon he and Andy Prescott would be on-board. The kid had a date in county court. And not long after with the hangman.

Drew knocked off at noon and called Al Stamper. There was no need to be frightened, and he told himself he wasn't, but he couldn't deny that his pulse had kicked up several notches.

"Hey, Drew," Al said, sounding just like himself. Sounding strong. "How did it go up in the wilderness?"

"Pretty well. I got almost ninety pages before a storm came along —"

"Pierre," Al said, and with a clear distaste that warmed Drew's heart. "Ninety pages, really? *You?*"

"I know, hard to believe, and another ten this morning, but never mind that. What I really want to know is how you're doing."

"Pretty damn good," Al said. "Except I've

got this damn rat to contend with."

Drew had been sitting in one of the kitchen chairs. Now he bolted to his feet, suddenly feeling sick again. Feverish. *"What?"*

"Oh, don't sound so concerned," Al said. "It's a new medication the doctors put me on. Supposed to have all kinds of side effects, but the only one I've got, at least so far, is the goddam rash. All over my back and sides. Nadie swore it was shingles, but I had the test and it's just a rash. Itches like hell, though."

"Just a rash," Drew echoed. He wiped a hand across his mouth. *CLOSED FOR FUNERAL,* he thought. "Well, that's not so bad. You take care of yourself, Al."

"I will. And I want to see that book when you finish it." He paused. "Notice I said *when,* not *if.*"

"After Lucy, you'll be first in line," Drew said, and hung up. Good news. All good news. Al sounded strong. Like his old self. All fine, except for that damn rat.

Drew found he could laugh at that.

## 30

November was cold and snowy, but Drew Larson barely noticed. On the last day of the month, he watched (through the eyes of Sheriff Jim Averill) as Andy Prescott climbed the stairs to the gallows in the county seat. Drew was curious as to how the boy would take it. As it turned out — as the words *spilled* out — he did just fine. He had grown up. The tragedy (Averill knew it) was that the kid would never grow old. One drunken night and a fit of jealousy over a dancehall girl had put paid to everything that might have been.

On the first of December, Jim Averill turned in his badge to the circuit judge who had been in town to witness the hanging, then rode back to Bitter River, where he would pack his few things (one trunk would be enough) and say goodbye to his deputies, who had done a damn good job when the chips were down. Yes, even Jep Leonard, who was about as smart as a rock. Or sharp as a marble, take your pick.

On the second of December, the sheriff harnessed his horse to a light buggy, threw his trunk and saddle in the back, and headed west, thinking he might try his luck in California. The gold rush was over, but he longed to see the Pacific Ocean. He was unaware of Andy Prescott's grief-stricken father, laid up behind a rock two miles out of town and looking down the barrel of a Sharps Big Fifty, the rifle which would become known as "the gun that changed the history of the west."

Here came a light wagon, and sitting up there on the seat, boots on the splashboard, was the man responsible for his grief and spoiled hopes, the man who had killed his son. Not the judge, not the jury, not the hangman. No. That man down there. If not for Jim Averill, his son would be in Mexico now, with his long life — all the way into a new century! — ahead of him.

Prescott cocked the hammer. He laid the sights on the man in the wagon. He hesitated with his finger curled on the cold steel crescent of the trigger, deciding what to do in the forty seconds or so before the wagon breasted the next hill and disappeared from sight. Shoot? Or let him go?

Drew thought of adding one more sentence — He made up his mind — and didn't. That would lead some readers, perhaps many, to believe Prescott had decided to shoot, and Drew wanted to leave that issue unresolved. Instead, he hit the space bar twice and typed.

THE END

He looked at those two words for quite a long time. He looked at the pile of manuscript between his laptop and his printer; with the work of this final session added, it would come in at just under three hundred pages.

*I did it. Maybe it will be published and maybe it won't, maybe I'll do another and maybe I won't, it doesn't matter. I did it.*

He put his hands over his face.

## 31

Lucy turned the last page two nights later and looked at him in a way he hadn't seen in a very long time. Maybe not since the first year or two of their marriage, before the kids came.

"Drew, it's amazing."

He grinned. "Really? Not just saying that because your hubby wrote it?"

She shook her head violently. "No. It's wonderful. A western! I never would have guessed. How did you get the idea?"

He shrugged. "It just came to me."

"Did that horrible rancher shoot Jim Averill?"

"I don't know," Drew said.

"Well, a publisher may want you to put that in."

"Then the publisher — if there ever is one — will find his want unsatisfied. And you're sure it's okay? You mean it?"

"Much better than okay. Are you going to show Al?"

"Yes. I'll take a copy of the script over tomorrow."

"Does he know it's a western?"

"Nope. Don't even know if he likes them."

"He'll like this one." She paused, then took his hand and said, "I was so pissed at you for not coming back when that storm was on the way. But I was wrong and you were rat."

He took his hand back, once again feeling

feverish. "What did you say?"

"That I was wrong. And you were right. What's the trouble, Drew?"

"Nothing," he said. "Nothing at all."

## 32

"So?" Drew asked three days later. "What's the verdict?"

They were in his old department head's study. The manuscript was on Al's desk. Drew had been nervous about Lucy's reaction to *Bitter River,* but he was even more nervous about Al's. Stamper was a voracious, omnivorous reader who had been analyzing and deconstructing prose his entire working life. He was the only person Drew knew who had dared to teach *Under the Volcano* and *Infinite Jest* in the same semester.

"I think it's very good." Al not only sounded like his old self these days, he looked like it. His color was back and he had put on a few pounds. The chemo had taken his hair, but the Red Sox cap he was wearing covered his newly bald head. "It's plot-driven, but the relationship between the sheriff and his young captive gives the story quite extraordinary resonance. It isn't as good as *The Ox-Bow Incident* or *Welcome to Hard Times,* I'd say—"

"I know," Drew said . . . who thought it was. "I'd never claim that."

"But I think it ranks with Oakley Hall's

600

*Warlock,* which is just behind those two. You had something to say, Drew, and you said it very well. The book doesn't pound the reader over the head with its thematic concerns, and I suppose most people will just read it for the strong story values — the what-happens-next thing — but those thematic elements are there, oh yes."

"You think people *will* read it?"

"Sure." Al seemed almost to wave this away. "Unless your agent's a total dummocks, he or she will sell this easily. Maybe even for a fair bit of money." He eyed Drew. "Although my guess is that was secondary to you, if you thought about it at all. You just wanted to do it, am I right? For once jump off the high board at the country club swimming pool without losing your nerve and slinking back down the ladder."

"Nailed it," Drew said. "And you . . . Al, you look terrific."

"I feel terrific," he said. "The doctors have stopped short of calling me a medical marvel, and I'll be going back for tests every three weeks for the first year, but my last date with the fucking chemo IV is this afternoon. As of rat now all the tests are calling me cancer free."

This time Drew didn't jump, and he didn't bother asking for a repeat. He knew what his old department head had actually said, just as he knew part of him would keep hearing that other word from time to time. It was like a splinter, one lodged in his mind instead of under his skin. Most splinters worked out without infecting. He was pretty sure this one would do that. After all, Al was fine. The deal-making rat at the cabin had been a dream. Or a stuffed toy. Or complete bullshit.

Take your pick.

## 33

To: drew1981@gmail.com

**THE ELISE DILDEN AGENCY**

January 19, 2019

Drew, my love — How great to hear from you, I thought you were dead and I missed the obituary! (Joking! ☺) A novel after all these years, how exciting. Send it posthaste, dear, and we'll see what can be done. Although I must warn you the market is barely making half-steam these days unless it's a book about Trump and his cohorts.

XXX,
Ellie

Sent from my electronic slave bracelet

## THE ELISE DILDEN AGENCY

February 1, 2019

Drew! I finished last night! The book is WUNDERBAR! I hope you aren't planning to get fabuloso rich from it, but I'm sure it will be published, and I feel I can get a decent advance. Perhaps more than decent. An auction is not entirely out of the question. Plus-plus-plus I feel that this book could (and should) be a reputation-maker. I believe when it's published, the reviews of *Bitter River* will be sweet indeed. Thank you for a wonderful visit in the old west!

XXX,
Ellie

PS: You left me hanging! Did that rat of a rancher actually shoot Jim Averill????

E

Sent from my electronic slave bracelet

### 34

There was indeed an auction for *Bitter River*. It happened on March 15th, the same day the season's final storm hit New England (Winter Storm Tania, according to the

Weather Channel). Three of New York's Big Five publishers participated, and Putnam came out the winner. The advance was $350,000. Not Dan Brown or John Grisham numbers, but enough, as Lucy said while she hugged him, to put Bran and Stacey through college. She broke out a bottle of Dom Pérignon, which she had been saving (hopefully). This was at three o'clock, while they still felt like celebrating.

They toasted the book, and the book's author, and the book's author's wife, and the amazing wonderful kids that had sprung from the loins of the book's author and the book's author's wife, and were fairly tipsy when the phone rang at four. It was Kelly Fontaine, the English Department's administrative assistant since time out of mind. She was in tears. Al and Nadine Stamper were dead.

He had been scheduled for tests at Maine Medical that day (*tests every three weeks for the first year,* Drew remembered him saying). "He could have put the appointment off," Kelly said, "but you know Al, and Nadine was the same way. A little snow wasn't going to stop them."

The accident happened on 295, less than a mile from Maine Med. A semi skidded on the ice, sideswiping Nadie Stamper's little Prius and flicking it like a tiddlywink. It turned over and landed on the roof.

"Oh my God," Lucy said. "Both of them,

gone. How horrible is that? And when he was getting better!"

"Yes," Drew said. He felt numb. "He was, wasn't he?" Except, of course, he had that damn rat to contend with. He'd said so himself.

"You need to sit down," Lucy said. "You're as pale as windowglass."

But sitting down wasn't what Drew needed, at least not first. He rushed to the kitchen sink and vomited up the champagne. As he hung there, still heaving, barely aware of Lucy rubbing his back, he thought, *Ellie says the book will be published next February. Between now and then I'll do whatever the editor tells me, and all the publicity they want once the book comes out. I'll play the game. I'll do it for Lucy and the kids. But there's never going to be another one.*

"Never," he said.

"What, honey?" She was still rubbing his back.

"The pancreatic. I thought that would get him, it gets almost everybody. I never expected anything like this." He rinsed his mouth from the faucet, spat. "Never."

## 35

The funeral — which Drew couldn't help thinking of as the FUNNERAL — was held four days after the accident. Al's younger

605

brother asked Drew if he would say a few words. Drew declined, saying he was still too shocked to be articulate. He *was* shocked, no doubt about it, but his real fear was that the words would turn treacherous as they had on *Village* and the two aborted books before it. He was afraid — really, actually afraid — that if he stood at the podium before a chapel filled with grieving relatives, friends, colleagues, and students, what might spill from his mouth was *The rat! It was the fucking rat! And I turned it loose!*

Lucy cried all through the service. Stacey cried with her, not because she knew the Stampers well but in sympathy with her mother. Drew sat silent, with his arm around Brandon. He looked not at the two coffins but at the choir loft. He was sure he would see a rat running a victory lap along the polished mahogany rail up there, but he didn't. Of course he didn't. There was no rat. As the service wound down, he realized he'd been stupid to think there might be. He knew where the rat was, and that place was miles from here.

### 36

In August (and a mighty hot August it was), Lucy decided to take the kids down to Little Compton, Rhode Island, to spend a couple of weeks at the shore with her parents and her sister's family, leaving Drew a quiet house where he could work through the copyedited manuscript of *Bitter River.* He said he would break the work in half, taking a day in the middle to drive up to Pop's cabin. He would spend the night, he said, and come back the following day to resume work on the manuscript. They had hired Jack Colson — Young Jackie — to truck away the remains of the smashed shed; Jackie in turn had hired his ma to clean the cabin. Drew said he wanted to see what kind of job they'd done. And to retrieve his watch.

"Sure you don't want to start a new book there?" Lucy asked, smiling. "I wouldn't mind. The last one turned out pretty well."

Drew shook his head. "Nothing like that. I was thinking we ought to sell the place, hon. I'm really going up there to say goodbye."

### 37

The signs on the gas pump at the Big 90 were the same: CASH ONLY and REGULAR ONLY and "DASH-AWAYS" WILL BE PERSECUTED and GOD BLESS AMERICA. The scrawny young woman behind the counter was also pretty much the same; the chrome stud was gone but the nose ring was still there. And she'd gone blond. Presumably because blonds had more fun.

"You again," she said. "Only you changed your ride, seems like. Didn't you have a 'Burban?"

Drew glanced out at the Chevy Equinox — purchased outright, still less than 7,000 miles on the clock — standing at the single rusting pump. "The Suburban was never really the same after my last trip up here," he said. *Actually, neither was I.*

"Gonna be up there long?"

"No, not this time. I was sorry to hear about Roy."

"Should have gone to the doctor. Let it be a lesson to you. Need anything else?"

Drew bought some bread, some lunchmeat, and a sixpack.

### 38

All the blowdown had been trucked away from the dooryard, and the equipment shed was gone as if it had never been. Young Jackie had sodded the ground and fresh grass was growing there. Also some cheery flowers. The warped porch steps had been repaired and there were a couple of new chairs, just cheap stuff from the Presque Isle Walmart, probably, but not bad looking.

Inside, the cabin was neat and freshened up. The woodstove's isinglass window had been cleaned of soot and the stove itself gleamed. So did the windows, the dining table, and the pine-plank floor, which looked as if it had been oiled as well as washed. The refrigerator was once more unplugged and standing open, once more empty except for a box of Arm & Hammer. Probably a fresh one. It was clear that Old Bill's widow had done a bang-up job.

Only on the counter by the sink were there signs of his occupancy the previous October: the Coleman lantern, the tin of lantern fuel, a bag of Halls cough drops, several packets of Goody's Headache Powder, half a bottle of Dr. King's Cough & Cold Remedy, and his wristwatch.

The fireplace was scrubbed clean of ash. It had been loaded with fresh chunks of oak, so Drew supposed Young Jackie had either had the chimney swept or done it himself. Very efficient, but there would be no need of a fire in this August heat. He went to the fireplace, knelt, and twisted his head to stare up into the black throat of the chimney.

"Are you up there?" he called . . . and with no self-consciousness at all. "If you're up there, come down. I want to talk to you."

Nothing, of course. He told himself again there was no rat, had never been a rat, except there was. The splinter wasn't coming out. The rat was in his head. Only that wasn't completely true, either. Was it?

There were still two crates flanking the spandy-clean fireplace, fresh kindling in one, toys in the other — the ones left here by his kids and those left by the children of whomever Lucy had let the cabin to in the few years they'd rented it. He grabbed the crate and dumped it. At first he didn't think the stuffed rat was there, and he felt a stab of panic, irrational, but real. Then he saw it had tumbled under the hearth, nothing sticking out but its cloth-covered rump and stringy tail. What an ugly toy it was!

"Thought you'd hide, did you?" he asked it. "No good, Mister."

He took it over to the sink and dropped it in. "Got anything to say? Any explanations? Maybe an apology? No? What about any last words? You were chatty enough before."

The stuffed rat had nothing to say, so Drew doused it with lantern fluid and set it on fire. When there was nothing left but smoking, foul-smelling slag, he turned on the water and doused the remains. There were a few paper bags under the sink. Drew used a spatula to scrape what was left into one of these. He took the bag down to Godfrey Brook, tossed it in, and watched it float away. Then he sat down on the bank and looked at the day, which was windless and hot and gorgeous.

When the sun began to sink, he went inside and made a couple of bologna sandwiches. They were sort of dry — he should have remembered to get mustard or mayo — but he had the beer to wash them down. He drank three cans, sitting in one of the old armchairs and reading an Ed McBain paperback about the 87th Precinct.

Drew considered a fourth beer and decided against it. He had an idea that was the one with the hangover in it, and he wanted to get an early start in the morning. He was done with this place. As he was with writing novels. There was just the one, his only child waiting for him to finish with it. The one that had cost his friend and his friend's wife their lives.

"I don't believe that," he said as he climbed the stairs. At the top he looked down at the big main room, where he had started his book and where — for a little while, anyway — he had believed he would die. "Except I do. I do believe that."

He undressed and went to bed. The beers sent him off to sleep quickly.

## 39

Drew awoke in the middle of the night. The bedroom was gilded silver with the light of a full August moon. The rat was sitting on his chest, staring at him with those little black bulging eyes.

"Hello, Drew." The rat's mouth didn't move, but the voice was coming from him, all right. Drew had been feverish and sick the last time they conversed, but he remembered that voice very well.

"Get off me," Drew whispered. He wanted to strike it away (he wanted to *bat the rat,* so to speak), but he seemed to have no strength in his arms.

"Now, now, don't be like that. You called me and I came. Isn't that the way it works in stories like this? Now just how can I help you?"

"I want to know why you did it."

The rat sat up, holding his little pink paws to his furry chest. "Because you wanted me to. It was a wish, remember?"

"It was a *deal.*"

"Oh, you college types with your semantics."

"The deal was *Al,*" Drew insisted. "Just *him.* Since he was going to die of pancreatic cancer anyway."

"I don't remember pancreatic cancer ever being specified," said the rat. "Am I wrong about that?"

"No, but I assumed . . ."

The rat did a face-washing thing with his paws, turned around twice — the feel of those paws was nauseating, even through the quilt — and then regarded Drew again. "That's how they get you with magic wishes," he said. "They're tricky. Lots of fine print. All the best fairy tales make that clear. I thought we discussed that."

"Okay, but Nadine Stamper was never a part of it! Never a part of our . . . our arrangement!"

"She was never *not* a part of it," the rat replied, and rather prissily.

*It's a dream,* Drew thought. *Another dream,*

612

*got to be. In no version of reality could a man be lawyered at by a rodent.*

Drew thought his strength was coming back, but he made no move. Not yet. When he did it would be sudden, and it wouldn't be to *slap the rat* or *bat the rat.* He intended to *catch* the rat and *squeeze* the rat. He would writhe, he would squeal, and he would almost certainly bite, but Drew would squeeze until the rat's belly ruptured and his guts erupted from his mouth and his asshole.

"All right, you might have a point. But I don't understand. The book was all I wanted, and you spoiled it."

"Oh boo-hoo," said the rat, and gave his face another dry wash. Drew almost pounced then, but no. Not quite yet. He had to know.

"Fuck your boo-hoo. I could have killed you with that shovel, but I didn't. I could have left you out in the storm, but I didn't. I brought you in and put you by the stove. So why would you repay me by killing two innocent people and stealing the pleasure I felt in finishing the only book I'll ever write?"

The rat considered. "Well," he said at last, "if I may slightly change an old punchline, you knew I was a rat when you took me in."

Drew pounced. He was very fast, but his clutching hands closed on nothing but air. The rat scurried across the floor, but before he reached the wall, he turned back to Drew, seeming to grin in the moonlight.

"Besides, you didn't finish it. You *never* could have finished it. I did."

There was a hole in the baseboard. The rat ran into it. For a moment Drew could see his tail. Then he was gone.

Drew lay looking up at the ceiling. *In the morning I will tell myself this was a dream,* he thought, and in the morning that was what he did. Rats did not talk and rats did not grant wishes. Al had cheated cancer only to die in a car accident, dreadfully ironic but not unheard-of; it was a shame his wife had died with him, but that was not unheard-of, either.

He drove home. He entered his preternaturally quiet house. He went upstairs to his study. He opened the folder containing the copyedited manuscript of *Bitter River* and prepared to go to work. Things had happened, some in the real world and some in his head, and those things could not be changed. The thing to remember was that he had survived. He would love his wife and children as best he could, he would teach the best he could, he would live the best he could, and he would gladly join the ranks of one-book writers. Really, when you thought about it, he had nothing to complain about.

Really, when you thought about it, everything was all rat.

# AUTHOR'S NOTE

When my mom or one of my four aunties happened to see a lady pushing a pram, they were apt to chant something they probably learned from *their* mother: "Where did you come from, baby dear? Out of the nowhere and into the here." I sometimes think of that bit of doggerel when I'm asked where I got the idea for this or that story. I often don't know the answer, which makes me embarrassed and a little ashamed. (Some childhood complex at work there, no doubt.) Sometimes I give the honest answer ("No idea!"), but on other occasions I just make up some bullshit, thus satisfying my questioner with a semirational explanation of cause and effect. Here, I will try to be honest. (Of course that's what I *would* say, isn't it?)

As a kid, I may have seen some movie — likely one of the American-International horror flicks my friend Chris Chesley and I used to hitchhike to see at the Ritz in Lewiston — about a guy so afraid of being buried alive that he had a phone put in his crypt. Or it might have been an episode of *Alfred Hitchcock Presents.* Anyway, the idea resonated in my over-imaginative child's mind: the thought of a phone ringing in a place of the dead. Years later, after a close friend died unexpectedly, I called his cell phone just to hear his voice one more time. Instead of comforting me, it gave me the creeps. I never did it again, but that call, added to the childhood memory of that movie or TV show, was the seed for "Mr. Harrigan's Phone."

Stories go where they want to, and the real fun of this one — for me — was returning to a time when cell phones in general and the iPhone in particular were brand new, and all their ramifications barely glimpsed. In the course of my researches, my IT guy, Jake Lockwood, bought a first-gen iPhone on eBay and got it working. It's nearby as I write. (I have to keep it plugged in, because somewhere along the way someone dropped it and busted the on/off switch.) I can go on the Internet with it, I can get stock reports and the weather. I just can't make calls, because it's 2G, and that technology is as dead as the Betamax VCR.

I have no idea where "The Life of Chuck" came from. All I know is one day I thought of a billboard with that "Thanks, Chuck!" line on it, along with the guy's photo and 39 GREAT YEARS. I think I wrote the story to find out what that billboard was about, but I'm not even sure of that. What I can say is that I've always felt that each one of us — from the kings and princes of the realm to the guys who wash dishes at Waffle House and the gals who change beds in turnpike motels — contains the whole world.

While staying in Boston, I happened to see a guy playing the drums on Boylston Street. People were passing him with hardly a glance, and the basket in front of him (not a Magic Hat) was mighty low on contributions. I wondered what would happen if someone, a Mr. Businessman type, for instance, stopped and began to dance, sort of like Christopher Walken in that brilliant Fatboy Slim video, "Weapon of Choice." The connection to Chuck Krantz — a Mr. Businessman type if ever there was one — was natural. I put him into the story and let him dance. I love dancing, the way it frees a person's heart and soul, and writing the story was a joy.

Having written two stories about Chuck, I wanted to write a third one that would knit all three into a unified narrative. "I Contain Multitudes" was written a year after the first two. Whether or not the three acts — presented in reverse order, like a film running backwards — succeed will be up to readers to determine.

Let me jump ahead to "Rat." I have absolutely no clue where this story came from. All

I know is that it felt like a malign fairy tale to me, and it gave me a chance to write a little bit about the mysteries of the imagination, and how that translates to the page. I should add that the Jonathan Franzen lecture Drew refers to is fictional.

Last but hardly least: "If It Bleeds." The basis of this story existed in my mind for at least ten years. I began to notice that certain TV news correspondents seem always to appear at the scenes of horrific tragedies: plane crashes, mass shootings, terrorist attacks, celebrity deaths. These stories almost always head local and national news; everyone in the biz knows the axiom "If it bleeds, it leads." The story remained unwritten because someone had to catch the trail of the supernatural being masquerading as a TV news correspondent and living on the blood of innocents. I couldn't figure out who that someone might be. Then, in November of 2018, I realized the answer had been staring me in the face all along: Holly Gibney, of course.

I love Holly. It's as simple as that. She was supposed to be a minor character in *Mr. Mercedes*, no more than a quirky walk-on. Instead, she stole my heart (and almost stole the book). I'm always curious about what she's doing and how she's getting along. When I go back to her, I'm relieved to find she's still taking her Lexapro and still not smoking. I was also curious, frankly, about

618

the circumstances that made her what she is, and thought I could explore that a little . . . as long as it added to the story, that is. This is Holly's first solo outing, and I hope I did it justice. Particular thanks to elevator expert Alan Wilson, who walked me through the way modern computerized elevators work, and the things that can go wrong with them. Obviously I took his info and (ahem) embellished it, so if you know this stuff and think I got it wrong, blame me — and the needs of my story — rather than him.

The late Russ Dorr worked with me on "Mr. Harrigan's Phone." It was our last collaboration, and how I miss him. Thanks are due to Chuck Verrill, my agent (who particularly enjoyed "Rat"), and my whole Scribner team, including (but not limited to) Nan Graham, Susan Moldow, Roz Lippel, Katie Rizzo, Jaya Miceli, Katherine Monaghan, and Carolyn Reidy. Thanks to Chris Lotts, my foreign rights agent, and Rand Holston, from the Paradigm Agency in LA. He does movies and TV stuff. Big thanks also — and big love — to my kids, my grandkids, and my wife, Tabitha. I love you, honey.

Last but not least, thank *you,* Constant Reader, for coming with me again.

Stephen King
March 13, 2019

# ABOUT THE AUTHOR

**Stephen King** is the author of more than sixty books, all of them worldwide bestsellers. His recent work includes *The Institute, Elevation, The Outsider, Sleeping Beauties* (cowritten with his son Owen King), and the Bill Hodges trilogy: *End of Watch, Finders Keepers,* and *Mr. Mercedes* (an Edgar Award winner for Best Novel and an AT&T Audience Network original television series). His novel *11/22/63* was named a top ten book of 2011 by the *New York Times Book Review* and won the *Los Angeles Times* Book Prize for Mystery/Thriller. His epic works *The Dark Tower, It, Pet Sematary,* and *Doctor Sleep* are the basis for major motion pictures, with *It* now the highest grossing horror film of all time. He is the recipient of the 2018 PEN America Literary Service Award, the 2014 National Medal of Arts, and the 2003 National Book Foundation Medal for Distinguished Contribution to American Letters.

He lives in Bangor, Maine, with his wife, novelist Tabitha King.

The employees of Thorndike Press hope you have enjoyed this Large Print book. All our Thorndike, Wheeler, and Kennebec Large Print titles are designed for easy reading, and all our books are made to last. Other Thorndike Press Large Print books are available at your library, through selected bookstores, or directly from us.

For information about titles, please call:
(800) 223-1244

or visit our website at:
gale.com/thorndike

To share your comments, please write:
Publisher
Thorndike Press
10 Water St., Suite 310
Waterville, ME 04901